Further praise for *Rides of the Midway*

"Comic though it is, *Rides of the Midway* engages serious concerns. . . . Durkee has given the coming-of-age novel enough twists to make his version seem something else entirely—a ghost story, perhaps, mixed with a sexual comedy and slice-of-working-class Southern life. . . . Much of the book's strength, of course, derives simply from the likableness of its hero. . . . Dark and exhilarating."
—*New York Times Book Review*

"Mississippi-raised author Lee Durkee portrays his hero's feckless dissolution with considerable comic flair and a sharp eye for regional manners, good and bad. . . . Readers will finish the book feeling they've been treated to quite a ride."
—*Time*

"This book gave me the heebie-jeebies, and almost nothing gives me the heebie-jeebies these days. It's a damn good novel."
—Pinckney Benedict

"Horrifically comic. . . . Masterly. . . . You've got to love a coming-of-age story in which Lynyrd Skynyrd's plane crash plays a pivotal role. . . . A vivid personification of that classic adolescent territory between responsibility and freedom, which, in this impressive debut, can often look like a prison."
—*Los Angeles Times Book Review*

"Welcome to the hallucinatory world of first-time novelist Lee Durkee. It's a world that contains both the youthful yearning of *The Catcher in the Rye* and the spectral oddity of *The Sixth Sense*. . . . [Durkee's] gift is in conjuring the ghosts and shadows, bringing them to a convincing kind of life."
—*Austin American-Statesman*

"A wonderful debut. . . . Lee Durkee is a marvelously inventive writer, both moving and comic in turn, who packs up surprises on every page and writes sentences that any other writer will envy. *Rides of the Midway* was a joy to read."
—Stephen Dobyns

"Southern literature teems with healers, zealots, saints, and non-believers of all stripes. . . . Lee Durkee's assured, richly imagined debut novel is a raucous tour through this scorched landscape of faith. . . . Durkee handles Noel's odyssey with grace and style, crafting sentences so beautiful that you stop to read them twice."

—*Time Out NY*

"Bracing. . . . Boy, does this make *The Sixth Sense* seem like Dick and Jane. . . . [A] stunning, startling tale. . . . [Noel] may be the most engaging literary antihero since Holden Caulfield. . . . From first electrifying page to last, Noel Weatherspoon lives in a surreality from which you may be loathe to emerge. This is dark poetry, dementia with a smile, and unbelievably good storytelling." —*Philadelphia Weekly*

"What an exciting new voice we have in Lee Durkee! Every sentence in *Rides of the Midway* bristles with joy and danger and surprise."

—Lewis Nordan

"*Rides of the Midway* is filled with thrills and chills as it rockets toward its amazing and strangely graceful conclusion, in which we are reminded that only 'the truly wretched' can really sing 'Amazing Grace.' " —*New Orleans Times-Picayune*

"A work of manic brilliance that depicts a gorgeous inverse of America you haven't seen in print before." —George Saunders

"Durkee renders both the anguished, absurd inner life of a hormone-addled pubescent boy and his creepy, nouveau Southern Gothic milieu in loving and ferocious detail. . . . Durkee's dark bildungsroman reaches for the universal. In its grim, haunted, and often outrageously funny specificity, it becomes almost allegorical—a Pilgrim's Progress through the valley of the shadow of the late twentieth century."

—*Bookforum*

"Lee Durkee chronicles one young man's hilariously knotty adolescence in mid- to late-70's Mississippi. . . . Durkee creates a deeply specific, stifling southern town. It's one where Billy Graham is on every television set, each passing thought is a possible sin, and the local underachiever dedicated to drugs and arena rock just may have more going on behind those mirrored sunglasses than you think." —*Spin*

"Durkee writes with the verve of a young Philip Roth or Thomas McGuane. . . . Deft and toothsome hilarity. . . . Durkee calls to mind the early Barry Hannah—rattling his lingual sabers, jitterbugging on the edge of absurdity, lobbing firecrackers at his startled audience. *Rides of the Midway* is a manic, sloshed, whiny, fizzy, horny, noisome and wondrous novel. . . . This coarsely graceful novel feels . . . vital and involuntary—as vital and involuntary, that is, as the truest art."

—*Salon*

"A memorable first novel, its darkness lit by wisdom."

—Shelby Hearon

"Compelling and accomplished. . . . The novel is so enthralling and its prose so streamlined that one might be tempted to devour it ravenously in one long sitting. But such is the book's richness of detail and depth of character that it is equally tempting to take it in over several days, savoring its playful satire, evocative imagery, dense allusion, and hard-won humanity. . . . Beautifully exciting. . . . What Durkee has created in this remarkable debut is a lively, loving ode to Southern adolescence, its crude confusions, and its strange freedoms—in short, to its fierce deities." —*Memphis Commercial Appeal*

"Tremendously energetic. . . . Durkee combines haunting lyricism . . . with blatantly crude comedy that will have readers laughing out loud despite themselves. First-timer Durkee writes with a southern accent that doesn't smother a unique voice, and his roller-coaster ride of a story leaves a reader breathless and waiting for more."

—*Kirkus Reviews*, starred review

"A marvelously rich book—thick with life, dark-humored as a night in the funhouse, smart as the guy who guesses your weight."

—Lee K. Abbott

"Sharp and engaging. . . . Durkee's darkly humorous debut sorrowfully and sincerely portrays a boy's self-damnation. . . . In the tradition of Anne Tyler, this promising first-timer has taken great care to resurrect smalltown living in the '70s and '80s without a hint of sentimentality."

—*Publishers Weekly*

"This is not your father's coming-of-age tale. . . . A wild, unforgettable ride. . . . Wickedly disturbing. . . . Undeniably funny. . . . *Rides of the Midway* will have you howling, laughing, screaming and holding on tight."

—*Winston-Salem Journal*

"This is one of those books that resonate in the mind long after the last page has been turned. . . . A classic coming-of-age tale. . . . The book's great strength is that the reader never loses sight of the person inside— an extremely likable kid whose misfortune it is to be utterly helpless before the tempests of life. . . . *Rides of the Midway* is a headlong, apocalyptic, picaresque tale, as gut-wrenching and addictive as the Black Dragon, the fairground ride on which Noel last saw his father, and which gives the book its title. It is tragic, funny and, in the end, even optimistic. Noel is an unlikely hero, but his story of love, death, brotherhood, and hope rings true." —*Seven Days* (Burlington, Vt.)

"A beautiful whirlwind of a novel, one whose sentences make you want to uncork some wine and toast Lee Durkee. Good French stuff, I might add, for this debut is that impressive." —Dale Ray Phillips

RIDES OF
THE MIDWAY

RIDES OF
THE MIDWAY

A NOVEL

Lee Durkee

W. W. NORTON & COMPANY   NEW YORK   LONDON

For information about permission to reproduce selections from this
book, write to Permissions, W. W. Norton & Company, Inc.,
500 Fifth Avenue, New York, NY 10110

The text of this book is composed in Sabon with the display set in
Franklin Gothic.
Composition by Thomas Ernst
Manufacturing by Maple-Vail Book Manufacturing Group
Book design by BTDnyc

Library of Congress Cataloging-in-Publication Data

Durkee, Lee.
    Rides of the midway : a novel / by Lee Durkee.
        p.   cm.
    ISBN 978-0-393-32290-3
    1. Teenage boys—Fiction. 2. Mississippi—Fiction. I. Title.

PS3554.U6865 R53 2001
813'.6—dc21   00-062219

W. W. Norton & Company, Inc.
500 Fifth Avenue, New York, N.Y. 10110
www.wwnorton.com

W. W. Norton & Company Ltd.
Castle House, 75/76 Wells Street, London W1T 3QT

1 2 3 4 5 6 7 8 9 0

To my dad,
who was a bit of a cautionary tale himself

ACKNOWLEDGMENTS

A VERSION OF CHAPTER FIVE originally appeared in the *New England Review* under the title "Sacrilege."

Special thanks to Neil Giordano, Tabitha Griffin, Jay Mandel, and Margo Rabb.

PROLOGUE

HALF GHOST, HALF SKELETON, and tethered to his body like a
dog in a yard, Ross wanted only to fly out the one window. But as
it was, being neither quite dead nor quite alive, he could not soar
through the hospital window except in the dream fits that overtook
him without warning so that no event could be altogether trusted.
He could float, sure, and sometimes he could pass through the
walls into the neighboring rooms or into the bright hallway with its
ice-tray lights and food carts, but, for instance, he could not change
the TV channel nor could he unplug the city of machines that sus-
tained his body nor could he taste the food he swiped off the carts.
In fact, when he studied the cart, he would see that he had not
stolen the food at all. There it was, both in his hand, dream food,
and still on the plate, real food.

On weekends his dad switched the TV to baseball. Those were
the best times. Then Ross could forget about being a ghost and
watch Johnny Bench.

As to his own body, his real body, Ross had long ago grown bored with that, though for the first year he had been fascinated by its decay. This fascination gave way to a period of revulsion as the skin yellowed and caved in upon the flowering skeleton. But now Ross only noticed the body when it became the room's focal point, such as when his family visited or when a nurse came in to rotate his limbs or when his older sister Amber talked to him on the Ouija board.

The Ouija board proved another lesson in frustration. Not only had his spelling deteriorated into a type of dream spelling, but moving that plastic puck to where a single letter was centered inside its eye exhausted him. Meanwhile, Amber's limp black hair spilled over the alphabet. With her thin bones and white skin and the blue map of veins on the undersides of her forearms, she seemed to Ross as fragile as his own body on whose lap she had propped the Ouija board. And they both knew Ouija boards to be mildly satanic, at least that's what their parents had taught them. On some level Ross was still worried about getting into trouble.

Then one day while Amber was manning the Ouija board and asking him for the hundredth time what it was like to be brain-dead, someone had entered the private room, and in a panic Amber had thrown herself under the bed. Ross froze, his fingers perched on the plastic puck. At the foot of the bed stood an older boy, a teenager maybe, clutching a black baseball cap that said CAT. He had long black hair, skull-shaped and dirty-looking where the cap had been set, and he had slightly Mongoloid eyes that made him appear suspect, maybe retarded, maybe stoned. The boy studied first the largest of the machines, a cabineted ventilator, and then lowered his eyes along Ross's skeleton until they came to rest upon the Ouija board on its lap. He began tucking in the front of his white T-shirt. Finally, in a stunted whisper, he spoke. He said, "Look, I'm sorry I ran into you, all right? I guess I shoulda slid." He beaked his lips. Speaking more deliberately, he added, "Thing is,

I'd never had an in-the-park homer before. I'd never had any kind of homer." Glancing out the window, he said, "Just stay outa my dreams, okay? Please. Leave me the hell alone."

He backed away from the bed, but before leaving the room he turned and regarded the TV a long moment, then he reached up and changed the channel all the way around the dial to *Dark Shadows*.

As soon as he was gone, Amber crawled out from under the bed. She changed the channel back to *Guiding Light* and asked, "Who was that? He's cute."

It took a painstaking fifteen minutes, but eventually Ross managed to dictate: "*H-E-W-A-S-O-U-T.*"

Counterclockwise

What but design of darkness to appall?—
If design govern in a thing so small.

—*Robert Frost*

CHAPTER ONE

NOEL'S FATHER, WHEN LAST SEEN, had boarded a ride called the Black Dragon on the final evening of the Great Mississippi Fair, which in a matter of hours and direction would transform itself into the Great Louisiana Fair or the Great Tennessee Fair or the Great Alabama Fair. Though Noel was never positive he could remember his father, he would always remember the Black Dragon because it kept coming back with the fair every year and it was rumored to have once killed a boy by decapitating him. At night, streamlined with hundreds of small clear bulbs, it resembled a polished black octopus, the spinning cockpits slingshotting toward earth, the tentacles engraved with a fierce red calligraphy. In later years it would return to town disguised under bright shades of metal-flake enamel and bearing various demonic aliases and blasting the latest heavy-metal soundtracks, but Noel always recognized the Black Dragon on sight and rode it dozens of times. As he got older he rode it drunk and stoned and once he rode it with a Polaroid of a naked woman in his back pocket.

He was failing first grade when his father was declared MIA. This prompted his mother to explain, "That means he's dead somewhere in Vietnam, but they don't know where yet. His bones always were hard to find."

Noel stared into the lined pages of a Blue Horse notebook he had been drawing pictures in, while his mother, a tall attractive woman fond of props and postures, rolled a wineglass filled with grape juice against her bottom lip. Before leaving the room, she knelt to where he sat on the rug and inserted a black and white photograph into his notebook.

It took Noel a moment to recognize her inside the photograph. Hiding a cigarette behind her back—the feathery smoke gave it away—his mother wore a white headband, a black dress, and stood wide-shouldered and thin-waisted and torpedo-breasted, listing into a man who, slim and tall, wore a baggy dark suit that seemed in wanting of a hat, a cigar, and a machine gun. Only his mother's shocked expression accounted for the whereabouts of the man's right hand. It was an old photograph with serrated edges, and someone had put out a cigarette on the man's heart. Because of this, it was difficult to separate his expression—the half sneer, the sun-slitted eyes—from the ridged wound melted through his chest that Noel now held up to the light and fit his eye to, as if to a keyhole, as if to the future.

At ten he played Little League for the Standard Oil Red Sox. One spring Sunday while trying to score off a triple, Noel shattered the collarbone of the opposing catcher. The catcher had to be carried off the field, the ball still clutched in his fist. Noel had been called out. He tried explaining this fact to his mother after the game while she paraded him past the grandstands. Her hair had been dyed blond the day before, actually more yellow, and she wore it in a short-banged fashion she called a butch. During the drive home Noel kept putting his red baseball cap on her, and she kept brushing it off and saying *stop that*. Suddenly she hit the brakes, and the white station wagon drifted into a familiar yard. For a moment they sat silent in the car while she adjusted the studious look on her face. Then, apologetically, she shrugged and suggested they have quick look inside. "Just hello and goodbye," she promised over Noel's protests.

Aunt Carol, the family spinster and one of his mother's five sisters, had a beagle name Archie that she pampered like an only child. Her front door had been left wide open that afternoon. They entered the house and called out hello and walked into the kitchen and there they found both Archie and Aunt Carol in a bad way. The beagle, its eyes sealed shut, was heaving away on a blue nylon blanket while Aunt Carol, wearing a pink bathrobe and no makeup, her hair bound in blue curlers, circumnavigated the blanket and remained frighteningly unaware of their presence, as if she were an apparition already passed into the spirit world awaiting the arrival of her dog.

Still in cleats and the red and blue uniform, Noel guided his aunt outside to the Rambler and placed her in the front seat then got into the back. While they waited, a wave of rain hammered over the car and vanished down the length of hood. His mother, who had been on the phone, tied a clear plastic bonnet over her hair then started across the yard carrying Archie. She placed the dog, a wet corpse for all purposes, upon Noel's lap in the back seat. Noel stiffened, shot out his limbs, and right at that moment a strange coincidence took place, one that would impress his born-again relatives far more than it would impress Noel himself. At the moment Archie touched Noel's lap, the beagle roused itself and seemed indisputably cured. Within minutes Archie was caroming about the yard sniffing out tennis balls. Archie even chased their station wagon when they finally left.

In the sideview mirror, the beagle faltered into a neighbor's yard. Noel turned and half accusingly asked his mother, "How'd you know to stop the car?"

. . .

Noel's stepfather bore an uncanny resemblance to Billy Graham, one he cultivated by sweeping back his hair in the same high-banged fashion. Roger had even assumed some of Billy's mannerisms, such as stabbing at the air in front of him with steepled hands. The house fell silent only during Billy Graham Crusade Specials when Roger required Noel, Matt, and their younger half-brother Ben to huddle before the TV and shut up. Roger had also installed a rotation system of grace. Before supper—which had become supper, no longer dinner—the three brothers took turns saying *bless this food to our use and thus to Thy service.*

Noel launched out of grace and into the play-by-play of how he had tried to take home off his triple. Matt and Ben listened with the reverence due an older brother who had broken someone's collarbone. But just as Noel was lowering his head to spear the catcher, Roger interrupted to ask, "Noel, isn't tomorrow the day your class goes to that zoo?"

Noel ignored the question the same way he had ignored the third-base coach, who had signaled him to stop. Noel had not wanted to stop. He wanted a homer. So he kept digging and rammed his helmet into the catcher, spearing him just above the chest protector. Then, after untangling himself, Noel had limped to the dugout through the loudest applause he had ever heard. "Ya killed him, Weatherspoon!" someone cheered from inside the dugout. That had caused Noel to stop and turn around. The catcher, sprawled facedown over home plate, had yet to move.

Noel did not get this far into the story before Roger interrupted him again.

"Noel. Did you hear me ask you a direct question?"

Noel said yes sir his class was going to the zoo. "And I haven't had any trouble breathing, not for weeks, ask Mom if you don't believe me."

Instead Roger said pass the salt. While sprinkling it over his spaghetti, he recalled, "We spent over a hundred dollars on those allergy tests. I think it's assumed we're going to heed the results."

Matt made a clown's crying face at his older brother.

"But I'm allergic to the whole planet," Noel protested.

"No, what you're allergic to, the main thing," Roger clarified, "is animal dander. Which is why we are not going to get a dog, Ben. And why we are certainly not going to get a snake, Matt. And knowing what we know, I'm wondering why we're even entertaining the notion of letting Noel go to that zoo tomorrow, especially since the last time he went there—correct me if I'm wrong—he had another asthma attack."

"I tested positive to grass, that don't stop me from having to weed your garden all the time."

"That's because your mother and I want you to grow up normal."

"He *is* normal," Alise said.

Roger picked up his fork, the fork he used to eat french fries and pizza; at breakfast he poured ketchup over his scrambled eggs.

"What's so normal about failing first grade?" he asked.

"Normal boys sometimes fail first grade. Then they study harder the next year and pass it, like Noel did."

"Going to the zoo is normal."

"He's not allergic to snakes."

Roger jabbed the fork at Matt, who was wearing a white T-shirt with a snotty collar. "Matthew," he said. "I don't want to hear one more word about snakes come out of your mouth for the rest of your life, understand?"

The phone began to ring, but no one dared answer it, not during supper. It rang a dozen times. Only after it had stopped did the family resume eating their spaghetti, everybody except Noel, who tipped back his chair and started over, "Okay, I'm rounding second, right? And Coach is waving his arms like crazy, yelling for me to stop. But I don't wanna stop. . . ."

· · ·

A bright slew of candy-coated pills awaited Noel at the breakfast table. Sometimes his mother arranged these pills in a cross shape, sometimes in a happy face, sometimes in the V-pattern of migrating geese. After everyone else had left the table, Noel handed her the permission slip. She widened her green eyes upon the purple mimeograph then scribbled her name boyishly at the bottom. "Don't breathe a word," she warned. Noel stood, but she touched his wrist. "Noel, there's something we need to discuss. It has to do with that boy. Ross Altman."

"Who?"

"The boy that got in your way, the one with the mask on. He had some kind of seizure after yesterday's game. They don't know what's wrong with him yet, but whatever it is, it's not your fault, okay? They can't get Ross to wake up. He's in a coma."

"In a what?"

"A coma. That means the doctors have to figure out a way to make him wake up."

"Is he gonna die?"

"No. Well, nobody knows yet. It's possible, I suppose."

Noel nodded and folded away the permission slip. As he started to leave the table, Alise said, "Wait. First let's find you some more blue pills. For the zoo. Just in case." Rummaging through the pill drawer, she murmured, "I don't know why I'm letting you go. I hate that place. Those poor beasts. Sometimes I think burning that zoo to the ground would be a pure Christian act." She tucked some blue pills into his shirt pocket and found two other pills already there, white nubs that had survived the wash. She dropped these into the disposal and while fanning her fingers under the spigot said, "Never mind. I didn't say that."

Kamper Park reeked of lost enthusiasm. It had survived two decades as an abomination of a small-town zoo where somnambulant animals huddled in cramped wet cages. Through the steel bars monkeys stared at the pine trees. The lion's tongue lagged out while it blinked and blinked at the boys who tried to rally it with their own roars and bared teeth. Eventually the boys took to pelting the lion with peanuts. Only the baboons had enough gumption to return fire—flinging pawfuls of shit between the bars at the boys. The llamas would not spit, though there were signs promising they would if annoyed. A mangy brown bear paced in its sleep, whisking an inch away from the bars at each turn.

After the zoo, the class brown-bagged lunch in a pavilion beside a playground containing a military tank and a red caboose. For this occasion each child had been allowed to bring one bag of candy. Noel had selected a jumbo sack of bubblegum cigarettes, each one wrapped in paper tinged red at one end. When blown into, the cigarettes would issue a few puffs of powdered-sugar smoke. They looked real, and everybody wanted one. Noel started the bidding at a quarter each. And although he cleared over six dollars that day, he did not care so much about the money. He cared about the power he felt, jacking up the price, denying a customer, slipping a freebie to a friend or a pretty girl.

When the rain started, the kids were herded under the pavilion. They crowded the rail nearest the street and posed with their cigarettes and timed their measured puffs to coincide with traffic. Some cars slowed, others honked, then a dirt-brown Buick jerked to the shoulder of the road and a man in a brown overcoat stepped outside and walked to the back of the car and leaned against it. He cocked one leg backward onto the fender and studied the pavilion.

"Look!" a girl cried out. "It's Billy Graham!"

. . .

That afternoon Alise took Noel to the clinic for his weekly allergy shots, three in his left arm, two in his throwing arm. Doc Martin broke off the needles with his thumb and gave Noel the syringes to play with. Halfway home, Noel had an attack. Alise got him home and propped him up in a makeshift bed she created by pushing Roger's recliner up against an easy chair. After using up the last of his inhaler, Noel sat bolt upright and began to rock. And that's how Roger found things when he arrived home from his security job at Pine Belt Airport. Roger was wearing his blue jumpsuit, and he had a rolled newspaper clamped under the same arm that toted a silver lunch pail. He stopped just inside the door, as if tactically absorbing the scene, but before he could say one word he was sent to the pharmacy for a new inhaler.

Noel used this reprieve to confess that he had been spotted at the zoo. Alise took in the news resiliently and then walked into the kitchen. She opened the freezer, said *goddamnit* into it, then let the door squeak shut.

The highlight of the ensuing argument was his mother screaming, "I will not have you following my children around like a spy in the dark!" Noel was recuperating on the back porch and pretending to read *Durango Street*, which was about this black kid who carried a switchblade harmonica. Noel had read the book a dozen times. Late at night, unable to sleep because of the synthetic adrenaline in his asthma medications, he would slip out of bed and wield that switchblade harmonica in imaginary gang fights until his chest seized up and he had to crawl back under the sheets, sipping from his inhaler and pretending to be bleeding to death in some ghetto alleyway.

Roger came out onto the porch and squatted beside Noel's rocking chair so that they shared the same backyard view: pecan and eucalyptus tree, budding garden, tall pine trees along the property edge. They stayed quiet until Roger reached up to steady the rocking chair and commented, "I suppose you think it makes a difference them being candy cigarettes." He raised a stop-sign palm. "Let me tell you a little story, Noel. Something you might find useful. Today, driving by that zoo, when I saw you under that wooden thing, I didn't recognize you, not at first. You ever have that happen, where you don't recognize somebody you know, and it's like, for those few seconds before you recognize them, it's like you're seeing them, *really seeing that person*, for the first time?"

"No sir."

"And it's like you can see their entire future."

"Yes sir."

"In this case I wouldn't call it a pleasant experience."

"No sir."

"Cut that out."

"Cut what out?"

"The yes-sir, no-sir crap."

"But you said always call you sir."

Roger exhaled wearily then continued, "You going to the zoo today, that was your mom's fault, not yours. I'm not punishing you for that." He steepled his hands, flexed the fingers. "But I was right about your asthma, wasn't I?"

"It wasn't the zoo, it was the allergy shots did it."

"Noel, be reasonable. Nobody's allergic to allergy shots."

"I am. I'm allergic to everything."

"No. Not everything. But you are allergic to that zoo. And when a man's wrong, he steps up and admits it."

"When was the last time you did?"

"Did what?"

"Admitted you was wrong."

Roger explained that he was not the one on trial here. A muddy hummingbird dive-bombed wasps off the juice feeder. When Noel reopened his paperback, Roger stated, "And another thing. Your mom and I, we're worried that you use those inhalers too much. We're considering taking them away from you."

Noel closed the book on his hand. Very carefully he stated, "But if you do that, I won't be able to play baseball."

"Baseball's not everything."

"It is to me."

"Well, what else can we do, Noel? Your hands shake—look at them. You can't sit still in class. Can't concentrate. That's what your teachers say. You've got bags under your eyes, like an old man does. You went through that last whiffer in two weeks. They're supposed to last you two months."

Noel banged the back of his skull against the headboard of the chair. Then he did it again, harder.

"Two months, that's what Doc Martin said. And now, to top it all off, you're out smoking cigarettes."

"*Candy* cigarettes."

"That's not the point—quit hitting your head, please—the point is . . ." He started rocking Noel's chair like a cradle, but Noel anchored the chair backward by stiffening his legs. "It's like this, Noel. Every time you use that inhaler, you know what it does?"

"It lets me breathe."

"It speeds up your heart." He lowered his hands onto Noel's knee. "It speeds up your heart."

LEE DURKEE

"So?"

"So! Think about that. A heart's only going to beat so many times—correct?"

"I guess."

"No guessing to it. It's a scientific fact. A heart is only going to beat a given number of times. So what you're doing, Noel, every time you use that thing, you're wasting heartbeats. You're shortening your life." Roger stood with a groan. Trying to sound jocular, he added, "Mom says pork chops in five minutes. And no, you're not getting off the hook, you're going to Aunt Paula's with the rest of us after supper."

Roger started inside, but Noel said, "Mom said you were going by the hospital today."

Roger ran his tongue around the inside of his mouth. He said, "That was none of your fault what happened. Boy was born that way. Something on the brain. It woulda happened sooner or later, even if you hadn't creamed him."

"He's dead, isn't he?"

"No. Not dead, not alive. Somewhere in the in between. They've got machines breathing for him. Which ain't right, if you ask me."

Noel asked if Ross was going to get better. It felt strange to call him by his first name.

Roger shook his head and said no, probably he wasn't. "If he was just a little more brain-dead then they could take him off those machines. Way it is, though, they got to leave him running. Like a car with the keys locked inside it. That's what the law says."

At supper, the family joined hands beneath the dining table, their arms forming an upside down crown. Roger said, "Matt, if you would," and Matt lowered his face and piped, "Good food, good meat, good God, let's eat." An occult silence ensued. Outside, setting behind pine trees and gray clouds, the sun became a full

25

moon and filled the dining room with the fuzzy consistency of a newspaper photo. Ben, his head barely showing above his plate, blinked his brown cow eyes at his two older half-brothers. Noel had sunk into laughing convulsions so severe they rippled through the crown of arms; Matt stared crucified into his own lap, refusing to cry out even though Roger was caving Matt's palm in lengthwise. Finally Roger rebowed his head.

"Ben," he said, "if you would."

♦ ■ ●

Hattiesburg already had a Pizza Hut. On the drive to Aunt Paula's, they passed the new McDonald's, its much-heralded grand opening still weeks away. Across the street loomed a billboard that for years had displayed a giant cartoon likeness of Noel's oldest cousin, Bible in hand, standing before a spearheaded gate that imprisoned a dark and smoldering castle. Gold letters against industrial gray sky spelled out, THE LOST TRIBE CHURCH. RATTLING THE GATES OF HELL! Cousin Rod pastored at the Lost Tribe, a disc-shaped church renowned for glossolalia, a beautiful-sounding word for a truly ugly phenomenon, one which Noel had yet to witness firsthand, though he had watched his cousins imitate it, and at school he had once overheard a girl say that scientists had recorded a man speaking in tongues, and when they had played it backward it had said, "Satan is king." Now McDonald's had confiscated the billboard, and Cousin Rod's black suit, Bible, and industrial hell had been replaced with the visage of a carnivorous clown.

At Aunt Paula's, the brothers veered into the TV room to join their cousins beneath an arabesque tent made out of blankets and sleeping bags draped over furniture. A color TV glowed from inside the tent. Most of his mother's family were jaw-set Methodists, and typically at these weekly gatherings their cousins let Noel and Matt know that, what with them being Baptists, they were going straight to hell. Noel believed them only to the extent that he could blame his stepfather for his eternal damnation. Ben alone seemed ostracized from this dire forecast, perhaps because even at five there was a yoked saintliness about him, an instinctive goodness that seemed mostly to embarrass him. Ben was simply not the same species as his older half-brothers. He had grown up worshiping Noel and Matt, but at the same time he had grown up observing them too, like a small good-natured anthropologist.

Their cousins were treating them too gingerly on this evening, even letting Noel commandeer the TV. Noel did not understand why this was until Cousin Angel returned from the kitchen with an extra ham sandwich and announced to Noel, "They're talking about you in there. You laid hands on Archie."

His eyes soaking up television glow, Noel muttered, "Uh-uh, he was like that when we got there."

"Rod says you might got the calling. Says it runs in our family. Except I heard him ask if you used your right hand or your left hand, because, if you used your left hand, that means you called on the power of Satan."

Angel held out the sandwich. Noel accepted it suspiciously, then checked under the bread. All his cousins were mayonnaise freaks. After he started chewing, he asked her what kind of calling. Angel, a lanky tomboy two years older than Noel with long straight hair the same color yellow his mother had so recently achieved, placed the heel of her palm against his forehead and told him, "To heal—like Jesus done." Then, toppling Noel over backward, she hissed, "*Get thee behind me, Satan!*"

During the next set of commercials Noel walked into the kitchen to spy on the grown-ups. They were in the den, the women sitting on a crescent-shaped white couch, its circle completed with straight-backed chairs that the men occupied, everyone except Roger sipping coffee. Aunt Carol, replacing her cup in its saucer, said she didn't care what anybody said. "I saw it with my own eyes—and so did you, Alise." Alise frowned and claimed to have seen no such thing, at which point Aunt Carol felt it necessary to reiterate the story of Archie and Noel. Listening, Noel launched spit bubbles off his tongue until his mother interrupted by saying, "Carol, if I ever catch you talking that way in front of my boys, I'll wring your neck."

The way she had said it, without the least hint of humor, halted the conversation. Alise blushed then massaged the scar where her ear had once been pierced. She seemed to be fighting the urge to apologize.

"It might help him be a good Christian," Aunt Mary suggested timidly.

"That's exactly what I'm afraid of."

Alise stood and made for the kitchen, passing Noel in the doorway. As she refilled her cup from the blue-flowered percolator, Noel was recalling what she had said about burning down the zoo. He was remembering her taking the Lord's name in vain. He wiped his buttery mouth on his wrist and asked, "Why come you don't want me to be a good Christian?"

"Because." She blew steam off the coffee at her own reflection in the dark window. "Good Christians bore the pants off me."

•   •   •

All that summer, while Ross Altman's corpse was being rhythmically inflated, Alise kept Noel stockpiled with balls and plastic weaponry and seemed genuinely impressed with his bloody noses and torn clothing and with whatever damage he had inflicted upon the neighborhood children. In spite of her best efforts, though, by mid-July Noel had become born again. Simultaneously the Gospel of Archie graduated from a simple laying-on-of-hands to an outright resurrection. Archie had been brought back from the dead! More than once, Noel heard himself likened to Jesus, though one afternoon Cousin Rod took him aside and warned him not to take any personal credit for the miracle but to ascribe his healing powers to the Holy Ghost. "Otherwise you're just an ol' sorcerer."

Soon both Archie and Noel were receiving preferential treatment at family gatherings. Noel was showered with Jesus paraphernalia, most notably a New Testament for kids and a red T-shirt that said, JESUS, THE REAL THING! in Coca-Cola lettering. Noel liked that shirt, and when it became shredded in its very first wash cycle he suspected foul play. To get even with his mother, he took to reading the New Testament in front of her. Alone in his bedroom he placed onionskin paper over the New Testament's color plates and traced the cruciform bodies of Christ and the two thieves, then he colored in the picture and clamped it to the refrigerator with magnets. He also began to frequent Aunt Carol's Feed My Sheep Bookstore, where he bought with his own money a paperback called *I Believe in Miracles*. Late at night he cut short switchblade fights to raise the dead.

It wasn't until late August that his salvation began to unravel. One Sunday afternoon, when he was supposed to be weeding the garden, Noel was sitting beside Ben on the love seat watching a horse race on their black and white TV. The race at Belmont, billed the "Battle of the Sexes," pitted that year's Kentucky Derby winner, Foolish Pleasure, against an unbeaten three-year-old filly named Ruffian. The race would run a fast mile and a quarter, which meant the network had to fill the hour time slot with interviews and highlights. One expert explained that the horses would try to *break each other's hearts*, meaning they would run the entire distance at top speed until the winner *cut out the heart* of the loser. It was this use of language that stopped Noel from turning the channel to pro wrestling to watch his hero Dusty Rhodes, the man who had lispingly coined the expression *payback is hell.* The second announcer noted that in body type and margin of victory, Ruffian was the only horse to rival the great Secretariat. Then they showed Ruffian—large-bodied and thin-shinned and appearing solid black on the TV—running to a slow-motion victory in an earlier race.

"They say the lady's never been tested," the first announcer reflected. "But since her granddaddy is Bold Runner—that's Secretariat's daddy, mind you—nobody I've talked to today expects Ruffian to suffer from a glass heart."

Ben gazed at the TV while spooning at a bowl of ice cream and chocolate syrup. Noel sipped from a mug of instant coffee he'd made from the stash his mother kept hidden from Roger, who did not allow coffee inside the house. He took a sip and asked Ben which horse he wanted to win. Ben blinked fiercely, a habit he had before answering any question, then he said, "The girl one."

Noel frowned at that, but before he could correct his younger brother's loyalties, the race had started. Ruffian broke from the gate ahead of the smaller Foolish Pleasure. The filly held her lead, about two lengths, as they circled the track, both jockeys staying at the whip. Approaching the home stretch, Ruffian was still in front when all at once the camera followed Foolish Pleasure pulling ahead into that great solitude he was no doubt accustomed to. The camera panned, trying to encompass both horses, but Ruffian was nowhere to be found. "She's gone," Ben whispered, which made Noel think of *rapture,* a phenomenon his cousins had recently explained to him. Only after Foolish Pleasure had crossed the finish line did the camera begin to scan backward in search of Ruffian. It found her staggering along the outside rail on a shattered foreleg that flapped in the air when she reared. She landed on the leg, which buckled outward, and Noel's mind began to swim. He watched through his fingers as a squat van and an ambulance converged near Ruffian. Three men jumped out of the van to assist the jockey in settling the horse. Within seconds they had stripped the saddle and placed her leg inside an inflatable splint. Next they prodded Ruffian up a retractable ramp. The van sped away into a tunnel beneath the grandstand.

The instant replays began—the leg exploding again and again in slow motion.

    • • •

The world's greatest horse specialist was flown in to operate on Ruffian. He explained that if the injury had occurred a mere six months earlier, they would have had to *terminate her immediately.* As it was, the operation would be *precarious at best.* Alise had allowed Noel to stay up late and watch the news on the condition he not tell Roger, who always went to bed at nine sharp. When the segment ended, Noel said goodnight; then, on his way upstairs, he veered into Ben's bedroom and flicked on the overhead light. Ben was sucking his thumb through the sheets. Noel sat on the bed and could not stop himself from confiding his plan. He was going to heal Ruffian.

Ben sat up, his head cocked backward. Squinting, he asked, "How you gonna do that?"

Noel explained he would simply think about laying hands on Ruffian all night. "It's just one lousy leg," he pointed out.

All night long he dream-healed Ruffian. In one dream that startled him awake, he had pressed both his palms against Ruffian's chest, as if pushing her backward, and he could feel the bucketwork of her heart. His last dream had nothing to do with Ruffian, though. It had to do with Ross Altman. Ross was standing at the foot of Noel's bed. He was wearing a short-sleeved blue jersey with BLUE JAYS written across the chest. He had limp blond hair and sad blue eyes, and he had been watching Noel sleep. Noel woke up to find him there, and they looked at each other.

Then Ross faded away to nothing. Noel did not become scared until after Ross was gone. He told himself it was just a dream, just a dream. He was too afraid to go back to sleep, so he stayed awake until first light, then he turned on the clock radio and waited for the sports news, where he learned that Ruffian had been "put to sleep" during the night. The voice of the surgeon, after explaining that it was the humane thing to do, said that the operation had failed because, even under heavy sedation, Ruffian would not stop pumping her legs. "We couldn't stop her from running," he said. "She was still trying to win that race."

After a while Noel walked downstairs and stood over Ben's bed until he awoke of his own accord. He looked up at Noel, who told him the bad news. "She died, Ben. She died." Ben balled a fist into one eye and covered the other eye with the flat of his palm. He said, "I know she did. I dreamed I was riding her up to heaven."

Later that afternoon, strolling home from baseball practice, Noel came upon a dead squirrel in the road. It had no outward injuries other than a red bulb emerging from its mouth. Noel looked around then dropped his glove and squatted down and slowly placed his right palm upon the squirrel's rib cage. Closing his eyes, he tried to envision the color plates inside his New Testament. Suddenly he felt very observed. He sprang to his feet and glanced around wildly. Only after he was positive he was alone did he squat down again. He began to lower his left hand toward the squirrel. But at the last moment he chickened out and instead he picked up a long pine stick stripped of bark and began poking at the squirrel's eyes and at the artery inside its mouth. He carried the stick with him the long way home past the hospital.

Noel stood outside the hospital, gazing up at the countless windows reflecting the setting sun. When the sun had set in all of the windows, even the top ones, he walked inside, into the air-conditioning and breezed through the maze of corridors until he found what he was looking for. Then he set down the stick atop the cigarette vending machine then plunged his hand deep into his pocket, full of hard change.

CHAPTER TWO

BY THE END OF THE SEVENTH GRADE, which he narrowly averted having to repeat, Noel was the tallest white boy in his class and strutted the hallways wearing flannel shirts flyaway style above white T's tucked haphazardly into jeans and low-billing a black Cat Diesel Power cap. His straight black hair hung almost to his shoulders. During classes he rehearsed tattoos on notebook paper—guitars, daggers, UFOs, syringes, and especially the Zig Zag Man, his trademark of choice—before copying them onto his forearms using black, blue, red, and green ballpoint. Between classes he trapped kids against lockers and made them admire his latest tattoo and bragged that he was going to hitchhike to New Orleans and get this one done up for real.

Not even the blacks would fight him anymore. Like everyone else, they knew what had happened on the baseball field. Noel missed having enemies almost as much as friends. On the last day of the school year he followed the only Jewish kid in his class home, taunting him, trying to get him to fight, but instead they ended up in the mall together shoplifting. Noel's parents, however, did not approve of this new friendship. Not only was Tim Jewish, but he did not play sports and had straight brown hair even longer than Noel's. Tim's mother, a nurse, was divorced and attractive. And there were rumors about her too.

Roger designed a chore chart that summer. Each day the boys had to check off boxes and sign their initials, although Noel usually cut short his yard work for baseball practice. After practice he headed straight to either Pasquale's Pizza, where he had a job washing dishes, or to Tim's house.

A tidal pool of junk ran throughout Tim's household: dirty laundry, lipstick-filtered ashtrays, fast-food wrappers, snipped-out fashion magazines, bills, tabloids, and abandoned meals. Tim's bedroom was awash in comic books, and he had a box of pornographic magazines stashed under the bed. It was there that Noel had seen his first photograph of a naked woman. *That's where it goes*, he had thought to himself. That's where it goes. But when he finally spoke, what he had said was, "Somebody took that picture."

The only clean room in the house was the den, where Tim's mother had hung her own artwork, thick acrylics of nude cubist women. Miss Weiss did not get home until seven each night. Most afternoons Noel found Tim in his bedroom suctioning in a new comic book. Today the Green Lantern's ring formed an emerald sun that beamed down onto a desolate ice-locked planet. Noel studied his friend a moment—the dark complexion, the intent, slightly moving lips, the aquiline nose, and girlish eyelashes—then grabbed up an old comic off the floor and fanned the back pages until he found the ad for X-ray glasses. In it, a cartoon kid was watching the bone structure of his hand while his older brother, also wearing the glasses, whistled at a pretty girl. For the next quarter hour Noel lost himself inside this world of inadvertently naked women and wheeling skeletal birds.

Then Tim was laughing at him.

"You weren't even hearing me, were you, Weatherspoon? I asked do you want to listen to some Richard Pryor, maybe smoke some weed?"

"You got some?"

"You know I don't. You?"

"Yeah, but I'm running low."

Noel had been scoring pot at work, which was pretty funny because it was Roger who had gotten him hired at Pasquale's.

Tim led the way into his mother's bedroom and put on *That Nigger's Crazy*. The disheveled king-size water bed had a paneled stereo built into its headboard. Four peach crates, filled with jazz albums and topped with a bendable lamp and a clock radio, served as the bed table. There was a large, mostly empty bookshelf of untreated pine containing disordered encyclopedias as well as a small cache of Edgar Cayce paperbacks. They sat on the wooden floor between the bed and the open window. After turning on the fan, Tim brought out the stethoscope and unscrewed the metal drum, which revealed a perfect bowl. They removed the earpieces then inhaled hookah style through the black tubes. While they smoked, it occurred to Noel how easy it would be to spy in on Miss Weiss from the backyard. For some reason this thought unnerved him. He tried to dismiss it by examining some albums, but every so often his glance wandered outside again, and he saw himself standing in the starlit backyard spying into the bright room. Just above the tree line he could see the very top of Forest General Hospital, where Miss Weiss was now at work and where, as Noel imagined it, the robotlike breathing machines were forever crowding Ross Altman's bed.

Over the years Noel had taken to bragging about the home-plate collision, telling teammates, *Yeah, and now he's brain-dead!* But he had never told anybody about the dreams that had haunted him for years now and that were turning him into an insomniac. In these dreams Ross Altman appeared in his bedroom and called Noel by name. Nor had Noel told anybody about his recent visit to the hospital room and the dehydrated corpse with the Ouija board on it.

Although he had not told Tim about that visit, he did half expect Tim to ask about it, because as soon as he had left Ross's room that afternoon, he had run into Tim's mom in the hallway.

"Noel, what were you doing in there?" she had asked.

The whiteness of her uniform had paralyzed him for a moment. Then he lowered the bill of his Cat Diesel Power cap and told her that he'd just wanted to see what he looked like, that's all. "He's from way out in Petal. I'd never even met him before. . . ."

"And?" she asked. "What did you think?"

"He looked like he'd been buried and dug up."

She nodded and knelt down and adjusted her white shoe, using her finger as a shoehorn. She was wearing white hose, and the knee that stuck out when she knelt was white too. Still on one knee, she had looked up at him and said, "Between me and you, Noel, I wish someone would come along and unplug that poor boy."

Noel blew more cannabis smoke toward the hospital, and for a moment he thought he heard Ross call his name again. That was how Ross always woke him up at night, by calling out his name all forlorn and wind-carried. Noel. The same name as his dead father's. Properly pronounced in one quick syllable, never two, except by older boys looking for trouble and trying to make it sound like a girl's name or something to do with Christmas. In Noel they often found trouble. He'd fight them, no matter how much bigger they were, then he'd pick himself up and fight them again.

"You ever seen a ghost?" he asked Tim.

"A ghost?"

"Yeah. There's this girl at work says her dad comes and visits her at night. He got stabbed to death when she was a baby. She says it's not scary. He just likes to watch her sleep."

"A ghost," Tim repeated, even more sarcastically.

Tim's tone dissuaded Noel from pursuing the subject.

"Your mom listens to a lot of black people," he noted.

"Are you seeing ghosts these days, Weatherspoon?"

"Nah. But I kinda believe in them, don't you?"

Tim just smirked and turned his head away, staring at the stereo speaker as if it were a TV. Chastened, Noel picked out a Fats Waller album and began to read the back. The album felt weighted wrong, though. He looked inside it and found a bulky envelope stashed there. He took out a rubber-banded deck of Polaroids. At first he tried to conceal this discovery, but Tim leaned over and touched the Polaroids, as if to jerk them away. But he didn't; instead he too sat mesmerized by the chlorinated colors of naked women.

Most of the women had thick bones and short hair, and they were all posing somberly naked on the water bed. Noel sorted the deck top to bottom, allowing about ten seconds for each photo. The very last Polaroid was of Miss Weiss. She was smiling and naked on the water bed, her hands thatched behind her raised head, her legs raised and bent so that the soles of her small feet were pressed together prayerlike.

Tim snatched away the photos. Then he recrated the album and shunned the room, calling back sharply, "Come here. I got to show you something."

But Noel lingered, gazing at the water bed. When Tim called again, Noel followed the voice into the garage, where he found Tim perched on a cinder block, a Virginia Slims cigarette protruding from his mouth. Tim lobbed a small green disc across the garage at Noel and said, "Worm dirt." Noel caught the disc, opened it. He held the tobacco to his nose. "You go first," he said, but Tim was already pointing with both index fingers to the cigarette duckbilled in his mouth.

"Hey, I'm not the one has asthma attacks every time he lights up these days."

"Hell, son, I taught you," Noel muttered, but he went ahead and tucked in a large pinch of the Skoal. Tightening his bottom lip, he mumbled, "Them pictures—"

"Don't spit on the damn floor."

Tim handed over a large McDonald's cup, then streamlined smoke toward a cardboard box. "Look inside there," he said. Noel did and removed two pairs of boxing gloves stitched out of stained crimson leather.

"They used to belong to my dad."

"He was a boxer?"

"I dunno. He used to beat up my mom."

"Your mom . . ."

Tim lashed the gloves onto Noel's wrist so quickly that Noel had no time to get rid of the Skoal. After Tim had laced on his own gloves, using his teeth, the two boys squared off, Noel feeling alternately nauseous . . . dreamlike . . . aroused. He parried with his left, roundhoused with his right, but soon his arms grew heavy. The garage began to gyroscope around him. He was just about to call time-out when Tim came in hunched low, then straightened up and flurried into him. The back of Noel's head hit cement first. His eyes had not shut. He had absorbed the whole backward sweep of his fall. Brown spit seeping between his lips, he lay there, his face in the afternoon sun, his body in the shade of the garage, while Tim stood over him with tears on his jaw and neck.

"She's an artist! That's what artists do, that's how they paint. *They all* do stuff like that!"

Then Tim turned and slammed the door, leaving Noel spread-eagled on the driveway. After a few deep breaths, he flopped over onto his boxing gloves and knees. Holding that position, he spat out the tobacco, then shed the gloves and tested his legs. "I called time-out," he lied, before staggering the mile home under a headache like a jet taking off.

• • •

Noel's house was in a much poorer suburb than Tim's, but it was the only two-story house on the block. The house was brick, and the windows of the two upstairs bedrooms stared out upon Mandalay Drive like eyes. His mother, barefoot and wearing a short lime-green dress that showed off her legs, met him at the door and told him there was someone here to meet him. She ushered Noel by the shoulders into the den, where a tall man sat all arms and legs inside the green La-Z-Boy recliner. He had the footrest up, and the chair had just twirled all the way around and was coming to a halt.

"Noel," Alise began. "I'd like you to meet Tommy Weatherspoon, your dad's baby brother and heir apparent. You've met him before, but you don't remember it."

"How you get outa this thing, Alise?" Tommy asked, locking his eyes on Noel in a quick, confidential manner. Alise replied that she would rescue him in exchange for one of those cancer sticks, and instantly Tommy righted the chair and offered up his pack. That's when Noel saw the ponytail. Ribbed with red elastics, it ran along his spine almost to his belt. Noel had never before seen a man with a ponytail, nor had he seen his mother smoke, something she did with a familiar flair, tapping a cigarette out of the pack then leaning into the lighter Tommy Weatherspoon held forth. After she had it lit, she went around the den opening doors and windows until the air filled with sun streams and dust. She kept using her free hand to smooth her hair, which had grown back to brown.

She warned Noel, "Don't you dare tell, or I swear I'll hide the coffee where you'll never find it." Then she came over and pushed her palm across his forehead. "What happened to your shirt? Is that blood?"

Noel backed away and explained he had been in a fight, that's all.

"Yeah, you tag 'em one?" Tommy Weatherspoon wanted to know. He had an amused, sleepy way of asking.

"Naw, but I know where he lives at. And payback is hell."

Tommy grinned from Noel to Alise, then to her bare feet, then to the open window.

"Not far from the tree, huh?" he said.

"Not far enough." Alise moved in front of the window, as if to intercept his gaze; then, pretending to be studying something outside, she said, "I don't know where Matthew's off at—you, Noel?"

"Matthew?" Noel said, because nobody ever called him that but Roger. Matt had ball practice, he reminded her. "Like always."

The wind tailed inside and slammed shut first the front door, then the door to the kitchen. Alise put her hand to her heart and said *ghosts*. She seemed to be enjoying herself. Smiling approvingly, she walked around the couch and began to tell Noel all about *Mr. Weatherspoon here*. The first time they'd met, he was just a boy fond of spying on people. She said it was hard to believe little Tommy was a grown-up businessman now.

Tommy wavered his hand in the air and replied, "Hell, we own a coupla frydog stands is all."

"We?"

"Yeah, but we want to sell them off, use the money to open a restaurant down in the Keys. At least that's the plan. But you know what they say about plans." He shrugged and asked, "Hey, you play ball good as your old man did?"

"What's this *we*? You hitched up, Tom?"

"Hell no, Alise."

Still studying him, as if she doubted the truth of that answer, she added, "Tommy's company owns almost a hundred concession stands, Noel. They rent them out. Cotton candy ones, fried dough, candy apples, onion rings . . . stuff like that. Spread out over what— a dozen fairs? What is it with your family and fairs?"

He laughed and said it wasn't just fairs, it was rodeos and bluegrass festivals too. "And I don't think anybody's ever called us a company before." Whenever he quit talking, the rubbery grin took over his face.

"My dad used to play double-A," Noel said.

"I know he did. I watched him pitch a no-hitter once."

"He pitched a no-hitter?"

"Hell yes. Your mom never told you that?"

"She never tells us nothing about him. She says the less we know, the better."

There was a long silence in which Tommy studied a shard of sunlight on the green carpet, and Alise raised her eyebrows, as if daring anybody to object. Finally Tommy said, "Yeah, he pitched a no-hitter. Walked a good dozen of them boys. And he must've set some sort of record for bean balls that day too. He never was big on control. Hell, the other team scored three runs."

Suddenly Noel understood why his uncle was here.

"They found him, didn't they, his bones?"

"His bones?" Shaking his head slowly at first, then faster, Tommy said, "No. Hell no. Not yet, they ain't."

"His bones always were hard to find," Alise offered out.

"She always says that. She thinks he's dead. You think he's dead?"

Leaning forward and appearing less awkward, Tommy nodded sagely and predicted, "If he is, you can bet ol' Goose took down some gooks with him."

"Goose?"

"That was his nickname." Again he glanced at Alise. "Because our family was from Goose Creek. And because he looked like a damn goose too. It's what we all mostly called him. His family did—including your mom here."

"What I mostly called him will have to remain a secret, for now, but I can promise you it was not Goose."

Noel remarked that he never much liked the name *Noel*.

"Neither did your old man, at least not when he was a kid. Guys used to call him No-el. Like that song. They'd call him *the first No-el*. They do that to you?"

"Yes sir. But they only do it once," Noel said, then he asked what was a gook.

"Gook's a Viet Cong. Used to be the enemy."

"It's not a word we use in this house."

"No reason to." He spread his palms upright and winked at Noel as a longer breeze entered the room.

"Tommy served in Vietnam too."

"You did?"

"Yep, eighteen and just barely stupid enough to qualify. Weapons specialist, they called me, though to this day I don't know why. Mostly what I did was practice my picking. I was the best damn banjo player in Vietnam."

"My stepfather," Noel reported, "had flat feet."

"Your daddy had webbed toes. That's another reason they called him Goose."

"Had what?"

"Webbed toes. Webbed like a duck's. The army don't mind that, though. Now, flat feet, that's different. Can't hump on flat feet."

"Can't what?"

"Hump. March."

Tommy looked down at his wrist. There was no watch there, only a pale band of skin topped by a pale medallion. He slapped his knees but did not stand. Averting his eyes, he said, "Your daddy, he was a hero, your mom told you all that, right?"

Noel had to wait for his mother to quit laughing before he could answer.

"Yes sir. I mean, I guess she did."

"Your mom, she doesn't want me to tell you this."

"Tell me what?"

"What I'm about to tell you."

Alise stood and said she thought she'd go check on supper. "Roger'll be home in half an hour," she noted, as if to herself.

Tommy watched as she left the room. Then he said, "She hasn't been telling you the truth, Noel, not exactly." He held his breath and released it with a *phaaa* sound. "Alright. Ready or not here goes. See, about five years ago this badass Marine escaped from a POW camp in Vietnam, one of those mobile units out in the Happy Valley. Nothing happy about it, though. That's *jungle* jungle, nowhere you ever want to be. And this fella ends up giving a pretty good account of maybe your dad being kept a few hootches over. A private. Who answered to Goose. Was from down south but spoke fluent Vietnamese. Said he looked like a bunch of sticks all tied together."

"Goose," Noel whispered.

"Yeah. Goose. Now, see, the army, it's got something it likes to call Title Thirty-seven. Title Thirty-seven says they had to switch your dad from MIA to POW and to notify his family. Which they did. But your mom, she didn't notify you. Didn't want you getting your hopes up, I guess." He fit one work boot inside the shard of light he had been studying. "Okay. Now fast-forward. In '73, we traded all our prisoners for all theirs. Supposedly. Operation Homecoming, they called it.

LEE DURKEE

But your dad wasn't one of the ones came home. Am I going too fast?
I don't talk to kids much."
    Noel asked what a hootch was.
    "Hootch is a hut. Made outa bamboo."
    "My dad spoke flu-what?"
    "He spoke Vietnamese. He didn't before, but prisoners tend to
pick it up real quick. They have to." Tommy allotted five seconds
for another question, then continued. "Alright. No American
POWs were left alive in Vietnam, that's the official word from DC.
But it's a crock of shit—lies, I mean—as far as I'm concerned it is.
Something not right is going on over there, Noel, and it has to do
with what they call *pearls.*"
    Before Noel could ask, Tommy began to explain that a *pearl* was a
POW held for ransom, and that during peace negotiations that ass-
hole Nixon had promised the Vietnamese billions of U.S. dollars to
help them rebuild their country. But then Watergate had hit, and
Congress had vetoed giving away all that money. "Meaning the
Vietnamese lost face. And so, during Operation Homecoming, the VC
kept back a few hundred pearls because Nixon had lied to them just
like he'd lied to everybody else he'd ever opened his mouth in front of.
Our boys got sold down the river—treason, pure and simple—by
Nixon and that other bastard Kissinger. So maybe, just maybe, your
dad's still alive over there, rotting in some prison cell. It's possible.
Point is, if he shows up now, he'll make those Pentagon boys look
awful bad, and they just ain't gonna let that happen. So what I'm
telling you, Noel—what I'm trying to tell you—is this. Even if your
dad is still alive—and he probably ain't—he's better off dead."
    Noel's headache had swarmed to his brow during this explana-
tion, which was anything but clear to him. Having finished, Tommy
pushed down on the armrest to stand. It was at that moment that
Noel realized who it was that his uncle reminded him of: the scare-

45

crow in *The Wizard of Oz*. Except Tommy was much taller, coming
in at about six-foot-four. When he stretched himself out, the rattle
of a snake tattoo slid out from underneath his shirt cuff.

"I gotta go sell a man a busted Frialator," he said.

"Matt'll be home soon. You could stay for supper."

That made him smile. "You trying to get me shot?"

"No sir."

"I'll meet Matt next time I pull through town. Besides, your
mom says he's too young to hear this. Maybe she's right. Maybe
she's right about you being too young too."

"No sir, she ain't right."

"Good. Because I'm gonna try and send you letters, keep you
posted." He put his hand out. After they had shaken, he said,
"Noel, always look a man in the eye when you shake his hand."

Noel looked his uncle square in the eye and said, "I play shortstop. I once put a kid in a coma who tried to block the plate on me.
He's been there years now. He's *brain-dead.*"

. . .

It was like a field of electricity, his insomnia was, hovering and
crackling above his bed. He turned on the light and took out pencil
and paper and began to draw Miss Weiss from memory. He could
see her clearly, if fleetingly, a distinct image that faded to white like
a Polaroid developing in reverse. He outlined her limbs first, the
cocked elbows, the monkey-prayer feet. Then the dark hair, short
and tucked behind tiny ears. He touched in the slight hook of her
nose, the pressed smile, the catlike eyes, then he paused to use his
inhaler before penciling in her breasts, practicing the curves over
and over before hardening the line. Next his pencil followed the
hip bone, coasting along her thighs, then upward, but slower,
slower, as he entered a vortex, that dark tunnel where he forgot to

breathe and his bed jarred forward as if pulled through the night by chains.

The next morning he announced he wanted a camera for his birthday. His mother finished pouring her orange juice, then replied, "That's still months away. You'll change your mind a dozen times before then."

• • •

Hattiesburg's small Jewish community lived in an affluent neighborhood, the one exception being the Weisses' small A-frame with its overgrown lawn and peeling gray paint. Tim and Noel were in the TV room on the L-shaped couch that half enclosed a coffee table covered with the desiccated remains of a Burger King meal. The blue curtain had been draped across the sliding-glass door in order to cut the glare off the TV. They watched a game show in silence. Neither of them had mentioned the events of the previous day. After a while Tim stood and said he wanted to go down the street to the minimart and see if the new *Daredevil* was in.

Not taking his eyes off the set, Noel handed over a crumpled bill and said, "Bring me back a Coke, alright?"

Tim hesitated but then took the dollar and left. As soon as he was gone, Noel tore into the back bedroom. He found the Fats Waller album, then separated the Polaroid of Miss Weiss and clamped the photograph atop the peach crate. With his scalp resting against the warming cradle hood of the lamp, he dove into the photograph and sharked around, threshing deeper and closer to Miss Weiss's nakedness until suddenly, from the above world, he heard a door slam shut. Following a series of false starts, he crammed the Polaroid into his back pocket, slid the album into the crate, then darted for the bathroom. Five minutes later he flushed the toilet and returned into the TV room.

It wasn't Tim who had slammed the door, it was Tim's mother. Miss Weiss stood there aiming the remote control at arm's length toward the TV and clicking the device to no effect. She had on the same short white dress, and she was so petite that she looked more like a precocious sixteen-year-old than anybody's mother. Frowning, she turned to Noel and asked where his sidekick was.

"My God, it's a beautiful day out, what in the world are you two doing with this thing on? Jesus, how do you turn it off, Noel? Help me out here, will you?"

He covered the distance between them. Then, while taking the remote from her hand, he received a fishhook of static.

"Oh," she said. "You feel that?"

He squeezed hard around the battery compartment and clicked once. The picture shrank into a blue cube.

"How did you do that?" she demanded, but before he could demonstrate she had turned to open the curtain. "Like a couple of vampires." She lit a long cigarette and blew smoke against the glass door.

"Well, where is the little shit?"

She turned again and had just seemed to notice something wrong with Noel's face when Tim bounded into the room holding two cans of Coke. Wielding her attention upon Tim, she asked, "Do you want to explain to me, young man, what this television is doing on?"

Tim attempted a charming smile and asked what she was doing home.

"Never mind what I'm doing home, what I want to know is what this TV is doing on. Didn't we have this discussion already? I'll sell it, Tim, I swear I will."

"I turned it on," Noel said, though at first no one seemed to have heard him. He cleared his throat and explained that at home his stepdad would not let him watch any TV. "He says TV is run by devil worshipers in New York City."

"Excuse me?" said Miss Weiss.

"Sometimes he says devil worshipers in New York." Noel shrugged apologetically. "And sometimes he says it's the Jews in Hollywood."

He paused to let the washboard thrill of the lie pass through him. He had heard these theories not from Roger but from his cousins. Noel looked down at the remote in his hand and explained that he had made Tim turn on the TV.

"See, you squeeze it around the batteries—like this."

And he held out the remote to her.

"Oh my God." She winced then reached out and touched Noel's jaw, flicking the smooth bone with her lacquered nails. "You poor thing."

CHAPTER THREE

LATE THAT NIGHT Noel shucked off his clothes and began pacing around his room holding the Polaroid in front of him like a psychic entering a trance. This trance led him downstairs into the dark kitchen, where he opened the refrigerator and let its light yellow his nakedness. He opened and closed the refrigerator twice more before following the Polaroid into the backyard to stand among the watery shadows beneath the pecan tree. There he began to pee in an arc that crested above his head. When he heard the footsteps, he could not stop peeing, and the warm urine lashed his legs as he grafted himself to the pecan tree. He scoured the yard, but found nothing there, at least nothing he could see. "Ross, that you?" he called out. No answer, just the footsteps, louder, closer. Finally he lowered his gaze just enough to spot the tortoise.

It was a huge one, too, its shell the size of a dinner platter, plodding through the pecan shadows toward the distant garden. Noel waited until it passed the tree, then he stepped up onto the damp shell. The tortoise froze and seized itself inward. A moment later, though, the legs reemerged, then the nub head, and it began to lug Noel out of the shadows and into the moonlight.

Throughout this painfully slow ride, Noel watched himself as if through the windows of his neighbors' homes, this tall and slender, almost feminine young man, monstrously aroused, forearms and biceps hieroglyphed with guitars and switchblades and UFOs, surfing across a moon-smoked lawn on the shell of a giant terrapin. After a few moments of this, the tortoise suddenly deflated again. Noel stepped down and carried it the rest of the way to the garden.

Even by starlight, the garden appeared too immaculate: beans sprouting under musical scales of twine, aluminum pie plates dangling from blueberry bushes, and tomatoes blooming inside spiral cages spray-painted white to match the staked ornamental fence. Noel took no pride in the garden even though he had done most of the work—everything but the actual seeding. Cucumber vines teased through the fence, and the tortoise began to chew the tiny yellow flowers there. Noel stepped over the fence and knelt beside his stepfather's prized watermelon. The melon was almost three feet long, still yellow underneath but green on top. Noel turned it over and found a stick and punctured the watermelon, then he shoved two fingers deep inside the sugary pinkness and tasted them.

Repositioning himself with palms flat on the dirt, he straddled the melon and began to couple with it. A minute later he came devastatingly into the watermelon as if dying in waves of pleasure, terror, and humiliation. . . . These waves did not soon subside, his groin gulping like some desert animal at a spring. Eventually he pushed himself off and rolled over beneath a blueberry bush, its pie plates cupping the moonlight, and he opened his eyes upon the synapse of stars bearing down on him, letting their codes merge with his own, a meeting of incomprehensions.

The rest of the night was spent slumped on the toy box by his bedroom window staring numbly into the Polaroid. He had fucked a watermelon and his shame knew no bounds.

The next night he fucked it again.

After that, Ross Altman began to visit him nightly and there was no such thing as sleep. Two weeks of no sleep. For hours on end he would keep the sheets pulled over his head and listen to Ross sadcalling his name. To escape this fate, Noel started getting dressed and sneaking out of the house and taking long walks deep into the world of night. He stood alone in yards and spied into windows, longing to see something he could not yet put a name to. Full of hope and dread, he walked into the Jewish suburb, but night after night her bedroom light was off. Next he would circumambulate the hospital, where only a scattering of lights showed. Before going home, however, he would return past the Weisses'. Finally, one night, into his third week of no sleep, he was staring at the dark A-frame when suddenly a light shot on inside.

He followed the driveway around back and dropped to hands and knees and spidered across the backyard until he was sitting directly under her bedroom window. Traces of saxophone penetrated the glass. Trying to get up his nerve to spy inside, he sat there for almost an hour with his head inches below the windowsill, his back pressed against the peeling paint, his feet almost touching the window's four-paned reflection on the grass. Twice her shadow passed across this green window.

Then the bedroom light went out, and the stars seemed to grow and flex. All Noel ever saw up there were dippers, hundreds of dippers. He sat there another ten minutes before crawling away and fleeing down the street. Feeling increasingly invisible, he backtracked to the hospital and began to stake out the emergency room. When an ambulance arrived, he slipped inside and made for the staircase then climbed to the seventh floor, where the stairwell window revealed a long, bright, empty hallway.

There are moments when the gestures of our dreams jar us awake. Noel seemed to awaken more with each footstep down the hallway—more panic, more adrenaline—and yet the dream never broke. He pushed open the door to Ross's room. It was dark inside except for the television glow, the screen showing a test pattern. The circular TV light—like the reflection of a giant clock—fell upon the bed's white sheets. Noel could make out the narrow mound of Ross's body. It was a small private room, he knew, but the severe darkness along the walls made the room feel infinitely large. Tiny red and green lights formed dissolving lines behind the bed. Every few seconds there was a beep followed by a hydraulic sigh.

Though Noel did not realize it, he had begun to breathe along with the rhythm of the ventilator as he took two strides to the bed and gently removed the pillow from under Ross's head. He placed the pillow over Ross's face and pressed down hard with both hands. The pillow was thin enough that he could feel the shape of the mouth and nose. He could even feel the teeth. The body did not kick or groan or otherwise object, but the lungs kept inflating, no matter how hard Noel pushed down. After a few minutes, he splayed his left hand over Ross's chest. The heartbeat was throbbing steadily against his palm when suddenly—as if separating itself from the pulse—there was the distinct *clip-clip-clip* of footsteps in the hallway. Noel ducked beside the bed. The footsteps passed, and after a while Noel quit hugging the pillow and stood, but as he did this his left arm became entangled in a plastic tube. He followed the tube with his hands until it slithered into Ross's throat. Biting his lip, Noel crimped the tube around his index finger. The next time the machine sighed, the tube strangled his finger. After a minute of this, the machine began to make a series of faster beeps, loud enough to be heard from the hallway. Noel's finger was throbbing, his lip bleeding. He wondered if there might be another alarm going off in the nurses' station. Finally he leaned down and pressed his ear to Ross's chest. There was no sound this time other than a hypnotic seashell-like hum.

The lights behind the bed continued to form short lines that dissolved and started over. The alarm continued to sound, and Noel knew he had to escape, but suddenly he felt too drained, too sleepy. He placed the pillow under Ross's head and did his best to wipe fingerprints off the plastic tube. Then, after adjusting the sheets, as if tucking Ross in, he leaned down and whispered, "You're supposed to go to the light. I read that somewhere." After saying this, he turned away and stared up at the test pattern.

He would not remember leaving the room or walking down the hallway or even descending the seven flights of stairs. He came to himself at the ground floor and from there escaped through a side exit near the gift shop. The night felt cooler than he remembered it because he was covered with sweat. He walked home using shortcuts, and battling sleep. His own house was as dark as all the others, and he entered it through the back door he had left unlocked. As he walked upstairs, he had the strange impression he was already asleep on his bed. He turned on the bedside light, then shed his clothes and crawled under the sheets and fell instantly asleep with the lamplight on his face and he did not dream.

• • •

Every Sunday before church, Roger cooked breakfast, black-scabbed French toast with slabs of black tangled bacon. Noel woke to the smell of burning bacon. He felt very peaceful until he remembered what he had done, and this new knowledge of what he was capable of made his own bedroom appear foreign to him, almost unrecognizable. The velvet black-light posters, the baseball trophies, the *Sports Illustrated* covers that his mother had wallpapered his room with years earlier . . . he felt like a trespasser here, a rested and hungry and potentially dangerous trespasser.

The kitchen was empty, and the door to the backyard had been left open. Noel sat alone at the table and had just swallowed the seven pills by his napkin when his mother called him into the back bedroom. He stood and walked down the hallway, looking at the photographs on the walls. The photographs had been hung chronologically, and as he walked down the hallway he moved from the realm of color to the realm of black and white. A new air conditioner hummed in the bedroom window, bright patriotic telltales streaming from its vents. The walls were painted such a soft shade of blue they appeared white in the morning light. His mother looked very beautiful and—like the photographs on the walls—not altogether recognizable. Wearing a beige slip and shaking earrings loose from her jewelry box, she smiled at him and told him that she had some bad news. Or maybe it wasn't so bad.

"That boy Ross Altman's heart quit beating last night," she said softly, as if afraid of waking somebody.

Noel's own heart stalled. Suddenly the bedroom held no sound. He watched his mother put away her jewelry box. She did this without taking her eyes off of him. The bed behind her had been stripped of sheets, a perfect yellow rectangle.

"He didn't just die, Noel," she continued. "He had some help. Someone snuck into his hospital room last night. Late last night someone did."

"He's dead?"

"He's been dead. For years. Now his heart's stopped beating is all." She started stroking the sleeves of the hangered dresses, as if to coax them from the closet. "Whoever killed that boy did the world a favor." Still touching the dresses, she told him that she'd found out something else too, that Ross's parents had known about his brain condition before they signed him up for baseball. "There were pills he could have been taking, to relieve the pressure on his brain. But they wouldn't let him take pills. Because they're Christian Scientists. They don't believe in pills."

"Don't believe in pills?"

"No. They think medicine's a sin. They think it's up to God to decide who dies. That's why they hired lawyers to get Ross taken off those machines."

Noel pushed his spine against the door latch and hooked an elbow behind each knob and leaned forward.

"How can you not believe in pills?"

She smirked, shook her head. "Don't try and make sense of it. You can't. Nobody can."

Without lipstick, her mouth looked thin and dry and boyish. She selected four dresses and draped them onto the bed one atop the other, and she seemed to be staring at the bottom dress through the top three. As if speaking to the dresses, she said, "Aren't you going to ask me who pulled his plug?"

"Pulled his plug?"

"Plugs, I guess. From what I heard, the whole room was unplugged, even the TV they kept running for him." She shuffled the dresses. "Three years of television. Could hell be worse?"

When Noel asked who had done it, Alise picked up a red dress and held it in front of her and frowned at it. "They don't know, yet." Next she held up a green dress, shimmying it from the shoulders down, but her expression remained forbearing. "Noel, somebody saw you inside his hospital room a few weeks ago. Ross's older sister saw you in there."

"Who did?"

"His sister. Is that true?"

Noel nodded slowly.

"What were you doing in there?"

"I don't know. I'd just never seen him before is all."

"Do you know Miss Myrick? Old Miss Myrick from church?"

He continued his nod.

"She lives near the hospital. She saw you walking through her backyard two nights ago. She says it was after three in the morning she saw you. Where were you going, Noel?"

"Nowhere. I was just out walking."

"At three in the morning?"

"I couldn't sleep. I can't ever sleep."

"Miss Myrick lives near the hospital."

"I know. You said that already."

"Did you do it, Noel? Did you unplug that boy?"

"No."

"Do you sleepwalk?"

"Sleepwalk? I don't even sleep. How could I sleepwalk?"

"Well, it runs in our family. Both Carol and Betty did, when they were little. Maybe you're doing it and don't remember."

"You think I killed him in my sleep?"

"No. I didn't mean that. I'm just thinking out loud."

"What if I did? What if I did kill him?"

"You didn't. Everybody knows his family wanted him off those machines. There was even an article about it in the paper. It's a shame, though, that somebody might go to jail for doing such a good deed."

She turned her frown upon the air conditioner then one by one she plucked off the streaming telltales.

"What kind of scientists did you say they were?" he asked.

"Not any kind. They just call themselves scientists to sound something other than crazy." She dropped the telltales in the waste-basket then picked up the black dress and folded it over the head-board. "We're not going to the funeral," she said. "We didn't know them. Besides, I don't want to see that boy's mother. I'd scratch her eyes out."

Noel asked if it was murder.

"Of course not." After saying this, she added, "Well, that depends." Finally, as if Noel were arguing the case, she conceded, "Okay, it is—*legally.*"

She kept staring through him the same way she had the dresses.

"What? Am I in trouble?"

"No. But the police want to talk to you. They called early this morning."

"The police called?"

"Yes. They want to ask you some questions. About why you were in the hospital that day. Just tell them what you told me, but don't mention anything about Miss Myrick's yard unless they ask you."

"Can I still spend the night at Tim's Friday? You promised I could."

"Is that all you're worried about right now?"

"I didn't do it."

"I know you didn't."

The last thing she told him was, "Roger wants to talk to you after breakfast. I want you to practice on him like he's the police."

• • •

By the time Noel rejoined the breakfast table, his two brothers were talking about going to the fair that night. He sat and half lis-tened to them, then after a while he asked where his pills were. Roger, who was cooking French toast, answered, "You musta took them already."

"No, I didn't," Noel replied. Studying the napkin ring, he began to wonder if something was wrong with his brain. He had no memory of unplugging the machines in Ross's hospital room, and he began to wonder if he had a secret life, one he kept hidden from himself. Suddenly it occurred to him that he must have left fingerprints on the plugs, but even so he remained calm. He felt no apprehension, no need for strategy or alibi—he felt only a great certainty that he would be caught. He was still trying to remember unplugging the machines when Roger placed a cereal bowl in front of him. The bowl was filled with watermelon balls.

Noel stared first at the bowl, then at his brothers, both of whom were feasting on the watermelon balls with their fingers.

"Is this *the* watermelon?" he asked after a moment.

Roger turned from the stove and, all but blushing, he admitted, yes, this was the watermelon. "Had to harvest it a few days early," he explained. "Snake got after him."

"Him?"

Roger was sock-footed and wearing a white V-neck tucked into the front half of his brown slacks. His dress shirt, brown tie, and leather belt were hung over the ladder-back of his empty chair.

"That the best watermelon you ever tasted or what?" he asked Noel.

"I don't like watermelon," Noel said.

"You don't *what*?"

"I don't like watermelon."

"But you're the one practically begged me to plant it in the first place."

"I don't like—"

"*Noel!* Everybody. Likes. Watermelon."

With Roger standing over him Noel slowly broke open one melon ball and examined its cross-section before placing half of it on his tongue and washing it down with orange juice. He had to swallow three more melon balls before Roger lost interest and sat across from him and went to work on his own bowl of watermelon. Roger had almost finished when he stopped eating and looked up and asked, "What're you grinning at?"

"Nothing. You want some more? I'll get it for you."

Roger nodded and said, "That'd be wonderful, Noel."

While Noel was topping off Roger's bowl, Alise entered the kitchen. Her hair was tugged back by a comb of tarnished silver, and she was wearing the black dress.

"Serve your mother while you're up."

Noel served her the French toast with black bacon, but Roger cleared his throat and asked if Noel had forgotten something. Noel returned to the counter and filled another bowl with the watermelon balls. He placed the bowl in front of his mother, then sat down and took up a knife and started scraping the black scabs off his French toast.

"STOP!"

After shouting this, Roger pushed away his bowl, set down his fork. They had forgotten grace! And on a Sunday too! He asked whose turn it was. Both his brothers pointed at Noel.

"Noel, if you would."

The family bowed heads, linked hands. Noel waited until everyone's eyes were shut, then he whispered, "Bless this food to our use and thus to Thy service."

•   •   •

A woman police officer arrived shortly after lunch. She had long white-blond hair and she chain-smoked. She did not seem to think Noel guilty of anything, and she spent much of the time asking questions about his parents. "Your mom, now, I talked to her on the phone, I'd say she's got some strong opinions about that boy being kept alive on machines. Did she ever go visit Ross?"

"I don't think so. But my stepdad did. A few times, I think."

"Your dad did?"

"Stepdad. Yeah, he was always really mad about Ross being kept alive on those machines. He used to say it was going against God, and that somebody oughta do something about it."

She took lots of notes.

It was Noel's inner certainty that he would be caught that allowed him to relax throughout the interview. He even asked her if the police had found any fingerprints in the hospital room.

"None worth bragging about," she replied.

Before leaving, she promised Noel his name would not appear in the newspaper.

"You look disappointed," she joked.

Noel was disappointed, even though it had never occurred to him that his name might be in the paper. And his disappointment would increase in the weeks to come when the national news picked up the story. Both CBS and NBC would run segments on the bizarre murder, and both reports would implicate the Altman family, who continued to refuse comment to the press.

• • •

Their mother did not like rides, didn't trust them, said they were put together by drug addicts; still, every year she ferried her boys to the state fair and read them the rules of conduct before disappearing into the green beer tent. On this night the Black Dragon was called the WidowMaker and was painted a smooth ebony with red hourglass lights on her tentacles and with hidden speakers blasting Lynyrd Skynyrd. Noel got stuck with Ben first. He guided his little brother between the light shows and ripoff booths, Noel saying, "I wasn't scared at your age." Saying, "Shit, Matt wasn't either. Damn, boy, you a little pussywhip or what?"

It did not take long before Ben had agreed to board the WidowMaker. There was no line, and no one seemed to mind that Ben was two inches shy of the minimum height cutout, a faded plywood clown holding out his hand. They were the first ones aboard and had to wait ten minutes before the ride heaved a hydraulic sigh and red lights began to flicker up and down the black tentacles. A man wearing a black silver-rimmed cowboy hat and with a burn scar across his throat leapt spiderlike onto the cockpit and locked the safety bar against their thighs. Only three other cockpits had filled. The WidowMaker heaved once more then lit up from the center outward. Next she started to deflate but then suddenly spurred forward, causing Ben to bang his head against the wickered metal— he was too short to reach the torn vinyl cushion. Throughout the entire ride, his eyes remained buried, his mouth pinched inward. After five minutes, the ride slowed and halted, only to stir again in the opposite direction, stretching the neon tubes of the midway into bright banners and slinging the two brothers into the battling lead guitars of "Saturday Night Special."

Usually while riding the Black Dragon Noel thought about his real father and those lost bones, but tonight as he held his arms over his head, in the posture of arrest, he simply allowed his mind to go blank. By the time the ride ended, Noel felt as dark and dangerous as the ride itself, as if he had somehow internalized the Black Dragon. Leaving, he made a point of walking past the man with the cowboy hat and the burn scar and staring him down hard. Ben was beside Noel, but Ben was walking funny, weaving. He staggered up to a truck trailer and propped his arms against it as if to retch. But he didn't retch, he simply stood there. Noel began rubbing Ben's back, asking him if he was okay. Ben said he was, he just needed to sit down is all, and so Noel led him to the grandstand area and they sat on the hard dusty grass between the bleachers and the metal stage to watch the hypnotist show.

The hypnotist was a pear-shaped man with the oily too-dark hair of a mechanic. He wore a frayed batwinged cape and a black silk shirt blackest beneath the armpits and unbuttoned low enough to reveal much chest hair and gold. Twelve volunteers sat in a line of folding chairs on stage. The hypnotist had positioned in front of the stage three small tables with a tulip vase centered on each table. Into each of these three vases he now inserted one long-stemmed rose, tightly budded. He turned to the volunteers and instructed them that they were now going to use their *hitherto untapped powers of mass concentration and visualization* to speed the roses into bloom.

While the volunteers tried to do this, the hypnotist turned to the crowd and announced that anyone in the audience wishing to be hypnotized tonight should stare throughout the show at the spiraling barber pole above the stage. Immediately Noel began doing this. The hypnotist returned his attention to the volunteers and lulled them into a deep sleep, then woke them up again. He made a farmer dance the Funky Chicken. He convinced a high school quarterback he was nine months pregnant and could feel the baby kicking inside of him. It was going to be a girl, the quarterback confided to the hypnotist's microphone. He planned to name her Melody. The quarterback, seated on the folding chair with his legs apart as if playing the cello, smiled blissfully while the hypnotist moved down the line, turning men into cheerleaders and women into farm animals. A blond woman in a black halter sprouted wings and swooped low over the stage, her freckled cleavage exposed to the crowd as she scoured the earth for mice and rabbits.

Toward the end of the show, the hypnotist put the volunteers back to sleep and told them that when he clapped three times quick—like this—they would awaken feeling refreshed and wonderful, but, he added, waggling a finger, "After you wake up, for the rest of the night, every time you hear the words *Great Mississippi Fair,* you will start jumping into the air like an Ole Miss cheerleader and you will commence to shout at the top of your lungs the last words of the immortal bard, who said—on his deathbed—and I quote: *We are such things as dreams are made of, and our little lives are rounded by a sleep."*

He repeated the quote once more, then he clapped. The volunteers slowly returned to their seats, all except the high school quarterback, who remained in his chair staring into his palms until one of his friends came and assisted him down from the stage. The hypnotist told the audience to give the volunteers a big hand. He thanked the crowd, said his farewells, and announced a midnight show *for adults only* inside the French Casino. He urged everyone to have a wonderful evening and be sure to come back next year to the Great Mississippi Fair.

Noel was pondering the words *for adults only* when Ben exploded into the air. At this same moment, a dozen other members of the audience jumped up too, all of them pumping imaginary pom-poms and howling various high-pitched misquotes of Shakespeare up at the stars. Noel wrapped his arms around Ben, pulled him down. "Whoa!" Noel kept saying, coaxing Ben to the grass. Ben's eyes had clouded over, and his broad smile seemed mismatched with his face. Then the smile collapsed. He sat down hard, hugging his knees to his chest. Ben's recovery was duplicating itself throughout the audience. When Noel glanced up at the stage, a plywood replica of the hypnotist stood there, the next-show clock on his heart set at nine-thirty. The replica was much more handsome than the hypnotist himself. All three red roses were in full bloom.

.   .   .

They wandered through the dark searching for Matt. Noel kept asking Ben what it was like to be hypnotized, but Ben didn't want to talk about it. He seemed embarrassed and mostly he just shrugged with his mouth hung open, his crew cut plastered with sweat over the monkey shape of his skull. The last time Noel asked, Ben shrugged and pointed and said, "There he is."

Matt was trying to dunk a clown by pitching baseballs at a bull's-eye. Not so long ago everyone had mistaken Matt and Noel for twins, but this last year had seen Noel shoot upward while Matt shot outward at the shoulders. Because of this, Matt had more coordination and arm strength. Noel and Ben joined the small group of adults who had gathered behind Matt. The clown, sitting on the platform above the tank of dirty water, was drenched and sullen-looking. Matt leaned in with a farsighted squint. He started his windup and fluttered his eyes and fired the ball home.

He dunked the clown two times with three balls, then someone bought him another set of throws and lined up the baseballs at his feet. Matt accepted the free throws without taking his eyes off the clown. He knelt and set two of the balls farther to his right, near where a giant stuffed bear sat, then he scooped up some dirt and feathered it through his fingers. His first throw nailed the bull's-eye again. The red stoplight flashed, a buzzer sounded, and two seconds later the clown cannonballed into the Plexiglas aquarium.

The clown was climbing back onto his perch when Matt nailed the target again. This time the clown went over backward and walloped his head against the tank. The applause slowed when there appeared to be some doubt as to whether or not the clown was drowning. But the clown rallied, and while everyone applauded and hooted, somewhat for the clown's tenacity now, Noel came up behind Matt and asked if he could throw the last one. Matt shook his head no, like a pitcher shaking off a catcher's sign, and told

Noel to go buy his own balls, which Noel did. Meanwhile, Matt nicked the target with his last throw, but the buzzer did not sound. The crowd was booing the mechanism as Noel stepped up and, pitching wild and hard, missed on all three balls. The clown stuck his thumbs in his ears and waggled his fingers at Noel, who cashed in another dollar and popped three more balls against the canvas. The clown blew Noel a kiss, then dangled his hand from his wrist. Noel shot him the bird then turned to answer a question.

Matt had asked if it was true about Ben being hypnotized. Noel shrugged and said, "Hell, I dunno," but then he got an idea and added, "It's all just part of the fun here at the Great Mississippi Fair."

Ben vaulted into the air wielding his pom-poms.

"We are such dreams as things are made of!" he shrieked. "And our lives are rounded by a little sleep."

The gleeful smile caved in much sooner this time. He dropped to one knee and pressed his fingertips to both temples, as if halving his skull back together. Matt studied his younger brother with outright disapproval. Finally he whistled and rubbed his own crew cut backward and said, "Ben, don't ever do that again."

Noel picked up the stuffed bear by one ear. It was a shaggy brown creature, nearly as tall as Ben, with a yellow bow around its neck. Noel asked where he had gotten it, and Matt spat and replied, "They gave it to me."

"Gave it to you?"

"For sinking the clown."

"Well, how many times did you sink him?"

"I dunno. Ten or so, I guess. Twelve."

"Twelve?" Noel stared at the target then back at Matt. "You spent twelve bucks sinking a damn clown?"

Matt said no, he didn't spend any but the first two dollars—the rest other people paid for. He asked if Noel wanted the bear, and

Noel gave him a jaded look. Matt offered it to Ben, but Ben would not admit to wanting a stuffed bear in front of his older brothers.

It was at this moment that Noel spotted the berserk clown. He had scaled the ladder out of the aquarium and was striding toward them. He was soaked through, his head bald, the red sadness still painted onto his face, and clenched low in his right fist was an orange wig and a billy club.

"You done flipped off the wrong damn clown!" he shouted at Noel.

. . .

They left the clown and the stuffed bear in the dust and took off across the midway. Later, after Noel had set Ben atop a white gold-saddled pony on the merry-go-round, Matt said, "You know Mom's in that green tent over there drinking beer?"

"Is that the French Casino?" Noel wanted to know.

Matt didn't answer; instead he started telling Noel about the sideshow where he had seen the tattooed lady. The tattooed lady was this real tall Chinese-looking woman, he said. She was real pretty, with long black hair. "Like pure silk," he added after a moment's consideration. "And she had all these tattoos. All over her."

"All over where?"

"All over everywhere. She was wearing this red bikini, but some of them went down underneath it. She started talking to me too. I was the only person in there."

"You're lying."

Saying that was a mistake because now Matt refused to continue his story until Noel apologized. Then Matt explained that the woman had this butterfly tattooed on her neck. "Right here." He clapped his palm under his ear like slapping a mosquito. "And she told me it was her first tattoo ever and that how she got it was that one time a real butterfly landed on her neck just when lightning struck. And it'd been stuck there ever since. Then she asked me if I wanted to touch it. She said it was good luck to."

"Did you?"

"What?"

"Touch her damn butterfly."

"Wouldn't you have?"

"Hell yes, I'd have touched more than that. Was it just you and her?"

Matt pointed back to the green tent and said, "Afterwards I went in there to borrow some money from Mom. You know what she was doing? She was swiggin' beer and lighting a cigarette off somebody else's—off some ol' cowboy's. She caught me spying in on her too."

"What'd she do?"

"Nothing. Just stared me down flat, like she didn't even know who I was, then she blew out all this smoke and picked up her chair and set it down on the other side of the table."

They both stared at the green tent.

"Damn," Noel said.

"Noel, you didn't have nothing to do with that catcher kid dying, did you?"

"How do you know about that?"

"I heard Mom and Rog talking."

"Do they think I had something to do with it?"

"I dunno. Did you?"

"Did I murder him, you mean?"

"Yeah, did you?"

"Hell yes, I did."

"You're full of shit."

• • •

The station wagon straddled the center line and only veered into the proper lane under the approach of headlights. Cars flashed, blinked, honked, but under no circumstances did the Rambler dim its brights. When these cars had passed, and the Doppler effect of their horns had faded, the station wagon lurched back into the middle of the road. During this ride, which was not unlike another fairground attraction, Noel imagined himself to be hypnotizing Miss Weiss. He had already made plans to go to the new mall and shoplift some books on the subject. When the car swerved into the driveway, their house was dark and only the porch light had been left on. Their mother made them remove their shoes then led them into the house like a team of cat burglars.

CHAPTER FOUR

WHEN NOEL ARRIVED for the sleepover, Tim was in his bedroom reciting Hebrew to truckers over the CB radio. Noel sat on the floor and started paging through an old *Hustler*. Dinner was a frozen pizza Miss Weiss had heated up. Her eyes were big and deeply brown, just like Tim's. As soon as they had finished eating, she smiled brightly across the card table and said, "Noel, I want to try some of your pot. What do you think of that?" She stood, wiped her hands on her white jeans, and started piling plates into the sink. "I always told Tim if he was going to experiment with drugs I'd rather we tried them together. I know both y'all smoke and that you're supposed to have some good stuff with you tonight. I'm not mad, but I am curious. I've only smoked once, a very long time ago, and I never felt anything." She squirted yellow soap over the plates and filled the sink with hot water. "Will I feel anything off this stuff you've got, Noel?"

Tim was grinning at him.

"It's redweed," Noel said weakly, more to Tim than to his mom.

"Is that good? Do we want it to be redweed?"

"Yeah. It means Colombian."

"And where did we get it?"

He hesitated before saying, "At work."

"That pizza place?"

"Yeah." Noel wiped his mouth and added, "My stepdad makes me work there. He keeps half my paycheck too."

"For college?"

"That's what he says. But the government's gonna pay for most of my college, because of my dad. Anyway I don't even wanna go to college. You don't need college to be a photographer."

"A photographer? What kind of photographer?"

Noel instantly regretted having brought up photography, especially since he had the Polaroid folded into his wallet. He wondered if she had noticed the missing Polaroid yet. And, if so, did she suspect him?

"The kind that takes pictures of sports," he lied.

Hearing that, she seemed to lose interest. "I guess I should have fed you something besides pizza tonight, huh?" she said. "What do you do at Pasquale's?"

"Wash dishes. But they're gonna train me on sandwich board soon as someone quits."

"Well, let's see the goods."

He reached into his sock. With Miss Weiss intent on his every move, he deftly rolled a joint, lit it, then passed the joint to her upright, a small torch.

"Hold the smoke in and count eight Mississippi," he advised her.

They smoked two joints. Afterward Miss Weiss poured herself the last glass of red wine from a bottle. She held the upturned bottle over the glass and watched it drip.

"Hey, what about us?" Tim asked.

"What about you?" she replied, still watching the wine drip. Noel had started rolling another joint, but she touched his wrist and said, "That's quite enough, Noel. That'll do."

"You feeling something?"

"Oh yes."

"If we're supplying the pot, what are you supplying?"

"Tim, you're not supplying anything. Noel is. And if Noel wants anything, I'm sure he's capable of asking for it."

"I think Noel wants some Southern Comfort," Tim decided.

She tasted her wine, made a disparaging face. "Is that true, Noel? Do you want some Southern Comfort?"

"If it's okay with you, sure."

"Only if I can have another joint, for later."

"Deal," Tim snapped. "But we both get a drink."

"One each. Small ones. And while you're in there, Tim, bring me another bottle of red, please. And take your time. I want to talk to Noel alone for a few minutes."

Tim headed for the liquor cabinet in the den. Noel, in an effort to calm himself, started rolling the joint for Miss Weiss. She watched him a moment then said, "Let me try that." He pushed over the workings to her. Her brown eyes burrowed as she arranged everything with her little-girl fingers. While mangling the first attempt, she said, "Noel, I'm going to ask you a question you don't have to answer." She shot the table an exasperated look. "But first, is there anything you want to ask me? You're quite the regular over here. Do you have any questions that need clearing up?"

He beaked his lips thoughtfully before shaking his head no.

"Your parents, do they ask you questions about me?"

"No," he lied. "What kinda questions?"

"Oh, I have no idea. Any kind." She seemed to be listening to some minute noise. "You know that feeling where it seems like you've dreamt all this before?"

"Yeah. That happens to me a lot." He plucked a new paper out of the pack. "Here. Start over. It's ripped, it's no good."

"Questions about my lifestyle. Does your stepfather ever ask you about that?"

"He doesn't like me coming over here, if that's what you mean."

"Because we're Jewish?"

"He thinks Tim's a bad influence on me."

"Tim's a bad influence on you!" She growled playfully then went back to rolling the joint. "Ahh, let's not talk about him. Anyway, that wasn't my question. Here's my question. The one you don't have to answer." She knocked over the empty wineglass. It didn't break, and Noel caught it just as it rolled off the table, then sat it back upright between them.

"I heard the police came over and talked to you, and that—"

"I didn't kill him," Noel interrupted her. "That's just a rumor started by people in my church."

"I wasn't suggesting you did. I'm just curious as to what you thought about it all."

"Did Tim tell you about it?"

"No. But I did ask Tim. And he told me the police questioned you."

"If Tim didn't tell you, then who did?"

"I work at the hospital, remember? It's all the talk over there. Like some soap opera. *Who killed Ross Altman?* The police even questioned some of us nurses. They think one of us might have been in on it." She pouted. "I am having the hardest time following this conversation."

"You were gonna ask me some question I don't have to answer."

"I was?" She rubbed her nose with her palm. "I thought I already had. Oh! I was going to ask why you were in his room that day in the hospital."

"Did you tell the police you saw me?"

"No. Should I have?"

"Naw, they already asked me about it."

"And what did you tell them?"

"The truth. That I just wanted to see what he looked like. They didn't believe me, though. Nobody does. Everybody thinks I killed him, especially the police."

"That's not what I heard. I heard his family did it. And that the police are about to arrest his father or his mother or somebody in the family."

"Who told you that?"

"A number of people. It's just another rumor, probably."

"You wanna hear something weird?" Noel asked. "When I went in his room that day, there was a Ouija board spread out on top of him."

"A Ouija board?"

"Yeah. Not on the table either, but right on his stomach. And you know what they say about Ouija boards, right?"

"I'm afraid I don't, Noel."

"They're used by devil worshipers. The whole company that makes them is devil worshipers. Milton Bradley is."

"Is that something your stepfather told you?"

"Yeah," Noel agreed, though once again it was his cousins who had told him this. "Have you ever read that book *The Exorcist*?"

"You mean the movie they banned here?"

"Not the movie, the book."

"No, can't say I have."

"This girl in it gets possessed. And that's how it all starts, with her playing on the Ouija board. That's how she gets possessed."

Noel had shoplifted *The Exorcist* from the mall Monday along with two books on hypnotism. Since then he had been staying up reading *The Exorcist* late into the night. Finally he would switch off the bedside lamp and try not to think about Satan, knowing that if Satan detected fear He could appear inside Noel's bedroom. He might be at the foot of Noel's bed already, bending over Noel, reading his mind—*hearing him think this!*—and waiting for Noel to open his eyes so that Satan could dive into his soul like into a river. . . .

"Did you tell the police about the Ouija board? That sounds like a clue to me."

Noel had not told the police. It had felt too much like a shared secret, like something that would incriminate him. He was about to try and explain this to Miss Weiss when she called out, "I can see your shadow. You can come out now and quit eavesdropping, Tim."

As Tim reentered the kitchen, carrying the bottles, Miss Weiss pushed her second mangled effort across the table and said, "You better take over, Noel." Turning to Tim, she reminded him, "One drink each." Then she covered her ears, as if her own voice were unpleasant to her, and very softly added, "I'm going into the den, to paint. Noel, this will be our little secret. You have to cross your heart that you'll never tell anybody about tonight. Do you cross your heart, Noel?"

He did. He crossed his heart.

*   *   *

After rebrimming their drinks for a third time, Tim thinned the Southern Comfort with water, then left a blurred note saying they'd gone out for a walk and would be back soon. Noel placed two fat joints beside the note. Then they stumbled into the carport and down the street, staggering into the night, yelling, "FUCK!" at dark houses. Yelling, "EAT ME!" Yelling, "SUCK MY DICK!" Later, inside a half-constructed house, they nested themselves in plywood to smoke the last joint and Tim started detailing ways he would fuck Layle Smokewood, "if she'd asked me to the damn Sadie Hawkins."

Sadie Hawkins was the first dance of the coming school year, the eighth grade, which began in two weeks. Much to his own surprise, Noel had been asked to the dance by three different girls. His voice became somber as he explained to Tim, "Hell, her dad's *our preacher*. What am I supposta do? Move in on her while he's driving us home?"

"What you oughta do is hypnotize her. Like you did me the other day. Turn her into one of those farm animals."

"You're just pissed off nobody invited you to the dance."

"Turn her into a cow then milk her titties all night long."

"I knew you were just pretending to be hypnotized. It works, it just doesn't work on morons. You have to be intelligent to be hypnotized, that's what Edgar Cayce says."

"Who's Edgar Cayce?"

"Hell, your mom owns every book he ever wrote."

In fact, that's why Noel had shoplifted the Cayce book on hypnotism. Now he passed the joint to Tim and began telling him about Edgar Cayce, this redneck kid from Virginia who had wanted to be a preacher and who, when he was failing fourth grade, discovered that if he slept on top of a book, then the next morning he would know the contents of the book by heart.

"Wonder what would happen if he'd slept on a *Hustler*," Tim commented.

"This was before *Hustler*," Noel explained. He closed his eyes and asked, "Is everything spinning around for you?"

"What's the matter, Weatherspoon? Can't handle your liquor?"

Noel frowned, then forced himself to continue his story.

After Cayce had grown up, he lost his voice one day and had to quit his job, because he couldn't speak anymore. No doctors could cure him. But then a fair had come through town, and the traveling hypnotist said he could cure Cayce.

"Here," Tim said.

"I don't want no more. We'll save it for later."

They crawled out of the plywood and started weaving down the street. Noel was seeing banners, like he was still riding the Black Dragon.

"EAT ME!" Tim screamed at a graveyard. "SUCK MY DICK!"

"That a cop?" Noel asked as headlights approached.

"Why're you always so worried about cops?"

"Hell, you would be too, if you were wanted for murder."

"You're not wanted for anything. You just want everybody to think you are."

They waited until the car had passed.

"So what happened next?"

"What are you talking about?"

"That Cayce guy?"

"Oh." Noel drew in a few deep breaths then said, "This hypnotist, he puts Cayce under. Then, all'a sudden, this weird voice comes out of Cayce's body telling exactly what's wrong with his throat. But this voice, it's using all these fancy doctor words, like Latin and shit. Cayce didn't even finish high school, he didn't know any damn Latin. And from then on, that's how it worked. Cayce never even met the sick person, he'd just hypnotized himself and then somebody would read off a name to him. He'd settle back and start talking in that super-scientist voice, saying, *We have the body in front of us.* Then he'd describe the exact room the sick person was in right at that moment, and he'd list off everything wrong with the person's body. Everything—old scars, missing teeth, cavities, broken bones. Then he'd list off what exact medicines they needed or what operations or what—"

Noel's legs tangled under him and he went down and scorched his palms on the blacktop.

"We have the body in front of us," Tim said. "It needs to quit falling down."

Noel stood up too close to Tim and bumped his chest into Tim's face. He asked if Tim had a problem or what.

"You're just drunk," Tim said. "Don't get violent on me, alright?"

"Don't tell me what to do. You're always act like you're so much smarter than everybody else."

"Hey, take your hands off me, alright? Please. Look, I got a plan for tonight—a good one—but first you have to let me go."

Noel released him, conditionally.

After hearing the plan, Noel balked. At least he did until Tim accused him of being pussywhipped. Then they veered west, toward the new Sunflower supermarket. The dark pools between streetlights chirruped and cricketed. Noel clapped his hands to try and silence the wilderness. The claps dissolved. He shouted, "FUCK!" into the woods then listened as the word pioneered through the trees.

Automatic doors sprung them into the otherworldly fluorescence of the supermarket. They quickly bought their supplies then left. Noel finished the soda and ricocheted the empty bottle into the pine tops.

"So one day these doctors," he continued suddenly, "without even warning Cayce, these doctors started asking him all sorts of questions about God. After he'd hypnotized himself. Just'a see what he'd say. And that same spooky voice started saying all this weird shit about reincarnation and higher selves and that the real Jesus wasn't nothing like the one in the Bible. Then, after Cayce woke up—and they'd told him what he'd said—it scared the blue pee outa him. Because he was still this regular born-again Christian guy, and everything he'd just said, even though he's the one said it, he thought it was all pure sacrilege."

Tim shifted the grocery bag into his left arm and asked what was sacrilege.

"What's *sacrilege*? It's like taking the Lord's name in vain. That's the only sin can't ever be forgiven. You burn for that, son."

"You mean like saying *goddamn.*"

Noel winced then continued, "Anyway, that's what Cayce thought might be happening, Satan possessing him. He didn't know whether he should stop doing it or not. Hypnotizing himself. Because every time he did it, he cured some little kid or somebody."

"You're really afraid of saying *goddamn*?"

"You burn in hell for that, Tim. That's what the Bible says."

"We don't believe in hell."

"Don't believe in hell?" That stopped Noel midstep. "Everybody believes in hell, Tim," he explained. "The whole world believes in hell."

"We don't."

"Not believing in hell, that's like not believing in Australia or something."

"We don't believe in Australia, either."

"You don't?"

"I'm joking."

A street lamp was flickering and clicking its light down upon the husks of dead frogs, flat and brittle as leaves, scattered over the road. Noel scuffed the husks along with his sneakers. He was feeling less dizzy now. Finally he asked, "Okay, say some guy spends his whole life murdering people, like Hitler, where does he go after he dies?"

"That's easy," Tim replied. "Mississippi."

•   •   ■

Set back from the street, the front lawn landscaped with magnolia and dogwood receding in perfect rows toward the still-lit windows, the Smokewoods' home resembled something out of a fairy tale, at least to Noel it did. The grass was as perfectly groomed as a golf course's. The dirt driveway was lined with railroad ties. Tim and Noel stood facing a moat of flower beds glowing white with chrysanthemum and hydrangea. Tim reached into the grocery bag and opened a package of white toilet paper then handed two rolls to Noel. They moved inward, launching the rolls into the air, watching them crest and unfurl over tree limb and power line, then retrieving the rolls to hurl them skyward again. Noel reached the shadow of the house and stepped into a bright pane of light beneath a window—he could see into the empty living room—and from there he lobbed a roll onto the roof and stood planted on the grass while it unwound down the slope and leapt the rain gutter. He caught it and threw it again. When their supply was empty, they went around gathering loose rolls and relaunching them until the house and trees and power lines were all draped a ghostly white. The whole process was as silent as Noel imagined snowfall to be, and for years afterward this was how he pictured snow.

An hour later he was lying on his back beside the road, staring up at the three tangential moons, his hands folded behind his head. They had just smoked the last half of the last joint, and now Tim was pissing into a nearby ravine. Suddenly a sheet of light inserted itself between Noel and his moons. Sitting up, he found himself blinking into an incomprehensible vehicle that appeared to be hovering above the ground.

Tim, using his most bitingly sarcastic voice, yelled out, "Hey, Weatherspoon, it's a cop!" A second later he added, "Oh shit, it really is a cop."

• • •

They were placed in separate rooms downtown. Staring at his shoelaces jumbled with briars, Noel informed a police officer that some guys driving a green Camero had thrown a bunch of beer at them. The cop, middle-aged with short orangish hair, a bird-beak nose, and rusty eyebrows that twisted upward like a mustache, was leaning forward behind his desk. His hands appeared to be clasping his head onto his shoulders.

"Weatherspoon . . ." he mused, "now why does that name sound familiar?"

Noel, who thought he was facing a whole roomful of orange-haired cops, muttered, "I was just out for a walk. I couldn't sleep."

After twenty minutes of interrogation, the cop shut his eyes and said, "Son, let's try working up from something small. What color is grass?"

When Noel answered green, the cop clapped and said, "That's real good, Noel. You didn't lie about something." He stood and came around the desk. "Let's try something a little harder now. For instance, you mind telling me what's this on your arm?"

And he rolled up Noel's sleeve. They both stared at the tattoo of the Zig-Zag man on Noel's upper forearm. Then the cop wet his finger and smeared the face.

"Who's that supposed to be, Jesus?"

"Yes sir," Noel agreed. "It's Jesus."

"Jesus don't smoke."

"No sir. It started off being someone else. Then kinda turned into Jesus."

"You a pretty religious fella, huh?"

"I guess."

"Look at me when I talk to you."

"Yes sir."

"What religion are you?"

"First Baptist."

"That why you got your hair so long, to look like Jesus?"

Noel shrugged, started to speak, but didn't. His stomach was doing strange things, as were his eyes. Opening his mouth did not seem like a good idea.

"Drawing pictures on yourself, that something you do a lot of?"

He shrugged and said, "Only when I'm bored."

The cop nodded a circular digestive nod, then he reached into his shirt pocket and asked, "What else you like to do, son, when you're bored?"

And he held the creased Polaroid in front of Noel's bloodshot eyes.

"I didn't kill nobody," Noel said.

* * *

Noel was shaking his head no, no, no, no . . .

The cop was asking, "You take that picture?"

He was asking, "Wait, let me guess. Some guys in a green Camero threw it at you?"

He was asking, "That your girlfriend?"

He was asking, "She's a bit old for you, ain't she?"

He was asking, "She the one sold y'all that wacky tobaccy?"

He was asking, "You know there's laws against this kind of behavior? This ain't exactly Louisiana."

Finally he said, "Son, you wouldn't know the truth if it waltzed up and kicked you in the balls. And quit shaking your damn head before I knock it off its cradle."

* * *

When Roger arrived, the redheaded cop started calling Noel *she* and *her* and *Cinderella here*. Roger, in slacks and a plaid shirt, his hair flattened on one side, announced that he was counting to three. "And when I get to three, you're going to wish you'd told the truth about where you got the alcohol." He began to count, pausing painfully long between two and three. Then they sat there waiting for Roger to do something. Noel kept looking at his shoes. The cop made a series of popping sounds with his tongue, like pebbles falling into a well. Finally he tossed the legal pad upon the desk and said, "There's another little matter."

.   .   .

Having returned the Polaroid to the officer, Roger's hand remained suspended in the air, as if holding an invisible cigarette. Ten more pebbles fell into the well before Roger's hand dropped out of the air and he turned on Noel and demanded to know, "*Who is that woman?*"

"I didn't do nothing wrong," Noel said. "He was born that way."

The cop asked Roger, "You've got no idea who she is?"

Roger shook his head no. He had never met Miss Weiss, not face-to-face, though they had talked on the phone. Noel was far too drunk to appreciate his good luck, and he was too drunk to panic a minute later when a young black cop entered the small office and said, "Other boy's mama's here." He had a pen sticking out of his mouth that twitched when he spoke. "Want her to come in and join the wingdig?"

The redheaded cop cringed and covered one blue eye. "Hell, make Carl handle her. He's good at mothers. He's about half mother hisself. She at crying yet?"

"Not the crying type."

"Well, thank God for small favors."

"Wouldn't go thanking Him just yet."

.   .   .

For the last time, I have no interest in your infantile little games, I want my son released, and I want him released now. If you have any charges you want to press, fine, have at it, but if you know what's good for you, sir, you'll give me my son back now, or I promise you I will have a whole fleet of the most Jewish lawyers you have ever beheld down here on your fat ass in about ten seconds flat—do we understand each other?

The redhead cop quit eavesdropping and pushed the door the rest of the way open. He led Noel and Roger into the main station, where the entire shift had pivoted to watch Miss Weiss. Wearing the white jeans with a red blouse, she sat facing a metal desk that encaged one bald cop holding up two pink chubby palms and smiling like they were old friends. Miss Weiss did not seem to share his nostalgia. The large room glowed under fluorescent tubes casting a light so nearly blue that the two most noticeable things about every cop there, including the framed black and white glossies of cops on the walls, were the bruises under their eyes and how badly they needed a shave.

The redheaded officer grinned in the direction of Miss Weiss, then he turned away and sat himself at an empty desk and lost his grin inside a form he began to fill out. If he had recognized her from the Polaroid, he made no indication of it. He motioned for Noel and Roger to sit in the two folding chairs facing the desk. The top margin of the Polaroid was protruding from his shirt pocket. Noel leaned over and willed himself not to get sick. Every once in a while he raised his head to glance over at Miss Weiss, hoping to catch her eye, but she never turned her head in their direction.

The next day, though, he would remember how she had looked right then—drained, tired, and angry—and it would start to make sense to Noel why no one had recognized her from the Polaroid. Trapped under that blue fluorescence, Miss Weiss had appeared every bit as haggard and sexless as the cops at their desks and the photographs of cops on the walls. She was simply not reconcilable with the naked woman sprawled inside the Polaroid.

The cop finished the form and tossed the pen on the clipboard in such a manner it appeared the pen had leapt from his hand. He stared at Noel expectantly.

"Answer him," Roger prompted.

"Answer him what?"

"Answer the man!"

"She ain't gonna answer me. Are you, Cinderella?"

"Throw me in damn jail," Noel replied and stared across the station to Miss Weiss. She turned very briefly, their eyes met, it was the last time he would ever see her. "I ain't telling you shit," he said.

It sounded like a whip crack the way Roger slapped him across the jaw. The aftershock was a near repeat of Miss Weiss's tirade except that now everyone was staring at the punk with the bloodshot Mongo eyes and the long hair who did not flinch from the slap but only thinned his eyes and released a slow tight smile.

"Maybe I did do it," he said to Roger. "Maybe you're next."

The redheaded cop balled up the form he had been filling out and threw it at Noel, bouncing it off his forehead.

"Get her outa here," he said. "Before I start slapping on her too."

· · ·

The next morning at sunrise, Roger hefted Noel up by the armpits and commanded him to drink a bottle of beer.

"And I mean every last drop."

Noel complied, turning the brown bottle upside down until it was empty. Immediately he felt much improved. He stared up at his stepfather with a confused and somewhat grateful expression.

Roger swiped away the bottle and held it up to the light and shook his head dispiritedly. As he lowered the bottle, his vision lit around the bedroom and lingered on a velvet black-light poster of Lynyrd Skynyrd.

"Get up and mow the yard, now," Roger ordered.

"It doesn't need mowing."

Roger started to yell but then caught himself. An idea lengthened his face. "Wait here," he said and clapped Noel on the shoulder as if to stake him to the bed. While Roger was away, Noel tried to piece together the night. The police station was mostly a blur, but he did remember making Roger stop the car on the drive home so he could be sick. He was still trying to remember when Roger returned up the stairs snipping the air with a pair of sewing scissors. He stood over Noel and said, "We're going to do a little mowing of our own."

Clamping his left hand over Noel's eyes, Roger channeled his way around the head, here nipping an ear, there burying the point into the scalp. It was more a wrestling match than a haircut. After five minutes, Roger stepped back from the bed and then tilted his chin to each side. Noel sat there on the bed surrounded by a dark wreath of his own hair. Slowly he began to rub his scalp, exploring its gullies and ditches. His fingertips came away whorled with blood.

Roger took another step backward and smiled.

"I seen worse," he decided.

CHAPTER FIVE

TWO MORE YEARS PASSED and still nobody had been arrested for the murder of Ross Altman. Everyone in town seemed to have forgotten about the incident except Noel, who saw himself perpetually through the lens of that murder. When he shaved, he was a murderer shaving. When he stared at his hands, they were the hands of a murderer. In this light, every good thing that happened to him seemed but a reprieve. And good things did happen. He had a girlfriend. He would be the starting shortstop on junior varsity this year. He had published photographs in the school paper. He slept at night, at least most nights he did. People in general seemed to like him, to be drawn to his mysteriousness. Girls especially liked him. But Noel knew it couldn't last. He knew what he was and what he was capable of. The certainty that he would get caught had been slowly replaced by the certainty that he would kill someone else, eventually.

It was October and he was in his room doctoring his driver's license with a needle and purple ballpoint when his mother called up the stairs to say there was a package for him in the mail. He bounded downstairs and found the lumpy manila envelope on the kitchen table. It was from Tommy Weatherspoon.

"Aren't you going to open it?" Alise said.

"I gotta use the bathroom first," Noel lied and took the package upstairs, where he opened it over his bed. Inside was a rolled-up T-shirt. The shirt was dark red and said *Sloppy Joe's Bar* and it bore a round silkscreen portrait of a man Noel would later learn was not Sloppy Joe but Ernest Hemingway. When Noel unrolled the shirt, a copper bracelet fell onto the bed. It was a POW bracelet, the name *Noel Weatherspoon* inscribed thickly into the copper band.

Later that day, dressed in ironed jeans and a green button-down shirt, and spitting into a tennis ball can, he chauffeured himself through the churched suburbs carved of piney woods in his '66 Mustang. He had the POW bracelet in his shirt pocket, and he was once again trying to recall his father's face, not from the photograph, but his real face on the night of the fair, the night he had boarded the Black Dragon and disappeared forever. For the first time Noel owned a different version of the events that had led up to that night at the fair.

Tommy had written, "Your mom gave your dad a choice, baseball or her. He wasn't making any money playing ball, he was always on the road, and he had two boys to support, so I'm not blaming your mom one bit. Anyway he left her and there's no excusing that, not in a million years. Your mom was the best thing that ever happened to Goose and he was a fool to leave her. He went on to play a few more years of ball and when that didn't work out he had to join the army. It's more complicated than that but I'm writing this on a dashboard and it was a long time ago."

Twice Noel stopped the car to take a picture but then changed his mind. Every time he lifted his camera these days he was flooded with dissatisfaction. The fault was not in the camera, a weighty box-design Nikon he was buying in installments from a pawnshop. The problem was that, to Noel, the Nikon was simply an accessory to an expensive telescopic lens he half worshiped inside the pages of *Photo* magazine. The Aleph 2000, the most powerful telescopic lens known to man. With the Aleph 2000, he imagined himself standing in his own backyard and taking pictures of Layle undressing in front of her bedroom window. Then, with a quick adjustment of the zoom, he would be taking pictures of women oiling themselves on the nude beaches of France. Zoom again and he was taking pictures of black girls washing away tribal paint under clear African waterfalls. If he stared through the Aleph 2000 long enough, he would eventually find himself standing in the backyard.

The Mustang was halfway up the Smokewoods' dirt driveway when Layle broke from the front door and hurdled a nest of hay, pumpkin, and purple corn to cut in front of the car. Noel slammed the brakes so hard that the spit can lurched between his thighs.

"*Drive!*" Layle ordered, swinging into the car and rolling up her window. "*Get me out of here!*"

Reverend Smokewood stood in the front doorway cross-armed between a scarecrow and a ghost. Noel averted his eyes and then began to pilot Layle backward and away from her father. The Mustang bottomed out against the road.

. . .

Tall, thin, strawberry blond, and eternally bitter at not being allowed to try out for cheerleading, Layle Smokewood had a sly way of subverting her beauty to roll her eyes white at the world. Like most girls in tenth grade, Layle had plucked out her eyebrows then stenciled them back on in high arcs above half-moons of aqua shadow, fixing herself with a look of perpetual surprise. But, unlike other girls, Layle had a rose-cheeked complexion, an expressive blush entirely under her control that years later would land her the role of the soft-focus virgin in an ABC soap opera, distinguishing her as the only famous person ever to emerge from Hattiesburg High.

Usually Noel had to talk to Reverend Smokewood a good ten minutes or so before Layle came downstairs. The reverend enjoyed masking his contempt for Noel by sitting him down in the kitchen and asking him difficult questions on politics or philosophy. Once he had even sounded out Noel's opinion on euthanasia. A more recent chat had concerned *The Exorcist*, a movie that for years had been banned in Hattiesburg but that lately a rogue drive-in was threatening to feature. Noel had shirked off an opinion that evening by explaining that his aunts had helped to organize the protests against *The Exorcist*.

Brushing at the underside of his bulb nose, the Reverend inquired, "So you are of the opinion the Bill of Rights is not applicable here?"

"Sir?"

"The Bill of Rights. You propose to throw it out the window and be done with it?"

Obviously the reverend thought the movie should be allowed to play. Wanting very much to impress the man, Noel admitted to having read the book.

"The book? The good book?"

"The book *The Exorcist*, sir. I read it kinda by accident a few years ago."

The reverend's face bloated. "Am I to understand they sell this book to minors?" He straightened, as if about to rise and begin litigation, then he grabbed at a legal pad, gouged off the yellow pages until he found a blank one, and dated it with huge numbers before demanding to know where Noel had obtained the book. After scratching down this information and adding a series of exclamation points, he set the pad on the table and in a confidential tone asked, "And you found this book . . . to be . . . *sacrilegious?*"

There it was again, that word.

"I dunno, sir," Noel replied. "All I know is it scared the blue pee outa me."

Having said this, he made a sharp, wet inhalation, like a vacuum cleaner flicked on and off. But, fantastically, or so it seemed to Noel, the reverend began to laugh. He laughed so hard he had to scoot his chair away from the table.

"Well stated, son," he said, after exasperating himself. "Very well put."

Noel had not for a moment thought the laugh legitimate.

At the first stop sign, he opened the car door and flung out his dip and poured the Skoal spit onto the street.

"Jeez-us, it looked like he was gonna bust out crying," he complained.

"He'll get over it." Layle reached over and combed her hand through Noel's black hair, which was once again down to his shoulders, except that his shoulders were much wider now. "Noel, let's get us some liquor tonight, huh?"

He pretended to bore out his ear. "You know what it sounded like you just said?"

Layle attempted a wicked smile. Mimicking Noel's drawl—something she could do disturbingly well—she said, "Let's get drunker'n Cooter Brown."

He drove to Pasquale's, where he was cooking four nights a week in order to finance car and camera. The booths at Pasquale's were sequestered by black metal gratings meant to convey a graveyard ambience but that instead lent the restaurant a penal quality. While Layle waited in the corner booth, the one nearest the jukebox and most patched over with duct tape, Noel went to the counter and got two large drafts served inside wax cups sealed with lids. They drank through straws so that no one could tell they were drinking beer.

Because cheerleading tryouts started Monday, Layle had a lot on her mind that evening. What it came down to was this: her father would not let her be normal. *He won't even let me take parts in school plays unless they exhibit moral character!* She rolled her eyes white then caught herself and said, "I do that too much, I know."

Noel listened dutifully, every so often getting up for more beer or to refill their platters from the buffet. He went into the bathroom to sip from his inhaler. Dates still spurred his asthma, even though he and Layle had been going steady off and on for almost two years now. October was the worst month for his asthma. He dropped a quarter in the jukebox and selected "Free Bird," then he sat across from Layle and began to tell her about the letter from his uncle and how he had invited Noel to visit Key West and how Noel planned to manage his uncle's restaurant someday.

"I practically run this place already," he pointed out. "Hey, don't look at me that way, I'm not gonna up and leave you here."

"If we go to California, to Hollywood, you could be a famous photographer and I could be a famous actress. You could be my personal photographer."

"I'm already your personal photographer," Noel said, which was the truth. He had hundreds of photographs of Layle stroking trees or holding up pets or striking cheerleading poses or attempting sultry stares.

She was staring at him rather sultrily right now.

"This is my first beer, *ever*," she said. "Who knows, maybe it'll be a night for firsts."

"What's that supposta mean?"

"You'll see."

He mulled that over until the free bird was soaring away upon the conflicting winds of three lead guitars, then Noel set the copper POW bracelet between them on the table and said, "Here. I want you to have this."

"Nobody wears those anymore," Layle stated briskly. Then she covered her mouth and said, "Oh. It's—y'all have the same name."

"You don't have to wear it. I know your old man'll shit a brick if you do. You can just hold on to it for me, if you want. But if you do put it on, then you can't take it off, ever. He'll die if you do—my dad will. That's what they say."

Layle slipped the bracelet onto her left wrist then clasped the band tight. They held hands across the table. Seeing his own name engraved there reminded Noel of the ballads they were studying in English, the ones where the doomed lovers ended up buried side by side . . . *and from his heart sprang a blood red rose, and from her heart a briar.* . . .

"You like?" she asked, rattling her wrist.

Noel spoke through the knot in his throat, saying, "He sees that, he's gonna make you break up with me again."

"I'll run away if he does."

"How come he hates my guts so much?"

"He doesn't, he just thinks you're . . . I dunno. Maybe if you'd get a haircut it would help."

"He still thinks I did it, doesn't he? Because of that Miss Myrick bullshit. Hell, everybody in our church thinks I did it."

"No, he doesn't, not anymore. But sometimes, Noel, it's almost like you want people to think you did it. You're always bringing it up, always talking about it."

He rolled his eyes, a dismissive gesture he'd stolen from Layle, and said, "Coach told me I had to get a haircut too. Before the season starts. Otherwise he won't let me play on the team."

"Are you going to?"

He shrugged, sucked in more beer, then stared down at the bracelet on her perfect wrist.

"If you want me to I will, for you." Then he added, "My dad, he's either dead or better off dead. That's what my uncle said in the letter."

Layle started shaking her head vehemently.

"He's alive," she said. "I know he is. I felt him the second I put it on."

. . .

They left to go parking at either the Circles or the Curve, Noel had not decided which yet. He was thinking about how every decision, no matter how small—even something like the Circles or the Curve—will change your life forever. Driving along Richmond Road, a road famous for head-ons and hairpins, he started flicking the headlight on and off to scare Layle, and it was during one of those moments with the lights off and the stars honed that the DJ broke into the middle of a love song to report that the band Lynyrd Skynyrd had just crashed its private jet into a heavily wooded area west of Hattiesburg and that Rescue-7, the new medical helicopter at Forest General Hospital, had been dispatched to the crash site.

Noel swerved into a used-car lot and killed the engine. Although his lips were moving, he did not say anything until Layle asked him, "What if Lynyrd Skynyrd was killed?"

"Skynyrd ain't a person, it's the whole damn band," he snapped without even looking at her. He placed both hands on the wheel and started whispering, "Not Skynyrd." Finally he nodded once, started the engine again, then churned the car out of the lot, heading away from the Curve or the Circles and whatever fate may have been in store for him there. He stopped at a convenience mart and bought a twelve-pack of tallboys.

"I thought we were going . . . I mean—"

"The landing pad," he told her. "We're going to the landing pad."

• • •

The landing pad turned out to be a fluorescent yellow circle with crosshair dashes painted onto a circular patch of blacktop behind the hospital. Around this blacktop circle, teenagers and bikers waited for the helicopter and held up lighters, as if a concert were beginning, while a dozen competing sound systems blasted Skynyrd tunes. Rumors of death and dismemberment wafted van to bike to car with the sweet-smelling joints. A joint came Noel's way and he hit it and passed it along to Layle, who leapt back, then blushed. To redeem herself, she opened a tallboy and inserted her free hand into Noel's back pocket.

Then a biker listed his hog toward Layle and wrapped his arm around her waist. He was still straddling his bike. A red bandanna was pirated across his hairline. The back of his leather jacket read:

DIAMONDBACKS
WHITE BY BIRTH
SOUTHERN BY THE GRACE OF GOD

Leaning farther into Layle, he asked, "You see their new album, sugar, see it, the cover I mean? It's got the whole of them on fire, like they knew—*the whole damn band's on fire!*"

Plunging her hand deeper into Noel's pocket, Layle tried to console the Diamondback, saying that maybe nobody got killed, but he only shook his head resolutely and stared far away. Then, with a distant nod, he asked, "What do you know about it, cunt?" He laughed, then he roared, accompanying himself as if his own laughter were something irresistible, contagious. Flashing jack-o-lantern teeth, he began to study the joint as if it had asked him an interesting riddle. With an inward smile, he replied, "Life-support systems for pussies," and passed the joint to Noel and quipped, "Ain't that how it is, chief?"

Noel tried to hit the joint in such a way as to give sufficient reply. Layle, beckoning to him with her green eyes, said she was going to wait inside the car. Noel nodded but did not offer to go with her. He watched Layle get inside the car, then he turned and stared up at the stars and at the October moon shaped like a boomerang.

The biker was talking about the plane wreck. He made it sound like he had been inside the plane when it crashed.

Noel passed the joint back and said, "This tastes kinda funny."

"Funny?"

"Good funny, though."

Smiling, then spit-whispering into Noel's ear, the Diamondback said, "Dusted."

"Dusted?"

"The dust of angels."

When Noel asked what that meant, the biker had to consult the heavens before answering, "Means I hope you ain't got no big plans for tonight." He had stated this very slowly, as if translating from the language of stars.

"Dust of angels?"

The biker put his arm around Noel's neck, squeezed it hard, and asked, "What they call you, man? On the street?"

"Spider," Noel said, because that's what his summer-league coach had nicknamed him because of how he crouched down at short. "Did I just smoke damn angel dust?"

"Spider! *Hey, Hanford!* We got us *Spider* over here!" Then he added, "Hanford's a niggername, ain't it?"

Hanford bellied over, eyeing Noel's beer. He was huge, all black leather and beard and mean-slanted red eyes.

"Ain't it a niggername?"

"Hold on," Noel said. He ducked inside the car and grabbed three tallboys. "You doin' alright in here?" he asked. "You gonna miss it bringing them down."

"I like it better in here," Layle replied, as if contently.

"They're saying Ronnie's head got cut off, and they can't find it nowhere."

She asked which one was Ronnie.

"One that writes the songs, the lead singer."

"You look Chinese."

"I feel about half Chinese." Before closing the door, he promised he'd be back in a minute. "First I gotta run these old boys some beers before they decide to rip my arms off."

He got his camera out of the trunk, then handed out the tallboys to the bikers and opened one for himself.

"It a niggername or it a niggername?"

"Not one I ever heard of," Noel replied.

Hanford opened his beer, slapped Noel on the back, and asked, "Why come they call you spider, Spider?"

* * *

A star had begun to distinguish itself above the hospital. Noel was not yet sure if it was Venus, a helicopter, or the onset of his angel-dust hallucinations. "Look there," he said softly to Hanford. "You see that?" The helicopter's spotlight was a straight white beam that dished at the end, a nail head of light. Soon this beam located the landing pad and then seemed to draw the helicopter down onto the pad. Wind began to flatten itself through the crowd as the helicopter, yellow on blue, landed by dancing from one pontoon to the next. Beer cans were skittering everywhere. Noel had just started taking pictures when two men in orange suits jumped out of the cockpit. They inspected the crowd, then one man ran back to the pilot and made a motion like keying a mike. Cops had arrived and were scything the crowd with orange-coned flashlights. The pilot tested the bullhorn. After a burst of feedback, he announced that Rescue-7 had already taken the survivors to Jackson. "*Please disperse. Repeat. Rescue-7 has already taken all survivors to Jackson. . . .*"

• • •

The Diamondbacks scrummed then set off for the vicinity of the crash site, a V formation of rumbling geese, vowing to find the lead singer's decapitated head. Noel's Mustang followed in their wake, but he was driving without compass, his world once again centrifugal, composed of brightly colored banners of light, one of which was the yellow center line on the road. He held Layle's hand as the radio listed off the names of band members confirmed to be DOA. The lead singer's was the first name on the list. They kept driving. Ten miles outside of town, Layle raised their knotted hands and pointed to the Beverly Drive-in, her copper bracelet absorbing the glow of the single streetlight. There, spelled out in crooked black letters along the wind-listed marquee, the T dangling: THE EXORCIST.

"Oh my Gosh!" she said. "We have to!"

• • •

Idling in line toward the yellow outhouse ticket booth, Noel was as yet unable to see the movie screen, only the bug-filled river of images above the parked cars. A group of protesters, twelve Christians strong, was moving down the ticket line laying posterboard signs over windshields and belting out, "*Mine eyes have seen the glory!*" They reached the Mustang. EVIL IS EVIL! the windshield suddenly proclaimed in red Magic Marker. Noel tried to max the volume on "Crossroads" but turned the defroster on by mistake. Layle visored her eyes and sank into the seat.

"Do you think they recognized us?" she asked afterward.

"Who?"

"Them! They were from our church. Some of them were—Mrs. Gillespie was. God, she looked right at me too. I think she did."

"Our church?"

"Noel, are you okay? Your eyes look like they're bleeding almost."

He thrust a wad of bills through a crescent-moon window to a woman eighty years old wearing sunglasses, then he found an empty slot alongside the swaying corrugated fence painted swimming-pool blue that surrounded the drive-in with the loose bay-and-inlet shape of a lake. On screen a man in a black suit was walking down a black alley. Noel fitted the iron speaker onto his window. The music was already giving him the creeps. A headlight passed close enough for him to glimpse Layle, her green eyes were blurred.

"How many beers you had, girl?" he asked.

"Four. Counting this one."

"You had four tallboys already?"

"Plus the two at the restaurant."

He took her beer away and said, "Your dad's gonna be waiting up on you."

"He'll get over it."

"Yeah, he'll get over it by not letting you see me for the next year."

This information seemed to annoy Layle, at least momentarily. She propped her blue-jeaned legs out the window and rested her head on Noel's lap and clamped the back of her palm to her forehead.

"I am so drunk I bet I won't even remember this. The last thing

I'll probably remember is waiting for that helicopter. You'll have to tell me everything after that, I won't even know unless you tell me."

Noel made the mistake of glancing at the movie screen, and instantly he was aboard the small bed twirling in midair.

Layle sat up suddenly and said, "I gotta go to the bathroom."

"You gonna be sick?"

"No, I just gotta pee."

As soon as she'd left, Noel fed on his inhaler then slid low into his seat and covered an eye with each hand. He was peering between his fingers at the screen when Layle opened her car door and almost gave him a heart attack. She was out of breath. She was saying, "Noel, you will not believe what just happened to me!" She was saying, "Look—I'm bleeding!" She opened the door so that the weak dome light bathed the front seat. They both stared at her bleeding ankle while she explained, "They had the movie speakers going inside the bathroom, going full blast, and I was just sitting there with all these humongous spiders about to drop down on me then you'll never guess what happened I swear this owl I thought it was an owl trapped in there making all these spooked-out noises just like a ghost *oooooooohhhhh* . . ." Layle turned her hands into spiders. "I never peed so fast in my life. Then, right as I stepped outside, that poor girl's head—did you see that part?—it was spinning around her neck, I had to run back inside I thought I was gonna be sick." She paused for breath and then lowered one spider onto Noel's wrist. "But it wasn't an owl at all, Noel. It was a couple, in the last stall, doing it, standing up doing it, I think—is that even possible?"

He shook his head and told her, "Nah, baby, it don't work that way."

She wedged her bleeding foot atop the opposite thigh and started dabbing a tissue from tongue to cut.

"You've done it before, haven't you, Noel? Don't lie, I know you have. I've got ears."

"Ears?"

She asked was it with anybody she knew. She assured him, "I'll die if it is."

Not even on angel dust would Noel confess to being a virgin.

He said, "Just some ol' girl out in Petal. After that first time your dad made you break up with me."

"*I knew it!*" She demanded to know what it was like. "I can't believe I'm asking you this . . . did she, you know?"

"Did she what?"

"Oh I don't know! You tell me. Did she . . . make those kinda spooked-out noises, you know . . . *out loud*?"

"Naw, baby, it wasn't like that."

"Was it that slut Amber Smith, she's from Petal?"

Noel hesitated long enough to implicate Amber Smith, whoever she was.

"It *was* her, *I knew it!* You're just protecting her." She bit her bottom lip. "She's the biggest road whore in all Petal. And that's saying something. I can't believe she's a cheerleader, she can't even do a split, not a real one."

"She did that night," Noel said.

"Oh-my-God, *she did*?"

The little girl on screen stabbed at her vagina with a bloody crucifix and yelled "*Fuck me! Fuck me! Fuck me!*" while Layle listed for Noel everything Amber Smith had ever done wrong as a cheerleader. A welt on the girl's tummy spelled out HELP ME. Noel's stomach began to writhe too. He recalled reading a newspaper article that had reported strange fires on the set of *The Exorcist*. And he recalled another rumor, one his cousins had told him, that the girl actress *really did get possessed* halfway through the filming and that they'd used a lot of this real footage in the movie.

Layle was demonstrating the right way to do a particular cheer by throwing her arms around the car, clanging her new bracelet against the rearview, and chanting:

WOMP! UP! SIDE-DA-HEAD! Say Womp-Upside-Dahead
HEY-HEY-HEY-WOMP!

She choreographed two more cheers, explaining the footwork, the hard parts, what certain girls did all wrong. Then she explained that she had learned to do the cheers *the right way* from sitting in the visitors' bleachers and watching the black girls cheer for the other team. She launched into a husky gospel version of "Hey-hey Number Nine Got My Eye On You," but then she stopped abruptly and told Noel that the black girls at Mary Bethune High even turned songs off the radio into cheers:

DAH ROOF   DAH ROOF   DAH ROOF IS ON FIRE!
SAY WE-DON'T-NEED-NO-WATER-LET-THE-FIRE-STATION-
BURN!

She touched her throat, paused, then she said, almost begging, "Noel, this is so gross I can't watch. Can't we go in the back and smooch?"

• • •

The soundtrack followed them into the back seat, where Layle was lowering her kisses between the buttons of Noel's shirt. She untucked his shirt and slid her cold hands up onto his ribs and wet his belly with her tongue. Noel's lungs tightened like fists as she undid first his belt, then his zipper. She pulled his jeans to his knees then tugged down the elastic band of his white briefs, exposing his erection to moonlight and movie light. Timing her breath like a diver, she slipped the wet ring of her mouth onto him.

It was like his asthma was boiling up inside of him. He had been trying to weather the attack discreetly, but now he was starting to panic. Finally he sat up and tried to scissor his torso over Layle's, stretching his right arm toward the inhaler inside his jeans pocket. He almost had it . . . but then, just as his hand closed on it, he felt himself jettisoning into Layle, whose head was trapped beneath him. She could not pull away, though she tried. Her body performed an unsuccessful push-up, after which she made a strangled gag, then vomited a long hot gush of pizza, spaghetti, and beer onto Noel's groin. . . .

When he finally opened his eyes again, Layle was crouched over his lap and connected to him by long sinews of mucus. She looked like a wild animal. A terrible stench had flooded the back seat. Noel closed his eyes again but not in time. He too struggled to escape, then he choked and began to empty his belly onto Layle's long shiny strawberry blond hair. . . .

The world we know is a machine, a design, darkly spinning: therefore God exists.

●　●　●

The speaker above the sink was sporadically broadcasting the movie while Noel scrubbed himself with brown paper towels in front of the mirror. A man had followed him into the men's room and now stood behind Noel holding a quart of beer and watching solemnly Noel's attempts to clean himself. He was almost as tall as Noel and he wore a tan soldier's uniform and he was smoking a hand-rolled cigarette. He was handsome even though his nose was kind of large and his eyes kind of too big and his neck kind of too long. Their eyes met in the mirror and Noel was just about to tell the soldier to fuck off when he noticed the hole bored through the chest of the soldier's uniform. The hole was about the size of a baseball and it was surrounded by pink blistery scar tissue, as if the uniform and his skin had been melted together. Every time the soldier inhaled his cigarette, the hole filled with smoke. When the smoke dissipated, Noel could see the turquoise wall behind the soldier through the hole.

"I ain't afraid of you," Noel said. He turned to face the soldier, but nobody was there. Noel was alone in the bathroom.

He returned to the car with more paper towels and did his best to mop out the back, then he slumped into the driver's seat to wait for Layle. Soon, he knew, he would drop her off in front of her house and as her porch light shot on she would gently set the copper bracelet onto the console between them, then she would trudge wet and dreadlocked toward the ghost and scarecrow guarding her father's door. Noel would never see her again. He knew this as clearly as an old man remembering it, remembering it bitterly. And the longer he sat there staring at the movie, the more he was beset with this grim clairvoyance. He remembered that Layle would not show up for school on Monday, the day of cheerleader tryouts, and that over the next week word would spread that she had transferred across town to Beason, the private all-white academy. Other rumors would follow, the most persistent one being that Noel had taken Layle to New Orleans for an abortion.

Slumping deeper in the car seat, Noel recalled another day yet to come in early spring, a sunny day that would find him standing outside the school cafeteria in the jock Skoal-dipping circle when a linebacker named Jimmy Rey announced that he'd heard Layle Smokewood had pulled a train for the whole backfield at Beason. Jimmy Rey was a monster, even taller than Noel and much wider.

"*Pulled a god-dog train!*" he repeated, jerking down the cord of an imaginary whistle. "Hey, you used to date her, Spider, how far'd you get with her?"

Just then Tim Weiss passed by on the cafeteria sidewalk, and Noel felt a sting of tenderness for his old friend, whom he had been shunning of late. Noel raised a hand, but Tim pretended not to notice. All the jocks laughed. They thought Noel was making fun of Tim.

"You know what I heard about his old lady?" someone asked. At the same moment someone else said, "Damn jewboy fag. Y'all know what they believe?"

"He's awright," Noel said.

"His mama eats pussy is what I heard," someone else said.

"So how far'd you get with her, Spider?" Jimmy Rey insisted.

The group fell silent. Finally Noel shrugged and said, "Ahh, just an ol' blow job, Jimmy. Out at the Beverly Drive-in." He spat into the dirt and added, "Same damn night it burnt to the ground."

That detail sidetracked the conversation, just as Noel had hoped it would. Now, while half the Skoal circle continued to roundtable the Jewish faith, the other half began to embellish the night of the drive-in arson. *I heard it got lightning struck. The damn KKK did it, I heard. Shit, them devil worshipers did. You see them pictures of it in the paper? You could see angel wings in the smoke. I heard it was Satan's face you could see. And they killed Jesus too. Hell, they go to church on Saturday and celebrate killing Jesus like it's their Easter.*

Jimmy Rey stopped this discussion by spitting a stream of bug juice near Noel's boot and asking if Layle Smokewood had swallowed or what.

Noel had been trying to imagine Layle pulling a train and how that worked exactly. He knew that if she had, it was his own fault.

Slowly Noel lifted his hooded eyes and replied, "Naw, Jimmy, she didn't swallow. It wasn't much of a blow job, if you wanna know the truth. Not nearly as good as the one your mother gave me last night."

Noel landed a few punches going down, then just shut his eyes and let the darkness take him.

Slumped inside his Mustang and still waiting for Layle to return from the bathroom, Noel could see these events as clearly as if he had the all-powerful lens of the Aleph 2000 trained on the future. So when the fire started, this too seemed to be something he was remembering. He did not react at first other than to grip the steering wheel. Then, after a minute or so, he reached down onto the floorboard after his Nikon and stepped outside the car. The movie screen seemed to undulate as smoke formed a backdrop then plumed upward from the bottom. A brown flowerlike stain spread across the picture, as if the film had jammed and the projector were searing that one frame. But the movie kept playing, even after flames had eaten holes through the stain, even after the entire screen was solidly ablaze, a wall of fire. Images played like holographs inside the flames until the screen collapsed backward.

CHAPTER SIX

AFTER EIGHT MISSISSIPPI, and with a cough of smoke, Matt asked, "Hey—I tell you? Guess who I got a letter from."

They were driving to church. Noel let another car slip between his Mustang and Roger's new-used Lincoln, then he guessed Tommy Weatherspoon.

"Who?"

"Our uncle."

"Oh. No, not—I mean, yeah, I got one from him too—but that ain't the one I mean."

Noel, who had written a barrage of letters to Tommy and had not received another reply in almost a year now, asked what it had said, the letter from Tommy.

"Beats me, I couldn't hardly read it. You know something weird, though. He thought it was you, not me, made all-stars. I think that's what it said."

"Mom musta wrote him and he got us mixed up."

"Yeah." Matt pondered this. "Hey, you think Rog ever hits Mom?"

"Rog?"

"In his letter, he kept asking me all these questions about Rog. Like Rog was some kind of escaped criminal or something."

"He better not hit her, I'd fuckin' kill him."

"Y'all two went at it pretty good last night."

"Yeah. I can't wait to finally graduate, get the hell outa here. He invite you out to Key West?"

"Who?"

"Tommy."

Matt opened the top of his window and aimed a stream of smoke outside before replying. "He said his restaurant was losing money, but that it was supposed to lose money for a while, and that we could visit him after things turned around. Said he'd have us cleaning shrimp." Admiring himself in the sideview, Matt added, "I ain't cleaning no damn shrimp."

"He said us?"

"Fuck a shrimp."

"He said both of us can visit?"

"Yeah. But that ain't even the letter I'm talken about."

"He didn't send you a shirt or nothing, huh?"

"Guess who it was from, the other letter?"

"Ernest Hemingway."

"Who?"

"How the hell do I know who it's from?"

"It was from State. From Coach Tylerson up there."

"Coach Tylerson?"

"At Starkville. Said he'd been hearing good things about me and I should come visit campus, said he'd give me a personal tour if I did."

"Hey, keep it low, Matt, we ain't advertising."

"Sorry."

"You going there?"

"State? Hell, I got two years to decide that. I don't even want to go to college. Fuck college."

They pulled into a drugstore parking lot to finish the joint and they watched across the street as the rest of the family filed into church.

"What's that Mom's carrying? Looks like a damn baby."

"Care basket," Matt answered.

"Yeah, who for?"

Matt bit his upper lip but allowed the grin to escape.

"I ain't gotta be the one to always tell you, do I?"

"To tell me what, Matt?"

"I thought the whole damn town knew by now."

It took a full minute for Noel to extradite the information from Matt, who finally shook his head and admitted, "Layle Smokewood. Ran off to California. With the drummer of some band called Furry Merkyn."

Matt went on to explain that two days after Layle had run away, the Smokewoods' maid had found the reverend unconscious in his library and had called an ambulance. "An accidental overdose of tranquilizers," was how the paper reported it, but Matt knew better. "They're not even letting him do sermons no more after today, that's what Mom heard. Hell, who's gonna listen to some preacher tried to kill himself like an old lady does with a bunch of damn pills?" Matt made a pistol of thumb and forefinger and inserted the fingertip into his mouth. "Didn't even up and do it like a man."

Noel whipped the Mustang into the church parking lot. They sprayed the car with Ozium and rubbed their fingers in Skoal and sweetened their breaths from a bottled Coke.

"Hey, you know what *Furry Merkyn* means? What it means in French?"

Noel was using the Clear Eyes. He wiped his eyes with the tops of his shoulders and said, "I don't even wanna know, Matt, just—"

"Hairy pussy," Matt told him. "She ran off with the damn drummer from Hairy Pussy."

The church stairwell was cordoned off with a velvet rope the same burgundy color as the carpet. Matt and Noel straddled the rope, sprinted up the stairs, then sat hunched low in the first row of the otherwise empty balcony. Above them, in the bow of the A-frame chapel, a stained-glass Jesus knocked on a large wooden door. Jesus had a lamb tucked under one arm. The sun was rising behind the pictorial and splashing watercolor light over the pulpit, where Reverend Smokewood sat dressed out but deflated-looking inside layered purple and white robes.

Noel checked to make sure Matt wasn't paying attention then closed his eyes and began to pray.

Not so long ago Noel had been one of the most popular guys in school, but these days found him fast becoming a sideshow. There were rumors about him and Ross Altman and him and Layle Smokewood and him and drug dealing, plus the ones about how he'd been kicked off the baseball team because he'd refused to get his hair cut and how he'd cussed out the coach in front of the dugout and how he'd almost gotten into a fistfight with him. But lately the rumors were spinning out of control. For instance, just the other day, Tim, whom Noel had gotten hired at Pasquale's, had overheard a born-again girl named Mona Campsong telling a group of like-minded friends that she'd heard that Spider Weatherspoon dealt heroin and that he shot it up under his tongue and between his toes. And although this rumor was not true—Noel only dealt pot and quaaludes—it had still pleased him to hear it. It was all part of his testimony. A testimony for his love for Layle, whom he still imagined as buried by his side, a red rose growing up out of his heart, a sharp briar twisting up out of hers.

"I'm sorry," he prayed now. "It's all my damn fault. Just don't let nothing bad happen to her out in California. Let it all happen to me instead."

He checked to make sure Matt wasn't looking, then dove back into prayer. This time he prayed not to be gay. He prayed for this because ever since the night of the drive-in catastrophe he had been failing miserably with girls, one after another. He had failed with girls in the back seats of cars, on couches and love seats and bean-bag chairs, in their father's beds, in the woods, and once in the shallow end of a swimming pool. The only thing worse than the actual failure was the next day at school wondering who knew or did everybody know by now?

He opened his eyes again. Matt was leaning forward and smirking down at the service, which was being conducted by the Reverend Blankenship, the second-string preacher from the vast liturgical bullpen of the First Baptist Church. When it was time for the sermon, though, Reverend Smokewood stood up slowly and stepped toward the podium and grasped it. For the first time that morning, he seemed to fully occupy his white and purple shroud.

His sermon concerned what he termed *out-of-body experiences*. As this sermon progressed, he began to throw his arms about in a jerky puppeted manner reminiscent of his daughter's cheerleading. The reverend also seemed increasingly unaware of the congregation. At times he wiped away imaginary sweat, imaginary tears. His eyes took flight chasing invisible birds among the rafters. *Lights at the end of the tunnel!* emerged as his refrain. Every time he repeated it, his tone thickened with scorn, although the first time the words rang out, he had made them sound the very promise of salvation.

"*Lights at the end of the tunnel!* We hear this phrase everywhere these days, on TV talk shows, in bestsellers on so-called miracles, in songs, in books about near-death experiences. Everywhere we turn, lights at the end of the tunnel! Guiding lights. A star for every wandering bark. Just waiting for us to die. The Bible of course contains such episodes," he thundered, quizzing the congregation with his eyebrows. "*The most famous out-body-experience in the history of mankind!*" he further challenged. Then, with measured disdain, he continued, "I speak to you, of course, of the Book of Revelations." Turning his back to the pews and raising both arms so that the blue suit cuffs were visible at the wrists and ankles, he shouted, "*And immediately I was in the spirit!* . . . So Saint John tells us. John the Divine. John the disciple, whom Christ most loved. John says *I was in the spirit!* Not in the body . . . but the spirit . . . the spirit . . . the spirit . . ."

From then on he continued to supply his own reverberation, which mingled inside the chapel's already disconcerting echo.

"And what did our beloved Saint John see in his quote-unquote out-of-body experience?" he asked, his back still turned to the congregation and his raised arms starting a slow-motion fall toward his sides. For the next ten minutes, as his arms continued their slow descent, he touted the vision of horsemen and of eyes melting out of sockets and of slain lambs and a sun pitch-black setting behind plagues of locusts behind a sky darkened with rain hail fire blood venom, blood swelling the rivers, rivers reddening the oceans, until even the moon high above our wretchedness yea the very moon itself was festered into nothing but one great clotted wound . . . wound . . . wound . . .

When his palms finally touched his robes, he gathered in a breath and wheeled on the congregation. Now he wiped away real sweat, real tears, and with a giant's sadness he interrogated, "Lights? *Lights*, you tell me? Lights? *Lights*, you say? Where? I ask. *Where* are these lights? *Where*? SHOW THEM TO ME! SHOW ME THESE LIGHTS!"

He lowered his head and shook it bitterly.

"Do not," he concluded. "Do not speak to me. Do not speak to me of such fables of light."

And he remained standing there until Reverend Blankenship grasped him by the elbow and assisted him back to his throne.

* * *

In heavy post-church traffic, Matt took in a dip and complained, "Man, I'm so hungry I could eat a pale horse."

* * *

Noel spent the afternoon in the darkroom he had built inside his walk-in closet. There, among canisters of stop bath and fixer, he had stashed a shoe box of neatly baggied dope, and among the sponges and clothespins and rubber gloves, he had buried a small library of *Gallery* magazines. The darkroom was the perfect front. Nobody could enter without knocking and expecting to wait, and nobody could enter in his absence for fear of exposing film. He killed entire sunny afternoons on the swivel stool smoking joints in the chemical darkness.

Unfortunately, he had neither the patience nor the touch for developing film. Usually he destroyed the film while trying to spool it in the dark. Or, if he got past that obstacle, he failed to get the solutions at consistent temperatures, so that when he unwound the negatives they were cracked and corroded. Lately, though, he had come to prefer these botched negatives. They reminded him of old daguerreotypes. But more than that, the damaged negatives seemed to him to be photographs of ghosts. And not just ghosts of people, but the ghosts of an entire landscape, of tree, rock, and sun—a specter world that Noel had always sensed abided alongside his own.

Because he was anticipating the negative more than the print, his photographs had gotten so bad that even the one magazine that had previously published two of his photographs was no longer writing him back. But that didn't matter to him, not much anyway, because the only magazine Noel cared about now was *Gallery*. *Gallery* was a men's magazine that published photographs of women sent in by their lovers and friends. Locked inside his darkroom, stoned day in, day out, Noel plotted endless strategies to get girls to undress in front of his Nikon, and then he imagined their nakedness locked inside the pages of *Gallery*.

Lately these plots had centered around Amber Smith. He had a date with Amber this coming Saturday. This date had seemed inevitable, not only because Amber had boldly pursued him, but also because their reputations and tastes seemed to coincide. A year ago Amber had swerved to miss a deer and driven her car into a ditch. She claimed to have been electrocuted back to life during the ambulance ride. Later, she emerged from minor brain surgery no longer the pert cheerleader but now a boylike creature: flat-chested, rail-thin, and with a monkish head shaved and stitched. The outside corner of her left eye had been left scarred and stretched-looking so that her eyes appeared mismatched. When her hair grew back, it came in no longer jet-black and wavy as before, but straight and silvery gray, the color of lake water or mercury, and also the color of her eyes.

Come Saturday Noel loaded his camera into the trunk and took Amber first to Pasquale's and then to a party out in Petal. Afterward he did not recall failing with Amber. He recalled only the familiar rush of emotions attached to failure, though he clearly remembered holding a black rubber flashlight inside a slatternly tree house and watching Amber fit back on her yellow bra. The tree house was located fifty-odd yards into the woods behind her home, which sparkled through the branches like the evening star. Noel sipped from a tequila bottle and tried to mem-orize Amber's nakedness.

"You know what he'd do if he found us out here?" she was say-ing. "I shit you not, Moon Man, he'd shoot us both *boom-bang*. He might not shoot you right away, if you get my drift. He'd shoot me first, but all I'd do is laugh at him. I been dead before, what's the big deal?"

"Moon Man?" Noel said.

"You've never heard anybody call you that before?"

Noel let his eyes burn out of focus on the twinkling light under which Amber's father may or may not have been loading a shotgun, then he returned his attention to Amber, to her nakedness that any moment now would close itself from him forever. He tried to clear his mind, to leave it a blank sheet so that her naked body could develop onto it like an image inside a chemical bath. Amber was standing before him in only the green midriff shirt and yellow panties, and stroking her short hair with a broken-handled red brush, tossing her silver hair forward and brushing it up from behind. While she did this, she asked if she could have some pot to take with her.

"Just a couple pinches. I'll show you my scars if you do."

Noel pulled his jeans the rest of the way up then stuffed a matchbox with the red-stitched buds. He slipped the matchbox shut and handed it up to her.

Amber smiled and asked, "This that same spooky-dooky trip weed?"

Noel said it was.

"He speaks," she chimed. "Back from the dead."

"You gonna show me those scars?"

She knelt and took his hand and guided it to the crown of her head and rubbed it there. "Feel that?"

He nodded that he did.

"That's from where I went through the windshield *boom!* See, like my own private railroad track *woo-woo! chuga-luga-chuga-luga* all the way down . . . to . . . feel that?"

She pirouetted to show Noel the back of one thigh, which looked to be coated with lacquer. "That's where they peeled off my skin and patched it back on . . ." Again she rotated and this time lifted her hair away from her neck. "Right here. Feel. Shaped just like a heart."

Next she used both hands to diamond-frame a jagged four-inch scar running just under her belly button and ending in a pink blemish. "Don't touch it, though, it's bad luck. I can't even have babies because of it." She took the flashlight and pointed it at this scar so that a pale mouth of light engulfed it. "Shaped like lightning hitting a tree, see?" she noted. Then she asked, "I guess that's how it always works with you and girls, huh?"

Noel stared at the scar a long time before saying, "What do you mean *always?*"

"It . . . you know, melting off on us like that. You were doing real fine for a while. We could try some more, if you want. I don't mind."

"Why did you say *always?*"

"Nothing. Just something I heard. You know, girl talk."

"What kinda girl talk?"

"Regular ol' girl-talk girl talk. Hey, don't get mad at me, I didn't do nothing."

"I'm not getting mad. Just tell me what it was you heard. Please."

But Amber remained hesitant until Noel offered up a fat joint. When she reached for it, he snatched it away.

"First tell me what you heard."

She scrunched up her face to answer. "Nothing much. Just that maybe you don't like girls as much as you think you do."

LEE DURKEE

"*What?*"

"That maybe you *only think* you like girls."

Noel's fake laugh sounded more like a cough. He relinquished the joint and took a long evil pull of tequila, then he shuddered. Amber had balanced the flashlight on the slat between them, its beam pointing up at the ceiling, where a hole had been cut and a knotted rope led outside onto the roof.

"Don't worry, Moon Man, I'll tell everybody you were the best ever," she said, and as if to prove this she leaned in and closed her mouth on his neck and started to suck there, not one long continuous suck but a series of short ones between which she pinched his skin with her teeth. "There. Now everyone'll think we definitely fucked." She admired the hickey. "You wanna give me one?"

At first her neck tasted salty, but then it just tasted like neck.

"Ow!" she cried. "Stop!"

Noel apologized. Then they examined each with the flashlight.

"Yours is like a crow flying," Amber reported. "What's mine like?"

He brought the flashlight closer.

"Like two ghosts. Holding hands."

"Crows and ghosts." She picked up her jeans and shook them out. Then, more like an accusation than a question, she asked, "You used to go with Layle Smokewood, didn't you?"

He nodded and mouthed yeah.

"She was real pretty." To this she quickly amended, "I heard she ran off to Hollywood with some drummer."

Noel said yeah, he'd heard that too.

"You know what'll probably happen to her out there? She'll probably end up making those movies. You know, with horses and all. That's what happens to all those small-town chicks in Hollywood. They get them addicted to heroin, then they trot out Mr. Ed. She was a preacher's daughter too."

"Horses?"

"Horses, heroin, and black dudes. You know what else I heard? That she had an abortion. That you took her to New Orleans and made her have it."

Noel heard footsteps outside, or thought he did. He tensed and listened, but whatever it was had fallen silent.

"That's the exact same as murder. Maybe that's why you can't . . . you know. Like maybe that little dead baby placed some kind of curse on you?"

Noel drank more tequila and kept listening for the footsteps.

"Did you even ask her to marry you first? I mean down-on-your-knees ask?"

He gave her a strange look then shook his head no.

"See. I bet that's why you can't . . . you know, anymore. 'Cause y'all murdered that little baby."

She finished buttoning her jeans then crawled over to the ladder and started down the hole in the floor. With only her head and arms visible above the floor, she asked if he was going home. Noel said he'd stick around here for a while, if that was okay.

"You're not gonna hang yourself up there, are you, Moon Man?"

"Hang myself?"

"Yeah. Every time I climb up here I kinda expect to find some-body hanging from that rope, don't ask me why."

Amber stared at the rope, knotted at the bottom, which dangled through the hole in the roof and was tied outside to a branch above the tree house.

"The left half of your face looks Chinese," he told her.

"Thanks. Thanks a lot." She stretched both eyes into slants and bucked her teeth. "Confucius say . . ." But then evidently she could think of nothing for Confucius to have said. She let go her eyes and the right one reshaped itself.

Noel asked how many girls knew about . . . you know?

"Not many, probably. Most girls I know think you're real hot. I guess that must be kinda sad, having all us chicks chasing after you and then you not being able to . . ."

Noel used his cough laugh again. Then he asked, "You ever have them dreams, the kind where you fall in love with someone, someone you don't even know in real life, but in that dream, it's like you'd known that person forever? Then you wake up and just kinda lay there all brokehearted. That ever happen to you?"

Amber nodded and whispered yeah, she'd had those dreams. "They're so sad," she agreed.

"Well, that's what my whole life is like. Like one of those dreams."

"What? You fall in love with me?"

"Sure. Kinda. Showing me your scars and all."

"Don't hang yourself, Moon Man."

Saying that, Amber went down the ladder.

"Hey!" he called after her. "Can you do a split? A real one?"

Her face reappeared above the floor. Looking at him quizzically, she replied, "I used to could. But not anymore. I got steel pins in both my knees." She stepped up one rung then leaned her body away from the ladder so that her elbows locked straight. "It's okay with me—if you want—you can tell guys we did it. If you want. I don't care."

Noel watched her a moment longer, then asked if he could take her picture.

"Take my picture? Now?"

"Yeah, I got my camera back in the car. I'll run get it."

Amber wanted to know what kind of pictures. Her voice sounded suspicious.

"Any kind you let me. Brushing your hair out in front like you just did."

She climbed the rest of the way up the ladder then sat with both legs dangling through the hole.

"Or maybe showing off them scars."

"Moon Man, you ever wonder why I asked you out in the first place?"

"I asked you out."

"Shoot. I practically twisted your arm." Amber knocked twice on the plywood floor. "Guess whose fort this is."

"I'll give you some more weed. Hell, I'll give you all I got here, plus I'll throw in some 'ludes."

"Does the name Ross Altman," she asked, "ring any bells?"

Noel glanced around the tree house then up at the hole in the ceiling.

"Ross was my half-brother."

"Your half . . ."

"But there wasn't nothing half about us. I can't even remember not knowing him."

"But your name's Smith."

"Yeah. I'm a Smith and he's an Altman."

"That's why you wanted to go out with me, because of what happened with your brother?"

"That and because everyone knows you got the best weed." She grinned and added, "Nah, I mean, yeah, I was curious, but ever since I first saw you I thought you were real fine. I still do."

Noel slumped forward, his elbows hanging over his knees.

"Don't you think it's weird us two being here together?" she asked.

"Weird?"

"Weird spooky weird. You're the one who ran him down and I'm his damn sister."

"That wasn't my fault. He shoulda been taking them baseball pills."

"Baseball pills?"

"The ones that let him play baseball, the ones for his brain."

"Oh. Who told you about that?"

"I dunno, my mom. She said your family couldn't take pills because you're some kind of scientists."

"We're not scientists. We're Christian Scientists. Or we used to be. Now only my dad is. My mom won't step foot inside church. And me, I'm not anything. I don't even believe in God, I don't think."

"You don't?"

She shook her head. They sat quiet. Noel was imagining Ross Altman playing in the tree house—not Ross Altman exactly, but Ross Altman's ghost.

"I heard the police talked to you about my brother."

Noel made a series of half shrugs.

"What'd they ask you?"

Suddenly he felt very tired, almost too tired to lie.

"Nothing. Look, I didn't do it. I know everybody thinks I did, but I didn't. I mean, if I did it, then how come nobody's arrested me yet?"

"Maybe they don't want to arrest you. Maybe the police don't think it's really murder so they didn't arrest you, because they knew you'd go to jail and it'd ruin your life, and you're just a kid who didn't really do nothing wrong."

The way she was scrutinizing him, it made Noel wonder if he looked different to her out of the one slanted eye.

"Did you know I was sleeping in his hospital room the night he was murdered?"

"You were?"

"All night long. On the cot. I used to sleep there all the time."

"You didn't wake up at all, not even when the alarm went off?"

"How do you know about any alarm?"

"I don't. I just figured there musta been one went off when his heart stopped beating. Like on TV."

Just then the flashlight fell over and rolled about a foot toward Noel.

"You see that?" Amber said, nodding as if proud of something.

Without taking his eyes off the flashlight, Noel said, "Hey, this ain't some kind of setup, is it? I mean, your old man ain't fixing to bust in here and shoot me down or nothing?"

It took her a moment to comprehend Noel's paranoia, then she laughed and assured him, "No. I ain't setting you up."

"Can I ask you something?"

"Sure."

"That day I was in his room, how come he had a Ouija board on top of him?"

"Did you tell the police that?"

He shook his head.

"Because I used to talk to him on it." Amber had said this without the least bit of embarrassment, like answering a dare. "You think that's crazy, huh?"

"I dunno, I never used one. My cousins always said they were for devil worshipers."

"I heard that too."

"What'd you ask him on it?"

"All sorts of things."

"You ever ask him if he was already dead or not?"

"I tried, but he never understood what I meant. He just kept wanting to know the way home. He still thought he was a little kid and that he was lost on his way home from a baseball game."

"You're supposed to tell them to go to the light."

"I know you are. But whenever I told him that, he'd always spell out, WHAT LIGHT? Except he spelled it wrong."

"Those boards, they really work?"

She snorted and said, "Shoot."

"What else did he say to you on it?"

"Different things, different times. But lots of times I'd get all these white-trash spirits pretending to be Ross. But I knew it wasn't him because they could spell better than he could and because they didn't know our secrets. And sometimes I got other patients in the hospital. They'd tell me their names and what room they were in and what was wrong with them. And they'd give me messages for their family, but I could never figure out how to give the messages without sounding crazy. I'd sneak into their rooms, though, and check to see if their names matched up."

"Did they?"

"Sometimes they did, most times they didn't. I think some of them had died in the hospital a long time ago and didn't know they were dead. Isn't that sad, not knowing you're dead?"

"What kind of messages did they give you?"

"*I love you* messages usually, either that or *please let me die* messages. You believe in ghosts?"

He took another quick look around the fort and whispered, "Fuckin' A."

"I've seen his ghost in here before. Ross's."

"What was he doing? Playing?"

"How'd you know that?"

"I just guessed it, since he was a little kid."

"He was still wearing his baseball uniform. Number five."

Noel slapped a mosquito on his wrist and rubbed it off.

"Do you think I did it?" he asked her.

"Nah. I know you didn't."

"You do?"

"Yeah, you're crazy enough but too sweet. Besides, you'd have messed it all up. Unplugged the wrong kid or something."

Noel whistled then ballooned out his cheeks. He didn't know

what else to say, so he whistled again, then asked if she wanted to split a 'lude.

"No way. Too many bad things happen to girls on 'ludes. They 714's?"

"Bootlegs."

"Uh-uh." She shook her head decidedly no before smiling one last time and descending two rungs so that once again only her head showed above the brace of two-by-fours. Noel offered her his flashlight, but she said that she could find her way home in the dark. "'Bye, Moon Man." She slipped out of sight and from below came the crunch of leaves. When the leaves quieted down, Noel set the flashlight sideways on the floor and started arranging his contraband within its beam. The joints, the matches, the baggie of weed, the five quaaludes, the tequila bottle, the can of Skoal . . . he arranged them in the order in which he would do them, quaaludes first, dip last. After he had swallowed the first of the thick lime-green tablets, he picked up the flashlight and pointed it up at the rope's stop knot. He got to his knees and leaned forward and tested the rope, like ringing a bell. He undid the stop knot and as best he could he fashioned a hangman's noose, though it did not much resemble the ones on TV westerns. He wasn't sure why he had done this, just something to look at maybe, that or maybe as a keepsake for Amber, who would find it there the next time she visited the tree house with some other stud.

He was still watching the noose when he once again heard the crunch of leaves. This time they were distinct and definitely moving toward the tree house. The ladder creaked and shifted. As fast as he could, Noel extended his legs straight out and shut his eyes. He let his head lag to one side and his mouth droop open. He held his breath, sprawled both arms.

"Hey, you okay, Moon Man?"

He sat up again.

"I thought it was your dad," he explained. "I thought I was about to get shot."

Amber crawled inside and settled herself beside him so that their knees were touching.

"I changed my mind about that 'lude." She took out the joint Noel had given her and blew along the wet seam. "Let's get all Chinese-eyed."

Noel made a vague welcoming gesture toward the flashlight beam of paraphernalia.

"You play dead real good," she told him. Then she added, "And I oughta know."

CHAPTER SEVEN

ROGER DRUMMED NOEL awake at dawn demanding to know, "*What happened to your car?*" He jerked Noel out of bed and then with a series of shoves propelled him across the room to the window above the toy box. The sunlight distracted Noel for only a moment before he saw, showcased in the front yard, his battered Mustang, the driver's door winged open, both fenders bashed and contorted, headlights shattered, one taillight dangling out of socket.

Pushing Noel's face into the window, Roger kept shouting, "*Well? . . . Well? . . .*" Noel's breath was fogging the glass in front of his eyes. He tried to speak, but his mouth was smeared against the window. Finally Roger released him, and Noel sagged onto the toy box then looked up at his stepfather and asked, "What happened?"

To which Roger screamed, "*You're asking me?*"

That our lives are little more than our memories of our lives, that we have secret playgrounds we visit from time to time that we keep hidden from the parts of us that claim to remember, that we have dark aliases, names we answer to that our memories balk at—these were notions testified to by the wrecked Mustang below him in the yard, notions he would ponder more and more over the next few weeks as he waited to be arrested for what crime he was not yet sure. For now, though, crumpled onto the toy box, naked except for a pair of white briefs, he simply broke down, and before he could stopper himself he had confessed too much to his stepfather, not only about his previous night's failure with Amber, but his whole history of such lackluster performances spilled out. "Something's wrong with me," he kept interjecting as he spoke nonstop a dizzying twelve minutes, a young man not accustomed to telling the truth and, oddly, feeling more than ever as if he were lying. The bedroom dissolved under his humiliation and only reappeared when Roger interrupted him by urging, "That's enough, Noel. That'll do." But Noel could not stop, not until Roger placed a palm across his mouth. A moment later, tentatively withdrawing the hand, Roger said, "I think I got the idea."

To give him credit, he tried, Roger did, but in the end the best he could do was to clasp Noel's shoulders, lift his raggedy body up off the toy box, then squint at his stepson in a harsh, reassessing survey that concluded with him squeezing Noel's shoulders inward and shaking him like a Coke machine.

"Throw me out the damn window," Noel dared him. "I know you want to."

That made Roger smile, and the smile made him glance away, out the window and then down to the wrecked car. The smile vanished and he flutter-cleared his throat and said he could at least explain some of what happened last night. "The part after you got home."

Around three in the morning, Roger began, Noel had banged into the house and made so much noise that Alise had gotten out of bed to check on things. She had found Noel in his bedroom, talking to himself, pacing and weeping. At first she could not make him notice her; then, when he suddenly did notice her, he started telling her, over and over, how much he loved her, only her. "You kept saying that even if you went to jail, that it didn't matter, that you still loved her. Do you remember any of this, Noel?"

He reared his head and shook it.

Still eyeing the wrecked car, Roger said, "Noel, there's been plenty of times I wanted to throw you out windows. This ain't one of them."

. . .

The rest of the family went to church while Noel slept in tics and starts. Later, Roger climbed the stairs wearing his navy blue pinstripe with a wide silver tie, the same color as his hair now, which was thinning and combed back over his temples. He nudged Noel awake then said he had run into Doc Martin after church and had made Noel an appointment. On Friday, he added with a hopeless shrug.

"You told him!" Noel shouted, wide awake now.

"Noel, we have to do something. We need to get this looked at."

Roger removed the green rubber band from the Sunday *Hattiesburg American* and tossed the paper onto the bed. Trying to make it sound like a joke, he said, "Probably you should check the paper, make sure you didn't run nobody over last night." He started nodding. His nods wandered the room, glancing off the posters. When he spoke again, he spoke haltingly.

"The insurance—won't cover this—but maybe—we can work something out—some sort of loan—against your college money. What I was thinking—maybe it'd be a good idea—for now—to keep it in the backyard—the car, I mean."

Hide the evidence, Roger was saying.

. . .

LEE DURKEE

Noel shook out the front page and began to search for himself among the headlines and police reports. No citizens had been side-swiped, no hit-and-runs, no high-speed chases ending in balls of fire. He studied a description of a young knifeman beneath a photograph of a liquor store that had been robbed, and he compared his physique and clothing with that of a suspicious character seen loitering outside a restaurant hours before it had burned to the ground. Another rape had been committed, the MO meeting that of the infamous Westside Rapist, his sixth victim. Noel studied the features of the artist's rendering until the penciled face of the rapist, like so many toothpicks fitted together, seemed to grin up at him.

A pang of heartburn caused him to lower the paper and that's when he spotted the Nikon. Set on the dresser's edge and facing the foot of the bed, the camera seemed to be watching him. Noel tried to ignore the camera by raising the paper again. It was not so much that the rapist's face seemed animate, it was that the individual pencil lines seemed intent on something. After a moment Noel had to pull back to even see the finished product as a face instead of as an army of lines. Finally he dropped the paper and got out of bed and limped across the room to the camera.

Just as he had feared, an entire roll of film had been shot. He rewound the film and removed the cartridge. Listening to the dwindle of a distant siren, he examined the camera for any further clues or abrasions, then he set it down again and entered the darkroom.

He took his time developing the negatives. After he had smoked half a joint, he turned on the overhead light and clipped and pinned the negatives. Then he lifted the magnifying glass and nudged the swivel stool closer.

The first negative showed a naked girl with straight grayish hair foamed out around her, as if she were lying in the surf. Her eyes were white slits that burned like wicks. The camera angle was that of

129

someone standing above her near her feet. Her breasts were small, the nipples fine white dots, her pubic hair a spray of white seaweed. Her left side was outlined by a white pool where the flash had created a shadow. Within this bright pool her body appeared dark and fertile and possibly afloat. The dark scars on both knees stood out like glyphs, and the stark white wound on her neck made it appear as if whatever had killed her had first fed on the whiteness inside her.

Now and again Amber's hands and legs had been repositioned, but never in such a way as to appear natural. In the last few negatives her breasts had grown larger, lending the impression that Amber had been sat up and propped against the tree house wall for these shots.

Is she passed out? Noel wondered. Or is she dead? Did she OD? Or did I kill her?

When he came down to supper, his mother was already seated and did not look up. She finished eating and took Noel's plate, which had not been touched, and scraped every pea and every scalloped potato back into the serving bowls, then she forked his minute steak onto the platter and carried his plate to the sink on her way out of the kitchen.

Noel waited until everyone had left the table, then he walked out the front door with the measured steps of an astronaut. In the half dark, with a chipped moon far away and waning, he inspected the damaged craft that would never get him home again. A rear tire was shredded, the front passenger-side corner a metal accordion. The headlights and casings were equally smashed, the front fender bent upward, the rear one downward. He knelt with one hand touching a whitewall tire. The section behind the door had sidelonged against something painted cherry red, lending the impression that the Mustang's white paint job was bleeding. A gorged taillight hung by wires.

Eventually he stood and opened the trunk, which was empty except for the usual garbage and spare. He began to breathe again and walked around and collapsed into the front seat. After recouping there, he turned the ignition. The speakers exploded full blast and he killed the engine then ejected the cassette. After waiting for his heart to lull, he started the car again and forced it into drive. The Mustang groaned into the backyard. He parked it behind the woodpile then sat in the broken automobile until well past dark and in all this time exonerated himself of nothing.

The passenger door opened and Matt slid into the other bucket seat. Matt was wearing a sky-blue tank top he only put on after lifting weights. Taking in a dip, Matt mumbled something Noel could not understand then added, "Man, I had to get outa there. Everyone's walking around like some kind of funeral."

"No kidding, I hadn't noticed."

Matt started pumping his left arm, stroking that bicep with his right hand.

"You even know what's on your neck?"

"Yeah. It's about the last thing I kinda remember."

"That's the biggest one I ever saw."

"Maybe I can enter it in that book of records."

"Yeah, right next to the world's biggest fuckup."

In his brother's voice, Noel detected something dangerously close to contempt; it was as if Matt were experimenting with ways that Noel could be approached other than with fear and admiration.

"Go easy, Matt, I been in better moods."

"You remember seeing me last night? After you came upstairs?"

Noel shook his head no, and Matt began to describe how at three in the morning he had been awakened by the commotion of Noel falling down the stairs. "You fell down it sounded like about three times and you was about to go over again, but I grabbed you by the camera strap and pulled you the rest of the way up. Then you walked right past me without saying a word, like you'd made it all by yourself." Their breathing had fogged the windshield. Matt reached up and scrubbed the glass with his right hand. Looking at the finger-paint pattern this left, he recalled, "It drives Rog batshit you do that with your hand. He won't say nothing, but he'll just about strangle the steering wheel."

Noel waited for Matt to continue.

"Try it sometime," Matt suggested.

"Is that when Mom came up?"

"You remember that?"

"No. Rog told me that part."

"Yeah, Mom. She stayed in your room a long time."

"How long?"

"I dunno. Maybe a half hour. Then, soon as she left, I tiptoed over, opened your door, and stuck my head inside. Know what you were doing?"

Noel massaged his fingertips deep into the corners of his eyes and waited and then asked, "What?"

"Praying. Down on your knees. Like dry-heaves praying. And your hair, man, it was sticking straight out every which way. It wasn't like any kind of praying I'd ever seen either. It gave me the creeps. Then you opened your eyes and stared straight up at me. Like you was about to suck my blood. I got the fuck outa Dodge, man. Locked my damn door too."

Matt leaned out of the car to spit in the grass.

"Praying," Noel said reflectively.

"Yeah. Praying like a damn vampire."

Noel sat there shaking his head at odd intervals. He had forgotten that Matt was in the car with him until Matt startled him by saying, "Hey, you still coming to my doubleheader Wednesday, right? It's against damn Petal, you gotta be there." There was a definite trace of reconciliation in Matt's tone. "You do, I promise you'll get some good shots of me going deep."

Matt left and fifteen minutes later someone knocked on the passenger window then opened the door and got inside.

"Hey, Ben," Noel whispered.

"Ya'alright?" Ben asked and Noel replied, "Yeah, I guess."

In his fourteenth year now, Ben had grown too tall too quickly. His jeans were highwaters, like always, and he was wearing a gray sweatshirt that had once been Noel's but that was still too big for Ben. His neck was too long and his reddish hair was short and bowl-shaped curly. They sat together a long time not saying anything. Then all at once Noel began to cry. He cried very rhythmically up and down, like someone riding a horse over rocky terrain. Ben put his hand on Noel's kneecap but did not say anything. When Noel's sobs got particularly bad, Ben would squeeze the knee a little. Finally Noel stopped. A few minutes later he said gruffly, "Shit, maybe I should go back to bed, huh?"

"Yeah, that sounds like a good idea," Ben replied softly.

*   *   *

Noel crept downstairs to the phone and dialed Amber's number. It was late, he wasn't sure how late, and he had just awakened from a terrible nightmare. On the eighth ring a man answered the phone very curtly. Noel whispered, "Go out and look in the tree house, now, it's real important," and hung up the phone.

*   *   *

"Here, this is for you. I'm damn retired." The two of them were alone in Pasquale's. Noel was working sandwich board and register, Tim was working pizza board. Even at work Tim dressed neatly: starched shirt, creased jeans, and a white twice-folded apron. Tim opened the shoe box and whistled into it.

"Are you crazy? There's seven whole lids in here. At forty a pop, that's—"

"Quit sounding like the damn ACTs. It's yours, just shut up and take it."

Tim stashed the box under the counter then continued assembling the electric cheese grater.

"So what's the verdict?" he asked. "You fuck her or what? You'd be about the only guy in history who didn't."

Noel composed his thoughts, abandoned them with a shrug, then explained, "We did some 'ludes, that's all."

"I heard she's got brain damage."

"Yeah, well, you don't fuck her brain."

"You did fuck her, then."

Following an even longer hesitation, Noel said, "No, I didn't. At least I don't think I did."

"You're lying your ass off."

Tim was slicing plastic wrap off the blocks of pale cheese and periodically brushing the hair away from his face with his knife hand. He balled up the plastic and shot it at the trash can, but the plastic unraveled in midair and the shot fell short. He said, "Speaking of ACTs, I heard you were the first one out of the auditorium."

"Yeah." Noel flicked a quarter so that it spun across the cutting board. "I didn't even know they were giving those today." The quarter spun so quickly that both its heads and tails sides were visible at the same time. Noel watched this until the quarter died tails up. "I was so stoned I just filled in the dots, spelled out my name with dots."

"Weatherspoon is to smoking dope as sunset is to . . . ?"

"You probably aced it, huh?"

Tim said yeah, probably, he usually scored okay on those types of tests. "Besides all you need is a fifteen to get into USM. Even someone with brain damage could make that."

"Not me. Anyway I don't even care about USM. As soon as I graduate, I'm heading straight to the Keys and getting a job bartending at my uncle's restaurant down there. I already wrote him I was coming."

"At that chop-suey joint?"

"It's Vietnamese—his wife's Vietnamese. Chop suey's Chinese, I think. Too bad that wasn't on the ACTs, I'd have gotten one right."

Quartering the blocks of cheese, Tim said, "If Weatherspoon's boat is traveling, in reverse, at sixty miles an hour on a sunny day and leaves the dock at two A.M. into a ten-knot wind with fifty-three gallons of gasoline, a kilo of redbud, eight fifths of tequila, and sixteen quaaludes . . . then, taking into account the Doppler effect, how long will it take his boat to reach the bottom of the sea?"

The phone rang. Noel grabbed it and said, "Pasquale's."

"First off, why'd you call my house last night?"

"I didn't call your house."

"He went out there."

"What are you talking about?"

"My dad. He found that tequila bottle plus some roaches. I'm grounded for about a year. Thanks a lot, Moon Man."

"Somebody called your house?"

"You are such a liar."

"Hey, take it easy. Maybe one of your neighbors saw us out there and called—you ever think of that?"

"Speaking of my neighbors, did you get into a wreck that night after you left?"

"Hell no."

"Well, somebody plowed into our neighbor's Chevy. It was parked on the street. They said the car that hit it was white."

"Who said?"

"The police. They came around asking if we'd seen anything. It was you, wasn't it?"

"Hell no it wasn't. Hey, you didn't go telling the cops it was me, did you?"

"I don't tell cops nothing. Besides, I was in bed so hungover I could hardly breathe. Which reminds me. Did anything else happen that night? I want to know if it did."

Noel had already pulled the receiver as far away from Tim as the cord would allow. Now he turned his back and whispered, "Look, I'm sorry I called your house, okay? I was scared you were dead out in the tree house, OD'd or something. I had this dream you were hanging from that rope. It was the most real dream I ever had."

"Are you gonna tell me what happened that night or not?"

"You don't remember?"

"Shoot. I remember swallowing that 'lude, that's all she wrote."

"Nothing. Nothing happened."

"You swear?"

"I swear nothing happened."

After a pause, she said, "You're about the only guy I'd believe that coming from." Then she hung up.

. . .

The day, back in tenth grade, when Noel had been kicked off the team, that was the day he had stopped begrudging Matt his success in baseball. Now, every time Matt stepped to the plate, Noel sprawled forward over the home team's dugout to focus his Nikon. Matt was deserving of a personal photographer. Although only a junior, he had already begun an assault on the school's record books. Doubles and stolen bases were the first milestones to fall, but it was ground-rule doubles that were Matt's specialty. Something about his stroke, from either side of the plate, dictated that the ball take one grasshopper leap and skid over the fence. Also, with the help of a sympathetic home team scorer, Matt had played the entire season errorless at third base. His arm was a gun. He could throw runners out from his knees. Noel had documented this a number of times, and two of his shots had made the local sports page. All the sportswriters fawned over Matt, what with him being the most prominent white athlete to come through Hattiesburg High in years. The only broken record the sportwriters did not dwell upon in their columns was the fact that Matt had been ejected from five games in one season.

In the opening game of the double bill that evening, Matt hit for the cycle, going four for four in an abbreviated seven-inning rout. During his last at-bat, Matt had turned a double into a belly flop triple. The scorekeeper neglected to mark a throwing error so that Matt got credit for the cycle.

Noel killed time between the games by using his pawnshop zoom, a Zahyr that had seen better days, to search for Amber in the visiting bleachers. When he could not find her, he used the zoom to spy on his own family. Finally he just started zeroing in on random girls.

By the last inning of the second game, Matt needed only a single to hit for the cycle again. This time the crowd was hushed as it stood for his last at-bat. The first pitch was in the dirt. The second was way outside. That got the crowd to booing. The third pitch was outside and in the dirt, but Matt leaned out and fanned at it. He stepped out of the box and yelled something at the pitcher. The crowd was yelling too. Matt dug in. The fourth pitch was a loop change-up that the catcher caught standing up. A much deeper chorus of boos swarmed the field. The pitcher stepped off the rubber to polish the baseball. The last pitch, ball four, was wild and inside. Matt ended up on his butt in the dirt but did not stay there for long. He sprang to his feet, whirled the bat at the pitcher, then charged the mound.

In the photograph, the pitcher has his right arm cocked behind his ear, as if about to deliver a blow, but his face has already been churned sideways, toward the camera, by Matt's haymaker left. The pitcher's head is outlined with a spray of sweat, like a halo. His eyes are clenched shut, his teeth bared, and his face is pear-shaped from the punch.

Both benches cleared. Noel abandoned the camera on the dugout roof and jumped onto the field and clotheslined the opposing catcher just as he was about to blindside Matt. Then Noel straddled the catcher and started punching him. Every once in a while, though, Noel would stop and glance up, searching for Amber's face above the Petal dugout.

· · ·

On the same day his photograph made the front page of the sports section, Noel got his hair cut short, as a sign of yet further repentance. Less than an hour later, he went to the mailbox and found this letter awaiting him:

Dear Noel,

Thanks for all the letters and pictures. I'm afraid I got bad news though. I've been beating my head against the wall trying to keep this restaurant afloat. To top it off now Kim's 6 months pregnant. Truth is I can't offer you a place to stay right now. Probably if you'd ever been around pregnant women you wouldn't be asking. And what with the cost of living down here you'd have one hellava time meeting rent on what I could pay you. Why not give college a shot first? As far as I know you'd be the first Weatherspoon to go. I'll tell you something else, something I'm not supposed to tell you. Your mom called.

I guess she thinks I have some kind of sway over you, and basically she wants me to tell you to go to college. Seems she knows all about your plans to head south. You have been infiltrated. Anyway we talked it over and decided this. If you go to college and make good grades then I'll line you up a job here next summer. I'll put you behind the bar and teach you to sling drinks. There's lots of sweet young things down here running around in next to nothing.

You asked me about why your dad joined the army and thats a long story I'll try and sum up. Goose ran with the wrong crowd, always did. He liked to gamble and wasn't much good at it. He joined the army the day after he pitched that no hitter and ever since then there's been much speculating. Rumor has it he was supposed to throw that game, to lose it on purpose, and that he'd been payed alot of money to do this. But then he got caught up in pitching the no hitter and instead he won the game. Meaning he had to get out of town quick. He kinda pitched his way into Vietnam, so to speak. I'm not positive this story is true but it's the only explanation I've ever heard that makes any sense as to why he joined up. Never knew Goose to be much patriotic before that. I guess this doesn't cast your dad in a great light either, but he was always a good older brother to me and I miss him. I miss him alot and wish I'd been a better uncle to you and Matt.

You take care of Matt and take care of yourself too. Y'all are brothers and need to look out for each other. Try to stay outa your stepdad's way. And please give your mom my regards.

Tommy

After Noel had finished reading the letter, he balled up the paper inside his fist and put that fist through his bedroom wall and then dropped the letter inside there. Later he had to hang a poster over the hole in the wall.

Friday arrived, and Roger drove Noel to the new medical plaza. They walked together up the brick steps to the brick fountain, Roger with the collar of his lime-green sports shirt flicked up. At the top step Noel halted and said he had changed his mind. He planted himself on a scaffolding along the edge of the fountain bright with new pennies while Roger locked his fingers behind his head and gazed out over the fountain as if it were an ocean. Here I am, Lord, he seemed to be saying, a man doing his level best.

Finally he asked, "Noel, what's the worst thing that can possibly happen in there?" When Noel mumbled, "I dunno," Roger nodded as if that were an intelligent response, then he asked what was the best thing that could happen.

"*I dunno,* I said."

"So what do we got to lose, huh?"

What Noel had to lose became abundantly clear at the check-in window when the worst thing that could possibly happened promptly did. He recognized the girl behind the sneeze glass from school. He could not recall her name, but she was the same girl Tim had overheard saying that Spider Weatherspoon shot up heroin under his tongue. Did she already know the reason for his appointment? Was that written down somewhere? Horrified, Noel scratched his signature then shoved the clipboard back toward her while offering up a sphincter smile. Her name would not come to him. He knew she had once been very fat and was not fat anymore, though her breasts remained huge, her face plump. Behind her in the office, four older women typed and filed. Did they know too? Did everyone know?

Reading his name off the clipboard, she said, "Noel," with an approving smile, then she added, "I never heard your real name before." Next she asked, "Got your ears lowered, huh?" The anatomy of the question left him dumbstruck until she laughed and touched her own bangs and said she liked it short. "You don't even know my name, do you?"

"My memory's a little shot." He made his hand into a pistol, aimed it at his temple, then shrugged. She told him her name then, Mona Campsong, and asked how Noel had done on the ACTs. He replied, "I don't even wanna know." Jerking his thumb over his shoulder, toward where Roger was seated, he said he'd best be getting home now. And since that made zero sense, he quickly added, "He ain't my real dad," then he whirled away and staggered off full blush.

"Hey, what's my name?" Mona called out, loud enough that everyone in the waiting room looked up. He had to stop. He had to stop, turn around, and face the aquarium of secretaries.

"See, I can't even remember," he said, shooting himself again. "And you just told me, huh?"

Twenty minutes later his name was called by a large black nurse with dangling Jesus-on-the-cross earrings. She led him into an examination room and took his blood pressure, his temperature, read his pulse, then she shifted her ballast in the chair and asked the nature of the visit.

"The nature . . ." Noel repeated. "It's kinda personal."

Without raising her head—she seemed to be addressing the clipboard—the nurse said, "Well, hon, how we supposed to help if you don't tell us what's wrong?"

Noel remained silent.

"Is it something to do with your hands?"

He looked first at his right hand, at the purple and yellow knuckles and the scabs. Then he looked at his left hand, which wasn't bruised as badly. He shook his head and told her, "It involves . . . sex."

"Ah-huh," she said and asked if by any chance he had contracted a sexually transmitted disease. "STD," she added.

He quickly agreed that he had. "Kinda."

That made her lift both her pencil and her eyebrows. "It has been my experience, as a nurse, that either you do or you don't."

"I do."

"Any discharge?"

"Discharge? . . . Yeah, sometimes."

"What color?"

"Yellow?"

"You asking me yellow or telling me yellow?"

"Sorta yellowish."

She repeated *sorta yellowish*, stretching out the two words to last as long as it took her to write them down.

"Burning when you pee?" To this, she tacked on, half resentfully, "Urinate."

He said yeah, a little.

"Stains on your drawers? Your underwear?"

He cocked his head as if trying to recall, then he said no.

"Not even in the morning?"

"Oh yeah, then, sometimes."

"Sometimes. Blood in your urine?"

"Blood?" He pursed his lips before consenting, "Yeah, blood."

"What about on the rim of the john—the commode—more blood?"

"More blood."

"And the last time you had intercourse? . . . was . . . ?"

It had been a while, he explained apologetically.

"What's that mean? A week, a month?"

"A few weeks."

After recording a few more such lies, the nurse arranged a series of scissorslike instruments on the steel counter, then she handed him a blue bib and told him it tied in the back. "Doctor Martin'll be in shortly."

Alone, Noel picked up the nearest instrument and fit his fingers into its handle. He made the motion that with scissors would have spread the blades. The thin metal probe divided itself into two thinner probes with a disconcerting half-inch margin between them. He set the instrument down but did not take his eyes off of it as he undressed and tied on the bib.

Doc Martin entered the room still laughing at some hallway joke. While skimming the clipboard, he drummed his fingers against it. Then, very abruptly, he shut the door and paused to consider the chart hung there, a cross-section of the human liver and kidney, then, just as abruptly, he turned toward Noel and smiled grandly. They had known each other for as long as Noel could remember, though recently Doc Martin had grown a white goatee that framed his mouth in a perfect square.

"Well, Noel, old friend, let's have a looksee." He patted the bed behind Noel, who reluctantly stretched himself out. Doc Martin fitted a white latex bib over Noel's lap then milked Noel's penis and testicles up through a small hole in the bib. He took a giant tube of ointment and squeezed the cold lubricant onto Noel then massaged it in. Suddenly Noel was very aware of a draft inside the room. The doctor rearranged the instruments on the metal table before saying, "Physicians have different theories when it comes to this moment, Noel. Some think it only fair to warn you. Others think that just makes it worse. Me, I come down on the side of fair warning. At least that way if you scream bloody murder you won't feel guilty for it. Noel, this is going to hurt like all get-out. Scream away, young man."

Instead of screaming, Noel began to talk for all he was worth.

Not that what he blurted out was the exact truth; instead he made his impotence sound a recent phenomenon, a curiosity that had followed upon an otherwise active sex life. When he had finished and opened his eyes, Dr. Martin was wiping him off with a towel and chuckling, "Well now, that's a horse'a different feather." He removed his rubber gloves and asked Noel had many times this . . . *condition, let's call it* . . . had happened.

Noel held up three fingers, shrugged, and said, "I dunno, a couple maybe."

"Son, I'm no Sigmund Freud standing here before you, but it's my guess you wouldn't be here if it had only happened twice."

Noel nodded, whispered, "Yeah, more'n twice, I guess. A lot more."

The doctor nodded sympathetically then began tapping his right temple with his index finger.

"The mind," he said, "is a funny thing, Noel."

"Yessir."

"And an amazing thing."

Noel continued nodding and then tried to make a joke by suggesting that maybe he was allergic to sex.

"Heaven forbid," the good doctor said and crossed himself.

*   *   *

Doc Martin was one of those men fond of informing the public that if he had it all to do over again he would not change a thing, as if his own current character and outlook were so satisfying to him that any number of trials would be happily reendured. "No sir," he liked to say. "Looking back, I'd do it all over again."

The first thing Doc Martin did was to explain to Noel how very rare impotence was, especially in boys his age—"almost unheard of." Next, after making a series of henlike clucks, he launched into a reminiscence where he admitted it did crop up in wartime, what with all those soldiers driving over potholes in those blasted jeeps—"hell on the prostate." He picked up Noel's chart, scanned it, then scribbled something down and announced they were going to play a little game, the two of them were. A simple game, really. Or maybe not so simple. He was going to leave the room. To check on another patient. And while he was gone, he wanted Noel to do something. Or rather not to do something. "While I'm gone," he instructed, "I want you not to think about pink elephants."

He stared at Noel too intently and asked if he understood the rules of the game. Noel, who had been straining to read his chart and simultaneously imagining all of the places that chart might end up, kept bobbing his head even after Doc Martin had left the room. For the first full minute alone, Noel stared at a colorful poster of the male reproductive system. Then he slid off the table and pressed his face against the second-story glass and pictured himself splattered across the parking lot. He drafted a suicide note or two and imagined the fuzzy consistency of his obituary photograph. Which photo would his mother select? He was still considering this choice when some giant humming mechanism a floor above him shut down. He had not been aware of the loud hum until it stopped. He listened for laughter in the hallway, but there wasn't any. There seemed not a sound left in the world. A capsizing silence filled him.

He felt an odd washboard quiver. The floor shifted, or seemed to, and Noel lurched into the wall. *Earthquake!* That was his last coherent thought, but in truth what happened was more like a flash flood, one that picked him up and swept him away and then set him down again, gently, and left him staring down into an open manhole, an imperfect circle framed by an octagon of two-by-fours. The manhole appeared to be covered with dead leaves. Slowly he raised his head. The wall he was facing swam a moment, then solidified into raw plywood. He was cold and knew he was naked, but his body felt so strange to him that he was afraid to look down at it. He touched his stomach and then his fingers began tracing the edges of a jagged scar just under his bellybutton. Finally he raised the hand to his neck and felt the noose there. He looked down again and saw that his feet were not touching the floor.

Mona Campsong was about to pour water through a coffeemaker when she saw Spider Weatherspoon come out of the examination room wearing the blue bib. Her mouth opened, but instead of speaking she held the pot higher up, pointing it at him, and she watched in this manner as he pivoted away from her and walked toward the staff phone mounted at the end of the hall next to a sign in Mona's own handwriting that said, *No Calls Longer Than 3 Minutes!!! This Means U!!!* She could see the acne on his butt. His steps were smallish, heel to toe, and his hips swayed. The walk seemed noticeably wrong to Mona, who carried the coffeepot a few steps forward before stopping again. It was the voice she heard speaking into the phone that had halted her. During the next few weeks she would learn to imitate the voice. When she told the story—and she would tell it often—she made it very clear that it was not Noel's voice she heard at all, no, not a boy's voice imitating a girl's, *it was a girl's voice coming out of Spider Weatherspoon's body*, a girl's voice that Mona could not quite place, not at first anyway. This voice said into the phone, "Mom, it's me, I'm in the tree house, there's a rope 'round my neck. Help me. HURRY!"

Then, as Mona would later explain it, many times over, "He just hung up and walked past me, except this time, right as he passed me, he said, still using that same girl's voice, he said, *Hey, Mona.* Just like that. That's when I recognized the voice. I almost dropped the coffeepot. He went back into the room and closed the door, and I just stood there, like some kind of statue. I was still standing like that when Dr. Martin went into the room. I think he said some kind of joke to me, but I didn't even hear it. I get goose bumps now just thinking about it. Look." After extending her arms, which had recently been treated with electrolysis, Mona would add, "That was the same afternoon that Amber Smith tried to hang herself in her dead brother's tree house and that her mom found her just in time to get her down alive. I used to know Amber. At 4-H camp. We lifeguarded together." Here Mona would time a mental drum-roll before concluding, "Now, if they ever let her out of the crazy house—and they probably won't—but if they do, then she's going straight to jail, that's what I heard. For murdering her baby brother. She confessed to it, that's what everybody says. That's why she tried to kill herself."

• • •

Doc Martin paused to reflect on the chart of the human liver before turning around and straddling the metal stool, which rolled forward two feet under his momentum. "So," he began, but then he paused to deliver a rakish grin. "Noel, what have we been thinking about?"

The sound of his own name startled him awake. He had been dreaming. In this dream he had been given an Aleph 2000 made of pure gold. While looking through it for the first time, he had seen a montage of beautiful women, like a quick shuffle of photographs, dozens and dozens of beautiful women. And in this dream he had known with a wonderful certainty that he would sleep with all of these women. Staring into the Aleph 2000, Noel had understood, however fleetingly, that not even pain was permanent, that life was long and contained possibilities unimaginable. That's when he heard the sound of his name being spoken.

Noel, who owned no memory of the hallway incident, and who furthermore had no memory of who this goatish man in front of him might be, searched the room for a clue as to where he was, but instead he found actual words to speak. And even though the words were nonsensical to him, he felt a tremendous gratitude for them. Looking at the older man, whom he suddenly recognized as Doc Martin, Noel replied, "Pink elephants, sir."

Clockwise

Oh Arjuna! the Lord abides in the hearts
of all creatures, whirling them
by his power, as if they were mounted
on a machine.

—*The Mahabharata*

CHAPTER EIGHT

POPLARVILLE WAS VERY SMALL, very dry, and very Baptist. Downtown was a Sonic Burger drive-in flanked by a strip of stores, hardware, fabric, and five-and-dime. Most of the windows staggering these shops were covered with plywood or cardboard. The junior college, called Pearl River, was surrounded by the agriculture school, which was surrounded by local farms, mostly soybean and corn, and these farms were surrounded by the De Soto National Forest. Inside this wheel within a wheel within a wheel, girls plotted pregnancy and marriage as they hugged their books to class or attended pep rallies with religious fervor, and guys sat on tailgates and passed quart Budweisers in the woods at the western shore of the pine forest and discussed things they had shot or things they had almost shot or things they damn well intended to shoot.

Noel lived in Huff Hall, a white-pillared brick dormitory he would in due time cause to be evacuated and cordoned off with yellow police tape. But, for now, he was growing fond of Huff in spite of the persistent drone of Jimmy Buffett in the hallways. Buffett,

Pearl River's one famous alumni, was an acoustic-raunch guitarist who had made the big time with the hit "Margaritaville." He had lived on the same floor of Huff as Noel, the second floor, and at PRC the dorm floors distinguished themselves much as fraternities did in universities. Small tours took place in which newcomers were guided into Buffett's old room and shown the drawing on the bottom of the top bunk attributed to Buffett, a jackknife and ink engraving of a disembodied vagina with the words *The Pink Pussycat!* scratched under it.

Noel, heavily into the Clash and the Wailers these days, hated Jimmy Buffett with a hate beyond all scope and reason. In a way it was how he distinguished himself in the dorm, he was the one Jimmy Buffett hater. Buffett aside, Noel had few complaints. Here at PRC he was enjoying a renaissance of sort. Here, he simply did not allow himself to think about Ross or Amber or murder or suicide; he closed the door on that part of his life. Often he would fall to sleep shushing his own mind, making the *shhhhh* noise over and over, not allowing himself to roam over old battlefields. Here, at the River, as everyone called it, he had even found friends; in fact, during the first week of class, his neighbor in the dorm, a lanky big-eared kid named Jay Underwood, who was part Mormon and part Cherokee, and who could not even manage the spidery mustache the rest of the freshmen were growing, lent Noel a rifle and took him out early one fall morning on a squirrel hunt.

Not a single squirrel showed itself, though. Around ten A.M., after they had met up again and were stationed under an orange-dead pine tree smoking pot from Noel's brass one-hitter, Jay pointed up into the tree and asked if Noel saw that big hoot owl way up there. Noel could not distinguish any owl inside the dead tree. When he said as much, Jay asked, "You want me to shoot it down?"

Noel said sure, go ahead. "Nothing up there to shoot."

Lying on his back, Jay aimed the .22 and fired. Branch to branch, down fell a brown horned owl about the size and heft of a decapitated head and absolute dead weight by the time it crashed into Noel's lap. Noel wailed and began crabbing away from the owl, all of which got Jay swamped in laughter. He seemed honestly unable to quit. Meanwhile Noel did another couple of hits then traded the one-hitter for the Nikon. Thrusting the dead and bloody owl at Jay, he said, "Here, hold this and quit laughing. You're scaring all the squirrels."

As they drove back to campus, Jay kept pointing to the roadside and saying, "Look at that redtail," or "Check out them does." But Noel never saw anything there. Jay was driving his black pickup very cautiously, because Noel was still smoking and there was a cop behind them three cars back. Jay had a paper-thin crewcut and large spearhead-shaped forearms. They were both dipping, Jay spitting into a pried-open Dr Pepper can, Noel into a crusted Saints mug. Meatloaf was playing, and Noel was scavenging through Jay's tape collection searching for something better.

"Hey, you got a brother, don't you? Plays third?"

Noel waited too long before he admitted yeah, he did. The way he said yeah sounded so resentful that even Noel noticed it. After a moment he added, "Sometimes I get tired of hearing about Matt all the time. Maybe if he was the older brother it'd be different. Way it is, though, hell, I taught him practically everything he knows, how to switch-hit, to bunt, to slide headfirst, and now he's about to go pro."

Jay laughed and said for Noel get used to it. "Besides, it's no biggie, he's just your brother. It's not like he's your old man or nothing."

Noel asked what that meant.

"Nobody's told you about my dad yet?"

"What about him?"

He said never mind then changed the subject back to Matt. "Your friggen little brother, we played y'all our first home stand my senior year. I pitched. That punk pulled three doubles on me, three in a row, the last two were ground-rule ones. Weren't bad pitches neither. Then we brought in our lefty, our ace, and what does your brother do? Switches sides and bounces over another one. Not only that, he runs it out full speed, even though he knows it's ground-rule and he can trot."

Noel listed off some of the scholarships Matt had been offered, then explained, "But he don't want to go to college, he wants to go straight to the minors. He's already got letters from the Braves and the Reds both."

Jay whistled then asked, "He that good?"

"Good enough to tag you."

"Hey, I just pitched to keep in shape for football. I only had two pitches, the pill and the water balloon. If he'd had any real power, he'd of taken me deep."

Noel pressed his fingertips together to explain that Matt was more a contact hitter, a nickel-and-dimer. "A natural-born lead-off man, that's how I taught him. What're you laughing at now?"

"You. For someone who don't like being his big brother, you sound awfully proud of him."

Noel pointed to an empty meadow. "Look at them bucks. Three of 'em. Standing over there. See 'em?"

"Bucks standing together?" Eyeing the meadow skeptically, Jay recalled, "His last time up that night, we let him have it. Nailed him square in the back. I'm talking *bing*. But he just dropped the bat and took off full speed to first. Then he stole second. Then he stole third. Stole third with an eight-run lead! Man, we hated his guts by then. We had guys waiting for him in the parking lot after the game." Jay smiled and added, "I was one of 'em."

•　•　•

Not only was Poplarville dry, but there was no pot to be had either, none, so on weekends when the Huffheads all went home, they tried to score off old high school connections. Noel always bought from Tim, who, after taking over Noel's shoe box, had applied his 33-ACT intellect to drug dealing. Basically Tim was now fronting kilos with student loans. Around Huff, Tim's weed had a reputation for being choice, and it was not long before Noel was dealing bags on the side. With this extra income, he bought a giant TV. And since the room already had extra space—his roommate having been the first to get a girl pregnant and drop out—Noel's room became a gathering point, especially on Mondays when everyone wanted to watch *Monday Night Football*.

It was on Monday afternoon getting late in the semester when Jay came into Noel's room, held out both fists, and said guess which hand. Noel guessed left, and Jay opened that hand. Resting on a nest of tinfoil were two small squares of paper with yellow and red eyeballs tattooed onto them. "Twenty-twenty," Jay whispered, but before he could elaborate, someone else barged into the room, and Jay snapped shut his fist and touched a finger to his lips.

It was Timmy-Tom, a first-floor gnome who always wore the same flower-embroidered denim shirt and who had taped Buddy Holly glasses and who currently was holding a curled-up magazine like a baton. He marched past them and flipped on the TV and sat on the bottom bunk as *Love Boat* materialized on screen. They both stared at Timmy-Tom. Jay cleared his throat. Noel made the motion of screwing in a light bulb, a gesture of high sarcasm around Huff. Timmy-Tom, oblivious, uncurled his magazine and asked if they'd seen this one yet. He spread open the coverless issue to a section entitled BIG PUSSY WOMEN. It was a contest, leading page by page from the numerous runners-up to the winner.

"Boy, you'd better strap a two-by-four 'cross your ass," Timmy-Tom warned. Then he added, "Or'd you fall in."

Jay and Noel winced through the four-page spread of the winner, which was about three pages more than needed in order to award the trophy. She was indeed Big Pussy Woman. The next page started a different contest, this one featuring guys with freak-show cocks. One guy had his tied in a knot, which caused Timmy-Tom to conjecture, "Wonder what'd happen if somebody came along and pulled on that."

"You find yourself thinking about that a lot, Timmy-Tom?" Noel asked. "Pulling on black guys' dicks?"

"Somebody oughta introduce these folks," Jay observed, flipping pages back and forth. He took one last wince, then passed the magazine back to Timmy-Tom. "Where do they find these freaks anyway?" he wondered.

"California," Timmy-Tom assured them, then he started in on some lie about a second cousin of his who took pictures of naked women in California. At Pearl River you were always hearing unreliable stories about cousins. Second-cousin stories were the worst. This particular second cousin of Tim's went around with great success convincing women he was a *Playboy* photographer.

"You oughta give it a try," he urged Noel. "You're the one always taking everyone's picture."

As soon as *Love Boat* ended, Timmy-Tom asked Noel to front him a bag. Noel laughed and turned off the TV and asked if Timmy-Tom would *please leave us alone now*, because, *as is our custom*, Jay had promised "to give me a big blow job after *Love Boat*. You understand, of course."

"We got some business to take care of," Jay clarified. "If you don't mind."

Timmy-Tom grinned and started to leave, but then got sidetracked by the photographs of Layle tacked onto the wall behind the small refrigerator. He squinted at the shrine and asked, "She from around here?"

Jay quickly replied, "That's our boy's honey . . . out in Hollywood, if you believe that. Supposed to be some kinda model. Oh yeah, and a cheerleader for the Rams too. Is it the Rams or the Raiders, Spoon?"

Noel grunted it was the Rams, then he busied himself brushing Skoal off the bedsheet. "Damnit, Timmy-Tom, you done spilled shit everywhere."

"She's real pretty," Timmy-Tom said.

"Hey, aren't they playing on TV tonight? The Rams?" Jay asked.

"I don't think so," Noel replied slowly.

"I think it's the Rams. Hey, why you looking so pale all'a sudden, Spoon?"

"Who's looking pale?"

"She ever let you take ones of her naked?" Timmy-Tom wanted to know.

Noel grabbed him by the collar and winged him at the door and kicked him in the butt.

"Goddamnit, Timmy-Tom! Leave! Leave now 'fore I throw you out every window in this dorm!"

And off he shuffled with his magazine.

"Jeeezus," Noel complained.

What Jay had hidden in his fist was a type of LSD he called Oklahoma 20/20. A second cousin of his had mailed it to him from an oil field there.

"This is real medicine-man acid," Jay explained. "They use it for ceremonies at the reservation there because they can't get real peyote anymore. There's some kind of cactus disease going around."

"What kinda ceremonies?"

"Stuff like vision quests."

"Vision quests? What the fuck's a vision quest?"

You were supposed to go out into the woods, Jay explained. And surround yourself with this big circle of rocks. To keep out evil spirits. Then you stay inside this circle of rocks for days or weeks until your vision arrives. And that vision, it tells you what you're supposed to do with your life . . . whether you should be a medicine man, a brave, a farmer, whatever.

Jay kept on talking about vision quests. And after a while it occurred to Noel that Jay was actually trying to coerce Noel into taking the acid, as if there were still some decision-making process left between Noel and any available recreational drug. Jay had launched into a spiel concerning the Mormons, the Hopi Indians, and some missing tribe of something or other. Noel was not really listening; he was worrying about the Rams game and all the drunken, half-blackout lies he had told about Layle and him.

Jay must have sensed this lack of attention because he changed tacks and tried scaring Noel, telling him how LSD was a powerful drug, how you had to show it proper respect. Then he told the story about the guy on acid who had climbed a fire tower and tried to fly off it. Noel had heard the fire-tower story before, a number of times, although the story was never exactly the same. Now he tried to imagine himself doing that, jumping into the air with his arms spread out like an eagle, and as he imagined this he loaded his one-hitter and passed it to Jay, who was already shaking his head no.

"If Cindy smells it on me again tonight, I'll be in the doghouse forever. I swear that girl's got a nose on her like a bluetick. Ever since she busted me last week, now she's always smelling me when we kiss. I can see her doing it too, her nostrils pumping in and out." He grew solemn a moment then laughed. "Maybe I should take her out hunting."

Cindy McGee played cymbals in the school marching band, which was something that Jay caught endless grief about inside Huff, partially because it was cymbals and partially because Cindy had breasts that would seem to impede the cymbals.

Noel called him pussywhipped and sucked the pipe clean.

"Hey, I tell you, Cindy's got that good-looking friend of hers, that Rebecca chick—the one with red hair? We met her at the

Sonic, remember? Well, believe it or not, she thinks you're cute. Even though you're a damn hippie with an old-lady mustache. You want, we could double, take the ladies out to a drive-in or Cash McCool's or something."

Noel had been holding the smoke inside his lungs and watching himself inside the blank TV. He had not for a moment considered the double date, even though he had thought Rebecca very beautiful. If he failed with Rebecca, then the truth about him would get back to Cindy, then to Jay, then to the rest of the dorm. No, Noel was laying low for now. That was one of the reasons he had resurrected Layle. He turned his head from the TV to aim smoke out the window.

"Shit. Layle'd kill me. Besides, it ain't red hair, it's damn orange, clown-wig orange." He stared back into the TV. There, inside the black-green convex screen, he saw both their reflections captured, sitting on the bottom bunk, like two inmates in prison. He could see the whole dorm room trapped inside there, even the minuscule reproductions of *National Geographic* photographs on the walls.

"Submitted for your approval," Noel said.

Which was a saying he'd stolen off Rod Serling's *Night Gallery*. Every time something weird happened around Huff, Noel would say, "Submitted for your approval." Now he had other guys saying it.

Before Jay left for his date, they made plans to drop acid the following night, in the woods.

Left alone, Noel tried to remember why in the hell he had made up that story about Layle being a Rams cheerleader. He even considered sabotaging his own TV, but instead he retreated to his upper bunk. Braced for the worst, he began rereading *The Sun Also Rises* and he hardly glanced down from the paperback as his friends crowded into the room. Skipper, Ace, Hutch, Moose, Waterhog, Preacher, Brain . . . most everyone had nicknames, though the freshman ones were less established. Noel himself had three floaters. Mongo, which he hated. Spoon, which he liked okay. And Wasted, which was his favorite.

After the beers had been opened, the dips and plugs taken in, the kickoff silenced the room. The receiver backed into the end zone, caught the ball, and dropped to one knee. The Rams were not playing. Jay had made that up, yet another of his practical jokes. As soon as Noel realized this, he raised the paperback again and began to consider the LSD. The fire-tower story had spooked him. He kept imagining himself jumping off a tower. It did not seem out of character. Soon, though, his mind went to work conjuring up many a scenario worse than false flight. For example, after taking the acid, he might confess everything to Jay. Everything. From perpetual virginity to relentless impotence to murder one. Or worse, what if the acid roused the homosexuality he feared might be slumbering inside him? Or worse-worse, what if he tried to explain to Jay the jealousy he experienced whenever Cindy was around? Hell, what if he made a pass at Jay? Or murdered him? Come to think of it, flying off fire towers seemed the least of his worries.

Howard Cosell's impossible voice wafted up to the top bunk along with the rancid smell of tobacco. It was like being trapped in a curing shed. Noel considered opening the door, but then the RA might spot the beer. He edged closer to the open window and had just stuck his head outside into the night when he heard Cosell say, "Dandy, I've got some news here that's more important than any football game."

A silence akin to the opening kickoff ensued, except that the hang time of assassination proved longer. The silence endured nearly fifteen seconds before someone asked, *He the one with the big nose?* Waterhog replied, *Naw, that's damn Ringo, I think.* Then, *He that Hairy Hairy Krishna one?* Again a pause, then Moose answered, *Hairy who-what?* Someone turned up the volume, and

Noel had to raise his voice to say, *He's the one with the weird Chinese chick they took pictures together of naked.* That statement had a brief hang time of its own. *Naked?* someone asked. *Yeah,* Noel replied. *Naked.* Then Moose said, *Joko Yoko Noko, somethin' like that* and Preacher stated, *I'll tell you who he is, he's the one came out said he was Jesus Christ. WAS JESUS?* Moose said. Preacher kept on nodding. *He even called a press conference to announce that he was Jesus.* That appeared to ring a bell because suddenly Hutch recalled, *Hey, ain't he the one that Helter Skelter guy worshiped, you know, the guy who cut them babies out of that actress?* Preacher said, *I know one thing, I wouldn't want to be where he is right now. Must be a trifle warm.* Then everyone started talking at once. *I didn't even know Beatle season had opened yet. Hell yes, it opened today. Ol' Mark David got him his Beatle opening day. How many points you reckon it had? I heard they taste pretty gamey, them Beatles do. Yeah, but they're good in stew.* Finally it grew quiet again, then Hutch belched and said, *Damn waste a good bullet you ask me.*

After that they all sat there very silent watching the motion of the game. To anybody entering the room, as Timmy-Tom had just done, it would appear as if the game were in the final seconds of overtime. Not that Timmy-Tom took much notice of this. Timmy-Tom had a mission. He was holding a batoned magazine, as usual, and he walked straight to the small refrigerator, his head starting to bob as he consulted first the photographs on the wall and then the magazine in his hand. Finally he turned and bravely inserted himself between the TV and the bottom bunk. Holding up the newest *Gallery,* as if to protect himself from the insults being hurled at him, he began to jab his finger at one specific photograph.

"Look. It's her! Her in the magazine! I knew it, I knew I'd seen her someplace!"

The magazine was snatched into the world of the bottom bunk. Timmy-Tom returned to the wall to resume his chant. *It is her!* Soon the bottom bunk emptied and everyone fanned out along the same wall, where Hutch now held the magazine clamped to the wall with his palm, and everyone was slowly agreeing. *Fuckin' A. He's right. That's the same chick. Damn, it's her awright!* Noel started climbing down off the top bunk. This seemed to take him about an hour. Finally he reached the wall, where he saw the magazine photo. It was Layle, all right, however blurred and overlit. At least his first impression was that definite. During the next twenty hours, he would stare at the photograph so tenaciously it would lose all coherence, like a word repeated a thousand times over. The caption did not use Layle's name but stated that the photograph had been taken by *L's friend Lid*. In the photograph, Layle was standing on a beach, the surf in the background, and the sun, judging from her dwarfed shadow, directly overhead. She was topless and holding her red bikini top trapped between her hip and left hand. Both elbows were winged out, though at different angles, and her hip was cocked to the left. Her hair was longer and redder than Noel remembered it. And her face was hard, not smiling. Her breasts, which Noel had felt but had never seen before, were neither large nor small but perfect and astronomically freckled, the closer to the nipples, the more freckles. Because of this, the circles around the nipples were not precisely round. The bird finger of the hand trapping the bikini top against her hip was extended across her belly button.

Noel was in no way prepared for what happened next. It wasn't just that he escaped ridicule, no, what astonished him was the flood of admiration. He was patted on the back and consoled by tapering whistles. Soon Waterhog began to herd everyone into the hallway, where they lingered outside Noel's closed door. And although no one recognized it at the time, this moment at Huff, on the Monday night John Lennon was assassinated, marked the beginning of the Noel Weatherspoon legend at PRC, a legend that would end in search warrants and stuttering blue lights.

* * *

Behind that closed door, Noel paged through the *Gallery*, but there were no more photos of Layle. In fact, there were no other photographs even similar to Layle's. Hers was by far the most coy and inept photograph in the entire magazine. Layle's tall gawky beauty had just barely overcome the idiocy of whoever had operated the camera. Staring into her face, Noel had the impression that, during the moment the photograph was snapped, Layle had been thinking about Noel. For a moment her gaze seemed to invigorate the photograph and to zoom in and find Noel there at Pearl River. Noel, her first photographer.

"'Bye, Layle," he whispered.

The TV channel was broadcasting a special report about Lennon's death when Noel stood and began removing the glossies from the wall. By the time the special report ended, the olive-green paint behind the refrigerator was speckled with Scotch tape. He took out his one-hitter, loaded it. He knew there would be no sleep tonight. The TV played the national anthem then filled with snow.

CHAPTER NINE

HE DID NOT COME OUT of his room until late the following afternoon when Jay pounded the door with a fistful of Oklahoma 20/20 Second-cousin Visionary Acid.

Silent in the black pickup, they journeyed by backroads into the eye of the De Soto National Forest and parked in the woods called *nowhere woods* and went to work building a teepee fire. Since it was not yet dark, they left the fire unlit and set out gathering extra fuel. In purply dust and without much ceremony, beneath a sky of scouring nighthawks, they placed the LSD on their tongues and studied each other's expressions for signs of mortality. To settle their nerves they began tossing a football in the small clearing, Jay spiraling it up unbelievably high over the unlit fire and Noel fielding the throws as if they were punts, and all the while the nighthawks crisscrossing behind the ball. When it became too dark to catch the ball anymore, Jay lit the fire, and they opened new beers and watched the liquid flames shoot out the top of the teepee and trail into the night like messengers.

The evening turned cold. Jay returned from the truck wearing a high school letter jacket, red with gold sleeves, a big red corduroy *L* on the right arm. Inside the *L* were two stitched baseballs and four stitched footballs. The fire reddened as night closed over them. *You feeling anything yet?* Jay asked. They had been trading the question for the last hour. A gauze of moths and gnats and mosquitoes capped the fire. *Not yet, Mother,* Noel replied. He watched his breath slip into the dark and then put on the camouflaged hunting coat that Jay had handed him. And nothing happened and nothing happened and nothing happened and then all at once electrical waves were sluicing through Noel's limbs and his stomach began to shunt and tumble.

The fire snapped and more sparks shot into the air, the wind dragging the sparks off through the pines. Noel concentrated, trying to decide if Jay seemed worried, but the fire showed Jay's face stoic and hypnotized. What if Jay leapt into the flames? Noel wondered. Could he move to pull Jay out? Could Noel drive to a hospital? Jay said something, but Noel only noticed the shapes Jay's mouth made. Then Jay spoke again and asked if Noel was okay. Sure, Noel said, cutting his eyes to the fire.

The radio was playing inside the truck, both doors left open. It was a Louisiana station, one Noel sometimes liked, but whatever it was they were playing right now bothered him. He kept checking his pocket for his inhaler. What if he forgot how to breathe? He was putting the beers away pretty fast too, but not as fast as Jay, who drank faster than anybody Noel had ever seen. Every five minutes he'd toss another empty can into the fire.

Noel glanced at the scant light the fire cast into the nearby trees. He felt certain he was being watched from out there, from that periphery of darkness. The wind changed and his eyes began to burn. He felt panic light inside him like someone striking matches in a dark room. Two men were out there in the woods, he sensed, standing in the dark pools, watching him. He listened very hard and before long through the music and the wind he began to make out a gentle murmuring of curse words and hoarse laughter. It sounded like someone was telling a long tiresome joke about Pollocks and the Pope, but Noel could only pick up certain words. Soon he got to where he had to talk, just to drown out the joke. "When I was a little kid," he said, then held his breath a moment. "When I was a kid," he began again, "I wanted this pair of shoes, these sneakers I'd been begging for a long time called PF Flyers. In the commercial this kid puts on a pair of PF Flyers—it's a cartoon commercial—he puts on a pair of PF Flyers and suddenly he's off running, rescuing all these other kids from fires and everything—"

"Whoa. Slow down, Spoon. You're talking a mile a minute."

"He's off rescuing all these other kids." Noel rested here. "Because he can run so fast now." Again he rested. This was how he continued his story, each sentence followed by a pause. "So my mom bought me a pair. White and green ones. I put them on. I thought I'd be like the Flash, you know? And that's what it felt like too. Like I was on fire when I ran. I mean, I know I wasn't running any faster than I was before. But it felt like I was. A million times faster. But the weird part was when I stopped. Stopped running and just listened. I could hear all these kids crying for help. Like now I was supposed to go rescue them because I had the damn PF Flyers! It kept happening. Every time I put them on I'd hear those voices crying out for help. My stepdad was about to kill me because I wouldn't even wear these expensive sneakers I had begged him for. He made me wear them to school. I'd sit in class all day listening to all these cries for help coming from . . . I don't know where. Everywhere. That's part of the reason I failed first grade. The teacher'd call on me and I'd look up at her like I'd never even seen her before."

Noel laughed nervously then tried very hard to remember what he had just said.

"You failed first grade?"

"Yeah. And nobody oughta be allowed to fail first grade."

Jay hung back his head to drain another beer. His jugular fisted and breathed, fisted and breathed. Then he shovel-passed the can into the fire and told Noel *wait here,* and he walked off into the woods. Noel wanted to yell out, *Wait! Don't go out there!* but instead he wiped his eyes with his coat sleeves and tried not to listen to the river of curse words, the endless bad joke murmuring from the dark.

Twice Jay returned and dropped a shirtfront of rocks onto the ground. Then he arranged them into a circle and told Noel that anybody who stood inside this circle of rocks would be protected from evil spirits.

"You believe in evil spirits, Spoon?"

"Hell yes. Will you please build me one too? I'm too scared to go out in the damn woods."

"This one is for you. You looked like you could use one."

Noel quickly stepped inside the circle and squatted down.

"Aren't you gonna build you one?" he asked.

Jay tapped a finger to his lip and said, "*Listen.*"

At first Noel assumed it was the two men drinking whiskey and telling bad jokes that Jay heard, but, no, Jay was listening to something else, something perhaps even more sinister than drunken ghosts.

"What is it, Jay? Quick, get inside here with me."

Aiming his box flashlight toward the truck and its gun rack, which contained a double-barreled twelve-gauge and two rifles, Jay asked, "This that guy got shot?"

"Got shot?" Noel took this to mean a zombie, some bullet-ridden corpse about to wallow out from trees and shred Jay apart while Noel watched helplessly from inside his rock fortress.

"That dead Beatle guy," Jay added, which served only to affix a name and additional unsavory details to Noel's imaginary creature. The Dead Beetle Guy. Noel was considering a mad dash for the shotgun when Jay whispered, "Dead-man music."

But there was no music. Noel listened, but the music had stopped. Then a DJ came on and announced he was going to continue playing John Lennon commercial-free for the next hour. He put on something slow then, a song very feminine and reassuring about imagining this, imagining that. Noel told Jay to turn it up, but Jay said he didn't want to run down his battery, a statement that made no sense to Noel, who eyed Jay suspiciously. Noel wanted the music cranked up loud enough to exorcise the woods. The music sounded to him like the forces of good prevailing. The song ended and gave way to a new one about watching wheels go around. Noel's shoulders began to unclench. His spine loosened and turned into a green stalk and then into a beam of light. High above them a new moon pulled free of the pine tops like a black kite.

Neither of them spoke until the radio tribute had ended.

"You feeling anything yet?" Noel asked then.

"I feel like I glow in the dark."

"Yeah, me too." Noel picked up a stone and squeezed it. Then he stepped out from the circle of rocks. "You can have this back, for your whatever thing. I'm alright now, I think."

"Don't need it," Jay replied. "I've always known what I wanna be." He stood and rolled the log he was sitting on closer to the fire. "I've always wanted to be an architect. Ever since I was a kid."

"An architect." Noel bobbed his head. "Like one who builds buildings, huh?"

"Yeah, Spoon, like one who builds buildings. What about you? What you gonna be when you grow up, Spoon?"

"Hell, all I ever wanted to be was to take pictures of naked women." He stepped between Jay and the fire. "Don't tell nobody else I said that, though." He crossed his arms. "Damn chilly willy."

"Can't see through muddy water."

The statement made no sense to Noel, who ignored it and continued to stand there watching the flames. Then he started throwing on more fuel. While he did this, he asked Jay if he'd heard about what had happened yesterday night.

"You mean Timmy-Tom and them pictures? Yeah, I heard."

"It wasn't pictures. It was just the one. And it didn't show nothing hardly."

"Yeah, that's exactly what I heard."

"Besides, she ain't my girlfriend, not anymore. She used to be. I guess I'm kinda still in love with her is all."

"Nothing wrong with that." Jay tapped Noel on the hip with another beer. Noel took it and drank it half off then noticed he was sweating and stepped back from the popping wood. The radio was playing commercials now. Jay went over and turned it off. When he came back, he said, "Can I ask you something personal?"

"I guess."

"Promise you won't get mad?"

"Yeah."

"Did you ever take her picture that way? Without any clothes on?"

"Layle? No. Hell no. She wasn't like that. Not when I knew her."

"You ever taken any girl's picture naked?"

Noel nodded that he had. Once, he said. But they'd both been fucked up on 'ludes and none of it had turned out any good.

"You wanna be a photographer for one of those magazines, like for *Hustler* or something?"

"Naw, not for *Hustler*."

"What? For *Playboy*, then?"

"Maybe. I dunno. It's more like for some magazine that hasn't even been invented yet. You know what I'd like to do, I'd like to work for *National Geographic* and just go off into the jungle and take pictures of whole tribes of naked women. Women who don't even know they're naked." Noel had stated this very deliberately but without much hope of being understood. Then he asked if Jay thought there was something wrong with doing that, with taking pictures of naked women.

"You mean for a Mormon to?"

"Oh yeah, I forgot, y'all can't hardly even dance."

"We can dance."

"Is it true you can have all these wives? A whole harem of them? Can't Mormons do that?"

After Jay had dispelled this rumor in his usual neutral manner, Noel asked what exactly Mormons did believe. Jay shrugged and said they believed Jesus had reappeared in America after dying on the cross, and that Jesus had taught here, to the Indians, and also some Mormons believed in stuff like astral traveling and guardian angels, and they all believe that after you die, if you've lived your life real well, then you get to become god of your own universe.

"God of your own universe," Noel repeated and whistled. That made an impression, but at the same time it made him suspect that right now he and Jay could be trapped inside most any fool's universe, and that got him to thinking about those state fairs and the drug addicts his mom always claimed assembled the rides of the midway. Noel did not mention any of this to Jay, who seemed fairly sensitive about the whole Mormon subject. Instead Noel asked, "Astral traveling, what the heck's that all about?"

It was sending part of your soul out away from your body, Jay explained. So you could explore outer space or China or wherever. Jay did not seem particularly anxious to discuss astral traveling either. "Anyway, only certain kinds of Mormons do weird stuff like that, most of us just get up and haul our butts to church like the rest of the world."

Noel fueled more wood onto the fire until the flames were once again over his head. By now the LSD had given him a near-swaggering confidence; suddenly he wanted to be around women, just to watch them. But when he asked Jay what he wanted to do next, Jay took the question more philosophically.

"After the River? I'm gonna apply up to Starkville, to the architecture school there. It's supposed to be like boot camp almost. I started working construction, gofering, when I was ten. I know how buildings work, how they go up. Then, once I get that degree, I'm heading straight to either New Orleans or Saint Louis, and I'm gonna design these big-ass skyscrapers made out of nothing but glass and mirrors. Kind you stare right at but all you see is sun and clouds."

"You gonna take Cindy with you to State?"

"No. I already told her I'm not getting hitched up until after my first building's finished. These local gals—you better watch yourself, Spoon—they come to the River for one reason, and that's to latch on to some guy and show him the field or the factory. That ain't for me."

"Ain't for me neither."

"Know what my old man told me once? Back when I had my first real girlfriend. I was about thirteen. He took me fishing, rowed us out to the middle of a lake, then he crossed the oars at his feet and looked me hard in the eye and he said, *Son, just 'cause a girl lets you play with her peehole, don't let her get you by the balls.*"

"Naw," Noel said, giggling. "Your old man said that?"

"I swear he did."

"He used to play pro ball, didn't he, your dad? That's what everybody around Huff says. That your old man played safety for the Saints."

Jay did not answer, only stared into the fire. Finally he said, "Hey, I got an idea," and he walked to the truck and began rummaging inside its bed. He returned with a long thick rope coiled around his neck. The rope was knotted at foot-long intervals and tied to a grappling hook. He was carrying a can of spray paint with a red top and an extra flashlight.

Noel grinned, asked what all this was for.

"Somethin' I designed special. I hadn't planned on using it tonight, but now I'm thinking what the hell? C'mon, get up. Follow me."

He handed Noel a flashlight and set off into the woods.

Noel hurried to catch up. For the first hundred yards or so he paid little attention to where they were going, but then he began to worry about getting lost. They kept following their flashlight beams, Noel occasionally wriggling his up at strange sounds inside the trees. After about a mile, they stepped into a round clearing that contained a circular fence fifteen feet tall that listed outward. The fence, topped by four orbits of barbed wire, enclosed a water tower that also seemed to loom in their direction. It had one flashing red light on top and two smaller ones along its catwalk. The word POPLARVILLE was belted in black letters around the bulb, which appeared powder blue in the starlight.

Not using his own voice but imitating somebody at the dorm, somebody Noel could not pinpoint, Jay said, "Well, will you looky here. And they just repainted her too. Not one lick'a graffiti up there."

Noel moved in to investigate. Already he had spotted a gap in the barbed wire. The fence had black triangular signs crimped onto it. He came closer and saw that the black triangles contained red lightning-bolt logos. He had just turned to warn Jay that the fence was electric when Jay shot past him, sprinting full speed at the fence and then hurdling into the air. His hands and upper body hit first. The fence caved inward then trampolined back out but did not throw Jay off. His body shivered, then his head lagged away from the fence, but still he clung there like a locust husk. Noel stood ten feet away, his own arms and shoulders making involuntary jerks and starts, as if he were the one being electrocuted. Then, riding a wave of curse words, he hurled himself at Jay and half hooked, half blocked him off the fence and onto the grass.

An ant bed of electricity crawled out of Noel's body and vanished into the ground. Jay was sprawled facedown beside him. Noel touched Jay's arm like whisking a hot iron, then he turned Jay over and splayed one palm over his chest. But Noel's own heart was thudding too hard inside his hand for him to ascertain anything that way. He lowered the side of his head to Jay's chest. At first he did not hear anything except an eerie seashell noise, but then he heard something different, something deeper, like a low rumble rising out of Jay's chest, an avalanche rolling closer that balled up Jay's body as laughter poured out of him into the night.

The laughter contorted Jay. Again and again he tried to uncurl and apologize, but he could not. After ten minutes of this he was on his knees, still trying to stop laughing. His cheeks were wet and he was in pain and holding his ribs. Finally he managed to say, "I'm sorry, Spoon, I couldn't help it. I swear. They did it to me first. Hutch and some other seniors did. Don't be mad." Recovering a bit more, he glanced up and explained, "It's another of their traditions. And I shoulda known better too, because we used to sell the same lightning-bolt signs at the hardware store where I worked. Hey, don't be mad, Spoon. I built you that circle of rocks, remember? Anyway, now you can do it to someone else."

Noel marched to the fence and fed his hands to it, then he climbed to the top and straddled the gap in the barbed wire. He dropped down and stalked beneath the insect legs of the water tower into the crisscrossed darkness and there he stopped to wipe at his eyes. The shadows from the stays and shrouds formed a giant spider's web upon the grass, which was tinted red from the catwalk lights high above. Noel remained standing there until Jay had climbed over. From the darkness, dry and deadpanned, Noel called out, "That rope for what I think it's for?"

Jay apologized again, this time without laughing, and said yeah, he'd come up with a plan. "To get even with Hutch. Hell, you don't like him any better than I do, right? Didn't y'all two get into it once back in the fall?"

They could hardly see each other. Noel grunted and said, "Yeah, him and two other seniors tried to throw me in the shower. I tagged him one, kinda by accident, split open his eye. I was just trying to get loose. Then he went around telling everybody how he was gonna kick my ass. But he never did shit." Noel curbed the happiness in his voice and spat. "I was the only freshman not thrown in the shower."

"See, that's another of their damn traditions. They do whatever they feel like to us freshmen."

"I thought you was dead back there. It wasn't funny."

Jay apologized again, then he warned, "But if we do this, Spoon, you gotta keep your mouth shut afterwards. You can't go telling anybody it was us."

"Don't worry, I can keep a secret. What you gonna write up there anyway?"

"*Hutch is a fag!*"

Noel winced. "That's cold," he said.

"You can see it from town, the tower," Jay said. "And from the highway."

"Well, we gonna climb that son-a-bitch or what?"

Jay removed the rope from his neck and took two steps backward and started swinging the hook, feeding it more and more line so that its circle widened. When he released the slack, the hook soared up and clanged against the iron ladder. After a dozen throws, he snagged the bottom rung then jimmied himself up using the knots as handholds and letting his legs drag limp behind him. Noel went next, clawing with hands and boots. Soon they were both climbing the ladder toward the blinking red lights. The canopy of pine tops passed beneath them. Sweeps darted out from their nests along the bottom of the tower. Noel's cheap cowboy boots kept slipping. Twice he banged his chin on the ladder. The last time he did this, he dropped his flashlight, which somersaulted down in loops of light, then shattered into darkness.

Eventually the ladder gave way to the catwalk, which circled the tower, a few yards below the word POPLARVILLE. The bulb's outward curve formed a slanted roof they had to duck under as they explored the flashing red-lit perimeter. *Hey, Jay, I'm a damn bird!* Noel kept shrieking and then pretending to launch himself over the rail. Once he did this so convincingly that Jay grabbed the neck of Noel's hunting coat. They ended up sitting on the leeward side with their knees up, their backs pressed against the tower. From there, they watched the treetops sway in the wind. The can of red spray paint was set between them.

"I'm just about ready for this shit to wear off," Noel said.

"Yeah. But it's supposed to last all night, at least."

"That wasn't funny, what you did back there."

"I said I'm sorry. Anyway, it's not my fault, it's like some kinda disease everybody in my family has, like the practical-joke disease."

Noel was watching Jay's hands as he said this. The hands appeared to be playing castanets. Jay held them draped over his knees, and whenever he spoke, it was like one of his hands was asking the other one a question.

"What else you hear about my dad, besides that he played for the Saints?"

After a moment of adjustment, Noel replied, "Nothing, I don't think."

Jay straightened his legs so that, from the shin down, they stuck out through the rail and were tinted red. He said that his father still held the Saints' team record for most interceptions in one game. "Three snags." He pressed the tip of his tongue upward, which made him appear to have a swollen upper lip. "Really it just tied the old record. Some other guys had done it too." It was his right hand that appeared to be talking now. "I don't even remember him playing football, all I remember's him limping around that car lot smiling them gold caps at everybody and trying to interest them in a damn Pacer. After he blew out his knee, that's what he did, opened an AMC dealership in Laurel. And built us a pool in the backyard, because my mom always joked she'd leave him if he didn't build her a pool. She used to be a Miss Mississippi, a long time back. My dad, he'd come home from the lot every day and make himself a big ol' martini, then just start staring down into that pool, like his best friend had drowned in it. Wouldn't even answer us. We'd be yelling out that dinner was ready, nothing, he just kept staring into the deep end. Next morning there'd be another martini glass down on the drain I'd have to dive in and get. You ever tasted a martini?"

Noel shook his head.

"They're nasty."

Noel blew air through his lips then wished out loud that they'd brought some beer up here with them. "I could use a cold one right now."

"Yeah. Hey, you hear I played quarterback in high school?"

Noel said no, he hadn't heard that either. But it was easy enough for him to imagine Jay at quarterback. Tall, lean, and clean-cut, the kind of lopingly graceful kid that coaches love.

"My senior year we went oh and ten," he confided. "Oh and ten—you believe that?" He packed his can of Happy Days, making the *clap clap clap* sound in the dark. "It wasn't my fault either," Jay said after taking in a dip. "No D. No front line. I was like the Archie Manning of high school ball. They'd just prop them boys up in front of me, like cardboard cutouts or something." Jay spat through the grillwork floor and laughed. "And I wasn't half bad neither. I could chunk it. And could scramble too. Coach knew it. Knew it wasn't my fault. He used to apologize to me after games. And my old man, he shoulda known it better'n anybody. But oh and ten, that's hard to take. I don't know about Hattiesburg, but, shoot, in Laurel, when it comes to high school ball, people take that shit way too personal. It was like my old man was the laughingstock because his son played quarterback on the losingest team in school history. Every game I'd be out there scrambling my ass off—I was the leading rusher on the team—but all that mattered was oh and ten. Nobody was buying his cars either. And he blamed me for it. I know he did. He never said it outright, but he dropped all these little hints, made sure I knew. I mean, the man was selling AMCs, the most suck-ass vehicles in the history of the automobile. Pacers, man. Shaped like UFOs. You ever seen a Pacer?"

Noel nodded and said yeah.

"Not many you ain't. They're ugly as hell, aren't they?"

Noel agreed that they were.

"Look just like UFOs, don't they?"

"Yeah. Fuck a Pacer. Hey, didn't AMC make them Gremlin things too?"

"Gremlins, Pacers, Brats, Marlins. All the classics. Let me tell you, it didn't have nothing to do with oh and ten."

They fell quiet. Later, when they started talking again, it was about the real Archie Manning. Noel said that his mom had been about half in love with Archie. She'd get tears in her eyes watching the Saints crumble every week with Manning all bandaged back together. Jay was describing how one time Manning had passed underhanded, with three men on his back, forty yards downfield. *Underhanded! And on the damn numbers!* Jay thumped his chest. Then, as if there were some logic connecting that pass to his father, he said, "My old man killed himself, you probably heard about that too, huh?"

Noel had not and said as much.

Jay was nodding vigorously. "Last summer. I'm the one that found him, in the car lot. He had a garden hose leading in from the exhaust. He was just sitting there in the driver's seat, both hands still on the wheel, like he was driving. Inside a maroon Pacer. One he musta known wasn't nobody ever gonna buy anyway. That's why he picked it, I bet. A purple damn UFO Pacer. Man died inside the ugliest car in the universe."

Noel could not think of anything to say to that. His legs had started vibrating. A shooting star forked overhead, and Jay pointed to it and said make a wish. Unable to stop his lips from moving, Noel was letting different conversations play out inside his head. These conversations felt very real to him. He even suspected he might be communicating with Jay telepathically. Noel was telling him all about his own father and him disappearing that night at the fair. Then he told about the no-hitter and about Vietnam. And maybe Noel was using telepathy, because suddenly Jay asked, "What about your old man—what's he do?"

Noel reeled off most everything he had been thinking. He finished, then caught a breath and added, "My uncle, he thinks my dad might still be alive over there, in Vietnam. But he ain't. Alive, I mean. He's dead. I know he is."

"How do you know that?"

"I seen his ghost is how."

It took a moment before Jay asked when Noel had seen this ghost.

"Why you damn whispering, Jay?"

Jay repeated the question a bit louder, but he still hushed the word *ghost*.

"I seen him lots of times. Whenever I get fucked up enough."

"You seen him tonight?"

"Hell, he's sitting next to you right now."

Jay jerked around to check, and Noel started laughing.

"Naw, he ain't up here. Yet. But I heard him out in the woods earlier, at least I think I did. Had some drinking buddy of his out there with him this time."

Jay wanted to know if the ghost had ever said anything. "It ever tell you how it died? Ain't that what ghosts always do?"

"It ain't a it, it's a he, and besides, I already know how he died. My mom put a cigarette out on him."

"Say again?"

"My mom, she put a cigarette out on him. On this old photograph of them together. Melted a hole all the way through his heart. Way I figure it, right then, the second she did that, boom— he got bayoneted or shot or something."

"She did *what*?"

Noel tried explaining it again. Then he added, "That's why I don't let nobody take my picture, if I can help it. It's like giving them a voodoo doll of you."

"You're the one always taken everybody's picture."

"Yeah, I know, but don't you think it's weird that somebody can be looking at a picture of you right now and you don't even know it?"

"No."

"Well, I do. And you know what's even weirder? You ever see a picture of some beautiful chick smiling up naked at you, and it's about a hundred years since she died of old age? Now, that *is* weird," he said, resolute.

He cracked the knuckles on both fists against the catwalk floor, then he unbuttoned the hunting coat. He could not see his breath anymore, but he could still hear the wind blasting against the opposite hemisphere of the tower.

"You should tell him to go to the light. That's what you're supposed to tell ghosts to do."

Noel snorted and said yeah, he'd heard that too. "I don't think it's that damn simple."

When the talk dwindled, Noel once again took up the conversation inside his head. His own hands were playing the castanets now. Noel was the left hand, Jay was the right hand, like a puppet show. The left hand started describing all its many problems, including its failures with girls, but the right hand interrupted and said, Hey, that's alright, Spoon, no biggie, I know you ain't gay or nothing. Hell no, I ain't, insisted the left hand, then it went on to confess that it had lied about Layle too. She probably wasn't a Rams cheerleader, though she might be, she was pretty enough, and anyway they'd been broke up since tenth grade. The right hand laughed, said, Hell, everybody lies about chicks, Spoon. Then the left hand began to describe the murder of Ross Altman and how it had felt, feeling someone die underneath you, and how it was a head rush, kinda the same way getting into a fistfight was a rush. The left hand described what it was like to step back and see a dead body there and to know you'd made it dead and how from then on you knew that was something you could do . . . how it was like the beginning of something instead of the end.

He wedged his left hand under his thigh. Turning to Jay, whose eyes stared straight ahead unblinking, Noel asked, "Did I say anything out loud just then?"

"Whoa," Jay said, hugging himself. He glanced warily at Noel. "Swear to God, Spoon, I'as just astral traveling my ass off."

"You wasn't any fuckin' astral traveling."

"I swear I was. It was like I just rode on outa here."

"Where'd you go to?'

"I don't even know. Outer space, I guess. There were all these stars passing by on both sides of me."

For the next few minutes Noel tried to astral travel but instead ended up daydreaming.

"Hey, your old man," he said. "You reckon he ever got his own universe? For getting all them interceptions?"

Jay did not answer at first, but finally he whispered, "Man, I wouldn't wish that universe on a dog."

The deflated way Jay had said that made Noel want to cheer him up. He picked up the can of spray paint and asked if Jay was ready to do some damage. But Jay shook his head and replied nah, he'd changed his mind. He wasn't in the mood anymore. "Anyway, I wasn't planning it for tonight, I was planning it for the night before Christmas break. We'll come back and do it then. Leave a little Santa Claus for ol' Hutch."

"Hell, you're just scared."

"No. Can't stand up is all."

Noel took the can and ducked around the catwalk into the wind until he saw the sprinkle of lights he figured to be Poplarville. As he shook the agitator, he longed for something more spectacular to write than *Hutch is a fag!*, something so startling that the town below might never recover from it, something they'd be talking about for years. He kept clapping the agitator until an unfortunate inspiration came to him. At the time it seemed very funny and near-perfect, like a gift. Later, though, he would have a lot of trouble explaining this feeling to Jay.

To reach high enough for his design, he had to prop himself up on the guardrail and list his body into the bulb, bracing his free hand to its surface. Using this method, and stretching his painting arm, he made the top curve of a giant eye. Then he made the bottom curve and reddened in the eyeball and filled the whites with squiggly veins. He thickened the outside lines. Then he stepped down off the rail and had a look. He shook the can as he thought. Below the eye, he wrote the letter s. Shuffling along the catwalk, he finished the word SATAN, blood red on baby blue. He came down a line and added IS KING! Then next to this he painted a huge red pentacle. Finally he looped in the number 666 and tried to circle it except he ran out of paint before he could enclose the top. The Number of the Beast appeared cupped, as if riding a boat.

Noel's heart was racing now; he felt suddenly overwhelmed by what he had done and no longer certain that it was strictly hilarious. In the soft darkness he kept studying the giant bloodshot eye until something resembling hunger bloomed inside him. He stretched arthritically and loosened up his legs by shaking them, then he hunch-paced around the catwalk to where he spotted false dawn, a red saw-blade sun cutting through the horizon of pine.

"Jay," he called out after a moment, his voice sounding almost bored. "The damn woods are on fire."

CHAPTER TEN

THE FIRE HAD FANNED OUT in two directions. Inside the clearing it seemed to be slithering under the pine straw and only occasionally surfacing to consume a fallen tree and then moving along that tree like a bridge that led back underground. One of these red veins had crept dangerously near the pickup, and there was the strong smell of burnt rubber in the air. The high flames were off in the distance, but now the wind had changed again and was lashing the fire back into the clearing. Noel, his cheeks scorched with tears, searched through the area more from memory than from sight. He had already found the ice chest and thrown it into the truck bed. Jay was gunning the engine and screaming at him to get inside, but Noel stood his ground and surveyed the camp one last sweep. Finally he dashed across the dead fire pit and grabbed up the football, which had Jay's name markered across it, and carrying the ball like a fullback he bowled himself into the front seat of the moving truck.

On back roads they worked their way north and half an hour

later emerged from the woods with the sun breaching the treetops and deer bolting across the highway. Noel was already grilling Jay. If anyone asked, they'd been in Bogalusa all night. He made Jay recite the names of certain Bogalusa bars and he affixed a chronology to their night. "And I swear, Jay, if you tell one person the truth—you listening?—just one, then it'll get out, it's guaranteed to. Don't even tell Cindy. She already thinks we hit Bogtown last night, right?"

"She kept accusing me of us going to that strip bar there."

"That Pink Paradise place?"

"Yeah, the one where Hutch and them said you can finger off your waitress for five bucks."

Noel grew thoughtful a moment before deciding, "Don't say we went there. I don't think that place even exists. Maybe it used to, but not anymore. I think we all made it up somehow." He snapped his fingers. "What we need now is a car wash—the kind where you plug in quarters. And tomorrow morning, early, you gotta drive to Laurel and get some retreads put on—I'll pay for it—but don't get them anywhere around here 'cause people might be asking questions."

"Damn, Spoon. You got a good . . . criminal mind."

They returned to campus after washing the truck. From the top floor of Huff, they stared out the hall window at the black cauliflower-shaped cloud to the south. Then they showered and changed and went to the cafeteria. The LSD had not yet finished with Noel. His heart stormed and he had to keep fighting back waves of euphoria. The cafeteria was empty at this early hour. Its buffet resembled the plastic food inside the refrigerators at Sears. Noel was still hungry, but he couldn't eat. All he got was coffee. Same with Jay. Rolling the go cups in their hands, they walked back outside and headed to the center of campus, to the small amphitheater there.

The amphitheater was old and dilapidated. Gray pigment mottled
the pillars backing the stage, each pillar supporting the weight of one
virtue printed on top of it in uncial lettering. TRVTH, Noel read.
Weeds pushed through the concrete stage. Yellow danger ribbons
cordoned off one whole section of seats, and dried sunflowers and
old newspapers ratted from inside the chorus pit. They sat a dozen
rows up from the grass courtyard and Noel had just started grilling
Jay again when Cindy McGee yelled their names and came jogging
down the steps toward them.

Breathless and tanned and with nest-brown eyes, Cindy wore a
yellow running suit with a yet yellower bow tied around her long
brown ponytail. Noel watched her descending the steps, and as he
was doing this, the acid flared inside him and suddenly it was as if
he were wearing X-ray glasses. The yellow running suit kept dissolving and revealing her naked and so beautiful that it hurt to
look at her. Her breasts were large and had centers like brown
flowers. He had to look away.

And while he looked away, he was remembering something Jay
had told him. A few weeks earlier Jay had confided that Cindy's
left breast was considerably larger than her right.

"She's even got names for them," Jay had added, nodding gravely.

"Names? Like what?"

Jay had hesitated then said, "Like Sleepy and Doc."

"Sleepy and Doc! Those are damn dwarves."

"I know they are. She's got names for everything."

"For *everything*?"

Noel stole another glance at her while she kissed Jay, but her
jogging suit had reappeared. Then Cindy reached down and played
with his hair and asked about Bogalusa. She always held her breath
as she spoke, and the longer the string of words, the faster she had
to say them.

"Bogalusa's Bogalusa," Jay replied matter-of-factly.

"Yeah," Noel said. "Same ol', same ol'."

"Y'all went to that girlie bar, didn't you? You did, I can tell just from looking at you two."

"No way," Noel replied. "We knew better than to disturb you at work."

He peeled back the cup lid. Inside the blackness of his coffee, he began to watch Cindy on stage, her large mismatched breasts hidden by feather and cymbal and wild ropy hair. When he blew across the coffee, she commenced to tremble and dance. Using a circus-man's voice, Noel barked, *Ladies and gentlemen—I give you Cindy McGee and her sexy cymbal review! Submitted for your approval!*

Nobody laughed except Noel, who had set down his coffee to make a crashing cymbal motion. His laughter collapsed him onto the cement bleachers and left him staring up at the blue sky.

"Hey, that Rebecca friend of yours," Noel asked from that angle, "she still wanna go out with me?"

"Not after last night," Cindy replied very dryly.

"Last night?" he asked and shot Jay a stay-calm look. "What about last night?"

"Y'all two weren't the only ones who had a night on the town. Becky and I went into Hattiesburg, to that disco Pat McCool's, and we ran into some girls from your old high school, Noel." She stopped jogging in place to stare him down. "They said you used to get suspended for fights all the time and that you were a drug pusher too."

"Pusher," Jay said and giggled.

"Who told you that?" Noel asked, surprised at how unconcerned his voice sounded.

"I can't tell you her name, she made me promise not to. It was like she was scared of you. She said everybody used to call you *Moon*

Man, and that you once killed a boy in a baseball game, that you were a pitcher and hit him in the head with the ball and it killed him."

A flock of small crows landed in the oval of grass beneath the stage. Noel sat up and watched the crows and made a scooping motion with his chin as if he were about to reply, but before he could Jay asked, "That true, Spoon?"

"Yeah, I guess." He waited a bit longer, then said, "But it wasn't with a pitch, it was with him trying to block the plate on me and I ran into him. That's why I quit playing baseball."

"Jesus," Jay said.

The crows scattered overhead, and Noel pretended to take a forlorn interest in their flight. Every once in a while he'd steal another glance at Cindy just to make sure her clothes hadn't dissolved again.

"I was all-stars and everything. Better'n my brother Matt even. I probably could'a gone pro too, but I didn't want no one else to get hurt. I was like the Shane of baseball."

Cindy wiped at her brow with her biceps then turned to Jay and put her hand under his shirt around his ribs and hinted, "I think Noel wants to be left alone right now."

Which was not true either. Being left alone meant having to rummage through another plane-wreck of lies. Still, he received her stage direction and nodded. "Yeah," he said, "that'd be cool, if y'all don't mind."

Jay patted him on the back and asked if he was okay.

"Sure," he replied. "No biggie." Then he stared away and inhaled sharply, his gaze falling a few rows below them to where a class was gathering. All the students were carrying identical white paperback Bibles.

"You sure?" Jay asked, but Cindy had already taken him by the arm and was leading him up the stairs.

Noel did not watch them go but instead imagined them looking back down at him from the top of the amphitheater, at the figure of solitude he cut there.

As soon as they were gone, he started replaying the conversation in his head. He'd had the strangest impulse while talking to Cindy and Jay. Though he had overcome it, he had been overwhelmed by the sudden desire to tell the truth. He had felt it tugging upon him, the urge to confess to the murder of Ross Altman the exact way it had happened. Until that moment, the truth had always seemed to be his greatest obstacle, not something that he could use to explain himself to other people and maybe even to himself. He rolled the warm cup in his hands while his mind balked at all the lies. A life's work of them. Lies sprawled as far as the eye could see. What else was there in his universe? Lies and pornography and lies and drugs and lies and petty violence? Thinking that, he laughed. Then he laughed harder because it had just occurred to him that his alibi for the forest fire was a strip bar that did not even exist. For a long time he sat there, as if riding a seesaw, rising with euphoria, plummeting with paranoia, and all the while eavesdropping on the class below him.

It was, best he could figure, a Bible class. The students did not appear nearly interested enough for it to be a devotional group. The teacher was in her mid-thirties, with a wide, attractive mouth and short blondish hair feathered back and tucked behind her ears by a pair of red-rimmed sunglasses pushed back like a headband. Her accent was tough to pin down. It sounded precise and aristocratic and a bit fake. Kentuckian, he guessed, though he had never met anybody from there. Her clothes were equally odd. A tight white T-shirt he could see the pattern of her bra through and baggy yellow pants that tapered at the ankle. But the oddest thing about her was her tongue. It was bright green.

Midway through her lecture, she reached down and unbuckled her leather sandals and took them off and held them behind her back as she tried to rally a discussion, urging everyone to speak out, "Even you girls, God forbid." But the girls in the class remained moody and remote. What discussing took place, the boys accomplished. Every few minutes the teacher would visor a sandal to her forehead and smile Noel's way. Meanwhile, the class discussion kept lagging and finally it stopped altogether. The teacher pouted and dropped her sandals and started updrafting her hands, but the class remained definitely mute. She stared up at Noel again, as if in him she had found an advocate, then she announced very vindictively that she was going to tell the class another story. The students groaned in unison, and that made her smile.

"Our story," she began, "will be about Saint Thomas, who seems to have mystified us into silence. But it is also the story of the human soul. Or so its authors would have us believe. Though we can't always trust stories, can we? Stories, like authors, and teachers, are often suspect."

Two army helicopters, one with double rotors, thundered over the amphitheater, drowning out her voice. Noel, who had a pretty good idea where those helicopters might be heading, watched them grow smaller against the blue sky. After the roar had subsided, the teacher continued her pantomime, gesturing wildly and mouthing her words. None of her students thought it was funny, although Noel did. Finally she stopped her gesticulating. She took a breath and said that perhaps we did not know that Jesus had a brother. "But he did," she confirmed. "Two at least. And one of these was his twin. And not only his twin, but his identical twin. Yes, Saint Thomas and Jesus were identical twins. Or so the Bible tells us. And we all know the Bible to be infallible, the word of God. If you don't believe me, just go ask your parents."

Noel, in spite of himself, began rummaging through the carnage of lies. He was still constructing various alibis when three girls stood, the prettiest one tapping her wristwatch. Smiling acidly, the teacher watched them ascend the cement steps. A few minutes later the class scattered from the amphitheater, the teacher shouting out some last threats about the upcoming final. Noel leaned back on his elbows and sniffed the air and closed his eyes to let the lids absorb the sunlight.

A woman's voice said to him, "Pearls on the swine. Wouldn't you agree?"

She was sitting down beside him and also leaning back on her elbows, glancing over at Noel as if to attune her posture to his.

"Those little tramps, they were passing notes again, weren't they? I should have confiscated them and read their little fantasies out loud to the entire class and scarred them for life. That's how they used to do us back in Virginia." She scanned Noel's face for a reaction. "Ahh well, it didn't go so hot today. But maybe I gave them something to think about while they're staring up at the ol' ceiling fan. One never knows the full effects of one's dealing— true?"

Noel pushed himself up and asked, "What kind of teacher are you?"

She answered him too honestly, which, he guessed, was how she answered most questions. She said, "The kind who is about to be fired. A fact which is not lost on my students and which robs me of any authority. And, like most things wounded, makes me very dangerous." She sighed and while flexing her toes in the sunlight she introduced herself as Lily Frank and held out her hand for Noel to shake. Her upper teeth had a slight medicine stain along the tops. She wore an Irish wedding band that Noel noticed when she leaned forward and wrapped each hand around an ankle then arched her back and neck. Holding this posture, she asked if she might have a sip off of that coffee.

"I'm a caffeine junkie," she told him as she removed the lid. She took a sip, then stuck out her green tongue and thrust the coffee back at him and complained, "That's colder'n a witch's tit, Noel."

"Yeah, sorry, I kinda forgot to drink it."

She brightened and said that happened to her too, especially with wine. Sometimes when she cleaned up—which wasn't very often—she found three or four full glasses hiding around the house. "Poor lost wine," she lamented.

Noel asked what other classes she taught.

"Comparative Religion," she said. "I lobbied for that class for months and then nobody signed up for it and I got stuck with two sections of Bible Study, again."

After saying this, she burped very loudly.

"Do you know your tongue is green?" he asked her.

"Green?" she said, as if she would have preferred most any other color. "Oh damn, the jawbreakers." She opened her wicker purse and tilted it at Noel. Her wallet and keys rested on a sea of candy. "Leftovers from Halloween," she explained. "And I'm stingy as hell with it. It's got to last me all year." Then she asked, almost suspiciously, if Noel wanted a piece, and when he shook his head no—he still could not imagine eating—she pretended to be greatly relieved. She removed a folded handkerchief from the purse and began to lick it. "God, no wonder they were staring at me like I was the Wicked Witch of the East." She showed Noel her tongue and asked if it was still green. It was, but not as brightly so. He told her it was okay now, then he asked why she was getting fired.

"What a rude question." She had a way of nodding and squinting and focusing with her mouth. She considered the question in this manner, then admitted there was no getting around it. "Blasphemy.

Utter blasphemy. And they would have fired me right on the spot except my husband teaches here too—everybody thinks he's Mr. Wonderful—so now, during Christmas break, I get to appear before some judicial board, which I'm quite looking forward to, even though the verdict is a foregone conclusion. After that, they burn me at the stake. But at least I get to finish out this semester. The class that just fled"—she made a motion like slapping someone with the back of her hand—"I'm going to fail them all. Except for maybe one cute guy. My little way of saying *Sigh Oh Nara.*"

"What kind of blasphemy?"

She shrugged, again seemingly with her mouth. "Let's see. I guess I pretty much ran the blasphemy gamut, Noel. A to Z. Adultery to Zoroastrianism. I'm a pariah. Can't you tell?"

"I don't even know what that is."

"A pariah? It's a fish. A very dangerous fish. Indigenous to the Amazon."

Then she started asking Noel about his religious upbringing, and he told her he was raised Baptist but that he didn't hold with that anymore.

"I don't believe in God anymore," Noel said.

"Oh yes you do," she said. "You're too young to really not believe in God yet. You're just being fashionable and trying to impress me."

"I don't," he insisted.

"Well are you agnostic or atheist?"

"What's the difference?"

"An atheist says there is no God. An agnostic says maybe there is, maybe there isn't, but it beats the hell outa me."

"I guess I'm that last one."

"Ahh. Do you by any chance read, Noel? It's a strange question to have to ask a college student, you'll agree?"

When he told her that he did, she did not appear convinced and asked which courses he was taking. He listed them off then explained that he wanted to be a photographer but that the college did not offer photography courses. Yawning, she asked who was his favorite author. He told her Ernest Hemingway, and she sat up, saluting to block out the sun, and said, "Egad!" Then she changed the subject again, this time back to her class and what Noel had really thought of it. She asked this daringly, as if she had secret misgivings she might share. Noel only shrugged and said all that religion stuff bored him.

"Well, Ernest Hemingway bores me," she countered.

Staring down at his imitation snakeskin boots, Noel very slowly began to recite a few lines from *A Farewell to Arms*. Every so often he had to stop and scratch his cheek as he struggled to recall the next part. The passage was the famous one about knowing that the things of the night cannot be explained in the day and that the night can be a dreadful time for lonely people once their loneliness has started.

When he had finished, he glanced over at her and grinned.

"Oh my God," she remarked. "You must be knocking them off with a stick." Noting his confusion, she clarified, "The girls, Noel. The girls."

He blushed—he couldn't help it—then lowered his head.

"So that's what you were up to, huh? Sitting up here, doing your best to look like some rock star, and scoping out the talent in my class. Deciding which ones you wanted to undo with your little snippets of macho-boy poetry? Well, let me say, I suspected as much."

"I'm not trying to look like any rock star."

"The heck you aren't, Noel. There are some pretty ones in my class too. Especially sweet Cecilia. She'll be at our house tomorrow night, by the way, lusting after my husband."

Noel asked which one was Cecilia.

"She was that very tall, very tanned girl with the long brown hair, the one that left early." She examined Noel even more keenly. When she spoke again, she had a pink smear of lipstick on her front teeth. "And between boyfriends, at the moment, I might add."

"And she's snaking after your husband?"

"I couldn't have put it better myself. She's snaking after him, alright. Just out of curiosity, Noel, given the opportunity, since you're a photographer, how would you take her photograph? She's a twirler, you know. You might want to figure that into the equation."

"A twirler?"

"A Dixie Darling. Halftime and all that dog-and-pony show."

After a moment Noel decided, "I guess I'd have her waiting for one of those baton things to come back down. But she'd have to be holding another one so people'd know what she was looking up after. And maybe a clothesline or something in the background."

He did not elaborate that the clothesline would have her underwear pinned on it, though he felt certain it would.

"And what would you have her wearing in this photograph— spangles?"

"I dunno, that depends on what she's like. Maybe one of those real short shirts, the kind that hike up above the belly button."

"Midriff," Lily said. "The area from here . . . to here." She made a slicing motion, as if dividing that portion from herself. "Otherwise known as the oven." Sitting up straighter and blinking dramatically, she wished out loud that she had brought her sunglasses with her.

"They're on your head."

"Oh. So they are." She slipped them down. "I find it very annoying to talk to anyone wearing sunglasses. You can't see their eyes. They could be thinking most anything. Something diabolical. It's a very strange cultural phenomenon, sunglasses are. Almost as strange as wristwatches. Which I see you don't wear. Good for you."

"You don't either."

"No, but perhaps if I did I wouldn't let my class run overtime and make my students want to murder me."

"What religion did you say you were?"

"I didn't."

"Well, what religion are you?"

"You have to guess."

Noel guessed Mormon because he wanted to impress her with his new knowledge on the subject.

"Oh God! Do I look Mormon?"

"You kinda got them Osmond teeth."

"Wonderful. First a green tongue, now Osmond teeth. And why are you staring at my mouth so much?"

"It's still kinda green."

She licked her palm, studied the saliva.

"No, I'm not a Mormon, though I find them fascinating."

"You believe all that angel Moroni stuff?"

The tilt of her head indicated she just might be impressed. "To tell you the truth, Noel, the jury's still out on ol' angel Moroni. What about you, you believe all that angel Moroni stuff?"

"Hell no."

"It must be nice," she said, "to know things so absolutely."

"If you're not a Mormon, then what are you?"

If he wanted to find that out, she explained, he'd have to come to her house tomorrow night. "Our Thursday night nondenom meetings. Led by my much-beloved husband. I suspect a few cute girls will be there. Cecilia included. Can we count on you being there, Noel? I can promise you it won't be boring."

She took his right hand and drew a map to her house on his palm. Then she made him write down his phone number on her own palm. That done, she glanced around and complained that she needed to know the time. She strapped on her sandals, told Noel it had been a unexpected pleasure, and smiled deeply at him. She stood and strolled down the steps, plucking up her leather satchel in passing, and continued down to the island of grass beneath the stage where there stood an old iron sundial that Noel had never noticed until that moment. She placed her satchel on the grass and was studying first the mechanism and then the angle of sunlight over her shoulder when from across campus the chapel bell began to ring. It rang ten times. Each time it did, she extended one finger down at her side. When the bell stopped, she adjusted the sundial then turned and walked away along the edge of the chorus pit while glancing into its depths.

CHAPTER ELEVEN

OUTSIDE HUFF HALL a green and seemingly endless convoy of military vehicles caterpillared through campus. After a while Noel refused to follow its progress outside his dorm window and instead assessed his Mustang in the parking lot below. Though it had been somewhat rebuilt after the wreck, the car was in sad shape. It was bent and dirty and needed a paint job. Finally he turned away from the window and began to stare into the mirror and into the black discs of his eyes. Earlier, while stomaching a bowl of cornflakes in the cafeteria, he had asked some devout-looking students if they had heard anything about the fire. Turns out, they had. It had been started by devil worshipers, they breathlessly informed him. They knew this to be the case because of the satanic graffiti painted on the water tower in some kind of animal blood. Not only that, but one of the firefighters had spotted men garbed in dark red robes fleeing just ahead of him through the smoke.

The mirror tugged on him like a magnet, but he pulled himself free and crawled into the bottom bunk, taking some magazines with him. He found the one with Layle in it, but even that could not arouse him. He tried another, and another, then gave up and reached under the bunk for the baby aspirin. Real aspirin gave him heartburn. He fell asleep chewing the dry orange tablets, the plastic bottle still in his grip, the aura of girlie magazines spilled out around him.

He awoke a long time later to a window gray-lit with the watery light of either a dusk or a dawn, he could not decide which. Someone was pounding the door, yelling about a phone call. Noel lurched into the hallway and fumbled after the receiver. It was her, the strange but pretty teacher, reminding him that the nondenom meeting started in an hour. "Do you need a lift?" she wanted to know.

Glancing at the map on his palm, Noel told her he had a car. He stopped at Jay's door on his way to the bathroom, but nobody answered. The bathroom was six curtained shower stalls, four doorless johns, five urinals, six sinks. Hutch was bending over one of the far sinks, carefully shaving around his goatee. Noel brushed his teeth two sinks over, spat, and asked, "Hey, Hutch, that Pink Paradise place, did y'all really finger off some waitresses there?"

Hutch consulted his own reflection. He was wearing a black Rolling Stones T-shirt, the sleeves ripped off, and very tight faded bootcuts. His hair fell in brown ringlets over his forehead. In spite of the bad blood between them, Hutch still scored pot from Noel most every Monday. Smiling at himself, Hutch said, "Shit, that's just something we tell you rookies to get y'all to roadtrip to Bogtown and bring us back beer."

"Like that electric-fence bullshit, huh?"

"You know about that? Hell, we was gonna do you next, Mongo."

"I'd go easy on that Mongo shit if I were you, Hutch. How's that eye of yours doing?"

Hutch suddenly noticed a spot he had missed shaving.

Noel shook out his toothbrush and added, "Besides, Jay already done it to me. About shit my pants too."

"You two were down at the tower last night?"

"Nah, not last night, about a week ago."

Hutch leaned back to study Noel in the long mirror they shared. He asked if Noel had heard about the fire. About five hundred acres torched, he reported. That's probably a couple million bucks worth of timber.

Noel lathered his face and said, "Know what I heard about that? I heard devil worshipers done it, that they found a bunch of cut-off dog heads and shit like that out in the woods. Devil worshipers from New Orleans is what I heard."

"No shit." Hutch massaged his cheeks then sealed his razor up in a plastic bag and asked, "What kind of dog heads?"

"How the fuck do I know what kinda dog heads?" Noel nicked himself in the jawbone and cussed. Pressing a finger there, he asked, "Hey, speaking of devil worshipers, that where you saw the Stones at, New Orleans?"

"Superdome."

"They on?"

"Kick-ass, son."

"They do 'Sympathy for the Devil'?"

"I dunno, I was too drunk to remember. I threw up all the way back."

"How do you know they was kick-ass, then?"

"'Cause they're the Stones."

While leaving, Hutch slapped Noel on the back, which caused him to drop his razor into the sink.

Noel went back to his room to brush out his hair, which was down past his shoulders now. He unbuttoned his green polyester shirt to the chest of the white undershirt, then looped on his belt, crafted in eleventh-grade shop, the word SPIDER seared into brown leather. He pulled on his plastic boots and stood back from the mirror, massaging his thin goatee. He figured he was about as non-denominational as they came.

The walk would do him good, he decided, though two blocks later he was already regretting that choice. The evening sky was lightning-filled, more like heat lightning than any kind that would strike you dead. Noel hated all lightning. Lightning made him feel like his mind was being read, as if lightning could detect fear or guilt and hone in on it. The map on his palm led him about a mile from campus to a remote single-story house on a cul-de-sac. The house had grayish bricks and bluish shutters, the window and rain gutters strung with blinking red and green lights, the flat-roofed carport supporting two plastic reindeer, both of them Rudolph. A life-size manger scene had been assembled in the front yard, mostly silhouettes and shadows. Noel stood at the end of the driveway near the mailbox wondering what the hell he was doing here.

He was still considering turning back when a wave of rain herded him under the carport. The doorbell reverberated a quick five-note melody and then a man he instantly identified as Lily's husband opened the door and with a handshake pulled Noel inside into a bright kitchen that smelled of eggnog and raisins. "We got some fresh meat here," he yelled as he ushered Noel into the den, which contained an oblong circle of some dozen students sitting on folding chairs. A few faces he recognized from campus, but nobody he knew by name. Cecilia was there, wearing a tan jumpsuit, her legs crossed at the ankles, her hands clasped in her lap, her brown hair shiny and limp, its part perfectly centered.

Lily was seated to his right but at such an angle it was hard to spy on her for more than a moment, just long enough to glimpse a long ribbed black skirt, a grayish sweater, a string of pearls, and an empty wineglass she was rotating on her fingertips. Already he was making plans to take her picture. There was something about her eyes, a brightening green that reminded him of the McCurry photographs he admired so much in *National Geographic*. Except for a quick half smile, Lily did not acknowledge Noel.

Kevin, her husband, seemed to be in charge. Maybe it was the swept salt-and-pepper hair, or the black turtleneck, or the way he wanded his hands, but he put Noel in mind of a symphony conductor. Kevin had steely blue eyes above a pondering jaw. He looked to be a lot older than Lily, but, of the two, he was the more striking. Behind Kevin, an upright vacuum cleaner stood in front of the fireplace. Every inch of wall space had been converted into bookshelves. After Kevin had made everyone introduce themselves *for the benefit of those of us new to the nondenoms*, he winked at Noel and then started the meeting with a few general announcements. Everybody was welcomed here, all forms of practice encouraged. "We've got a little bit of everything, a regular Christian smorgasbord."

The only other guy there not wearing a tie had the shoulders and neck of an offensive lineman. He wore a blue sports coat and was clutching hands, almost belligerently, with an emaciated girl with short red hair who kept giving Noel cold glances. Noel's attention returned to Cecilia, or rather to her clothes. It was easy to imagine the jumpsuit she wore pinned to a wax-paper pattern. Suddenly she caught his eye and smiled brightly at him and mouthed the word *hi* just as Kevin began reading aloud the story of Ruth, often using caricatured voices for the characters. Afterward he encouraged the nondenoms to "roundhouse" the story. Noel remained mute, as did Lily, until about fifteen minutes into the discussion, when Kevin prompted, "What about you, Noel? Any deep thoughts?"

"No sir," he replied, sitting up straighter in his chair.

Kevin fixed him with a clouded look, as if he suspected Noel of harboring great insights, then he nodded toward his wife and asked, "I thought you said he was smart?"

"No, I said he was cute."

"Oh. That explains it, then."

Next Kevin started talking about Abraham and Isaac, who, evidently, the nondenoms had roundhoused the week before. Kevin said that somebody—somebody who would remain nameless—this certain nameless somebody, who had stayed deathly quiet throughout last week's discussion, had made some very interesting observations about our friend Abraham after the meeting had adjourned. Lily fired off an unmistakable go-to-hell look, which Kevin fielded with a graveyard whistle followed by a burningly innocent glance around the den. He said, "Let me summarize. The question before us, if you'll recall, was Abraham's attempt to sacrifice his son Isaac—"

"If there's one thing I detest," Lily objected, "it is being summarized. What I said—privately to you, dear—was that if God really told Abraham to stab his infant son to death, then God was one sick son-of-a-bitch."

The sound of the rain swelled outside as Kevin gleamed at the prospect of such controversy. He made a point of meeting each of the many imploring eyes, going around the circle sharing his countenance of feigned shock; after which he leaned forward and assumed the exact position as Lily, who, upon noticing this, straightened her spine, untouched her fingertips, then stood and left the room, only to return a minute later carrying a blue-tinted goblet filled with purple wine. Reluctantly, she stated, "I'm not saying anything profound here. Anybody who's ever held a baby in her arms should not have to be told this."

"So you don't believe it was God who told Abraham to kill his son? Anyone can jump in and answer these questions. There are no wrong answers."

Following an obligatory silence, Lily replied dryly, "Of course there are wrong answers. What you're supposed to say is there are no stupid questions. But there are stupid questions, believe me. Thousands of them. I could write a book of them. *The Book of a Thousand and One Stupid Questions.*"

The nondenoms were breathing as a group now, as one hugely attentive beast.

"Getting back to what you said earlier—"

"What I said earlier, in the sanctity of our marriage bed"—here Lily smiled at Cecilia—"was that the only way to approach that particular story as anything but ghastly is to assume Abraham to be deranged. Mentally ill. Hearing voices, seeing visions, probably a manic-depressive. And that this illness or demon or whatever you want to call it infected him to the point where he heard a very dark voice from nowhere but inside his own sick psyche—if I may use such a word here—command him to slaughter his baby. Which he promptly set about to do. Jack Nicholson would make a fine Abraham here. But then, at the least last second, not even God could endure this atrocity, and so She sent an angel of mercy to intervene."

"She?"

"Acting as protector of children? Of course She."

Kevin wanted them all to feel free to argue. He urged, "I think what Lil is saying is that there are stories, and then there are *interpretations* of stories."

"She said God was a woman," the offensive lineman objected.

"Yes, it appears she did say that."

Lily sipped her wine. After a moment she stated, "God can be either a man, a woman, a burning bush, or a serpent, or nothing at all, but I'm concerned with Abraham here."

"Abraham," Kevin concurred.

"Yes. Let's face it, every time that man hit his knees, it must have terrified his family and servants. Like the time, after another so-called vision, when he lined up all his servants and kinsmen, every male in his very large household, and went down the line one-two-three with a razor mutilating their genitals."

"Circumcising them."

"That's a nice scientific word. I doubt such a nice word would occur to any of you boys here if Kevin came back from the kitchen with a big steak knife and started lining you up against the wall."

"Interesting," Kevin said.

"Yes, psychotic behavior often is. Interesting."

"Are we finished now?"

"We are very close to being finished. One last item, though. Whenever Abraham's clan went traveling through another kingdom, Abraham had a funny little trick he liked to play. He'd tell the neighboring king that his wife Sara—who was exceedingly beautiful—was not his wife but his sister. The king would then confiscate Sara as a concubine, and in return the king would shower Abraham with gifts. Abraham does this twice, at least, or so the Bible tells us. The term *cowardly wife-pimper* does come to mind."

Kevin's grin remained intact, but there was a frozen quality to it. "Wow," he said. "Again, all very interesting. Hey, can anyone else think of a Bible story that might stand up to more than one interpretation?"

But no one could. The beast of nondenoms straightened the laps of its dresses, fingered the knots of its ties, quelled burps, or passed gas silently until finally Lily said, "Let's roundhouse Sodom."

"Sodom. I think perhaps Sodom might wait for another occasion, yes?"

"No. You started it. Now I want to roundhouse Sodom."

"Then proceed with caution. Sodom being very dangerous territory. A wicked city. With a very high unemployment rate. The people there practicing very little in the way of discretion."

"Sodom. To begin, if you'll recall, some angels of God come down to earth to have dinner with Lot—Abraham's best friend and kinsman. Two angels, Lot, the wife, the kiddies. Little dinner, little wine . . . but meanwhile outside, all is not well. The men of Sodom—evidently a high-strung crew—have surrounded Lot's house. Why? It's interesting, you'll agree. Turns out, the crowd wants Lot to send out his guests so that the angels of God can be sodomized. And what does Lot do? It's quite the dilemma, one with few precedents—"

"Timewise, I'm afraid we're going to have to leave Lot and the angels inside the house—"

"Surrounded by Sodomites. Shall we read that passage aloud, Kevin?"

"I think we shall not."

"A shame. And you read so beautifully. Oh well, no need, I can summarize. Our friend Lot, being a resourceful fellow, and having two virgin daughters—who in the end turn out to be equally resourceful—suddenly Lot hits on a solution. He decides that instead of sending out the angels, he'll send out his two virgin daughters to be gang-raped by the mob. Here, you can start to understand why Lot and Abraham are such close friends."

Thunder rattled the house. Kevin, his face pursed, inspected the ceiling a moment before conceding, "Well, certainly a great deal to think about there. Maybe too much for one night, eh? Especially on an empty stomach. Perhaps we could make more sense of Sodom over Christmas cookies!"

Beast that they were, the nondenoms cheered, applauded, and rubbed their bellies while Kevin returned from the kitchen dragging a card table loaded with quarts of soda, with stacks of Dixie cups, and with paper plates filled with tree- and snowman- and elf-shaped cookies.

*   *   *

"The snowmen are the best," Cecilia informed Noel. "I made them."

They were standing near the fireplace, the rest of the nonde-noms having scattered between the den and kitchen. Noel topped an extra snowman onto his plate, nibbled it, and told her it was real good. She nodded, as if that were an understatement, then she leaned closer to whisper that she hoped the group hadn't made a bad impression on him tonight. Usually their meetings weren't like this at all. She brushed a strand of brown hair from her mouth, studied it, then insisted, "Usually she won't say a word. She just sits there drinking too much."

"Who?"

"Who do you think?" She glared toward the carport. "They're out there having another argument right now." Cecilia lifted a snowman off Noel's plate, then she asked if he wanted to see something really scary. "We'll have to hurry, though." She took his wrist and led him down a hallway through a cluttered bed-room into yet another hallway, this one dead-ending into a closed door with a green handbag hanging from its knob. They stopped there long enough for Cecilia to confess that Stacy had found it first, but it had scared her so badly she hadn't said a word to any-one for almost a month. "Besides, I didn't believe her until I saw it for myself. We're the only ones who know—me, her, and now you."

Cecilia opened the door just wide enough to insert her thin arm inside and fan it against the wall until a light flicked on. A sickly sweet odor, akin to sawdust and marijuana, escaped from the room. "Hold your breath," she warned as they stepped inside. They stood in a small room painted off-white. Cecilia quickly directed his attention to the window opposite them, where a makeshift altar of some complexity had been assembled atop a round table covered by a red silk tapestry. Twelve small crystal bowls filled with water circled the table edge like the numbers of a clock. Behind the bowls, and appearing magnified through them, were a scattering of incense cones and an inner cycle of statuettes— elephant-headed men, flared cobras, insect-armed demons—and at the center of this conglomeration presided a three-foot-tall statue of a naked black woman dancing upon a corpse. Her long red tongue was stretched down past her collarbone. She wore a neck-lace of human skulls and a skirt of dismembered hands. Snakes crawled between her heavy breasts and between her six arms, one of which was holding forth, by the hair, a man's decapitated head. Covering the window behind this statue was another tapestry, this one black and red and containing a garish mandala of vampires copulating in every imaginable position.

Before Noel could even begin to digest all of this, Cecilia plucked him from the room and led him back into the den, where they fit themselves into a corner and soon Cecilia began to narrate, with a hushed voice and a very inconsistent sympathy, the saga of Kev and Lil and how two years ago their baby girl had died myste-riously one night in her crib.

"Nobody knows how exactly, except that she suffocated to death. That used to be the nursery, where we just were. Lil, I heard she used to be real sweet. Before. Ever since, she's been crazier and crazier. That's why they're firing her—did you know that?—her saying all that weird stuff, like she did tonight. Poor Kev, he takes care of her no matter what she does. Everybody tells him he should divorce her. Nobody would blame him if he did—I think he should—don't you?

For his own good. But he won't. He's a saint. Who else but a saint could sleep next to her every night and be as sweet as he is?"

"Who's that staring at us over there?" Noel asked.

Another girl, large-jowled and a bit desperate-eyed, was glowering at them across the den.

"Oh, that's Stacy. She's just mad at me for showing you the room."

"That statue back there . . . what do you figure that was?"

Jutting her eyebrows, Cecilia replied, "You heard about that forest fire, didn't you? Everybody's saying the police found all sorts of satanic stuff in the woods, things like bloody robes and those real long curvy knives." She leaned in closer to Noel until their foreheads were almost touching. Then, using a voice hardly even a whisper, she asked, "Noel, what does *sodomize* mean?"

After cookies they sang hymns. Everybody sang except Noel, who moved his lips, and Lily, who guarded the kitchen doorway sipping coffee. The first few hymns were standards, but then they sang a few hymns Noel had never heard before. In one of these, while the boys sang *we're so happy we found Jesus*, the girls latched their thumbs under their chins, framing their faces with their hands, and piped *happy!-happy!-happy!* Halfway through this hymn, Cecilia's head dropped straight back. Her folding chair tottered and then out of her small mouth gurgled an obscene-sounding stream of O's and B's. Her shoulders began to bob and weave, her head to wobble. Her eyes spun white. The rest of the nondenoms began singing faster, as if purposely fueling the spell. The hymn took Stacy next. Sitting two down from Cecilia, she suffered a similar spasm that rendered her on her back on the carpet. Then the redheaded girl crashed to her knees and tilted the O of her mouth upward in a wolfish yowl. The hymn circled once more then veered in on the football player, who suddenly drooped forward, boneless, and his acoustic groans joined the ranks of girls baying and gurgling as the hymn continued its rounds, taking this student, sparing another.

• • •

Later, Lily carpooled them home through the storm in a station wagon with fake wood paneling. Noel was crammed in the first back seat next to Cecilia, who was chatting away. When she asked if Noel was coming back next week, he reminded her that next week was Christmas break. Maybe next semester, he hinted. This lie made her happy out of all proportion. In fact, everything he said seemed to increase her opinion of him. All in all, just as with Lily at the amphitheater, Cecilia seemed a trifle too attentive, too charmed, and Noel found himself wondering if it was all part of some larger scheme to save his soul. Still, he did take the opportunity to ask her out to a movie next semester. She said that would be fun. Using a black flair pen, she wrote her phone number on his left palm, the one without the map on it.

As the rain got harder, Lily kept leaning in closer to the windshield. Nobody had spoken to her at all. First she dropped off the girls, who ran shrieking into the rain; next she stopped at Myerson Hall, where the other three guys lived. At this point she invited Noel into the front seat. They were halfway to Huff when the storm got so bad she had to pull over. They parked near the stadium, Lily pointing to the roof and shrugging. She turned off the key, bit her bottom lip. "Well," she said, turning her face to Noel. "Tell me all about tonight. What did you think of our little half-time show?"

Noel whistled and said, "I've heard about that stuff, but I'd never seen it before tonight. I got cousins who do that."

Lily performed a quick spastic mime and banged her elbow on the steering wheel. "Ow!" she complained. While nursing her elbow, she resolved they might as well get comfortable. Saying this, she reached under the seat and inclined it backward.

"Does that happen every week?" he wanted to know.

"Like clockwork. The little sluts. They're faking, of course. But God knows it'll be good practice for them."

"Faking?"

"Of course faking. And it was for your benefit, at least partially. Tonight's the only night Cecilia's ever been the first to go belly-up. Usually it starts with fat Stacy. You should have seen Stacy's expression when Cecilia stole her thunder."

Noel whistled again and said that he'd never seen anything like it.

"Really? Not anything? Are you sure? Or are you just being a gentleman?"

A sound like an airplane passing overhead made it impossible to speak. When the sound had faded and the station wagon had quit trembling, Noel said, "That was a funnel cloud."

"Yes," Lily said. "Really, though—you've never heard anything like that before? Nothing?"

Noel shook his head.

"I guess I'll have to give you a hint, then. Do you like hints, Noel? Because this is quite a good one."

"What kinda hint?"

"The very blatant kind, I'm afraid," she told him. And she hated it—absolutely hated it—that she had to give this hint so quickly, but, on the other hand, she didn't know how much longer she could sustain the storm.

She took Noel's left hand and opened the fist.

"What's this? Oh my gosh, it's Cecilia's phone number, isn't it? Noel, you cad. How could you?"

She spit into his palm and began smearing the number with her thumb. Then, staring at him with those sad and aloof eyes, she lowered his hand onto his lap, pushing it against Noel's initial resistance, and began to scrub the number off against the bulge in his jeans. At first Noel felt acutely embarrassed, as if he should not be getting aroused by his own hand, but soon he began to feel less embarrassed. Finally Lily picked up his hand again, inspected it, then she lowered the hand into her own lap and began to massage the tops of his fingers and to push their coupled hands down between her thighs. Soon Noel could feel a texture beneath the skirt, then a wetness, then an emptiness his fingers began to groove in and out of. As he did this, Lily slid lower into the seat and began to pull up her long black skirt until Noel's hand had found its way beneath her panties. Soon she began to make a short thrusting noise, the same noise she'd made bumping her elbow. The thrusting noise became a gasp, then a series of gasps, and two of her fingers slipped in between Noel's fingers and then her mouth remained opened and she began to pant *ha ha ha ha*, like a sneeze that would never arrive, and she turned her head toward Noel and stared with those awful green eyes into his brown eyes and inside her eyes Noel saw nothing but sadness green and bottomless and by the time her breath had begun to slow, Noel had fallen in love again.

She lifted his hand to her mouth and kissed the palm before returning it to his lap. She left her hand there a minute as if to steady herself and then she leaned over and undid his belt and asked if he was ready for the next hint. . . . Soon her mouth had found him and almost instantly Noel began to cum. He kept cumming and cumming it seemed like for years or maybe lifetimes, and finally it blinded him or rather he must have shut his eyes, and he left them closed a long time—for hours, it seemed—until he heard her say, "Ecclesiastes."

He opened his eyes one at a time, very slowly. The rain had lightened, as if on command, and now the stadium began to emerge around them.

"That's what I thought of while you were cumming. And cumming, and cumming. All the rivers run into the sea, yet the sea is not full. Isn't it odd that I thought of that? And what were you thinking, Noel, while you were cumming, and cumming, and cumming?"

"Nothing," he replied after a moment and then began to pull up his jeans.

Watching him do this, Lily sighed and said, almost in singsong, "Gloss-oh-*lalia*."

Noel hesitated. The word sounded familiar, but he couldn't place it. He suspected it might be French for eating pussy, and he wondered if she wanted him to do that now.

"Do you know what that means, Noel?"

"Sure," he said.

"It's one of the many things women do better than men."

"It is?"

"Very much so. By the way, were you by any chance pretending that I was Cecilia just then?"

He said no. She asked if he was sure, and he said yeah.

"Well, I was," she admitted.

"Was what?"

"Pretending. That I was Cecilia. That I was the little hot-to-trot virgin about to suck my first hard cock. And that I'd go straight to hell for sucking it, but I didn't care, I was going to suck it anyway. It made it all quite spectacular. You can't beat hellfire for an aphrodisiac."

"You were pretending you were Cecilia?"

"What? Did you think I was going to pretend you were Cecilia? Cecilia with a big wet hard-on? Oops. Sorry. I've shocked you. Have I shocked you? Oh, Noel, how I long to shock you."

He refastened his belt and considered a boycott of the conversation.

"Well, now at least you've seen the real McCoy. Not that I really blame them for faking. Faking is how we girls learn. Especially when it comes to orgasms."

He crossed his arms, cupping an elbow in each hand, then gazed up through the windshield's blue tint and was about to make some comment about the rain slowing when she asked, "Does it bother you when I say *orgasm*?"

"It's slowing down some," he noticed.

"Orgasm. Orgasm, orgasm, orgasm."

"You know what they reminded me of tonight, falling off them chairs and all?"

"Orgasm, orgasm, orgasm."

"It was like they was possessed or something."

"That's a very astute observation, Noel—orgasm, orgasm, orgasm—because, in case you haven't noticed it, we women—orgasm, orgasm, orgasm—tend to spend the better part of our lives getting possessed. In one form or another. In orgasm. Orgasm, orgasm. In marriage. In pregnancy. My God, have you ever watched a woman give birth? Talk about possessed!" Then in a much more soothing tone she added, "Or mourning, for that matter. Out-loud mourning. Wailing. That's another type of possession. Again, for the gals only. Men never wail. That would never do. Have you been eating pineapple, Noel?"

"Pineapple?" He shook his head.

"Hmmm . . . I thought I tasted something pineapply." Lily made a series of smacking noises. "By the way, did I hear you ask Cecilia out to a movie?"

He nodded, then shrugged.

"Tell me what it is you most want to do to her, Noel. If you could have your way with her? In your wildest dreams, what would you have sweet young virgin Cecilia doing?"

Bluntly, and almost in self-defense, he replied, "I'd take her picture naked."

"You would?"

"Yeah."

"Oh my gosh. Can I help?"

"I don't think she'd be real big on the idea. She don't seem the type."

"You know the type? You've done this before?"

He shrugged again, this time with only his left shoulder.

"Well, I wouldn't jump to any conclusions. I mean, she might be the type. After all, she likes to parade herself in a spangled bodysuit in front of a grandstand full of drunk rednecks. And what you saw tonight, that was pure exhibitionism."

"Exhibitionism?"

"One girl speaking in tongues is all it takes. Other girls get competitive. Women are fiercely competitive, you know that, Noel, correct? Then maybe some guy wants to impress the gals. Toby, our jock, went belly-up tonight—that was a first. Probably he noticed the girls zeroing in on you. Anyway, one by one, they fall. Next thing you know, you've got a full-blown glossolalia orgy in your den."

"Has that ever happened?"

"You look confused, Noel."

He covered his eyes and muttered, "I think I need some sleep."

"Christmas cookies! That's what I tasted, not pineapple. Cecilia's Christmas cookies! I'll have to give her my compliments. She's quite the little baker."

Again Noel did not respond.

"Is this your first time committing adultery?" she asked him.

"I didn't commit nothing."

"Bullshit, Noel. Less than an hour after leaving a man's home

you swapped orgasms with his wife—orgasm, orgasm, orgasm—
and it's nothing to be proud of."

"Who said I was proud?"

"You looked a little proud. He's good in bed, you know? My
husband is. That's why I married him. He was good in bed, and I
was sweet seventeen. I was Cecilia. He was thirty."

"You were only seventeen?"

"He's also a good person. A bit too good at times. And you may
very well wonder why it is I'm telling you all this, Noel. And the
reason is—are you ready?—it's because I want you to understand
where my loyalty lies. And it's not anywhere in this car, Noel. Do
you understand that?"

He sensed that a nod was required and so he nodded and said,
"You told me if I showed up tonight I'd find out what you were,
what religion."

"And did you?"

He considered the black statue, the copulating vampires. . . .

"Something weird, I bet."

"Then you'll just have to come back next time to find out."

"Come back? And be in the same room with your husband and
them singing about Jesus?"

"Oh, don't worry, Kevin won't notice. He'll be too busy trying
to impress Cecilia, to get her all hot and bothered."

"They . . .?"

"No. And they never will. Nevertheless, she's got it running
down her legs. Speaking of which." She flicked on the overhead
light and pulled taut the lap of her black skirt, exposing a dark wet
oval there. "Look at what you did to me, Noel. I'll have to stand
out in the rain to destroy the evidence. One wonders what you'll be
doing after you get home."

She turned off the light, then started the station wagon and pulled out of the lot. "*Huff Hall!*" she announced a few blocks later. "Last stop! Everybody out! Hurry up, I'm already in enough trouble. Cecilia wasn't the only one performing for you tonight. I was trying to impress you with my brilliance. Were you impressed?"

Noel lunged over to kiss her, but she pushed him away and said, "Uh-uh, not here, sport. A time and a place for everything. *Ecclesiastes*, remember?" She pointed at the dorm and ordered, "Go on! Out! Now. There will be other opportunities, I promise." Then she caught the back of his arm and pinched it hard. "And don't you dare be thinking about Cecilia while you're up there in the dark tonight. You think about me. Think about me standing in the driveway holding my skirt up to the rain."

CHAPTER TWELVE

REVIVAL TENTS AND WANDERLUST EVANGELISTS began to
invade Poplarville along with a persistent rumor that Billy Graham
himself might soon jet into town to help cleanse the air of the
satanic cults known to have hailed from New Orleans if not
California. Noel had taken some pictures of the water tower being
repainted, and the next day one of these photographs made the
front page of the *Hattiesburg American*. On that same day the
Channel 7 News Team confirmed that signs of demonic ceremony
had been uncovered at the arson site. In complying with federal
investigators, however, the reporters could disclose no further
details. This, of course, rekindled speculation to the point where
many students fled home early for Christmas break. One girl left
without informing anyone, and for a day it was assumed she had
been kidnapped and perhaps cast in a blue movie. The last home
game at PRC's Wildcat Stadium, sparsely attended, held an uneasy
moment of silence prior to kickoff, then the marching band blared
its horns and the Dixie Darlings broke formation and scattered off
the field tasseling their fingers in the air.

"It was all a bad joke," Noel pleaded to Jay. "I was just trying to get even with you for that electric-fence crap. How was I supposed to know the woods were on fire? Hell, you're the damn Indian, aren't y'all suppose to know about putting out campfires and shit? And it was your LSD and it was your idea to go tramping off through the woods and climb the damn tower. Look, I'm sorry, alright? Are you listening, Jay? Did you just hear me say I'm sorry?"

On the last day of finals, Lily called to say she had the run of the house if Noel cared to venture over. He did and they spent the better part of the afternoon on couch and carpet. Even though Lily would not allow Noel to actually fuck her, he left campus for Hattiesburg the next morning feeling not quite the virgin. On his drive home he stopped and bought a six-pack of beer, which he then placed in the holiday-crowded refrigerator. He was a college student now. That changed things. By late afternoon the beer had been removed. Noel marched to the street and began foraging through the trash barrels. While he was doing this, Ben came outside. Ben these days left an impression mostly of Adam's apple, braces, freckles, ears, and neck. At sundown every night he had to attach an elaborate headgear that prevented his jaw from growing forward in the night. His curly hair had grown longer and brightened to a flame red, all of which made him easy to spot in the church choir.

Noel pried open one of the beer bottles with a lighter and offered the beer to Ben, who only glanced at the house and took a step backward. Using a voice too froglike for his soft features, he warned, "Dad's gonna look out and see you, Noel. You're just asking for trouble. Sometimes I think you like getting in trouble. What you got against Dad anyway?"

It was a fair question, but one that Noel could never explain truthfully, not even to Ben. Noel hated his stepfather for a hundred small humiliations and indictments, but, ironically, it was that one morning of kindness—a gentle hand placed across his mouth—that he would never be able to forgive. His greatest secret had been revealed, and from that morning forward it had been unbearable for him to be in the same house with Roger.

Noel just shook his head and with a quizzical faraway look in his eyes told Ben, "Wait here." He went inside and returned carrying a wooden rack that contained six vials of maple syrup that Roger had mail-ordered from Vermont. Each vial was a different color grade. One by one Noel dropped the vials into the garbage. He tossed in the rack then walked over and leaned against the basketball goal Roger had built for them a decade earlier. The goal had a plywood backboard and stood eleven feet high, one foot above regulation. This was yet another reason to despise Roger. Because of that goal, both Noel and Matt owned moon shots that sometimes would pop the net of regulation goals but more often than not would clang off the rim out of bounds.

Noel asked if Ben wanted to play some one-on-one. "Hell, you're almost tall as me now. We'll play to ten by ones, and I'll spot you five for five bucks."

Ben agreed to play but not for money. He could barely dribble and whenever he found himself trapped, he inevitably flailed the ball up into the air backward toward the goal. Noel won 10–5, and after the game they both lay down under the net and stared up through its blue circle, the tops of their head almost touching. Noel, beer bottle resting on his belly, began to tell Ben about college life. Noel had always enjoyed talking to Ben. Ben was never judgmental and always interested. Now Noel told him about Huff and all the drinking and smoking that went on there and about the LSD vision quest.

"Do you know what you want to be yet?" he broke off to ask.

"A veterinarian."

"Still! And spend your whole life sticking pills up dog butts?"

Ben laughed, like he always did at Noel's jokes. His laugh was musical, not at all like Noel's or Matt's. Matt was hardly home at all these days. He was always off on a date, a practice, a workout session. He still drank and got stoned, but not with Noel. He seemed to be avoiding Noel.

Ben wanted to know what being on LSD was like, and Noel was all too happy to oblige. Then he told Ben that he was fucking one of the teachers at school. Practically right under her husband's nose.

"Hey, that reminds me, how far you gotten with Tracy now?" Noel asked. Tracy was Ben's steady. She had brown scour-pot hair and wore braces. "You eating her pussy yet, Ben?"

Ben shook his head and blushed and grinned and asked, "You ever really done that, Noel?"

Noel sat up. He traded his empty beer for the brown weather-stripped basketball. "Sheet," he said and squeezed the ball between his palms. "Is the Pope Catholic? Does a bear shit in the woods?" From that sitting position he leaned back and took a shot and swooshed the net. The ball just missed hitting Ben on the head, then bounced back to Noel, who squeezed it again and began to reiterate how much he liked eating pussy. How, if he could, he'd eat nothing but pussy for breakfast, lunch, and dinner. Then he asked, "You at least getting any stinky pinky, Ben?"

Ben went through his retinue of grins, shrugs, and blushes before he admitted that yeah, he had. He was still lying flat on his back, but he had scooted over so that the ball would not hit him if Noel shot again.

"You made her cum yet?"

"Cum?" He chaffed at his bottom lip. "How's that work exactly, with them?"

"They don't cum like we do," Noel explained. "We cum on the outside, they cum on the inside. Besides, they don't really cum, they cream."

"They cream?"

"Yeah."

Ben widened his eyes and held a deep breath. After a moment he asked, "And they can only get pregnant when they're cumming, right?"

"I never heard that," Noel replied. "Who told you that?"

"Some guys at school. They said girls can only get pregnant when they cum, and they have to be cumming right when the guy is."

"So if she don't cum then you don't even have to use a rubber or anything?"

"I guess."

Noel considered that. He reached for another beer from the line of bottles he had extracted from the trash barrel.

"How many of them you gonna drink, Noel?"

"How many?" Noel wedged the bottle between his legs and leaned back and shot the ball again. This time it clanged off the rim and bounced into the street. "Many as it takes," he said.

* * *

Noel spent most of his vacation inside the darkroom developing a semester's worth of bad photographs. Or at least they seemed bad to him. Worse than bad, boring. But instead of tossing the prints away, which had been his first impulse, he began to experiment with them. It started when he placed a finished print, the one of Jay holding the dead owl, facedown onto a sheet of emulsion paper. Then, by anchoring the sheets with a pane of glass and letting them simmer under a thirty-watt bulb, he created a print of the negative image. Next he tried using the enlarger instead of the light bulb.

This worked even better. Soon he was experimenting with hotter temperatures in the baths, the result being a graininess speckled with pockmarks and spidery cracks that made Jay look like some long-dead Civil War soldier.

Throughout Christmas Eve day, Noel stayed in the darkroom, smoking dope and guzzling beer from aluminum cans that reflected the small red safe light. He did not come downstairs until called to supper, which started at five sharp minus Matt, who arrived unapologetically ten minutes late, causing Roger to backtrack grace over the carved turkey. Noel, both times, refused to bow his head during grace. He finished eating, took his plate to the sink, and without asking to be excused went outside and sat on the woodpile, where he had stashed a case of beer. Into a cold night, near-freezing out, Noel sat in his white dress shirt dipping Skoal and drinking beer and spying inside his own house.

Later his mother joined him outside. She draped one of Matt's letter jackets over his shoulders. "Man-o-man," she whispered, "you must be half froze." Noel was sitting high up on the woodpile, and she was leaning into him, trying to stay warm. Five minutes passed before she mentioned that there was a Billy Graham special about to start, and didn't Noel think it'd be a nice gesture, all things considered, if the family watched it together, "like we used to when y'all were kids?"

"But I'm agnostic."

"Yes, Noel, we're all quite aware you're agnostic. Maybe you could get that printed on a T-shirt and save yourself the trouble of announcing it every ten minutes. By the way, are you drunk?"

"I had a few."

"It's Christmas Eve, Noel."

"Not for me it isn't. It's just Friday night."

She sighed then wondered out loud what it would be like to

have a houseful of girls. This was her standard whimsical remark whenever exasperated by Noel or Matt. Noel's standard response was to put his arm around her and assure her it wasn't nearly as interesting. He did this now.

"I could do without the interesting," she told him. "You've supplied enough interesting for two lifetimes."

They went into the den together and joined Ben, Roger, and Matt in front of *A Christmas Eve Celebration* broadcast live from Dodger Stadium. Noel hated the Dodgers almost as much as he hated Billy Graham, who was now rehashing the nativity. Flashbulbs strobed the stadium each time he raised his large liver-spotted hands or extended them eagle-armed. Noel could not decide what he hated most, that sweep of hair or that lantern jaw or those quarterback hands. His hate was by no means confined to Billy Graham but spun outward upon Billy's followers with their eagerness to applaud and pray on cue, their steepled hands and trembling lips, their gullibility and suspected Dodger loyalty. Roger, his legs crossed womanishly, leaned forward and shut his eyes whenever Billy inaugurated a new prayer. After a while Noel winked at Matt and began to imitate Roger. This started Matt laughing. Roger opened his eyes. Noel quickly straightened his face and returned his attention to the TV, where Billy had settled into some serious lambasting of Bethlehem for its inhospitality. He further noted that, during the darkest hours of our history, the blight and sway of evil resides not only in the inner cities but in the smallest of towns. "Tiny Bethlehem," he emphasized. "Tiny little Bethlehem."

Tiny Bethlehem, Noel mouthed, when suddenly he heard, or thought he heard, the word *Poplarville.*

"Yes, that's right," Billy said, as if speaking directly to Noel. "Poplarville, Mississippi. Population two thousand. Where just last week the local authorities reported a series of arsons they attribute

RIDES OF THE MIDWAY

to devil worshipers, some of them suspected to be high school students." Billy paused to allow a shudder to pass through the stadium. "Thousands of acres of national forest put to flame in demonic ceremonies. Afterwards the police found the woods littered with occult images—satanic symbols carved into tree trunks the same way teenage boys used to carve in the name of their best gal. No longer. Now, instead of prom dates and ice-cream sodas, we have Kiss concerts and cattle mutilations. We have hardworking farmers finding livestock with their throats slit and their bodies drained of blood. This is not New York City I'm talking about, people! No, not Transylvania! This is Poplarville, Mississippi, Hometown USA!"

The red ignition behind Roger's eyes put Noel in mind of bad flashbulb photos. The rest of the family was staring at Noel, but that was different, they were just curious and hoping Noel might be able to elaborate on what Billy was now calling *the Poplarville Horror,* but Roger's red eyes—those same X-ray eyes he used to scour luggage at the airport—they peered directly into Noel's soul and knew that he *was* the Poplarville Horror.

Noel stood casually and walked toward the back porch but then stopped at the door he had just opened and turned to face Roger. Right then on the street in front of the house a car hit its brakes. A long screech tailed into silence. Noel smiled and unlocked his eyes from Roger's and called out, "Hey, Ben, you want a cold one?"

It was as if the La-Z-Boy contained an ejector seat. Roger, fists bunched low, eyes narrow and evangelical—like hell's own Billy Graham—flung himself at Noel. Sometimes you see it coming. This time Noel did, a slow-motion tomahawk, a punch he could easily have sidestepped. But he didn't. He stood there, smirking. If anything, he might have leaned into the punch. It exploded on his nose and down he went, collapsing through the open door and onto the porch, where he ended up balanced on his side, the warm blood filling the bowl of his hands. From that blurred vantage point he watched his mother step forward and gunshot-slap Roger from behind, half on the jaw, half on the neck. She was screaming, "YOU DO NOT—REPEAT, DO NOT—HIT MY CHILDREN IN THIS HOUSE, DO YOU UNDERSTAND ME? DO YOU?"

Matt was yelling too, and Ben was pulling Matt away from Roger, and Alise had picked up the phone as if to hit Roger with the receiver and everyone was screaming except Noel, who was testing his vision and trying to figure out how everything had lost coherence. The house was like a film running backward. Finally he sat up and lowered his cupped hands into his lap and tried to steady himself by staring into the blood, but the blood appeared to be rising from his hands back into his body, as if replenishing him. Alise, still wielding the phone, was threatening to call the police, and Roger was daring her to, and Ben was pushing Roger away from Matt, who was grinning and taunting Roger.

Nobody even noticed when Noel stood and walked upstairs to the bathroom. His nose had swollen out impressively, and a giant butterfly stain had spread its red wings across the white dress shirt. He lifted the shirt and saw that the red butterfly had soaked through to the T-shirt beneath. Gently he began pinching his way up the bridge of his nose until he found the bright diamond of pain where the nose was broken. He counted to three then pinched as hard as he could. When he emerged from the white flashes of pain, he found himself on his knees hooked to the sink by his elbows.

He took a hand mirror with a white plastic frame into his bedroom and sat on the bed and continued his examination. He was still staring into the mirror when blue lights began to wash against his face. Even then he did not lower the mirror. He just sat and waited, staring at his blue-strobed reflection. Finally it was here, the inevitable arrest that had broken down the doors of so many of his dreams. It took about fifteen minutes before he heard the slow heavy footfalls on the stairs. Two curt knocks were followed by a deep dry voice booming out, "Pleethe. Open up."

Noel opened the door to a stout black officer with a perfectly round face. His hat was crammed under his right arm, his nose was flat, his hairline low over the forehead. A Polaroid box camera was hung around his neck. Noel extended his hands forward, joined, as if already cuffed. The officer glanced up from Noel's shirt and asked if he needed to go to the hospital. The cop had a lisp, which, oddly, was not effeminate. Noel hesitated then shook his head no.

"Lookth pretty bad—you pothitive?"

"It don't even hurt."

"You intend to preth chargeth?"

"Me?"

"You're the one got athaulted."

The cop asked if his father had a history of such behavior. Noel shook his head and shucked his shoulders, the two gestures seeming to cancel each other out. "That a yeth or a no?" the cops asked. Then he raised the camera and took a Polaroid of Noel.

"He's not my father, he's my stepfather."

"Turn thideway, pleath." The cop took Noel by the shoulders and gently rotated him, then snapped a second Polaroid. While watching the prints develop, he urged, "If you preth chargeth, we can lock him up for the night. Then, if you want, tomorrow you can reconthider. That way y'all might thleep better tonight. He ever hit your mama?"

"He hit her?"

"No, calm down, but hath he ever?"

"I'da killed him already if he had."

The cop was squinting at the Polaroids so intently that it appeared the developing process was of telepathic origin. The flash cube had not provided enough backlight. Noel stared forlornly into the camera, his eyes voids, his hair appearing wet it was so straight and shiny black. His pale skin and black-blood goatee and crimson shirt all lending the illusion he had been executed.

Noel and the cop spoke at the same moment. Noel saying, "I look like I'm already dead." The cop saying, "It's like magic."

Noel sniffed in blood, then asked, "You're really not gonna arrest me?"

"No law againth being coldcocked I know of."

"I think you better arrest me anyway. You don't, I'm liable to go down there and kill that son-of-a-bitch tonight."

"But you ain't done nothing wrong. Bethide," he added, "you ain't no killer."

"Maybe I am."

The cop blew on the Polaroids, then told Noel, "I know killers, I've arrethted them. You ain't no killer, you juth a puthycat. Now, that fella down there, your old man, he hath that look, like he juth might kill thombody." He slipped the Polaroids into his shirt pocket. "Hereth what I'm gonna do, I'm gonna lock him up for the night. I theen too many of theth thithuations ethculate." He pointed a finger at Noel's heart. "Remember, though, tomorrowth Chrithmith."

"Yeah. That's what my name means. *Noel.* It means merry Christmas, in French."

"Well then, merry Chrithmith, Noel."

"Yeah. Merry Christmas."

*   *   *

Early Christmas morning Noel watched from his toy-box perch as his mother returned from the police station with Roger in tow. Noel, still holding the hand mirror, fogged its surface by saying the word *Poplarville*. "Not Transylvania. Poplarville." Roger remained in the passenger's seat until Alise went around and opened his door. "You juth a puthycat," Noel told the mirror.

An hour later he was summoned downstairs to open presents. He had not washed his face or changed his shirt. The purple lines cupping his eyes had thickened overnight. Matt took one look at him and busted out laughing. The tree was unlit and akilter. Ben handed Noel a teacup of eggnog, which made Matt laugh again. Roger kept his back turned to the tree and was harassing the yule logs with an iron poker, a handy enough murder weapon, Noel noted.

Usually Roger led the family in prayer before allowing them to open presents, but today all prayer was forsaken. Noel sat away from the tree in a stiff-ribbed rocker and watched with haggard, raccoon eyes as Alise carefully untaped and spread open the gifts for both him and Roger, as if they were invalids. Neither of them in any way acknowledged their presents. The last gift she opened for Noel was a two-hundred-millimeter Nikon telephoto lens. Noel stopped rocking but then forced himself to start again. The tag claimed that the lens was a present from Roger. Noel glared at his mother, who, he knew, had switched tags in the night so that Roger's present would be the one Noel had begged for. Roger continued feeding wrapping paper and bows into the flames, which changed colors and sent out sparks red green yellow blue.

After all the presents had been opened, Noel left the telephoto lens untouched under the tree and went back upstairs and packed two duffel bags with clothes and two laundry hampers with darkroom equipment. He loaded all this into the Mustang, then stood a long time in the den doorway watching his brothers watch some college all-star football game on TV. He remembered, or seemed to, a whole childhood of Christmas trees, year by year, propped in that same corner, all of them leading up to this last sorry tree, which might fall forward at any moment and collapse upon the new Nikon lens beneath it. Noel untugged himself from the telephoto lens, then from his brothers, then from the house itself, closing the door on his family and leaving his brothers to the Blue-Gray Game.

An hour of aimless driving and he stopped at Tim's on the theory Tim was Jewish and might be hanging around bored. Tim's apartment was on the second of five floors, a communal balcony overlooking an almost empty parking lot. When the door opened, Tim was naked except for a green towel around his waist. He appraised Noel's bloody shirt and concluded, "Coffee."

The giant TV was dwarfed by the stereo speakers enclosing it. Tim came back from the kitchenette with two mugs of coffee. He had apparently started lifting weights. And there was a cosmetic tightness to his features now, especially his eyes, which appeared too large for his face. Tim sat on the white couch across from Noel and took a sip of coffee, then ran his fingers through his long wet hair and said, "Weatherspoon, I'm afraid to ask."

Noel was halfway through his Christmas saga when Tim made the time-out hand signal. "Continue," he said as he returned from the bedroom holding a penny-size vial filled with dark brown glue. While Noel finished his story, Tim took out a sewing needle and scrape-painted six short slash marks of the brown goop onto a sheet of torn aluminum foil. Then he took a white pen and using his teeth he withdrew the catheter of ink from inside it. He picked up a black lighter buried among a week's worth of fast-food garbage on the coffee table, all of this shored up against the blue ceramic bong, and he held the flame on its lowest setting under the tinfoil until the first slash mark started to bubble, then he sucked its brown tail of smoke up through the hollow pen into his lungs and held his breath studiously in the way Noel had taught him so many years ago.

"Hash oil," he said after exhaling. "It's what they smoke in California now."

Noel smoked three of the remaining slash marks then forgot about his nose and his problems and stared into the blank TV until Tim got up and turned on some parade. Later they drove to Burger King, the only place open. When they returned to Tim's apartment, three other guys were waiting in the parking lot. A steady stream of customers began to arrive, all of them scoring pot with Christmas money. Noel sat there wearing a paper Burger King crown and smoking bongs and watching *It's a Wonderful Life*. Eventually a girl came over—she looked about fifteen—and Tim kicked everybody out.

Christmas Day afternoon, the sky polished gray, the sun a white circle. Noel, alone in his car, held a Burger King sack filled with six bags of pot, ten quaaludes, and five vials of hash oil. He had only ten bucks left in his pocket. The banks were closed and the dorm would not open for another week. He started driving the empty highways until he passed a green exit sign for Laurel and decided to give Jay a call and wish him Merry Christmas. He found a pay phone but had to crawl around the floorboard searching for a dime. Finally he found one, sooty and heads up, in the ashtray. Jay's mother answered the phone and said the boys were across the street playing touch football. At least she hoped it was touch. She gave Noel directions.

Even though he had changed shirts and washed his face, the game came to a halt as Noel walked up. Jay jogged over and placed his hand on Noel's shoulder, as if to claim him, and of course everyone wanted to know what had happened to him. Noel grinned and sat to the grass while both teams, including Jay's two younger brothers, huddled around Noel like he was the new quarterback. His version of events was still in the developmental stages, and he spoke with long pauses, all the while trying to make it sound funny and who-gives-a-damn.

For the next week he slept on a mattress on Jay's floor. The Underwoods' home was modest. The swimming pool, the size of a large trampoline, had been drum-skinned with a black tarp. Jay's mother did not look like a former Miss Mississippi except for the scope of her smile. She was a tall woman with the skin and spidery eyes of someone who has spent too much time in the sun. She insisted Noel call her Babs. Every afternoon the boys played touch football in the vacant lot across the street. The games lasted until dark, the players ranging in age from eight to fifty. Noel and Jay always had to be on opposite teams because they were the two best. Noel never wanted those games to end. The weather stayed blue and crisp. Then, on the last day of vacation, it snowed three inches, and the town lost its mind. Kids were sledding on torn boxes, building muddy snowmen, and pummeling cars with ice balls. Jay's youngest brother fell off a makeshift sled and broke his leg, and it was Noel who had to carry him the three blocks home. By early afternoon the snow was all used up.

CHAPTER THIRTEEN

NOT MUCH HAD SURVIVED of the crop circles, only a large oval erasure where the cornfield had been mulched over by a yellow Caterpillar harvester. The latest rumors held that the brown stalks had been matted down and woven into rattan passages that snaked deep into the brittle corn. Seen from above, these paths had formed a series of tentacles, each terminating in its own perfect circle and each radiating out from the one large central vortex, which was, like the smaller capsules, filled with an intricate system of hieroglyphics. All this was hearsay, as the crop circles, born overnight on Christmas Eve in the agriculture-school farm, had been destroyed by the time the students returned to campus. The yellow combine harvester remained parked inside this womblike absentness, as if a symbol of godliness and defiance, guarding the school against the encroaching UFOs and the vampiric butchers of cattle and the blue-movie mongrels from Hollywood.

Enrollment at PRC had been truncated. Countless evangelists still roamed the sidewalks. A house on Pine Street rumored to be haunted was now rumored to have been exorcised. Local dogs had started to disappear, and a strangely delicate and arabesque graffiti had begun gracing the sides of buildings and bridges, its message indecipherable though suspect.

"I will transform you into a cocksman," Lily promised Noel over the phone. "You will obliterate women."

Their affair was proceeding under certain impositions, the most controversial of which was Lily's rule prohibiting intercourse. Neither were they allowed to use the bedroom; instead, they made use of the blue sofa in the living room or the plush off-white carpet in the den. They met Tuesdays and Thursdays. Lily would set a portable round-faced cooking alarm. She also enjoyed startling Noel by asking, *What was that?* or *Did you just hear something?* But, as she later explained, there was little risk. Kevin had never cut a class short in his life. Add the fifteen-minute stroll to campus, which he did for exercise, then figure in office hours, et cetera, and the risk *was negligible.*

Over Christmas break the judiciary board had voted nine to one against Lily's appeal, and now she was unemployed and planning to enroll at USM to start a second Ph.D., this one in comparative religion. In the meantime she had no students save Noel, and this isolation had softened her disposition a little. There was still something totalitarian about Lily. In spite of her acerbic charm, she was not altogether likable. But now she seemed more aware of this fault and more bruised by it. All of which served to increase Noel's loyalty. It wasn't so much that he saw himself reflected in Lily, it was more that he felt spotlighted by her intelligence. She told him that he was special, that there were great things in store for him, that he was above all this.

But now, to make matters more confusing, Lily kept pestering him to ask out Cecilia.

"How are we ever going to get her to pose naked for us if you don't ask her out first?"

"I don't want her to pose naked, I want you to."

Lily's posture collapsed. She was sitting on the living room carpet and looking up at Noel on the couch and she was wearing a fishnet shirt over a black T-shirt and green pleated slacks. Noel sometimes wondered if she was color-blind. She lifted her knees to her chin and said, "I have to ask. How would you take my picture?"

"Like those Bellocq ones I showed you. Like you'd died a hundred years ago. And with you doing all that yoga stuff you do."

"And naked, of course?"

"Some, some not."

"Where?"

Noel took his time answering because he sensed Lily might be serious about it this time. He scratched his scalp above his right ear then grinned and told her, "In that weird back room of yours."

"Weird room?"

"Yeah." He fronted a smile. "Cecilia showed me it my first night here."

"She didn't? Oh my Gosh, she did!" Lily made a scraping motion down her face and momentarily left her fingers hooked into her bottom lip. "Do you realize what this means? They'll burn me at the stake. Noel, Noel, *Noel*!" she cried. "I didn't suck the blood out of those cows! I didn't set the woods on fire! I didn't call down the UFOs! You won't let Billy Graham burn me at the stake, will you, Noel? Will you protect me? You can be my alibi. Mr. Graham, I can prove I didn't eviscerate those cows, why I was right here in my own living room with this eighteen-year-old boy."

"I'm nineteen, and I'm not a boy."

Lily stared at him, her pout deepening.

"And what did Cecilia have to say about her little archaeological dig? Does she think I'm some kind of Satan worshiper?"

"Probably."

"Of course she does, I bet they all do by now." Lily feathered her hair behind her ears with the backs of her fingers. "And what about Noel? Does Noel think I'm a Satan worshiper? Because if he does, then that makes it all very interesting that he keeps trip-trotting over here twice a week."

"I don't care what you are," he said, but then he asked about the black statue.

That made her smile. "Follow me," she told him.

He assumed they were going to the back room, but Lily stopped at the large bookshelf in the bedroom.

"You're not gonna give me any more books, are you? I'll fail if you do."

"Just one more." And she handed over a paperback called *The Crying Heart Tattoo* and told him it was a novel about a married woman seducing and educating a young artist. She explained, "I'm showing you this to shed some light upon our affair. Upon the nature of affairs. I want you to understand the haphazardness of things. For instance, if I had not read this book, I would never have seduced you. And if I had never seduced you, then I would not be teaching you how to undo Cecilia. And so on, and so on, until a man gets shot in the back or a woman is burned at the stake—who knows how these things end? Perhaps right now some writer is finishing a book that will inspire a beautiful woman to pose naked for you. Or maybe she'll sew you into your bed linen while you sleep one night and beat you to death with a broom. Beware what you read, Noel. But beware mightily what those whom you believe you love are reading."

Noel turned the paperback over to read the back.

"By the way," she asked, "what are you reading these days?"

"*Crime and Punishment.* At least that's what I'm supposed to be reading."

"Egad." She took his hand and led him to the end of the hall, where they stood together in the open doorway like travelers waiting to be asked inside.

"Kali," Lily said, dipping her forehead, or perhaps bowing to the statue of the naked black woman. "Tantric goddess of Time."

"Is that what you are, some kind of . . . ?" No word came to him; instead he asked, "If she's a god, how come she's holding up that cut-off head?"

"The decapitated head symbolizes the death of delusion. Cut off with the sword of discrimination. And the necklace of skulls symbolizes—"

"What about the dead guy she's standing on?"

"Not standing, dancing. That's Shiva. Her consort. And he's not dead. Look, see that dagger he's holding? It's his erection. He's a voyeur. In Tantra, Shiva represents the masculine half of God. The half that is never born, never dies. Kali is the female half of God. The active half. The exhibitionist. Energy that crystallizes into matter. Into earth, into stars, into everything that's born and has to die. Into Lily. Into Noel. Into Kevin and Cecilia. Look at her earrings. Go on. She won't bite."

Noel moved closer and knelt with his hands on his knees.

"Babies?"

"Dead ones. Dead-baby earrings."

Noel asked what dead-baby earrings were supposed to mean.

"Simple. Dead babies mean dead babies. Babies die here. At a tremendous rate. Have you ever seen a Shakespearean play?"

He shook his head.

"Well . . . used to be, back in the olden days, they wouldn't let women act in them. So men had to play the female parts. A prepubescent boy played Juliet. Don't you find that intriguing?"

Not especially, Noel indicated with the flop of his shoulders. He had already turned his attention to the window covered with the tapestry of vampires.

"Think about it, Noel. If our whole universe is the feminine half of God, that means that everything inside our universe is essentially feminine. Meaning not only Lily and Cecilia, but Kevin and Noel too. Everybody. Kali's dance hypnotizes Shiva into seeing the world, but the world he sees is a feminine illusion, a play, stage. And we're the players, we're the actors so perfect that we've forgotten everything except our roles. It's the exact opposite of those Shakespearean plays. Here, instead of everything being essentially masculine, everything is essentially feminine. Here, it's the men who are by nature imposters. That's why it's so tough on men, this female universe is. Which might help explain why men are so wonderfully fucked up, yes?"

Noel turned full circle, pointing to each picture in turn and asking *what are those things, what's that, who the hell's that?*

"Herukas. Dakininis. That's Troma. That's Ugratara."

When he asked about the vampires, she replied, "Those? Oh, they're what the Buddhists call *fierce deities*. They symbolize the pure anger with which we battle delusion. They also represent the part of us that isn't afraid, not of anything, not even of hell. That's why they chose to look that way, fangs and all."

"They're all fucking."

"No, not all of them, just the lucky ones." She made a gesture that seemed to encompass the room, or maybe the world, then she dropped her arms and said, "You still want to take my picture in here?"

"Yes." Then he asked, "Any way I want?"

"Any way you want, Noel. But I get to keep the film."

. . .

An hour later, and mere minutes before the cooking alarm would go bing, Lily suddenly lounged backward onto the sofa and picked up her glass of wine, sipped from it, then peered at Noel over the top of the glass. Now she was wearing an oversized Jets football jersey, number twelve. She had read about this *jersey gimmick,* as she called it, in *some horrible women's magazine.* Men were supposed to find it devastating. She had a long list of such tricks. Often, as with the jersey, she revealed the source and kept inquiring, "Is this devastating you?" It became a pet phrase. "Are you finding this devastating?"

Noel was splayed backward on the couch.

"Aren't you gonna . . . *finish*?" he asked.

She picked up the ashtray then relit a joint Noel had brought over with him.

"No. Not until you make a certain phone call. To a certain twirler."

"You want me to call her now—like this?" He gestured to his own nakedness and in doing so accidentally strummed himself.

"Exactly like this." Lily picked up the phone and started dialing the number, but Noel took the receiver from her and hung it up. "Suit yourself," she told him. She advanced the alarm clock until it binged. "Goodbye."

"You're kidding me?"

"Oh, I don't think I am." She swirled her wine and gazed into its tides as if ascertaining there a bleak future. "Believe me, Noel, you will not be coming over here again unless you make that phone call."

"She won't even remember me. We only met that once."

"Oh, she'll remember you, alright. We've discussed you. Haven't you guessed? I'm your champion."

Noel hung his head, took the phone. A girl answered and ran off calling Cecilia's name. Lily had one ear pressed against the edge of

the receiver. Her hand was busy in Noel's lap. "Cut it out," he was
saying as Cecilia came on the line. Noel quickly tried to explain
who he was. Even though her reaction seemed lukewarm, she
agreed to go out with him. They were setting details when Lily
pulled away and picked up Noel's camera and began taking his picture while he talked on the phone.

"Oh, *Noel!*" Cecilia exclaimed suddenly. "I thought you said
Joel. I had no idea who you were."

"You were going out with me not knowing who I was?"

Cecilia dismissed the question and asked if Noel had ever been to
Pat McCool's. It had the biggest disco dance floor in all Mississippi.
"You like to disco, don't you?"

"Disco?"

"Dance. Do you dance?"

At that moment Lily submerged her head into his lap, and
Noel's body became a horse galloping off.

"Yeah," he managed to say. "Dance."

.   .   .

Lily, after teaching Noel to dance and otherwise coaching him
through his first date with Cecilia, demanded payment in the form
of intimate detail. She wanted to know everything. What had
Cecilia worn? What makeup, what jewelry, what perfume? What
had she been doing with her hands? With her legs? Her tongue?
What kind of shoes was she wearing? When you touched her breast,
right before she pushed your hand away, did she make any noises?

Her advice for the second date was, "Drink in front of her. Tell
her all about you selling pot and getting in fights. Then, boom, ask
her to pose naked. And when she says no, ask her to pose topless.
And when she says no again, ask her to pose in that little spangly
thing. Be a rogue. Head straight to third."

"Third? I haven't even got to second yet."

"Trust me, Noel. Sometimes it's best to run those bases backwards."

Come the following Tuesday, Lily poured them each a glass of wine, took a tentative sip, then assured Noel, "Okay, I'm prepared. Let's hear it. And don't you dare hide anything. I'll know if you do, I'm psychic today."

Once again she showed too much interest in any sounds Cecilia had made, even forcing Noel into re-creating them. She also inquired about his various techniques but interrupted herself to say, "Wait—don't tell, show." She shifted positions on the couch so that she was sitting on Noel's right. "Let's pretend we're in your car— v'room, v'room—and that I'm sweet young Cecilia." When Noel refused to attend to this game, Lily got up and repositioned herself on his left and took over the wheel. "Okay, have it your way, I'll be Noel, you be Cecilia."

On the fourth date Noel got to third, but only a vague hand-trapped third.

After hearing the details, Lily traced her lips with the tip of her tongue and concluded, "We have her. She's ours, Noel. Whatever you do now, don't call her for a whole week."

• • •

Over a week later Jay and Noel took the girls on a double date to the new drive-in in Hattiesburg. It had goofy golf out front, and the screen was a house the owners lived inside. "No!" Lily cried when Noel began to describe the make-out scenario. She was wearing only black panties and Noel's brown flannel shirt. Noel had on unbuckled jeans and no shirt at all. Twenty-odd photographs of Cecilia in Dixie Darling attire were fanned across the magazine table. When he had finished describing how he and

Cecilia had made out in the front while Jay and Cindy had used the back, Lily exclaimed, "Oh-my-gosh, what do you think would have happened if you two had gone back there and joined them?" She cringed. "Sorry. Never mind." Returning her attention to the photographs, she asked, "Did you so much as ask her to undress for these?"

"In the middle of a football stadium? In broad daylight?"

"It's empty, isn't it? And God only knows what kind of fantasies she harbors about that stadium."

"I couldn't even get her to quit smiling at the camera." He began fitting the prints back into the Eckerd's packet. Not one picture had come back from the drugstore to his liking. "I need my darkroom back," he complained.

"You still haven't gone home, not once?"

He shook his head.

"You're not giving up, are you, Noel? You look defeated."

"It's not gonna work. I mean, how am I supposed to get her to take off her clothes if she won't even drink?"

"That's the trick. You have to make her feel incredibly abnormal for everything she won't do. And not only that, you have to make her think you're going to break up with her because she won't let you take her picture naked." Lily focused an imaginary lens. "That's why we have to get her to pose first, before we fuck her. Because if we fuck her first—trust me—then we'll never get her to pose naked for us."

"You've thought about this a lot, haven't you?"

"Don't interrupt." She inhaled very slowly through her nose then exhaled very slowly through her mouth. She did this two more times. "Okay. Here's the game plan. Next time she won't pose for us, we get miffed and ask out somebody else. Somebody she knows and hates. Like a best friend."

"*Stacy?*"

"Oh. You're right. Stacy won't do. I've got it. Are you ready? We ask out *another twirler!*"

* * *

Jay parked his truck at the end of a dirt road that fed down a steep clay bank into the mud-driven Pearl. The road had been made by trucks backing in to dump garbage into the river. He pulled out the emergency brake handle and asked, "You gonna chunk it in?"

Noel tore a PBR off the warming six-pack. In the shadows across the clogged Pearl, the sun was setting blandly behind Louisiana soybean fields. Now and then a brave crow skimmed the water. Higher up, four buzzards circled something dying beyond the soybeans. A stripped wiper had left Noel's half of the windshield rainbowed with red dust. This, at least, lent some color to the sunset. He stared at the white-disc sun until his eyes burned. The cassette player was blasting David Allan Coe out of one speaker at a time, switching left or right arbitrarily.

"Hell, pilgrim," Noel said, imitating a guy on the third floor who could imitate John Wayne, "let's just smoke up all this hootch ourselves."

Passing the sheet of tinfoil and the hollow pen, they discussed the four high school guys who had gotten busted the day before, Noel describing in detail what he ought to do to them if they ratted. Hang them by the balls, cut off their nuts . . . the more he railed, the steadier he felt, but eventually Jay lost enthusiasm for the topic, so Noel let it drop.

The Pearl ran the color of topsoil and did not appear to be moving at all until an occasional styrofoam plank eddied past. Jay ejected the cassette and tapped it twice against his knee. When he inserted it again, the music came out both speakers. He turned it down and asked, "I ever tell you what my old man said to me after I got my first girlfriend?"

"Yep. Man said, *Pilgrim, just 'cause she lets you play with her peehole, don't let her get you by the balls.*"

They both started laughing. Noel laughed a lot harder than Jay did.

"Peehole," Noel said.

"So what you gonna do, Spoon?"

"I'm still deciding."

"You scared?"

"Fuck yes I'm scared. Selling hash oil and 'ludes to damn minors—shit, they'll throw away my key."

"Pretty stupid thing to do, you stop and think about it."

"One of them had a mustache better'n mine. How was I supposed to know they were high school? I thought they were from Myerson. Who the fuck told them about me anyway?"

"They're gonna come after you, the cops are. Four local kids get busted, one of them's bound to squeal."

"Squeal," Noel said and giggled.

"So you gonna chunk it in?"

"I'm damn deciding—if you let me I am."

"I wish you'd decide faster. I don't like having this shit in my truck. You want me to chunk it in for you?"

"I want you to shut up for a minute."

Jay gestured across the cardboard box between them and asked how much all this was worth.

"On the street? Clear a grand easy."

Jay whistled.

"That's nothing, I got twice that in the bank already."

"It's gonna float."

"It what?"

"Them scales'll sink, and them vials, but not all that pot or them horse pills. You need to weigh it down. There's a garbage bag in back. Tie it up in that. Them scales'll sink the rest if you squeeze the air out good first."

"Goddamn, son." A moment later he added, "Gonna be some happy damn fish."

"I don't think there's fish in there. Least I never seen nobody working it."

"If I do throw it in, let me tell you, I'm retired. For good. I mean it this time. Look at my hands. I don't need this shit."

Jay watched the tremble of the hand Noel held out, then he held out his own hand next to it.

"Yours is worse than mine," Noel said.

"I told you I don't like having this in my truck." Then he said, "Wouldn't you know Cindy's gone and got pregnant."

Noel remained quiet a long moment while tracing a phantom pinballing of grief inside him. When it had finally subsided, he made a series of small coughs then managed to say, "Damn, and I used a rubber and everything."

Jay stopped staring at the top of his hand and gave Noel a cautionary look and said, "I gotta marry her, Spoon."

"No, you don't."

"Yeah, I do."

"What, and get some bullshit shift down at Hercules Paper the rest of your life?" Noel shook his head. "Listen, here's what we should do. The two of us, we'll get my money outa the bank and head down to Mexico and live like kings. We'll take this shit with us and sell it on the way."

To Noel it seemed the perfect plan, but halfway through his itinerary of strip bars and legal switchblades, Jay interrupted him to say, "I gotta do the right thing by her. You know I do."

"Bullshit."

"Anyway, I got cousins can get me on the oil fields."

"In fucking Oklahoma?" Noel's face changed expressions as quickly as an actor about to go on stage. Like someone practicing a repertoire of emotion. Finally he said, "Take her to New Orleans. I'll lend you the money."

"Yeah, and how'm I supposed to manage that? Tie her up, throw her in the back? It ain't like we're talking accident here."

"She done it on purpose?"

"I don't know. Maybe. Anyway, it was my own stupid-ass fault for not using anything. She told me she had a tilted . . . something. Uterus? She said some doctor told her she couldn't get pregnant even if she wanted to."

"Uter-what?"

"A uterus. A tilted uterus. You ever heard of that?"

"What the fuck's a uterus?"

"I don't know. But hers ain't tilted."

Noel smoked the last slash mark then balled up the tinfoil and pushed it inside his empty beer can.

"You musta straightened that out for her," he said.

"Yeah. Musta have."

Jay was still staring at the river when Noel stepped outside. He bound up the contraband in the garbage bag and turned two hammer-throw circles before slinging it out into the middle of the river. He watched it sink with his arms crossed, then he stepped out of the mud and cuffed the instep of each boot once against the front tire and got back inside.

"Well," he said. "That's that."

"I guess I'm dropping out."

"I guess you are."

"It's only JC anyway. I mean, who ever heard of a junior college architect? Who ever heard of a junior college anything?"

Noel nodded.

Jay said, "I'm doing the right thing."

The sun came out for a moment and flattened the river and for that instant Noel saw the Pearl as a thick vein of topsoil—something fertile and waiting for seed, something he could get out of this truck and stride across.

"You a better man than me," he allowed.

CHAPTER FOURTEEN

IF IN FACT he had not lost his virginity that afternoon he might well have convinced himself he had . . . but, as it was, he bumped and grinded his way toward some pocketed ejaculation until finally Cecilia reached down and guided him into the depths of warmth and wetness in which there lies no doubt as to what you are doing. You are fucking.

Then, after they had finished, Cecilia climbed onto his back and whispered over his shoulder and into his ear, "Promise you won't show them to anybody else—ever?"

On Tuesday Lily met him at the door in a red-dragoned kimono breathing fire across black silk. Her hair was wet and dark from the shower, her eyes wrinkled with inquisitiveness, as if trying to detect anything, however minute, different about Noel. He cut short the inspection by holding up a black plastic container. Lily took the container from him and carried it like a ring bearer into the living room and centerpieced it on the magazine table. The two of them sat on the blue couch, thighs touching, and together they regarded the roll of undeveloped film.

"Let me guess. She took off her top but not her bra?"

Noel shook his head.

"Don't tell me you got her to shed her little training bra."

"Hey, she's got nice titties."

Lily slapped him. Not loud but hard.

"How dare you defend her titties to me. Haven't I taught you anything? A cocksman's loyalty is always *fiercely directed* toward the woman in his immediate proximity. That would be me. At the moment. Now please continue."

Noel sat there rubbing his cheek and probing the inside of the cheek with his tongue.

"And don't you be coy with me either. Remember, I created you." Then, suddenly childlike, she added, "Can you develop these?"

"Maybe. I could try turning my room into a darkroom, I guess. But I don't want to take any chances, not with these."

"To say the least."

"And Eckerd's won't develop them, that's for sure."

"Oh my gosh, I'm all ears. I'm one huge ear. Wait!" She hurried to the kitchen for a bottle of red wine, a corkscrew, and two glasses. She handed the bottle to Noel. He opened it then poured both glasses full and tasted his.

"And?" Lily asked.

He shrugged. "Some kind of cabernet maybe."

"Where from?"

"How the hell am I suppose to know where from just by tasting it?"

"You aren't. But you're supposed to make an elegant guess."

"Damn France."

"Correct. But inelegant. Now"—and she raised her glass—"believe me when I tell you that you have my undivided attention."

•   •   •

The monitor at White Hall, Cecilia's dorm, did not work weekends. Except for Noel, the whole campus was abandoned then. Usually he used these ghost-town weekends to catch up on his reading, but on this Saturday Cecilia had returned to campus early so that the two of them could share some time alone in her dorm room.

"How romantic. And what was she wearing?"

Cecilia was wearing a red tweed skirt and a white shirt with a Scotch collar.

"Field-hockeyish. Very kinky. And let me guess—startlingly white bobby socks?"

They drank white wine, which made Cecilia look different, older. Cecilia never looked the same way twice. She was always taller, curlier, tanner . . . something. Her makeup varied drastically, but on this Saturday afternoon she had simply spiked her lashes with mascara.

"And what had you chosen for the occasion?"

Noel had chosen his green button-down shirt with faded jeans and tube socks.

"Charming."

Nevertheless they had gotten in an argument. This was happening more and more. Noel hated these arguments because Cecilia was so deft at them that he suspected her of choreographing them in advance. This particular fight started when Noel refused to escort her to another nondenom meeting. He told her all that speaking-in-tongues stuff gave him the creeps, and he even performed a quick impersonation of it, all of which caused Cecilia to start crying.

"Satisfied now?" Cecilia demanded after finger painting the mascara down her cheeks. "Don't look at me! Noel, don't you dare. Put that thing down, I mean it. Don't. I am not going to smile."

Then, instead of smiling, she had shot Noel the bird.

"No! She didn't!"

"I swear she did. But I missed it. I had to ask her to do it again."

"O sweet Cecilia." Lily patted the film cartridge. She seemed relieved. "So that's what we have here, Cecilia giving us the finger?"

Noel smirked, billed his lips, shook his head no no no . . .

"What, then? Noel, don't make me beg."

He sipped his wine.

"Noel!"

"When I asked her to shoot me the bird again, she lost it and went crazy and started screaming that all I cared about was taking her picture. Then she started tearing her clothes off. It was weird. She was crying, screaming shit like, *Are you satisfied now?* Buttons bouncing off walls, her throwing clothes everywhere, until finally there she was. It was the first time I'd ever seen her . . . step-back naked." He stared deadpanned at Lily and rubbed the cheek she had scorched. "She was real beautiful. Even with that makeup streaking down her face like Alice Cooper, it didn't matter. She couldn't help being beautiful. And she knew it too. She just stood there with her arms on her hips, like the only thing stopping her from murdering me was me taking her picture. Then she said—I couldn't believe it—she said, *Now what do you want me to do?*"

"She didn't!"

"Hell yes she did. And I didn't even blink twice, I just grabbed up the nearest batons and handed them to her. I think that surprised her, but not for long, because *boom,* next thing I knew she was at it, twirling the hell out of those things. She was still pissed, but it was like she was taking it out on those batons. I couldn't even see them they were going so fast, like damn airplane propellers, like she was about to fly away. That girl can spin."

Lily was already refilling her wineglass. Noel noticed this and drank his off and held out the glass.

"First off." Lily set down the bottle and moved her hand away from it slowly, as if it were balanced there. "She wasn't angry, she was only pretending to be angry. It's like the girl who wants to get laid so badly that she pretends to be incredibly drunk. It gives her an alibi. Cecilia wanted you to take her picture, but she had to devise a way to do it that was . . . congenial."

"You didn't see her. She looked like that statue of yours back there. She was like the damn baton twirler from hell."

Hearing that pleased Lily. Another sip and she asked what happened next.

Noel raised both arms straight overhead.

"No," Lily said. It sounded like an order.

He nodded vigorously, arms still raised.

"You used a condom, of course?"

He lowered his arms, shook his head, then blew downward like a flutist before admitting, "I had one in my wallet, but I never even thought about using it."

"You carry a condom in your wallet?"

"Just in case."

"Just in case what? You didn't even use it. Did you at least pull out in time?"

"I don't even think that's possible."

"Was she ovulating?"

"Ovu-what?"

"Oh, never mind." She returned her attention to the black film container, as if it were the more reliable source. "And how did she stand up to our onslaught?"

Noel grinned. "She was like a house on fire."

"Uh-huh. Do you remember that night she spoke in tongues? Did she sound anything like she did that night?"

"Yeah," he said. "Kinda. Now that you mention it."

"I figured as much. That means she was faking."

"Faking?"

"Oh, don't look so crestfallen. It's not our fault."

"She wasn't faking."

"Have it your way then."

"She wasn't."

"Okay, then. Fine. She wasn't."

"You know what I think?"

"What do you think, Noel?"

"I think you're jealous."

"Fine. Wonderful. I'm jealous."

"This whole thing was your idea. You oughta be thrilled."

Lily began massaging her eyelids. While doing this she said *congratulations* very dryly, her mouth hidden by her hands. "It's just that . . . oh, it doesn't even matter. It all happened so fast. The little tramp . . . she seemed so, so . . . impenetrable. Noel, you do realize what this means, don't you?"

She stood and walked around the couch and then slumped against the couch back. He stood too, and turned around so that he was facing the fire-breathing dragon on the back of her kimono. From there he could see out a window into the front yard. The wooden nativity figures were still there, though a few of the life-size cutouts had fallen over.

"It's almost Easter," he said. "How come you still got Christmas stuff in your yard?

"Do you understand what this means, Noel?"

"What what means?"

"This," she said, spreading her hands in front of her. She spread them wider. "This!"

"It doesn't mean anything."

"It means you can't come over here anymore."

He walked around the couch to see her face better.

"Are you kidding me?"

"You can't visit here anymore, Noel, not ever again."

"Why not?"

"Can't you figure that out by yourself?"

He told her no, he couldn't.

"Because I can't compete anymore, that's why. Isn't that glaringly obvious?"

Noel had to force himself to speak rationally. Very deliberately he explained that he would break up with Cecilia, that she didn't mean anything to him. But this announcement only made Lily shake her head more resolutely and ask what possible difference that would make. After saying this, she smiled, but it wasn't a real smile, it was more like a wince.

"So tell me how it feels. I don't even remember, it's been so long."

"How what feels?"

"How it feels to suddenly not be a virgin anymore?"

"A virgin!" he shouted, then made straight for the front door, but when he reached it he only leaned his forehead against the frame.

"It's not so easy, is it? Walking out on somebody forever?"

Without turning around, he said, "I love you, not her. I don't care if you are a devil worshiper. I love you."

Lily was still standing against the couch back. Her eyes were shut. Noel saw none of this; he was staring down at the doorknob with the top of his head propped against the door. After a deep breath, Lily opened her eyes. She said, "Noel, that is the sweetest thing anybody's ever said to me. Thank you."

He turned around and then raised his head to face her. He said, "I'm breaking up with Cecilia."

"Fine. But it won't matter if you do."

"I want to be with you."

"I know you do. But you can't." Then her sympathy seemed to vanish and she crossed her arms and stood there regarding Noel as if he were a difficult math problem. "If I told you that my husband knows about us, would that make it easier for you not to come back here?"

"He found out?"

"Maybe he knew all along."

"No, he didn't."

"Are you positive? Marriages are dreadfully complicated things. Nothing but trapdoors and laundry chutes, one after another after another. And adultery—"

"Shut up. You're lying."

"Am I? Try checking the class roster. You might find that Kevin doesn't even teach on Thursdays."

"Doesn't teach—"

"Ask me where he goes on Thursdays, Noel."

But Noel did not have to ask. His throat constricted around Cecilia's name, though he couldn't make himself say it out loud. He wondered if he was in love with Cecilia too. It felt that way suddenly. This realization shocked him, and he backed away from Lily until the doorknob hit him in the spine.

Lily said, "I want to give you something before you leave. Wait here. Please don't leave while I'm gone."

As soon as she left for the bedroom, Noel walked to the magazine table and pocketed the black film container. Then he returned to the door and stood surveying the den, recalling vestiges there, moments shared on the carpet. Ten minutes passed that way before Lily returned. First she handed Noel a sheet of folded yellow stationery, then she handed him a gray film container.

"Put the note aside for later. I couldn't find the exact quote I wanted anyway, so I had to write it from memory. Read it when you don't hate me anymore."

"I'll never hate you."

"Don't be so certain about everything."

"He really knows about us?"

"Worse, he approves."

"He goes to Cecilia, doesn't he, on Thursdays?"

"Cecilia?" This surprised her, but then her face grew sad and she said, "No, not there, Noel."

"Where does he go then?"

She took five steps across the den and pulled open the hinged blue-shuttered folding door to the French closet. The closet was empty inside except for a row of coat hangers pushed to one side.

"He goes in here."

. . .

Noel exploded into the nativity. The turbaned Ethiopian folded into a karate kick. The gray-bearded wizard was first coldcocked, then neck-stomped, the gold-maned Sufi spun around and vaulted onto the garage roof between the two Rudolphs. Noel floundered through the manger, soccer-styling sheep pig gold myrrh frankincense, leg-sweeping Joseph Mary ducks hens, sending divots of straw into the blue air, showing no quarter until he approached the hay-filled cradle. A long moment passed before he lowered his leg and started to back away from the yard. He continued walking backward for one full block, past houses mailboxes trash cans neighbors dogs telephone poles . . . staring forward backward, walking backward forward.

By the time he had wheeled around and aimed himself at campus, the trajectory of his life made perfect sense to him. It made sense to him in that it had all been one long migration toward this moment and the murder he was about to commit.

He entered the small liberal arts building and began rooting the hallways until he found the right classroom, then he spied through the diamond-cut window, its shatterproof web dividing the front of the class into a graph. Inside the graph, Kevin paced along the green chalkboard, his mouth railing silently. As Noel's face filled the diamond, Kevin removed a piece of yellow chalk from a box and in looping cursive wrote *Maslov* onto the board, underlined it, then kept adding exclamation points until the chalk snapped. He exchanged the chalk for a textbook, found his place, and began to read aloud, only to clap the book shut midway through and recite the rest from memory. He was wearing a pink oxford shirt and a yellow knit tie and faggish brand-new jeans. Finishing, he bared his perfect teeth and pressed his fingernails into the top of the chalk-board, as if threatening to scrape down its breadth. A few minutes later, after listening too intently to a question, he clasped his heart and staggered backward as if shot. Right before class ended he lobbed an eraser at a napping student.

When the electric bell sounded, Noel stepped away from the door. His hands were pressed against his sternum. A loud colorful river of students began to pass around him. He waited. There seemed no hurry. The hallway had all but emptied of students again by the time Kevin emerged from the classroom inside a flock of devotees, all girls, four or five of them. His twinkling blue eyes— even this blueness seemed an affectation—snagged on Noel, then slitted, as if the real Kevin were inside spying out of the fake one. Noel stepped forward, calmer than ever. If there was any emotion in him at all as he raised his hands, it was simply relief. Kevin made a feeble attempt to block Noel's hands away and then tried to protect his neck. Then Noel was strangling Kevin's hands and Kevin's hands were in turn strangling his own neck. This hit Noel as funny and he smiled as they stared at each other, Kevin's face reddening and growing larger.

The voice Noel heard inside his mind was distinct yet lisped, and

LEE DURKEE

he heard it a half second after he realized he was not capable of
murder. The voice said to him, *You ain't no killer, you juth a puthycat.* Then Noel found himself standing in the hallway feeling greatly
alone, like an actor who cannot recall his lines. There was a whirlwind of screaming all around him, there were shouts, and Kevin's
mouth was forming some plea of desperation. Staring into the darkness of Kevin's mouth and feeling awkward and trapped and
increasingly embarrassed, Noel wanted to release Kevin but did not
know how until he was suddenly rescued by Cecilia, who stepped
forward out of the classroom, books clasped to her gray sweater,
static electricity luring threads of brown hair onto the gray fabric.
Cecilia, taller than ever, more perfect than pretty.

She stopped in the doorway, her mouth a perfect O, and
dropped her books. Noel watched them scatter, then knelt down
and began to gather them up. Released, Kevin sank to his knees,
his own hands still wrapped around his neck. Noel handed the
books to Cecilia.

"You just saved his damn life," he lied.

Kevin tried to speak, but Noel kicked him onto his tailbone, his
long thin legs sprawled in front of him. Then Noel moved closer to
Cecilia and lowered his head to whisper, "I'm sorry. I really am.
You've never done nothing but be nice to me." He started to leave,
but stopped and walked back and handed the film container to her.

Outside, the sky was sharply blue, a low sun binding his eyes to
the grass as he walked and walked. He was almost to Huff when he
realized he had handed Cecilia the wrong film container, not the
black one of her twirling naked but the gray one of Lily doing yoga
and Noel on the couch. He turned a slow 360 degrees while still
walking, but he knew he could not go back there. Cutting across
the cafeteria lawn, he glanced up for quick bearings and saw,
parked on the street in front of Huff, a small barricade of police

cars, four cars long and parked end on end, their blue lights silently revolving or stuttering. He watched the blue reflect off the dormitory's fluted white columns, which were lassoed with yellow police tape. Oddly, it did not occur to Noel that the barricade had anything to do with him. For once in his life he felt innocent.

CHAPTER FIFTEEN

TWO OF THE POLICE CARS were local blue and whites, the third a green state police cruiser, and the fourth an unmarked white sedan with front windows rolled down and a blue cup rotating sluggishly on the dash. At least fifty people had gathered in the parking lot and were gazing up at the dormitory as if watching an invisible fire. A disarray of yellow police tape blockaded both entrances. Joining the crowd, Noel heard his various names shouted from a number of directions at once and turned to where a car was closing off the back of the posselike circle that had suddenly formed around him. "Hey, Wasted," Hutch called out again. Shirtless in cuffed jeans, his muscular torso incredibly pale, Hutch was reclined against the hood and windshield of his green Camaro. "They searched that piece-of-shit Mustang of yours already." He made a slurping noise. "Took a Hoover to her and everything."

This news just served to make Noel more tired. He joined Hutch on the car hood. It was a beautiful day, at least, and Noel was in his element. He closed his eyes upon the spring sun and wondered if he could actually fall asleep here, waiting for the cops to come and take him away. It seemed possible.

"Got a friend spying on you," Hutch warned. "Look yonder."

A young hatless cop stood staring at him across the parking lot. Noel sat the rest of the way up and bummed a dip off Hutch's Copenhagen. As he checked the expiration date on the can, he did wonder what he was going to be arrested for, but he was too weary to begin narrowing it all down and anyway he assumed it was something cumulative. He had forgotten how much he hated Copenhagen. The unsweetened tobacco stung at the canker sores in his mouth. He leaned back against the windshield and offered his neck to the sunlight and muttered, "That's some nasty-ass shit."

"Yeah," Hutch agreed, as if Noel were commenting on the over-all situation. "They gonna find anything interesting in your room, Wasted?"

"Hutch, I tell ya, I can't even remember. Coupla machine guns maybe."

Hutch's laughter lured other Huffheads closer. Soon they had formed a horseshoe around the car hood and were all comparing notes on who might have what in his room. Noel did not open his eyes again until someone wondered out loud what was taking the cops so long. Then he stirred and suggested that the cops must have found Timmy-Tom's stash of magazines.

"Hell, they're all up there having themselves a big cop circle jerk."

That about brought down the house. Guys were staggering away buckled over with laughter. Noel found himself remembering that distant afternoon walking to the dugout through waves of applause with Ross Altman splayed facedown over home plate.

Hutch sat up and said look and pointed across the street to where a cameraman from Channel 7 was setting up equipment so that he could get both the dormitory and the four police cars in the same shot. *We're famous,* somebody commented, then somebody else said, *You're gonna be a star, Spoon,* and somebody else added, *Hey, ain't that the good-looking news chick what's-her-name inside that van?*

Noel was still calculating the camera angle when a balding senior called Tank came forward and asked, "Hey, Wasted, you ain't got any kinda little black book or nothing like that up there, you know, a list with our names on it, who you sell to, anything like that, do you?"

Noel glared at Tank then slid off the hood and stood too close to him and said, "Tank, if you think I'm gonna rat, just come out and say it—be a man about it—but don't give me this chicken-assed little black book crap."

"Whoa, whoa, Spoon. No problem, no problem," Tank was saying as he backed away and bumped into the young cop, who had just come forward through the crowd.

"We got a problem here?" the cop asked.

"Yeah, obviously he musta mistook me for somebody from Myerson Hall," Noel said as the cop stepped between him and Tank.

The cop told Tank to go stand over there, then he turned to Noel and asked if they could talk a moment. "Upstairs," he indicated. "You are Noel Weatherspoon, correct?"

Noel leaned over to let the plug of tobacco fall from his mouth, then straightened himself so that it was evident he was much taller than the cop. Sticking out his right hand, he said, "My friends call me Spoon."

Ignoring the hand, the cop replied, "Noel, how about you and me go upstairs and have a little chat?"

"I didn't catch your name," Noel said.

The cop frowned and tapped his nameplate twice. With an exaggerated squint, Noel leaned down and read the name out loud.

"Bedell. Now, that's some kinda name, ain't it?" he asked too loudly.

The cop did not reply; he just stared at Noel.

"Well, Officer Bedell, first off I want to thank y'all for cleaning out Mary Lou. I been meaning to get around to it myself, but—"

"Mary Lou?"

"My Mustang. That sweet '66 classic?"

"Oh. That. Yeah, we cleaned her up pretty good for you. Fact is, if you'll come along upstairs with me, quietly and all, we'll discuss something Mary Lou whispered to me."

"Y'all got a search warrant for all this, right? I mean, see, I watch a lot of TV, and the cops on TV—like Starsky and Hutch—they all have these search warrants. You ever watch *Starsky and Hutch*? This here's Hutch himself right here in person."

Once again his fellow Huffheads had to turn and stagger away.

"Let's go—now!"

The cop jerked Noel forward then shoved him toward the side entrance. Noel complained, "Quit damn pushing me, I know how to walk," then, as if to prove it, he sprinted up the cement stairs, ducked under the cage of yellow tape, and turned to face the crowd. He smiled and waved at the camera across the street, but the smile vanished the moment he spotted Cecilia and Kevin standing side by side on the cafeteria lawn. The cop reached the top of the stairs and started pushing Noel inside.

"I'm goin', I'm goin'," was the last thing his friends heard Noel say.

•   •   •

A German shepherd-collie mix flopped on the second-floor hallway, sniffed Noel's boots, then looked up at him with a sad expectancy. Next to the dog was a large pile of bed linens, pillows, men's magazines, books, albums, clothing—some of the shirts still hangered. Inside Noel's room two trollishly short police officers, both in their mid-fifties, were contributing to the pile. The one state cop, a rangy bespectacled man in an evergreen uniform, was waving a backward goodbye as he edged past Noel in the doorway.

"I was never here," he called back into the room. "None of this ever happened, I ain't never seen this boy, I never seen that sorry mutt either. Call me Tuesday, Buell, we'll look her over'n decide whether'not take the boat out. Have a good day, gentlemen."

The shorter of the two short cops was wall-eyed and had horse teeth, which he was displaying now in what was either a grin or a squint. After delivering Noel upstairs into their custody, the tall young officer positioned himself in front of the window and stared down at the crowd outside with such intensity as to make himself absent from the room. The midget walleyed horsetoothed cop, who wore a badged cap with a plastic weather visor, toed the wooden desk chair and told Noel to have a seat. "Make yourself at home, son."

As soon as Noel complied, this same cop came up behind him and began stuffing baggies of pot down Noel's collar and up his sleeves.

"Looky here, Clyde," he chimed to the second short cop. "We got us the marijuana scarecrow."

Clyde, the taller of the two short cops, came over then and said, "Oh my word, Buell, what have we here?" He took a plastic bag containing two quaaludes and one vial of hash oil and shoved it into Noel's shirt pocket. "Seems to be a controlled substance of some sort."

Clyde had large brown eyes with wax-drip polyps beneath them, like tears made of skin, and he had a flesh-tone hearing aid lodged into his left ear, which he kept trained on Noel as he ordered,

"Wipe that grin off your face, son, this ain't *Hee Haw.*" He picked up a sheet of notebook paper, placed it on the desk, leaned over Noel, and drew a near perfect circle the size of a golf ball.

"That's your asshole, son," Clyde explained. "About the time you get outa Parchman prison."

"It ain't mine."

"Not yet it ain't."

"The pot and all, whatever that stuff is, it's not mine."

Walleyed Buell speculated, "Well then, one might wonder what in the world it's doing down your shirtfront, boy."

"Y'all put it there."

Tapping the contraption in his ear, Clyde remarked, "Thank Jesus I didn't hear that. Sounded like the boy was accusing us of planting evidence."

The horsetoothed cop Buell, who could not have stood more than five-foot-four, and whose name tag said O'COCHRAN, stopped rooting through Noel's albums to note, "That'll make for an interesting story. I'm sure Judge Hammersmith will be sympathetic. It'll give us a lot to talk about next week while we're out fishing." He found a vial of Clear Eyes and tilted back his head to administer a drop into each eye. Batting his splayed eyes, the liquid streaming down his sunburned cheeks, he added, "Especially after we trot out a few of them high school kids to testify." He unscrewed a bottle of Aramis he found on the sink. He sniffed it, made a disapproving face, but then rubbed some onto the back of his neck. While using Noel's comb to groom himself, O'Cochran estimated, "Let's see now . . . possession with intent . . . and selling narcotics to minors . . . quaaludes . . . hash . . . adding to the delinquency of . . . whew . . . Lord . . . class-A felonies both, if memory serves." He whistled, not a regular whistle but a staggered birdcall. "Good for an extra four, five years each, something like that. Heck, they change them laws so often can't expect no one man to keep up. You got a calculator anywhere in this room, son?"

Clyde leaned over again, reanchored the piece of paper, and widened the diameter of the circle accordingly.

"One thing's for certain," Clyde predicted, "he'll never suffer greatly from constipation."

Somewhere in the next few blurred minutes Noel demanded a lie-detector test. Officer Buell O'Cochran blew his nose into a Kleenex, examined it, then said to the young cop at the window, "Taylor, we got that new portable unit in the car or should we hook him up to that old beat-up ol' lie detector down at the station and pray he don't get electrocuted like that last boy did?"

The young cop with the thick lips and the short colorless hair, still entranced by the view, replied, "Let's use the one downtown, it's more ack'rut."

Noel, who firmly believed he was going to be administered a lie-detector test, stood and let Taylor cuff him. O'Cochran went to work plucking the contraband from Noel's shirt and then fitting it all back inside a shoe box.

"Hey, Taylor," he asked while rubber-banding the box shut. "What was it that scarecrow had such a hankering after?"

"Scarecrow?" the young cop replied.

"The one in that movie with all them dwarfs running around that yella road."

"Oh. That scarecrow. Wanted him a heart?"

"No, I believe that was the fella made outa sheet metal, the one that kept seizing up whenever it rained."

"A brain," Noel said.

"Darn tooten," O'Cochran agreed. "'Twas a brain."

•   •   •

While the two other cops were parading Noel through the crowd, O'Cochran walked along whistling away on the if-I-only-had-a-brain theme. Taylor, the young cop, drove Noel downtown with the blue lights spinning. Twice Taylor honked and waved at people, as if proud to have a prisoner in custody, and once he pulled over and had a chat with an old farmer who kept glancing nervously at Noel through blue-flashing spectacles. The police cruiser passed the field outside of town that had been given over to the traveling evangelists, but in the hot daylight the field looked like a place you might be evacuated to or perhaps the dregs of some defeated army. The back of the courthouse had been adorned with the same inde-cipherable and arabesque graffiti that had appeared on all the high-way overpasses. Taylor guided Noel down a corridor past six offices and then through a dingy yellow door that had POLICE STN stenciled in black. After uncuffing Noel inside a large room barren save two large metal desks and a line of six wobbly school desks, he whirled the first school desk around so that it faced an empty cork bulletin board and told Noel to sit down.

Noel did. By the time the two other cops had arrived, dragging the mutt, Noel was hard at work practicing the truth inside his head, trying to stunt his heart whenever he approached another lie. The dog curled beneath Noel's desk and her tail began to thump his boot. The smell of collie and flea collar tightened Noel's lungs. Behind him the three cops were squabbling over how much trouble *the suspect* was in, how many years he would serve, and what awful things might happen to such a pretty white boy in prison. Every once in a while they would get distracted by the police-band radio.

"That old Ned in pursuit?"

"Pursuit? Ned ain't seen pursuit since before you was born. At his age pursuit's a bowel movement."

When the radio fell silent, O'Cochran asked, "Hey, college boy, you bother to search our suspect there?"

"I thought y'all took care of that," Taylor said.

O'Cochran shot back, "Great God, child, it's a wonder he ain't opened fire on the lot of us yet."

Taylor, after commenting that Noel did not seem the open-firing type, stood Noel against the corkboard and began to frisk him.

"Don't seem the type?" O'Cochran objected. "Hell, he's about to spend the next ten years of his life being gang-banged blind by large black men in prison, what's he got to lose by shooten me in the back, me with a family to feed?"

"What's this doohickey?"

"That's an asthma inhaler," Noel told Taylor. "I gotta have that. I'm allergic to that dog."

"Give me that thing," Clyde ordered. "I'll safekeep it."

After Taylor had removed Noel's wallet, jackknife, keys, change, the black film container, and also the yellow piece of stationery in his back pocket, O'Cochran began to gleefully sort through these belongings on his desk. Noel could see none of this. He was sitting again and facing the corkboard, but he could hear O'Cochran chuckling and calling Clyde over to come read this. Noel did not know what the note from Lily said. All he knew was that after reading it O'Cochran kept calling him "the child of immortality," as in: *The child of immortality there is looking a little green around the gills,* or *Hey, child'a immortality, ain't it your brother plays third for the Hubcats?*

Noel said yes sir it was, then he asked for his inhaler back. The snarling faces of animals had started to appear inside the pattern of cork. Clyde walked up behind Noel and clamped a hand to each shoulder and began a clawlike massage. While he did this, he spoke softly to Noel of the relationship in prison between big black cons and pretty white boys.

"Oh hell, don't go bawling on us," he pleaded.

"I'm not bawling, I can't damn breathe, I need that inhaler."

Clyde patted Noel's head and assured him not to worry, that they were trying to arrange it with the higher-ups so that Noel could spend one last night here in a civilized white man's jail before being shipped off to nigger central.

"Wouldn't wish that on a dog," he said. "Hey, speaking of which, where'd Esmerelda go off to? You kick her, boy?"

"She's over here. Licken my shoe," O'Cochran reported. "Musta spilt something on it."

"Let's practice her hide-and-seek."

O'Cochran shoved aside Noel's wallet and said, "Alright. I'll cover her eyes, you do the hiding."

"Where is it?"

"Back in the shoe box."

"She looken?"

"I got her eyes covered. Don't hide it there, I hid it there last time and if it had been a snake it'a bit her right on the nose. Hide it in the other room. Awright . . . ready? Here she goes. There you go, girl! Go on, Essie! Good girl. *Where's the pot, Essie, where's the pot?*"

"She's gonna pee the floor again you keep that up."

"Look at her, she's worthless. We should stick her outside and let the devil worshipers have her."

"There she goes."

They followed the dog into the adjoining room and did not return. After ten minutes Noel called out that he needed to use the bathroom. Fifteen minutes later he yelled, "I gotta go real bad!" Nothing. Just the occasional burst of static from the radio. He stood and turned to face the empty office, the two desks side by side, the radio perched on the windowsill beneath uneven venetian blinds. He searched the room for the inhaler but did not see it. Finally he called out, "Anybody here?" then he walked into the next room, empty save for one desk near the door. He yelled again. He had just reached the door to the hallway when O'Cochran burst in. The door caught Noel on the brow. O'Cochran tackled him onto the desk and twisted Noel around and pressed his face down into a scattering of paper clips across the day calendar.

"Resisting!" O'Cochran bellowed. "Attempted escape! Jesus, you almost made it too."

"I gotta use the bathroom," Noel tried to say.

"Feel that? Feel that cold blue steel, son? It's the last thing many a better man than you ever felt."

If he could have, Noel might have begged not to be shot, but as it was, he had no breath left for begging. Very slowly O'Cochran maneuvered his weight off of Noel until only the pressure against Noel's neck still pinned him to the desk. O'Cochran said, "Now I want you to turn around—but slow, real slow. And then I want you to give the barrel of this revolver a big wet kiss, son. It'll be good practice for prison, trust me."

Noel had to roll over on the desk. After he had accomplished that, he saw that it was not a gun, it was O'Cochran's index finger.

"Fooled you."

"Yes sir."

"Pull on it."

"Sir?"

"Pull my finger!"

Noel quit removing paper clips from his cheek and reached up and gripped O'Cochran's chubby index finger and gave it a soft tug. O'Cochran closed an eye, hiked a leg, farted.

"That's better," he said.

Still hyperventilating, Noel said he needed to use the bathroom real bad, and he needed that inhaler back, please.

"Number one or number two?"

It took a moment for the question to make sense.

"Number two, sir."

O'Cochran nodded sympathetically then sat Noel back down in the desk facing the corkboard and left him there.

Some twenty minutes later Taylor found Noel doubled over on the floor and helped him to the bathroom and stood guard in front of the doorless stall.

"Go ahead, get started. Might as well get used to it. You're in custody now."

As his stomach began to uncramp, Noel cringed and then covered his eyes to hide the tears welling up there. When Noel's stomach had finally quieted down, Taylor said, "Look. Noel, right? Noel, maybe this ain't as bad as you think it is. See, those two old-timers back there, they like talking tough, but the truth is we checked you out and you got a clean record. There's no way you'll sit more'n two, three years tops. I know, I know—you're gonna keep harping away on how it wasn't yours—"

"It wasn't. Mine."

"See, you just dug yourself deeper is all. It's your word against theirs. Plus they're gonna haul in all these high school kids who'll swear on the Bible that you sold them drugs. Which we both know is the truth. Now, look. Hell, I used to run a little wild myself. So I can relate. Kinda. But those two buzzards, they're old school, Noel. They see you, all they see's a drug pusher, one who sells dope to children. They want your hide. And they got it too. Still, they been around long enough to know it ain't that simple. It never is," he added, as if he were an old man and not someone three years older than Noel. "So tell me this. Simple yes or no. Are you someone amendable to a deal?"

Noel asked what kind of deal.

"Only kind in town. You gotta give up your source. Soon as you do that, you walk outa here. Pretty day outside, Noel."

"Turn narc, you mean?"

"It's like pulling off a Band-Aid. Faster you do it, the better."

"I think I want a lawyer."

"Maybe that's a good idea. Get everything real official. But I gotta warn you, the second you call in a lawyer, won't be no more deals struck. Once that blue suit walks in the door, everything goes by the book."

Taylor reached into his pocket and found a dime and held it up, tail side showing. "You sure you want this?" When Noel did not reply, Taylor asked, "Or are you someone who's amendable?"

Scratched into the stall just above the toilet paper dispenser was the advice: *Need help? Dial 1-800-EAT-SHIT!*

Staring at that, Noel replied, "I don't even know what I am."

By dark everyone had left the police station except O'Cochran, who was crooning along to a Willie Nelson tape. Noel, both his legs asleep under the desk, continued staring into the phantasmagoria of the corkboard. More than once he had reached up and touched the cork to see what would happen. But even the act of raising one hand panicked his lungs that much more. The dog was gone now, but the smell was as strong as ever. Around midnight O'Cochran called over and asked if Noel had had enough for one day.

"I can't even feel my legs."

"Pretend you're handcuffed," O'Cochran instructed. He guided the limping Noel down the hallway into the last room. This room was layered thickly with robin's-egg-blue paint and halved by a cell. The cement floor looked to have been freshly scrubbed. A wire bunk held a thin but clean mattress. A trickle of water bled out of a contraption on the wall that looked more like a sink than a toilet, and beneath it was a roll of unopened toilet paper.

"My wife," O'Cochran apologized. "She did everything but leave one of them paper bands across the shitter."

He handed Noel the inhaler and said, "My son's got one of them too. His is green, though."

Noel used the inhaler. His shoulders slumped then he took a deep breath and looked up and explained that the green ones weren't nearly as good. Plus the green ones made your hands shake and kept you up all night. "You oughta change over to the blue ones, even though they cost a lot more."

"Now, why don't that surprise me?" O'Cochran replied, but he took out a pen and copied down the name of the drug on a notepad. While he wrote he said, "My youngest boy—I got six, six kids, not all boys—he goes to that school you like to sell drugs to."

"I never even seen that school in my life, sir, I swear."

"Uh-huh. Take your clothes off, please."

When Noel hesitated, O'Cochran removed Noel's belt and pointed with the buckle up at the water pipe running along the ceiling. He clenched both fists like doing a chin-up. "Black fella hung himself up there one night. Using his own underwear." He dangled the belt over his head, stuck his tongue out sideways, and then crossed his eyes. "Next morning, guess who waltzes in. Hadn't even had my first cup of coffee yet. Hell, I didn't even know we had anybody in lockup. I threw open the door, and good morning— there he was. Still spinning." O'Cochran measured his palms about a foot apart. "Son, let me yell ya, you ain't seen much in this world until you've seen, first thing in the morning, the enormous cold-blooded hard-on of a hanged man." He regarded the space between his hands and said, "I don't take chances anymore. Now strip down."

After Noel was naked, O'Cochran backed him into the cell and gently pulled the door shut and tested it.

"We never even found out his name. That black fella's. No ID, no nothing. Picked him up drunk-disorderly. All we found out, he had these two little teardrops tattooed under his left eye. You know what that means?"

Noel shook his head

"Means he killed two men in prison. A teardrop for each man you kill." O'Cochran touched himself twice under the eye. "Prison ain't no place for you, child'a immortality. I want you to be thinking long and hard about that tonight. Because, come tomorrow morning, I'm gonna ask you one question and I'm only gonna ask it once." He flicked off the overhead bulb. When he pushed open the door to the hallway, a two-by-four of yellow light fell across the cement floor and halfway into the cell.

"By the way, you ain't handcuffed anymore."

Noel looked from the shaft of light to his wrists, which he had fused back together as soon as he'd finished undressing. Now he separated them slowly, as if released from a spell.

"You want me to leave the hall light on? I can wedge a shoe or something in the door here, work it like a night-light."

"I ain't afraid of the dark."

That made O'Cochran chuckle.

"Well, you're one up on me, then. Good night, child'a immortality. Heater's running. Guess you don't hold with ghosts either. Good for you."

* * *

The door shut and the darkness around Noel began to expand. Sitting on the cot and pressing his back to the wall and rocking with his knees near his chest, he kept thinking about Tim and Miss Weiss. Prison life . . . that took up its share of his imaginings too, as well as the ghostly presence of the hanged black man spinning above him. And Lily. And the look on Cecilia's face when she had stepped out of the classroom. Every half an hour or so his lungs tightened up again. He tried to ration the inhaler. The ache in his buttocks from sitting down all day swam into his thighs and calves. Hours passed this way before he finally fell asleep. He must have fallen asleep. How else to explain coming bolt awake, his right arm, which had been pillowed under his head, deadened past the pin-and-needle stage? It felt like a dead man's arm had been pinned to his shoulder. Noel tried to rouse the arm by cursing it and by flopping it around and by kneading blood into it. In his panic he stood, but his right leg proved equally bloodless and instantly he collapsed backward onto the cot.

It was not until he saw the soldier sitting on the far end of the mattress that he understood himself to be dreaming. This realization did little to calm him. It was strange, knowing that you were dreaming but still not waking up. After a few seconds of studying the soldier, Noel went back to curse-kneading his dream arm. The soldier, whose severe thinness made his cheekbones stand out effeminately, was grinning, perhaps maliciously, down at a large black and white photograph set on his lap. His teeth were blackened and a few of the front ones were missing. His bare feet were scarred and mangled and infected-looking along the bottoms of the toenails. He inserted a trembling cigarette into his mouth and began pulling the fire toward his lips in long sips, rearing his head back as he inhaled, and every once in a while glancing up to watch with some amusement Noel's attempts to flag blood into his right arm.

Eventually he broadened his grin and coughed and said, "Boo."

"I ain't scared of you and it don't even matter if I am, you're just a ghost or some kinda bad dream."

"Just a ghost?"

"Yeah."

"If I'm just a ghost then go ahead and say my name."

"Goose is your name."

"Not Goose, my real name. Say my real name."

"I don't have to do nothing just 'cause you tell me to. Anyway, where'd you get that picture at? That's my little brother."

The black and white glossy was of Ben. In it, Ben stood naked, his feet spread wide apart, his arms straight out from the sides, but there were dozens of arms, all extending straight out, forming a near-circle around him, as if he had been flapping his arms like wings with the shutter left open except that each arm was depicted clearly without the least blur of motion.

Not looking up from the photograph, the soldier asked, "Hey, I know it's none of my business, but you're not going to rat on that little jewboy friend of yours, are you? Because, if you ask me, these fucking damn cops, they just mind-gaming you."

"I ain't ratting on nobody."

"Well, you're sure as hell thinking about it, aren't you?"

"I think about lots of things, that don't mean I do them." Then Noel asked, "Hey, how'd you die anyway?"

"What makes you so sure I'm dead?"

"What—you ain't one of those ghosts don't even know he's dead, are you?"

The soldier's laughter got all mixed up with cigarette smoke. Finally he replied, "How'd I die? Let's see . . ."

"You got shot, didn't you? In the damn heart."

He did not reply at first, just shrugged and went on smoking his cigarette, which he was holding between his thumb and index finger. His fingernails were gnarled and yellow and very long. His hand kept shaking, and the line of smoke coming off the cigarette shimmied upward, forming little staircases of smoke.

"Yeah, I got it in the heart, alright," he admitted finally. "But from the back, while trying to escape. I'd of made it too, maybe, if they hadn'ta already broke both my damn feet after the first time I tried escaping. You wanna see the exit wound?" After saying this, he unbuttoned his torn khaki shirt. A strong gravitational field started to draw Noel across the cot. It wasn't really an exit wound, it looked more like a perfect black hole, more an entrance than an exit. Noel was sucked forward, inching along the cot, but then the soldier closed the shirt again and smiled. As if a proper threat had been administered.

"I ain't narcing on nobody," Noel told him.

They waited together in the large darkness of the small cell.

"I got about three, four things worth telling you."

"Maybe I got a few things worth telling you too," Noel replied.

"The first thing is this. Beware what you learn to do well in this world. Because you just might end up doing it the rest of your life."

"What the hell's that supposed to mean?"

"Means what it says it means. The second thing I want to tell you is something my grandfather once told me. He said to me, *Goose, drunk women'll do funny things.*"

"I already know that one."

"Well, here's one you sure don't know. Only break one law at a time, Noel. One law at a time."

"Sounds like you didn't know that one either."

"I didn't know any of them except the one about drunk women. That's why I'm telling you them, so you don't make the same mistakes I did. And this last one's the most important one." Again he opened his shirt, and this time Noel began a long journey, swept forward and entering into the black wound headfirst with his arms soldiered at his sides. The last thing he heard his father say to him was, "Go to the light, Noel. Go to the light."

. . .

He emerged as if squeezed out of a tube into a vast black womb and began a descent into a region of stars that, as he drew closer, divided into clusters and spirals and animal-shaped nebulae flashing pink and orange, and these he passed through or missed by millions of miles and then after a long time he approached a galaxy centrifugal in shape, its tail studded with a system of planets tethered around a small dim sun and slung out from it haphazardly at such diabolical speeds that he could scarcely imagine it binding together another moment and into the midst of this unraveling dreamscape he plunged headlong and as he did so the rotation of the planets slowed or seemed to slow as the bright orbs grew larger and more formidable and he began to pass them one by one, their moons rearing and winking then lost in the approach of a new planet, then another and another, this last one sparkling blue on a collision course and as he feathered into its bright atmosphere he saw ahead of him a blue sea, which he followed at gull level into the mouth of night and then up and over an ocean liner, its passengers on deck pointing at him and wasting flash cubes, then daylight swallowing him up and a beach bone-white and constellated with umbrellas staggered blue red yellow blue red yellow for miles with women sunbathing between these bright asters *the eye is a womb* every one of them naked or at least topless *the beach is full of naked women* and onward through the strobe of night-day-night-day with a quick flight through jungle, through abandoned heathen temples, through bamboo villages giving way to flooded fields, to women with hats shaped like smaller umbrellas a dozen different colors bending into rice paddies, then a monsoon, another ocean, a giant polluted river, then veering low along a smaller polluted tributary, skimming a water tower where someone had spraypainted JOHN 3:16, and lastly him swooping down to enter the courthouse window as if it were a cave and he a bat fluttering down the hallway through the last door and between the bars into the small cell, where he found himself alone on the cot propped against the wall and as he honed in and hung himself upside down inside his own body he awoke, except there was no sensation of awakening, rather the mute understanding that he was now awake where as before he had been other than awake and all the while the voice inside his head was chanting *the eye is a womb,* chanting *the beach is full of naked women,* and again his right arm deadened and again he tried to rouse the arm by thrashing it around the cell as a phone rang thinly in a distant room.

CHAPTER SIXTEEN

AT FIRST LIGHT O'Cochran entered the cell and handed Noel his clothes, all neatly folded. Noel got dressed, followed O'Cochran back into the office, and sat at the same school desk. The phones were ringing and O'Cochran snapped one up, listened petulantly, then barked, "Lady, you ain't alone, the whole town thinks the world's coming to an end. But I ain't got time to go check your barn. You gotta go check your own barn and then call me back if it landed in there."

The phone rang again as soon as he hung it up. The same thing was happening to Taylor, who was manning the second desk. Finally O'Cochran put someone on hold and came over and set a carton of doughnuts and a mug of coffee in front of Noel. Noel ate quickly then asked to use the bathroom.

"You know where it is," O'Cochran replied, his hand over the phone.

Noel rose cagily and moved through the two rooms and down the hallway. He was too exhausted to ponder escape. When he returned from the bathroom, he hesitated before sitting down. The radio had been turned low, the Mr. Coffee was gurgling, both Taylor and O'Cochran were still answering the phones. Clyde had entered the office and was watching despondently as the coffeepot trickled full.

"That's another one, Clyde," O'Cochran informed him. "That makes thirty-five sightings total, so far. Twice last week's record."

Clyde poured himself a mug of coffee then moved to the window and raised the blinds. Staring up at the blue sky, he whispered, "Make that thirty-six."

"Great God, no! Not you too, Clyde?"

Clyde continued staring up and out the window. Finally he replied, "Early this morning, right after you called me outa bed. It just about blew my car off Duck Pond Road. All these little windows going around it and shaped just like one of those Mexican hats. It wasn't very big either, couldn'ta been holding more'n a couple of 'em inside. My engine died and I just sat there in the middle of the road watching it disappear."

"Well, I heard it all," O'Cochran muttered resentfully, letting the phone ring beneath his hand. "Now I heard it all."

"Maybe the world is coming to an end. Maybe it's time to get right with the Lord."

O'Cochran frowned and asked, "You right with the Lord there, Taylor?" But Taylor was busy on the phone. O'Cochran shook his head and smiled at Noel next. "What about you, son? You right with the Lord?"

Still standing, Noel cleared his throat and asked for a lawyer.

"Son, before we do that, I think we agreed I was gonna ask you a question this morning."

"I want a lawyer."

"That your answer?"

"Yes sir. I want a lawyer."

"You don't need one, son. You free to go."

Spinning his chair around to face Taylor, who was still on the phone, O'Cochran stated, "In light of new information, we're being so kind as to suspend all charges until further review." He picked up the plastic bag that held Noel's belongings and tossed it over the desk to Noel.

"What kind of information?" Noel asked after a moment.

Again O'Cochran studied the young officer, this time with out-right disapproval, and while doing so he explained, "You need to call home, Noel. There's been a dread development."

"A what—?"

"A death in the family, I'm afraid. That all-star brother of yours, he was in a car wreck late last night."

"Matt's dead?"

"I'm afraid so. Your RA called us a few minutes ago."

He shoved the phone to the front of the desk and said dial nine to get out.

Noel dialed nine and then the number.

Matt answered the phone before it even rang.

This astonished them both.

Matt shouted, "Hell, Noel, I'as just picking up the phone to call you!" and Noel shouted, "I thought you was dead!"

Matt, though by all counts alive, sounded enormously drunk, especially for seven A.M.

"We been calling you since yesterday, Noel. Wherea'hell you been at?"

"Jail."

"Jail!"

"Matt, what's going on? I don't understand, they told me you were dead."

It occurred to Noel that if nobody was dead, then he might be going back to jail.

Matt had started coughing. He coughed so hard that after a minute of it he set down the receiver. Noel waited. Finally Matt's voice returned. "I thought I was gonna—" But the coughing erupted again. This time, instead of setting the phone down, Matt hung it up. Noel had to redial the number. Matt picked it up on the third ring. He was still coughing.

"Matt, let me speak to Ben, okay?"

"Noel, that you? I was just about to call you. Man, we been searching for you since . . . where'a hell you been?"

"Listen, Matt. This is important. Put Ben on the phone, okay? Wait! Don't set the phone down. Matt, do me a favor, please, I want you to tell me, real slow, take a deep breath, then tell me what's going on."

It took some deciphering, but what Matt seemed to be saying, between jarred hiccups that backtracked his sentences, was that Ben had been killed last night in a one-car wreck.

"We been calling you ever since, Noel. Where you been at?"

"Matt, you sure it's Ben that's dead?"

"He's dead, Noel. I swear he is."

"I believe you," Noel said. "Matt, I gotta hang up now. I'm on my way home. Tell Mom I'm on my way."

As soon as he hung up, the phone rang again. O'Cochran pointed his pencil at the neighboring desk and said, "Taylor here'll give you a lift back to school. It ain't your brother plays ball?"

"No sir. It's my younger one."

He nodded and said, "Taylor, get the boy started home."

•   •   •

"Back seat," Taylor ordered and did not say another word until, parked outside of Huff, he twisted around to face Noel through the wire cage. "Just for the record, all that stuff yesterday, that was a big acting job. You understand?"

Throughout the drive Noel had studied a pockmark in the window to his left. Now he reached up and tried to rub it, but the mark was on the outside of the glass.

Taylor continued, "I want you to understand this. That stuff we planted on you, we was never gonna charge you with that. That woulda been wrong. We were just trying to get information outa you. You understand?"

Noel nodded vaguely. He had just noticed his Mustang in the lot. The angle of the sun made it appear the headlights had been left on.

"We wanted to find out your source. To scare you into telling us. That's our job. We didn't do nothing wrong. Besides, you had it coming."

While Taylor waited for a response, Noel placed a hand on the door rest, fitting two fingers inside the hollow where the ashtray had been removed. His other hand was still holding the plastic bag.

"Good cop, bad cop. It's a trick. A technique. Look—never mind that—here's what I want you to remember. Listen up." He swatted the cage. "Hey, you listening? What'd I just say?"

"Good cop bad cop."

"Okay. Now here's the part I want you to remember. See, I was just doing my job yesterday, being the good cop. I'm not your buddy. I guess I'm sorry your brother's dead and all, but what I really want you to understand is that personally you make me sick."

Noel let his focus drift upward until he found the Bud-man sticker pasted onto his dorm-room window. He had the feeling that he was still up there, incredibly stoned, spying down at himself inside the police cruiser.

"What'd I just say?"

"You're sorry my brother's dead."

"What else?"

"I make you sick."

"Good. Now get out."

The locks on both back doors sprang up. This startled Noel, then he got out and started walking toward the dorm. He knew he had to pack before leaving. He knew he wasn't coming back here ever.

"And close the door!"

Noel stopped walking. He went back and shut the door. Taylor was rolling up the front window. As he did this, the sunlit glass dissolved Taylor's face and replaced it with Noel's.

He remained standing in the parking lot a long time after the police cruiser had driven off. As seen from behind the Bud-man sticker, Noel appeared to be leaning forward as if trying to recognize the invisible driver of an invisible car.

• • •

An ambulance was parked in the middle of the front yard, its red light rotating almost imperceptibly in the bright sunlight. Cars lined both sides of the street and filled the driveway and most of the front yard. Noel had to park along the side of the house. Before going inside—he did not want to go inside—he took out the yellow stationery and read it one last time. There was no letter from Lily, no explanation for anything. It was just some quote that made no sense to him. It said:

Do not speak to me of the wickedness of the world and all its sins. Deplore that you still see wickedness at all. Deplore that you see sin everywhere you look. If you want to help the world do not condemn it. Do not weaken it more. For what are sin and misery but results of weakness? The world is made weaker and weaker every day by such teachings. Men are taught from childhood that they are weak and sinful. Teach them instead that they are all wonderful children of immortality, even those of us who are trapped in its weakest manifestations.

The poet/saint Vivekananda

Noel crumpled up the letter and was once again staring at the spinning red light atop the ambulance when suddenly the front door to the house burst opened and two medics emerged from inside carrying Matt between them on a gurney.

At first Noel did not recognize his own brother. Matt's Irish features appeared too delicate and pale, angelic almost, as if in death he had found some inner serenity that had evaded him in life. But this serenity proved short-lived. Halfway across the yard Matt sat bolt upright on the gurney. Like a king on a litter. The medic behind Matt, a stocky blond man sporting a General Custer mustache, made to push Matt down and strap him to the gurney, but Matt seized the medic's arm and sank his teeth into the underside of the wrist. Together they tumbled onto the lawn, the gurney flipping over on top of them.

Matt came up first and had stabbed the steel toe of his boot three times into the medic's rib cage before the second medic caught Matt from behind in a full nelson and slowly bent him forward into the grass. This second medic was large and his arms were thick with black hair. He continued to hold Matt's face down in the grass. They were like a statue there.

Noel was content to watch, he did not want to fight, and anyway that should have been the end of it . . . but, no, General Custer climbed to his feet and while holding his ribs he walked over and delivered a kick to Matt's tailbone that knocked Matt over onto the ground. There was grass in Matt's mouth.

And suddenly Noel felt solid again. He shoved the crumpled note into his pocket, got outside, took a good running start, and blindsided Custer, spearing him in the back and also catching both of his arms. Next he planted the sole of his right boot into the medic's spine and pushed him away from his own hands. When the medic screamed, Noel applied even more torque then released Custer, who shot forward and sprawled facefirst into the red cross on the side of the ambulance. As he sagged to the grass, the burly medic started backing away from Noel and yelling to his partner, "Get up! Get inside! They're damn crazy!"

The ambulance worked its way between the parked cars, then, as soon as it hit pavement, it peeled out and began to fishtail down the street. The driver blared the siren then shot the bird out the window. The ambulance topped the hill and disappeared, but for the next ten minutes its siren kept threading off, then welling up again, as if the medics were circling the block, planning a final assault.

The peace after a fight is a peace nonetheless. You notice things. The life force of a pair of boots. The geometry of hubcaps. Sitting on the grass, Matt drew his legs inward and hunched forward over a wrinkled cigarette, which he attempted to salvage by smoothing between his fingers. He kept shaking his head as if someone were administering smelling salts. A thin red mustache lined his upper lip. It looked like something a kid might get from drinking Kool-Aid. Noel squatted beside his brother and made a flute with a blade of grass held between his thumbs. After blowing into it a few times, he said, "Saved your ass again, huh, bro?"

Matt frowned then lit the wrinkled cigarette.

"Shit," he said ruefully. A moment later he added, "Regular bunch of Florence Nightingales."

Noel listened to the siren. Their relatives were still crowding the front doorway, and their mom had started across the lawn toward them. She was walking too slowly, though. Matt lowered his voice to explain that Doc Martin had left a whole bottle of tranquilizers for Roger.

"These little bitty white pills. But Rog wouldn't take them. So I took them." He made a wrenching sound then spat. "Nothing happened. So I took more. Last thing I remember . . . hey, did we talk on the phone?"

Noel patted him on the back and shushed him and said, "Mom's coming." Then he stood and hugged her. Someone else must have put on her makeup for her. Her eyes shone glassy and swollen, and her hands moved with a thickness, an absentness. She was wearing a plain black dress that made her skin look very pale. Her dark hair was pulled back tightly and it was streaked with white strands. When she had finished hugging Noel and describing how sad she was and how badly Roger was taking it all, she turned to Matt and said, "Hon, I'm sorry, but I couldn't wake you up. I found these sleeping pills next to your bed." She shook the bottle to prove it was empty. "And I thought I'd lost you too. I thought I'd lost you both." Her whole body trembled then, but instead of crying she reinforced her smile and stared down the street, as if confused at the sight of all these cars.

"Sleeping pills!" Matt said. "Those were damn sleeping pills?"

"What did you think they were, hon?"

This information seemed to help Matt arrive at a strategy because suddenly he bowed forward onto all fours and while crawfishing backward he began to vomit in a straight line onto the lawn. Alise plucked grass from his hair as he did this. She warned Noel, "Don't pay any attention to Roger today. He's delirious. But don't turn your back on him either."

Then she resumed her long sleepwalk back across the lawn and into the house.

"Jesus," Noel said. "What they got her on?"

Matt ignored the question and fished his lit cigarette out of the grass and blew the mowing off of it.

"Shit," he mused. "Ain't this just like us."

Eventually they had to go inside. Roaming Baptist women were dousing the house with pie plates and casserole dishes. Male relatives Noel had thought long dead now stood propped inside every corner. The two brothers silenced each room they entered, Noel with his arm around Matt, guiding him. Only the kitchen had been posted off limits to the relatives. Quarantined by grief, Roger sat alone at the breakfast table, staring straight ahead, as if watching a very sad movie projected onto the refrigerator door. Noel helped Matt into a chair, then sat across from Roger, blocking his view of the refrigerator, and that stirred Roger awake. With deep sincerity, and even a logic, he focused on Noel and then asked, "Why not you, for that matter?"

"Hush! Don't pay him any mind. The doctor had to give him a shot. When he wasn't looking. Like you do a child."

Alise began thumping through the cabinets, as if this were a stranger's kitchen. Eventually she placed an apple pie on the table in front of Noel. An index card folded lengthwise was trapped under the cellophane. Noel's name was written across the card in purple ink.

"A pretty girl brought this by for you. She seemed disappointed you weren't here."

Noel opened the card, which said: *Noel, I am so sorry about your brother. I didn't know him but everyone says what a saint he was. Call me if you need someone to talk to. Love, Amber Smith.* PS: *I've never baked a pie before it's probably awful.*

His mother asked who was Amber Smith.

"Just some girl I used to date."

"Pretty. Skinny. But pretty."

She cut three ragged slices out of the pie with a butter knife. Neither Roger nor Matt touched theirs. Noel gulped down his portion and when he had finished, Alise scooped out some cold ham-and-cheese casserole onto his plate. Noel shoveled that down too, unaware of the look of disgust Roger had fixed upon him. Matt was experimenting with Noel's magic eight-ball key ring. He clasped the eight ball prayerlike in his hands before peering inside at its answer.

"Saw you on the news this morning," Roger whispered dryly. Then he leaned forward to add, "No, she doesn't know, but you can bet the whole rest of the town does by now."

Noel started eating again, but he was still staring at Roger.

Matt unclasped the eight ball and said, "Noel, it says here we should take a little ride. For our own safety."

He slung the keys across the table at Noel, who blocked them onto his plate.

"You gonna eat those too?" Roger asked.

Noel picked up the keys and started cleaning the cheese off them.

"You better drive," Matt said. "I'm still seeing double every-thing."

Alise asked, "Y'all are leaving already?"

"Yeah," Matt replied.

"Well, change into your black suits first."

They went upstairs to change. Noel came back into the kitchen with his suit on, but Matt headed straight to the car. Alise was sitting across from Roger now. Noel walked up behind her chair and she reached backward around his neck and whispered in a voice not alto-gether gentle, "Take care of your brother today. He's blaming himself.

And remember, the service at the funeral home starts in two hours. I want y'all there on time." Noel started to leave then, but she called his name and stopped him at the doorway. "Sober," she added.

Inside the car, Matt held out two pills, dull black and worn-looking. Noel asked what they were. Matt said, "I'll tell you afterwards," then gulped one down dry. Noel studied Matt's face a moment before swallowing the other one.

"Well?"

"Cyanide."

"That ain't funny, Matt."

"Wasn't supposed to be funny. C'mon, hurry up, we ain't got long to live. Closest one's next to Pasquale's now. Only it ain't Pasquale's no more."

"Closest what?"

"Closest what-do-you-think."

At the first intersection Noel put the car in park and revved the engine.

"I'm asking you nice, Matt."

Matt stopped fiddling with the broken air conditioner to reply, "I already told you. Rat poison."

Noel stuck his arm out the window and signaled the car behind them to go around.

"Where'd you get them fine boots at?" he asked.

"Some recruiter. From Tex-ass. Them Texas boys don't give up easy. I ain't going to Texas. Fuck Texas."

Noel leaned across the gear lever and ran his fingers against the boot scales. They felt like something still alive.

"Virgin snakeskin," Matt reported. "Exact same kind Tom Landry wears."

"Virgin snakeskin? What the hell's that supposed to mean?"

Matt hesitated. "Snake that's never been fucked."

"How can they tell that?"

Matt pouted and stared straight ahead.

Noel said, "Matt, this is the last time I'm asking you nice."

"I told you. Rat poison."

"Well, at least Ben'll be happy to see us."

"That's kinda a long shot, don't you think?"

"What do you mean?"

"Us and Ben in the same place?"

Pasquale's was now a Chinese restaurant called Hop Sing's. A police car was parked in front of it. Noel pulled into an empty slot near the liquor store next door.

"You got an ID?" he asked Matt.

"Don't need one. I'm like a movie star around here."

As soon as Matt stepped outside, a German shepherd in the back of the police car began to growl and scrape one paw against the window. Matt went inside the liquor store, and Noel sat in the Mustang diagnosing his symptoms. He considered having a quick look inside the Chinese restaurant, but the idea of it made him sad. A few minutes later Matt returned outside, opening a pack of Kools. A brown bag was wedged under his arm. Instantly the German shepherd began to snarl and to scrape its teeth against the glass. Matt halted. He shook his head, like someone reprimanding a child, then strolled over to the police car and knelt beside the window and pressed his face against the glass. The shepherd hurled itself forward, hitting the window so hard that Matt fell over backward. He stood, grinned, then fished out a cigarette and began to blow smoke against the window.

The German shepherd was still attacking the window when Matt walked back to the Mustang. Noel forced himself to drive away slowly. In the rearview, the police car was swaying, like there were lovers inside it. He let a mile pass before he began screaming at his brother. What he screamed made little sense, at least to Matt.

He screamed for a long time about cops and prison and black cons and about how he was through with all this bullshit.

Finally Noel calmed down and about five miles later Matt started calling out directions, saying he wanted to show Noel something real important.

"I'm not taking you anywhere until you tell me what kinda pill I took." He stopped the car, this time on the shoulder of the highway. "I'll break your damn throwing arm, Matt. Say I won't." Noel got outside and walked around the front of the car to stand just outside Matt's open window. "C'mon. Get out."

"Can't you even tell yet?"

"It feels like my damn hair's standing straight up."

"Like it does on speed? Like on Black Mollies maybe?"

"Speed? I thought that was just for studying."

Matt said hell no, he used speed for road games and double-headers. "Just like Pete Rose does."

Noel got back inside the car and started driving again. Passing the bottle of George Dickel, they followed a thin highway between a field of cows and a field of soybeans. Noel asked how much time they had before the service started, but Matt assured him there was no hurry. "Those things go on forever, and besides, the real service is in the morning. That's just the viewing today, that open-casket crap. Anyway, you know what I bet they do? I bet they nigger-rig Ben back together on purpose."

"What are you talking about, Matt?"

"I bet they do, I bet they rig him back together on purpose. So that his friends see what happens when you drink and drive."

"Drink and drive?"

"Fucken Rog is even having the wreck towed out to Ben's school. They're gonna stick a bottle of whiskey up on the dash, get one of those big cardboard tombstones up on the hood that say, DON'T YOU BE NEXT."

"Ben was drunk?"

Matt nodded severely. "Plowed. That's what the sheriff told us. And when he told us that—you shoulda seen it, Noel—everybody looked straight at me, like I'd poured it down his throat. That's why they had to give Rog that shot. Fucker chased me down the street with a baseball bat."

The car had slowed to ten miles an hour, Noel's chin almost hooked to the steering wheel. Noel made Matt repeat the whole story, and this time Matt explained that, on the day it had happened, Ben had called home from work to say he was going straight to Tracy's. "He was hoping they'd get back together."

"They broke up?"

"She did. Found her some other guy, I heard."

Noel whistled. "Ben worshiped her."

"No shit. You shoulda seen it too. After she broke up with him, it was like . . . it was like Ben turned into one of us."

"I never even seen him drink a single beer."

Matt did not comment on this, but then a moment later he yelled for Noel to pull over to the shoulder. They crossed the lane and skidded to a stop, and Matt grabbed the bottle and got outside and started walking away from the car over a flattened section of barbed wire into a fallow pasture. Sweating inside his black suit, Noel got out and followed. As soon as he noticed the tree, a thick blackjack oak, about fifteen yards off the road, he guessed what had happened there. The only tree in the pasture, the oak was scaled down to hardwood on the side facing the road. The exposed wood inside this scar was light gold and grooved, as if someone had started to carve a totem there. Matt reached the tree and lit another cigarette, then he tilted the flame from the Zippo against the scar. The silver Zippo had UNIVERSITY OF ARKANSAS inscribed on its side.

"Ben didn't have any clothes on," Matt whispered as Noel

walked up. "When he hit the tree he was stark naked. That's what everybody's saying."

The wide blue-yellow flame slithered up the wood.

"Do Mom and Rog know that?"

Matt clipped shut the lighter, shook out his fingers.

"I don't think so. The sheriff never said nothing about it to us, it's just what everybody else is saying." He squatted down and built a small mound of twigs and leaves beneath the tree, then he tried to ignite the mound. After a minute he dropped the lighter and began sucking his fingers. The lighter kept burning in the dirt between the tree roots.

"Everybody's saying Ben's head got cut off in the wreck."

"No, it didn't," Noel said.

"How do you know?"

"It just didn't."

"Well, everybody's sure saying it did. Three different guys already asked me if it's true."

Noel cleared his throat and spat.

"People are always saying shit like that after a wreck. Saying his head got cut off or how they never found his foot or his dick or whatever. Next thing you know, they'll be seeing his ghost on the road. Looking for its left nut or some such shit. It don't mean nothing, Matt. Quit that, you're wasting good whiskey. It ain't high enough proof to set on fire."

Matt quit sprinkling the whiskey onto the twigs.

"You know what else I heard? I heard it's not the busting through the windshield that kills you. It's like there's this giant rubber band that yanks you back inside the car. And it's the coming back in that fucks you up."

An orange Ford pickup crossed over the highway and parked in front of the Mustang. The truck had two teenagers inside it. The moment it came to a halt, Matt quit trying to set the tree on fire and started picking up rocks. As soon as he had a good handful, he sprinted at the truck and hurled the rocks so wildly that he fell forward into a somersault. The rocks pelted both vehicles but mostly the truck, which peeled out forward and then braked. By then Matt had vaulted to his feet and was giving chase. The truck kept staggering the distance between them, taunting Matt forward, but eventually it left him standing in the highway bent over and holding his sides. After a few minutes he straightened and marched back to the tree, where Noel was sitting in the shade and helping himself to more whiskey.

"No skid marks." Matt's suit was softened with orange dirt. "That's the big deal here. That's what all these yahoos are pouring out to see. That and to look for blood." He picked up more rocks and bounced them one by one off the tree trunk. Then he gathered up another fistful and leaned back and sprayed the rocks straight up into the branches.

"Wither, motherfucker," he shouted.

The rocks rained down on them and Noel covered the whiskey bottle with his arms.

They both pissed against the tree before leaving. Matt got to the car first and slid behind the wheel and said that he wanted to drive for a while, that it'd do him good to drive. Noel shrugged and got in the other side, but first he removed his suit coat and shook it out. About an eighth of a mile down the road, Matt stopped the car and fit the gearshift into reverse. Looking back over his shoulder, and placing his right arm behind Noel's seat back, he pinned the accelerator to the floor. Noel yelled something, not any kind of word, then glanced at the speedometer, which of course read zero. He was grabbing for his seat belt when Matt stomped the brakes so hard that the car whipped around and left the road.

Noel was slammed into the heater. He landed cubbied on the floorboard in front of the seat. Staring up at the nest of red, green, and black wires, he kept waiting for his anger to catch up with him, but it never did. A storm of orange dust had filled the car. From down there Noel could barely see Matt, who had twisted around to stare out the back window. Noel climbed into the bucket seat and sat there as the orange dust thinned, sweeping away in patterns to reveal the scarred totem of the oak tree just two feet away from the car hood.

They continued staring in opposite directions, Noel forward, Matt backward.

When the dust had finally lifted off the highway, Matt coughed twice then cleared his throat and said, "I got your damn skid marks."

CHAPTER SEVENTEEN

THEY LEFT THE CAR on a gravel road sectioned with cow guards and flanked to the east by a twelve-foot hurricane fence. Crimped to the fence were yellow and red warning signs. Yellow for no trespassing, red for guard dogs. Matt left his suit coat behind in the car and scaled the fence. Then Noel lobbed the bottle over to him and started climbing. From the top he could see off in the distance where rusted cars formed a margin along a green meadow and where black cows with white skulled faces stood grazing between the wrecks. He climbed down and caught up with Matt, who already had his head stuck inside the busted driver's-side window of Ben's devastated El Camino.

The brown car had been left crab-shaped by the wreck, its fender ends hooked like pincers around an invisible tree trunk. The windshield, or what was left of it, hung in strips. A canvas sneaker stained pink was wedged under the brake pedal. Next to the sneaker was a broken whiskey bottle held together mostly by the label. It was George Dickel too. Matt carefully removed the shards from the window then crawled inside onto the front seat. Rolling over onto his back, he began to kick the driver's door open with the bottoms of his boots. This took about a dozen kicks before the door gave way groaningly. That done, he turned on his side to eject the cassette tape from the console. Matt studied it briefly then placed the tape in his mouth and began searching under the car seat.

"What was he listening to?" Noel asked from outside. He was looking anywhere but inside the car.

"Wild-Eyed Southern Boys," Matt replied. "Full blast."

In the center of the junkyard was a crane pointing up into the sky like a giant finger. The clouds moving behind it made the crane appear to be falling forward. Noel watched the crane as he tried to combine the music with the race toward the tree. From under the seat Matt pulled out a nest of clothing congealed together with blood. A pair of jeans twisted around a short-sleeved plaid shirt. Socks. Some briefs stained orangish black. He lifted the coil, holding it up scruffed like a puppy.

They both stared at the clothes until finally Noel said, "It don't make no sense."

Before getting out of the car, Matt sifted through the ashtray and found the better half of a joint. He did not act surprised at this discovery. There was blood-black under his fingernails and his hand was gray with ash when he passed the joint outside to Noel. They sat beside the car and smoked the joint without speaking, then Matt ate the roach and stood and started walking around the junkyard, gathering up loose pieces of newspaper and anything else that would burn. He made a bedding with the paper then sat cross-legged on the dirt and placed Ben's clothes on top of the newspaper, the pink sneaker on top of the clothes, the cassette on top of the sneaker, then he lit the paper. The fire grew quickly. The cassette curled into itself and produced a black acrid fume. There was no wind, and the smoke rose as straight as a rope on a pulley.

They watched the flames for a while, then Noel picked up an old wiper blade and began prodding the fire. He said, "You got him drunk, didn't you? His first time?"

Dogs were baying off in the distance. At least Noel thought it was dogs. He couldn't tell for sure. Maybe it was just dogs inside his head. Matt was holding both hands over the dying fire. When he splayed his hands, the pooled smoke feathered up between his fingers.

"Yeah," Matt said softly.

"Hell, I got you drunk the first time."

"Yeah," Matt said again exactly the same way.

"So it's just as much me as you." Noel listened to the dogs some more. Their baying rose and faltered like something drowning. "Did you get him stoned too?"

"You did me."

"I know, I'm just asking's all." Noel poled the wiper blade upright in the ashes then wondered out loud if maybe Ben might have been on something stronger, something besides just booze and pot. "Something like LSD maybe?"

He was hoping that Matt would laugh at this idea, but instead he stopped chewing his bottom lip and whistled. He'd never thought of that, he said. "It makes perfect sense. That's why he took his clothes off, and all." Matt whistled again.

"Keep up that whistling, Matt. Them Dobermans need all the help they can get."

"Dobermans?"

Noel tightened the laces on both his wingtips.

"Hey," Matt said. "You ever hear that story, the one about the guy who tried to fly off the fire tower?"

Noel did not answer. He was too busy remembering. He was remembering the afternoon not so long ago when he had highly recommended LSD to Ben. "It'd do you a lot of good, probably," he had told his little brother. He folded his legs Indian style, just like Matt's were, and stuck two fingers into his mouth and whistled three sharp blasts. Instantly the barking seemed to divide. Judging the distance to the fence, he picked up the bottle, drank off a good three fingers, then passed it across the dead fire to Matt.

But Matt only stared at the bottle and asked, "What do you think happens to someone who dies real fucked up, Noel?"

"What do you mean?"

"I mean where do they go?"

Noel shook the bottle, but Matt still wouldn't take it.

"Because you know what I'm thinking we did?" Matt asked.

Noel shook the bottle harder.

"I'm thinking we got Ben sent straight down to you-know-where." He reached for the bottle. "That's what I'm thinking."

"This damn speed," Noel complained while watching his brother gulp whiskey. "Feels like I'm sitting on the damn electric chair."

Matt gauged the bottle to make sure he'd drunk off more than Noel had, then he passed it back over the dead fire. Noel took the bottle again and held it up to the sun. It seemed to him that at any moment now the dogs might appear over the tops of the broken automobiles.

■　■　■

An hour later Noel was parked behind a monument store and spying over a landscape of blank stones to where a whorled sunset filled the horizon behind the neighboring funeral home. Matt had passed out against the window, but Noel kept himself awake by reciting out loud the names of the mourners he tracked entering and leaving the building. He held mini-conversations with old coaches or with girls he had failed with. The morning-league team that Ben helped coach filed in wearing their green-and-yellow uniforms, and that got Noel to crying, jaggedly, an asthma attack of crying. He couldn't stop, even after it had started to feel fake. He cried himself passed out.

It was the slam of the car door that uprighted him. At first he didn't know where he was. It was dark. The parking lot across the street was empty, the funeral home was dark. Noel, feeling wide awake and jittery with the speed, got outside and leaned a shoulder against a small tree to piss. While he was doing this, the windows of the funeral home began to ignite, first room by room, then floor by floor, until every light in the building was on. A few minutes later, Matt came loping through the tombstones and announced that Ben wasn't inside anymore. "They musta hauled him off to church already."

Except for the staked white cross spotlighted from the grass, the First Baptist Church at night appeared forlorn and abandoned. They found an unlocked window in the kitchen and followed the blue-yellow flame of Matt's lighter down a long passageway stocked with canned goods. When the Zippo petered out, they stumbled deeper into the annex, bumping through velvety rooms or dragging themselves up banisters or brushing their hands against walls, searching for light switches. Then Noel got separated. He started calling Matt's name, but there was no answer. He had no idea in which direction to turn. It seemed impossible that he would ever extricate himself from this darkness. He was very close to panicking when the chapel lights suddenly soared into his unguarded eyes and he found himself to be standing one pew shy of the balcony rail. Below him in the increasing light he could see, alleywayed beside the chapel, a small soundboard above which Matt now stood adjusting various dials and switches. The three ceiling fans started to rotate. A plastic candelabra whitened by degrees. Twin floodlights shone forth onto the stained-glass pictorial of Jesus, who was holding the lamb under one arm and knocking on a large wooden door.

"Notice there is no knob," Matt called up, trying to sound like a TV preacher. "The door must be opened from within."

Noel lowered himself down the stairs, then he came around and sagged into the first pew. "I ain't letting in nobody hangs with sheep," he said, then cradling his head in his hands.

"You gonna be sick?"

"Not yet."

"I'm gonna go find Ben."

For a while Noel remained in the pew holding his head. He was hearing the dogs still. A whole prison-break worth of dogs. He tried to diminish their barking by staring hard at the bright red hymnal slotted in front of him. Then he got an idea.

• • •

That night he dreamt that he looked down into Ben's casket and saw his younger brother pieced together with stained glass.

He awoke at daybreak in his old bedroom and was attempting to repair the previous night into some semblance of time travel when his mother flicked on the light and ruthlessly announced breakfast to be ready. He limped downstairs into the kitchen, where Matt was slumped over his plate as if pegged to the chair back. The table was covered with food. Scrambled eggs, biscuits, gravy, bacon, sliced ham, sausages, grits, and one large coagulated bottle of squeeze ketchup that any moment now Roger would spurt onto his eggs. Roger raised the bottle. Pointing it first at Matt, then at Noel, he warned, "Just y'all remember something today. Ben would have wanted some good to come of this." Then he inverted the red bottle and farted ketchup over the mound of scrambled eggs.

After breakfast, Noel wandered outside to his car to search for his black tie. He had forgotten about the hymnals until he saw them scattered over the back seat. Fifty of them, at least. He leaned against the car a minute, regrouping. He was doing his best to hide the red hymnals under laundry and camera equipment when Matt came outside to smoke a cigarette.

"What are all them books doing in your back seat?" he asked.

"We stole them from the church. You don't remember that?"

"The church?"

They decided to leave early for the service. That way they might have a chance to replace the hymnals, and anyway Matt still wanted to view the body. There were already a few cars in the parking lot when they arrived. Noel followed Matt up the steps. There was a distinct boot print dead center in the back of Matt's suit coat. Inside, the church was cold and utterly silent. The clockwork shadow of ceiling fans spun over the pews. Beneath the slumbering pictorials, a boy was fitting candles into brass holders and a woman with pins in her mouth was attaching a red velvet curtain to the base of the elevated coffin. The coffin reminded Noel of a magician's prop, something from which a beautiful naked woman might emerge. They stood in the alcove beside a wooden podium that held an open guest book bisected by a pink ribbon. Matt had started to sign it when Noel said, "I don't think we're suppose to do that. We ain't guests."

Matt scratched out his name then let the pen hang by its yellow yarn. Almost shyly, he cut his eyes to Noel's scuffed wingtips. Then his focus drifted higher to encompass the entirety of his brother's suit and person. "Man, we look dug up," he concluded. He sighed, shook his head, then started marching down the aisle into the chapel and downhill toward the coffin. Noel watched the boot print on Matt's back. The woman with pins in her mouth stood and moved to the side. Reaching the casket, Matt fingered the lid before raising it. It locked into place and he released the lid cautiously before glowering down into the casket. His hands were steepled in front of him. Above the pulpit, the sun reached the stained glass and filled the back of the chapel with watercolor light. Noel backed away from the podium, but before he could escape outside he heard a noise that sounded to him like a turkey gobble.

This noise sent him reeling into the sunlit courtyard, his heartbeat pounding on his headache. He found a cement bench and rested there bent over until he heard more cars starting to arrive. Then he got up and staggered across the street to an air-conditioned drugstore. They didn't sell coffee, so he settled for a large bottle of baby aspirin. He crammed a fistful of the orange tablets into his mouth and made his way back to the street, but now he had to wait for a lull in traffic. Most of the cars were filled with relatives or family friends. He could not help but imagine how he looked to them. The devastated black suit. The long black unwashed hair blowing behind his shoulders. The redness of his eyes, the black circles beneath them . . . the giant aspirin bottle clutched in his hand. Watching the people inside the cars, Noel tried to time that instant of recognition, that fleeting moment where, according to Roger, a person can foretell your entire future.

After a number of false starts, he lunged across the road and worked his way through the courtyard, pinballing away from relatives, well-wishers, and do-gooders. Then he spotted Tracy. She was walking between her parents in a slinky black dress, her brown hair longer and less frizzy, her figure much more assertive than

Noel remembered it. Seeing Noel, she checked her parents and walked over. She did not smile but approached him slowly, like he was something wild and uncaged.

They traded awkward hellos and stared down at the sidewalk. Tracy was wearing heels with thin black straps across the feet. Noel's navy-blue wingtips were caked with orange dirt.

Tracy said, "I guess we should be going inside, huh?"

Noel did not look up or reply.

"Ben's going to have them spilling into the aisles."

"He was the best person I ever knew," Noel said.

Tracy made a wafting motion with one hand and asked, "Are you drunk?"

"No. Just hungover as hell."

"What happened to your suit?"

He stared down at his torso a long moment before shrugging.

Tracy hesitated then said, "Yeah, Ben was almost too good."

"Too good? What's that supposed to mean?"

"Too good for this world."

"Is that why you broke up with him?"

"You are drunk."

"Or was it that he didn't have a fast enough car for you, something like that?"

"Don't," she said.

Noel snapped his fingers, pointed at her.

"You're not wearing glasses! That's what's different."

"Contacts," she admitted, lowering her brown eyes. "Don't make me cry or I'll have to take them out."

"And you got rid of them braces too. Damn, girl, that's what it was, huh? You musta had all sorts of young studs asking you out."

"Goodbye, Noel."

"Wait!" After a confidential stumble forward, he glanced

around and settled on her shoes again, then he asked if she'd heard anything about Ben taking drugs on the night of the wreck.

She rolled her eyes to say, "You mean about him being on X? Everybody's saying stuff like that. I don't believe a word of it. Do you?"

"X? What's X?"

"Ecstasy. It's some new drug, supposed to make you love everybody."

"Ben already loved everybody."

"Maybe you could use some of that, huh?"

"Yeah, I could use a whole truckful about right now."

Tracy quit smirking to ask if it was true about Ben being naked when he wrecked. "That's just talk, right?"

"Hell no, he wasn't naked. And his head wasn't cut off, and his damn ghost ain't walking down the highway looking for its left nut either."

"What are you talking about?"

"I don't even know."

Her foot began etching in the sidewalk pine straw. There was brown pine straw everywhere. No grass to be seen.

Tracy asked, "You think it's my fault, don't you, that Ben killed himself?"

"He didn't kill himself."

"But I heard—"

"Shut up."

"Excuse me?"

This came from her father, who had stepped forward, but Tracy turned and told him to wait. Mr. Carmody halted, but very reluctantly. Almost as tall as Noel, he had a small head and black hair oiled sideways. He shingled houses for a living and looked strongly disproportioned.

"I can handle this," she told him.

Noel whispered, "Can I just ask you one question?"

"You're going to anyway."

He held the question in his mouth, tasting it. The taste was venom and bile, the taste of grief.

"If you hadn't broke up with Ben, you think he'd still be alive?" he asked.

The way she closed her eyes made her face appear, momentarily, to be smiling. She spoke slowly, as if from inside a trance. She said, "You want to know who it was I heard sold him X?"

"Yeah, I do," Noel replied, hoping that it wasn't Tim. "Because I'm gonna kill whoever did."

"I heard it was you."

All at once there was shouting, motion, then Mr. Carmody had both his hands on Noel's shoulders, a gesture that gave the appearance of condolence or benediction, but the grip was too tight and the hands were positioned too close to the jugular. Grittingly he stated that these were tough times. "Tough all around. My family's going inside now to pray for your brother. Who we always liked and welcomed into our home. Be that as it may, if you ever touch my daughter again, I'll break you damn neck. Do we understand each other, son?"

"I'm not your son."

"Do we understand each other?"

"All I said was—"

"Do *we understand each other?*"

"Yes sir, we do."

• • •

He found Matt sitting on the gravel lot with his back resting against the front wheel of the Mustang. He handed Matt the plastic bottle.

Matt shook out some candy aspirin and started chewing and then returned the bottle along with some comment wholly indistinguishable. Noel, after pouring more aspirin into his own mouth, had to tilt back his head to say, "I told you not to go look, didn't I?"

"It was like they'd—"

"Shut up, Matt. I don't want to hear it." While saying this, Noel had to stopper the aspirin back into his mouth.

They kept chewing, both of them squatted down in the shade like aborigines.

"We should head in," Noel said after a while and started to brush the orange pellets off his suit collar.

"It looked like they—"

"Matt. Shut up."

Matt picked up the front apron of his tie and used the back of it to wipe his nose. Then he said, "It didn't even look like Ben, it was some scarecrow of Ben, like something they'd burn of Ben at a football game."

Noel stood up and walked away toward the church.

•　•　•

Baptists know their songs by heart, especially the hymns they use to serenade the dead. The immediate family took up the front pew, Noel by the aisle, then Matt, Alise, and Roger. The Reverend Smokewood stood on the far side of the casket gripping the altar podium. Waiting for the perfect pitch of silence to begin the service, he stared down at the giant black leatherbound Bible as if trying to intimidate it. Roger had requested Smokewood for the service, and although Noel had anticipated this, he still had trouble recognizing the man. Smokewood's chest had dropped into his belly, and his baldness had subdued the military air that lingered now only in the metallic eyes enlarged by tiny round spectacles that made his head look tumorously large. This defeated appearance made it all the more startling when he began the service a cappella. His voice had survived, at least. The congregation moved their lips to "Amazing Grace," not sure whether or not they were supposed to join in. The reverend had a cigar smoker's baritone that boomed through the song until he came to the *saved uhh-uh wretch li-hike meeee!* part. The reverend knew better than to sing that part pretty; instead he hung it out to dry. Hearing it, you could tell, here was a man who has truly been wretched. It was the best rendition of "Amazing Grace" Noel had ever heard.

But then the eulogy began. Glaring directly at Noel and Matt, and standing so close to them that twice Noel had to blink spittle from his eye, the reverend came around the casket and Cain-and-Abeled them. At first Noel could not believe what he was hearing, but then he recalled Roger's warning at breakfast—that Ben would have wanted some good to come of this—and then he understood the eulogy to be part of some larger strategy to dog-catcher his soul.

The reverend clenched his fists and cried out, "And the Lord said unto Cain, *Where is Abel thy brother?*"

"You bastards," Noel said, more breath than words.

Now Smokewood assumed the cowering mannerisms of Cain in order to reply, "I know not. Am I my brother's keeper?" He mouthed the question, then began to repeat it over and over, his tone changing from that of Cain's trembling alibi into a stern philosophical dilemma. Am I my brother's keeper? The second time that Noel said *you bastards* it was audible throughout the church. Everyone heard it except perhaps for the reverend himself, who had been catching his breath to shout, "And God said unto Cain, *The VOICE of THY BROTHER'S BLOOD it CRIETH unto me from the ground. IT CRIETH! UNTO ME! FROM THE GROUND!*"

The last time Noel said *you bastards* he timed it so that it rang like a bell inside the church. Then he turned to Matt for some mirror of outrage, but instead he found his brother to be weeping, his chin held high as if hooked from beneath, his eyes locked into the reverend's. Noel elbowed Matt, elbowed him hard in the biceps, then stood to face Smokewood, whose eyes never wavered from reeling in Matt. Noel began to step backward up the aisle. Very solemnly. Like a groom in reverse. And as he did this, he called out Matt's name louder and louder as the distance between them increased. In a voice equally determined, the reverend was thundering, "And Cain said unto the Lord, *My punishment is more than I can bear. More than I can bear! I shall be a fugitive. A FUGITIVE! A vagabond on the earth. A VAGABOND!*"

The wooden front door to the church was enchantingly small. It was over three hundred years old and had been shipped from England. As a child, Noel's favorite moment at church was at the very end of the service when Reverend Smokewood would march to that elfish door and fling it open, allowing in a tunnel of sunlight, then he would bellow, "NOW GO OUT THERE AND DO GOOD!" Noel's back was now pushing against this door. The entire congregation had contorted around to stare up the aisle at him, everybody except for Reverend Smokewood and Matt. In that hushed and encapsulated moment, Noel braced his shoulders hard against the top of the doorframe, then he shouted his brother's name one last time before wheeling forever out of that church and into sunlight.

He walked across the courtyard and swung into his Mustang, banging its door into the neighboring sedan. As he backed the car around, he could hear the congregation singing, "Michael Row the Boat Ashore." He centered the church in the rearview and sat there pumping the brake pedal. "C'mon, Matt, c'mon," he kept chanting, but when the church door finally opened, it was not Matt who came out, it was a woman, and not his mother, and not anyone he recognized. Walking toward him, she started off looking older but by the time she reached the car she had grown much younger. Dangerously thin, dressed in a pleated black dancer's skirt with black leotards below and tight black ribbed shirt above, Amber appeared torn between death and disco. Noel might not have recognized her at all had it not been for the long mercury-colored hair that spilled into the car when she framed her face in the rolled-down window.

They studied each other a moment, then Noel grinned and thanked her for the pie.

"I bet it was awful." She smiled with the tip of her tongue touching her upper lip. "Hey, you remember calling me last night?"

"Last night?"

"About three in the morning."

"Nah, really? Did I say anything stupid?"

"No. You were real sweet. Most of it was hard to make sense of, but I was glad you called, it was sweet."

Noel checked the rearview and told her he had to get going. He asked if she needed a ride anywhere.

"You act like somebody's chasing you."

"I feel like somebody's chasing me."

Amber leaned inside the car and brushed against Noel as she plucked the black film container off the center console. "Still taking pictures, huh?" She shook the film cartridge next to her ear and asked if these were of his girlfriend. "I heard she's real beautiful, that she's a Dixie Darling and everything."

Noel geared the car into drive and pressed his foot on the brake. "She ain't my girlfriend, not anymore," he said. "I broke up with her."

"You did! Why?"

"Shoot. You ever hear that song 'Superfreak'?" He half sang a few lines. Then, as soon as he had Amber laughing, he reached out and took the film from her.

"I always liked that song," she said.

"Amber, I gotta be heading out. But there's something I need to tell you first."

"Is it about my brother?"

He nodded and said, "Yeah, it is."

"I'm sorry about that, Noel," she said quickly. "I'm sorry I tried to make the police think it was you. I never shoulda done that. If they had ever arrested you, I would have said something, I promise I would have."

"What are you talking about?"

"I did it," she said. "You know that, don't you?"

"You did it?"

"I thought you already knew. I thought everybody in town knew that I did it, that I unplugged him." Amber leaned farther into the window. She did this with unabashed pleasure, like someone telling a scary story around a campfire. The first thing she said was, "I've never told anybody this before, except doctors, and they don't count."

The night it happened, Amber explained, she had been sleeping on the cot in Ross's hospital room—something she did a lot—but on that particular night she'd had this dream. "Me, you, and Ross were walking around the hospital room unplugging all those machines. It was like a game the three of us were playing. Just a game. We were laughing and all, and singing some song I can't even remember now. Then, after everything was unplugged, Ross kissed me goodbye and flew out the window. And that's when I woke up. I woke up because some alarm was going off. I turned on the light and then I went around the whole room, just like in the dream, unplugging everything until the alarm finally stopped beeping. And then I went back to sleep and didn't wake up again until the next morning when the nurse found Ross dead."

"You didn't murder him," Noel said after a moment.

"I know I didn't. It took me a long time to figure that out, though. That it wasn't murder at all. For years I thought it was, but now I know better. It's the only thing I've ever done in my whole life that I'm proud of." Amber had tears on her cheeks, but she wasn't really crying. Her voice was level and her eyes were bright and happy. She wiped the tears away then looked at her hand and said, "It feels so good to finally tell someone. Someone who counts."

"You never told the police either?"

"No. But I think they kinda knew I did it. I kept expecting to get arrested. Every day of my life. Day after day. I just kept waiting and waiting and it never happened. And now I finally know why they never arrested me."

"Because they didn't want you to go to jail? Because they knew you were just a kid and you hadn't done anything wrong?"

"No, that wasn't it. I thought that too for a long time, but then just a couple of weeks ago my mom told me the real truth. They didn't tell me before because it was too . . . spooky, I guess. At least to them it was."

"Spooky?"

"Yeah, to them. The reason they never arrested me is because of fingerprints. When I unplugged everything, I didn't use gloves or anything, but the next morning, guess whose fingerprints they found all over those plugs."

"Mine?"

"Yours? How could they be yours?"

"I don't know."

"Ross's," she said. "A little kid's fingerprints."

"Your brother's?"

She nodded and smiled and made her eyebrows dance. Then she said, "It freaked the cops out so bad, they never arrested anybody."

"Jesus."

"In my dream it was Ross doing all the unplugging. Me and you, we were just walking around the room with him, just playing the game. We were all real happy. It was a beautiful dream."

She waited until Noel's face had tried on sufficient expressions of disbelief, then she said, "Why don't you come back inside with me? We'll go back in there together."

Noel shook his head, then asked her what today's date was. After she told him, he nodded severely and repeated the date out loud.

"Ask me where I'm gonna be a year from today, Amber."

"Where?"

"First, I'm gonna work my ass off bartending for my uncle, save up for a whole year. My uncle owns this Vietnamese restaurant down in the Keys. Then, a year from today—" He frowned. "Why are you crying?"

"Nothing. I always cry at funerals."

"Guess where I'm gonna be, Amber, a year from today."

"Where?"

"A year from today I'm gonna be on a plane to France. You ever known anybody that's been to France?"

She took out a tissue and shook her head no.

"Then, as soon as I get there, I'm heading straight to one of those naked beaches they got there, and I'm gonna take off all my clothes and throw them in the damn ocean. You think I'm lying?"

"No. I know you're not."

"You get inside this car right now, I'll take you with me."

Instead Amber knelt down so that her arms were folded on top of each other along the window's edge, her chin resting on top of her hands.

"We're praying for you, Noel."

"You're *what*?"

"Praying for you. We all are, everyone at my church is. I've been saved, Noel. Can't you tell? I've been born again."

He examined her face a moment, then shook his head and asked if she knew how people in France said goodbye.

"They don't. They just kiss."

She leaned in the window again and they kissed. As she pulled herself free, she took Noel's left hand and placed it under her right arm against the side of her breast. Noel could feel her heartbeat. Her face became very intent, then she smiled and said, " 'Onward, Christian Soldier.' "

"Huh?"

"Listen."

"Oh. That." He removed his hand and put the car in neutral and twice tapped the accelerator. "I'm gonna ask you one last time, Amber."

"We're all praying for you, Noel."

"They been doing that for years."

"I'm praying for you now."

"Good. You can. You got my permission."

"Goodbye, Noel."

"Say-La-V, Amber."

"What's that mean?"

"I got no idea, but it's all the French I know ain't something dirty."

As the car began edging away, Amber stood very straight and cupped her hands to her mouth and waited for him to get far enough away to merit the gesture, then she cried out, "Jesus loves you, Noel. No matter what you do."

He honked the horn.

At the first gas station he tore off his tie and pumped the tank full and got a large black coffee to go. Back on the highway, he flicked on the radio to some static-eaten zydeco gospel about a heart like a wheel and he blasted the accordion music over the roar of wind and engine, and then he reached into the back seat and one by one fed the red hymnals to the open window and watched them take flight in the rearview. He finished his coffee, then released the trembling cup to the wind and lost himself in the pureness of acceleration, in the shallow grace of not being the one left behind.